"That feeling you get when you curl up on the couch on a rainy Saturday, with a great book in one hand and a spiked hot chocolate in the other: that's the feeling you get when you read *Weather Girl*."

—Jasmine Guillory, *New York Times* bestselling author of *While We Were Dating*

"A sexy storm of a book."

—Sophie Cousens, *New York Times* bestselling author of *This Time Next Year*

"A delightful romance. Perfect for rainy days and sunny days and everything in between."

—Helen Hoang, *New York Times* bestselling author of *The Heart Principle*

"Rachel Lynn Solomon has crafted a magical story that celebrates hope, resilience, and love. My forecast: read it, and you'll be on cloud nine."

—Ali Hazelwood, *New York Times* bestselling author of *The Love Hypothesis*

"A tender, hilarious, and heartfelt love story you'll read in one sitting!"

—Tessa Bailey, *New York Times* bestselling author of *It Happened One Summer*

"[Solomon's] realistic portrayal of the internal struggles that come with the highs and lows of optimism and depression, and how it affects sex and relationships, is an important one."   —BuzzFeed

"Humorous, captivating, and delightful."   —*USA Today*

"Heartfelt charm, memorable characters, steamy moments . . . this rom-com has it all."
— *Women's World*

"Whether sunshine or rainfall, *Weather Girl* is the perfect read no matter what storms you're facing."
— The Nerd Daily

PRAISE FOR *THE EX TALK*

"A very funny book . . . . Rom-coms need tears the way bread dough needs salt, and here the mixture strikes a perfect balance between sweet and savory."
— *New York Times Book Review*

"*The Ex Talk* delivers. This book is quick, spicy, and sweet."
— Shondaland

"More than lives up to the hype."
— PopSugar

"*The Ex Talk* is so many things: a banter-packed laugh-out-loud rom-com, a meditation on how grief shapes our lives and our love, an ode to the joys of public radio and podcasting, and an all-around exquisite romance."
— *Entertainment Weekly*

"A glimmering, sharp, and delightfully feminist rom-com. *The Ex Talk* just crashed its way onto my forever-rec pile."
— *New York Times* bestselling author Christina Lauren

"With a crisp and affectionate attention to detail, Rachel Lynn Solomon breathes life across her pages that's so relatable you could sink right in."
— Rosie Danan, author of *The Roommate*

BERKLEY TITLES BY RACHEL LYNN SOLOMON

The Ex Talk

Weather Girl

Business or Pleasure

BUSINESS
or
PLEASURE

RACHEL LYNN SOLOMON

BERKLEY ROMANCE

New York

BERKLEY ROMANCE
Published by Berkley
An imprint of Penguin Random House LLC
penguinrandomhouse.com

Library of Congress Cataloging-in-Publication Data

Names: Solomon, Rachel Lynn, author.
Title: Business or pleasure / Rachel Lynn Solomon.
Description: First Edition. | New York: Berkley Romance, 2023.
Identifiers: LCCN 2022046231 (print) | LCCN 2022046232 (ebook) | ISBN
9780593548530 (trade paperback) | ISBN 9780593548547 (ebook)
Subjects: LCGFT: Novels.
Classification: LCC PS3619.O437236 B87 2023 (print) | LCC PS3619.O437236
(ebook) | DDC 813/.6—dc23/eng/20220923
LC record available at https://lccn.loc.gov/2022046231
LC ebook record available at https://lccn.loc.gov/2022046232

First Edition: July 2023

Printed in the United States of America
1st Printing

Book design by Daniel Brount

For anyone who took a little while to figure it out
and anyone who's still figuring it out—it's never too late.

I've been searching all the wrong places
I've been trying too many faces
Only one way to go
This is the way back home

—"MAPS" BY LESLEY ROY

BUSINESS

— *or* —

PLEASURE

chapter
ONE

"This book was a real labor of love," says the woman seated behind a table of hardcovers sporting her makeup-free face, scrunched mid-yelp as she attempts to drink from a garden hose. "I can't believe it's something I can finally hold in my hands! And the cover's not too bad, either."

The audience laughs right on cue. In the back row, I can practically feel Noemie cringe beside me. "I've made bowls of cereal that were more a labor of love than the effort she put into that book," she whispers.

She's not wrong—I experienced it firsthand. Still, I give my cousin a nudge. "Be respectful."

"I am. To the cereal."

I press my lips together to keep from reacting and focus on the stage, where Maddy DeMarco commands the room with a warm, practiced confidence bordering on emotional manipulation. The bookstore is filled with just a fraction of her 1.6 million Instagram followers: mostly women, mostly white, mostly dressed in sustainable linen they bought using her discount code MADSAVINGS10. At first I thought it was a cult, and to be completely honest, I'm still not sure. Her brand of saccharine positivity doesn't quite do it for me anymore—whenever I need self-love, it's more likely to take shape as something handheld and battery-operated. Which Maddy has devoted tragic few (read: zero) social media posts to.

She's built her career on empty affirmations and obvious advice. Case in point—the book is called *Go Drink Some Water: A Guide to Self-Care, Self-Discovery, and Staying Thirsty*.

"People often ask how I turned one viral post into a lifestyle brand," Maddy says, crossing one linen-clad leg over the other. Her natural waves are shined to perfection with an expensive oil I'm ashamed to admit I tried before chopping my ash-blond hair into a pixie last year. "And the answer is simple: I don't sleep." This gets a few more laughs. A muted groan from Noemie. "No, I want to be real with you guys. I was one of those people who never had their shit together—wait, can I say that? Are there kids here?" She makes a show of squinting out at the audience before barreling onward. "I would get so stressed that I literally forgot to drink water! It wasn't until I got so dehydrated that I ended up in the hospital that I realized I'd stopped doing things just for myself. I'm talking *basic*, keeping-yourself-functioning kind of things. Like drinking water. And I knew something needed to change."

I wrote three chapters of her book on that hospital visit, poring over her Instagram to make sure I was capturing her voice. Every fourth comment swooned over how relatable she was—and this is someone who sells wall hangings that say LIVE LAUGH GIRLBOSS.

All through the writing process, I tried to keep Maddy relatable: when she insisted on communicating with me only through her team, when that team sent me photos of notes she'd scrawled on compostable napkins, when she said the writing needed to feel *a little earthier*. I wanted to like her so badly, wanted to believe her posts were inspiring people to live their best and most carbon-neutral lives. Because the thing is, back before the book, I did like her. There was something both aspirational and authentic about her that had compelled me to hit "follow" a few years ago, long before the wall hangings and the constant #ads that clutter her feed these days.

Ghostwriting isn't a glamorous job, and even if nothing about this finished product screams *Chandler Cohen*, I've been strangely giddy over the idea of finally meeting Maddy—because some part of me is still a little starstruck. The book came out a few days ago, and I've made myself wait to get a copy until her Seattle tour stop, convinced her signature on the title page will cement this as a collaboration. I didn't even open the box of hardcovers that showed up on my doorstep last week.

In my wildest dreams, I've wondered if maybe Maddy will ask me to sign a copy for her, too. An inside joke between the two of us. And somehow, that would make up for all the eleventh-hour rewrites and irreversible, anxiety-induced damage to my cuticles.

Chapter 6: Harness Your Inner Optimist. Maybe the book really did make an impact.

Maddy lifts one arm in the air. "Can I get a show of hands—who here has ever posted a photo of themselves smiling when they were so far from happy, hitting the submit button almost felt like a lie?" Nearly every hand goes up. "There's nothing to be ashamed of. I've done it plenty of times. But it's not the photos of my smiling face that have enabled me to connect with so many of you—it's the photos of my crow's-feet. My frowns. Even my tears." She slips her phone from her pants pocket, scrolls through her own feed. "The next time you post something, think about how much it's representing your authentic self. And then don't just hit submit. Take a new photo. Write a new caption. Let your inner beauty do the talking."

"Then she's going to love my event recap," Noemie says.

A woman in front of us turns around, shoving a finger to her lips. Noemie goes silent and blinks wide, innocent eyes at her.

"You're going to get us kicked out," I say. "And then what am I going to say to my publisher?"

"You can tell them I'm living my truth and speaking my heart. Isn't that what chapter twelve was about?" Unfortunately, yes.

After another half hour of Maddy's sweeping proclamations about our on- and offline lives, infused with no fewer than four references to brands that sponsor her, she gets a signal from her assistant and claps her hands once. "I'm afraid that was all the time we have! I can't wait to sign these beauties for you, but before I do . . . I want you all to do something for me." A sly grin spreads across her face. "If you reach under your chairs, you'll find your very own bottle of water."

There's a flurry of eager, electric energy as those who didn't notice the water bottles when they came in discover them for the first time.

"Now I want you to open that baby up"—Maddy uncaps her water bottle, raising it high in a toast to the audience. I tap my recycled plastic against Noemie's with an exaggerated lift of my eyebrows—"and take a big, delicious sip."

"DOESN'T IT BOTHER YOU," NOEMIE ASKS IN THE SIGNING LINE, RUN-ning a hand along the book's glossy cover, "not seeing your name on it?"

It did. At the beginning. But now there's a sense of detach-ment that accompanies a book release. As a celebrity ghostwriter, I'm not hired to be anyone's coauthor—I'm supposed to write from their point of view. To *become* them. My first author, a *Bache-*

lor contestant who infamously dumped the guy on national TV after he proposed, was an utter delight, and she still emails asking how I'm doing. But I quickly learned that wasn't the norm. Because then there was Maddy, and the book I just finished for a TikTok-famous personal trainer with his own line of protein shakes that really stretches the definition of literature.

Maybe there's some satisfaction in clutching these several hundred pages I churned out at record speed, a tangible conclusion to all those late nights and canceled plans. And yet I can also completely divorce myself from this book in a way that's either great or terrible for my mental health. Maybe both.

"It's not my book," I say simply, taking another sip from my Maddy DeMarco–branded water bottle. It's like, weirdly good water, and I'm not sure I want to know why.

The signing line crawls forward, people asking Maddy to pose for photos before they head off to pay at the register. I can't fault any of them for loving her the way they do. They want to believe that changing their lifestyle can change their life—after all, it worked for her.

"Thanks for waiting with me," I say, and Noemie's eyes soften behind her tortoiseshell glasses, her cynical exterior cracking for a moment. "I know this isn't your ideal Friday night."

"Considering I spent last Friday explaining to a client why we couldn't guarantee them a cover story in *Time*, this is a definite upgrade." She's still dressed in her PR professional best: tapered slacks, daisy-patterned peplum top, a blazer draped over her arm. Long dark hair straightened and frizz-free, because she's not Noemie if she has even a single flyaway. Meanwhile, in my cords, faded Sleater-Kinney tee, and a black denim jacket that's too warm for early September, I must look like I haven't seen the sun since 1996. No vitamin D for me, thanks.

"Can't argue with you there." I pick at a speck of silver nail polish, a tell my cousin will be able to see right through. "And hey, the longer we're here, the longer I can pretend everyone else isn't at Wyatt's housewarming."

Noemie grimaces in this familiar way I'm never sure whether I learned from her or the other way around. Noemie Cohen-Laurent is both my only first cousin and my closest friend. We grew up on the same street, attended the same schools, and now even live in the same house, though she owns it and I'm paying a deeply discounted monthly rent.

We both studied journalism, starry-eyed about how we were going to change the world, tell the stories no one else was telling. The economy pushed us in different directions, and before we graduated, Noemie had already been hired full-time at the PR firm where she'd interned during her senior year.

"I'm guessing that means you decided not to go?" she says.

"I can't do it. You can go if you want, but—"

Noemie cuts me off with a swift shake of her head. "Solidarity. Wyatt Torres is dead to me."

My shoulders sag with relief. I haven't wanted her to feel like she needs to pick a side, even if there's no risk she'd pick his. Still, she's the only one who knows what happened between us a few weeks ago: one incredible night after years of pining I thought was mutual, given the desperate way his hands roamed my body as we tumbled into bed. I'd helped him unpack his new apartment, and we were exhausted and tipsy and just seemed to *fit*, our bodies snapping together in this natural, effortless way. Wyatt's dark hair feathering across my stomach, tanned skin shivering where I touched him. The way he dug his nails into my back like he couldn't bear to let me go.

But then came the *Can we talk?* text, and the confession, during said talk, that he wasn't looking for a relationship right now. And I was a Relationship Girl, he said, with all the distaste usually reserved for that one person who replies-all on a cc'd email. He valued our friendship too much, and he didn't want either of us to get hurt.

So I pretended I wasn't.

"We would have been good together, though," I say quietly, forcing my feet forward in line.

Noemie places a gentle hand on my shoulder. "I know. I'm so sorry. We'll have a much better time tonight, I promise. We'll go back to the house and order way too much Indian food, because I know how you love being able to eat leftovers for five days afterward. And then we can watch people on Netflix making bad real estate decisions with partners they absolutely should not be with."

Finally, it's our turn, one of the booksellers beckoning us forward. Maddy's smile has barely slipped, an impressive feat after all those photos.

"Hi," I say, thrusting my copy forward with a trembling hand, which is only marginally embarrassing. I wrote pages and pages pretending to be this woman, and now that she's three feet in front of me, I can barely speak. Someone take away my communication degree.

"Hi there," she says brightly. "Who should I make it out to?"

"Chandler. Chandler Cohen."

She squeezes one eye shut, as though trying to remember. Any moment now, it'll ring a bell. We'll laugh about her takedown of internet trolls in chapter four and roll our eyes at all the people-pleasing she used to do, documented in detail in chapter sixteen. "How do you spell that?"

"Oh—um," I stammer, every letter in the English alphabet fleeing my mind at once. "Chandler . . . Cohen?" Maddy gives me a blank, expectant look.

No. It's not possible, is it? That she wouldn't even remember my name after all the back-and-forth? All her demands?

"You don't know Chandler—" Noemie starts to say, but I silence her with an elbow to the ribs.

Sure, I communicated mostly with Maddy's team . . . but my name was on the contracts. The rough drafts. The endless email chains. I wrote this fucking *book* for her, and she has no idea who I am.

I must mumble out the spelling, but my vision blurs as she swoops her magenta sharpie over the title page, sliding in a bookmark and passing it back to me like a seasoned pro.

"Thank you," I manage as Maddy waves us away with a sunshine grin.

Once we're safely in the picture-book aisle, the one farthest from the stage, I let out a long, shaky breath. It's fine. This is fine. Obviously, she wasn't going to ask me to sign our book.

Her book.

Because that's the whole point of a ghost—no one is supposed to be able to see me.

"You should have told her who you were," Noemie says, one hand gripping her quilted Kate Spade and the other white-knuckling the water bottle. "I would have, if you hadn't viciously attacked me."

"It would have just made it more embarrassing." I clutch the book tight to my chest because if I don't, I might hurl it across the store. "Maybe she's not great with names. She meets a lot of people. I'm sure she just gets . . . really busy girlbossing."

"Right." Noemie's stance is still rigid. "Well, I'm still going to unfollow her." And to prove it, she takes out her phone, only to have something else catch her attention. "Shit, it's work. The wrong draft of a press release went out and the client is *livid*. I might have to . . ." She trails off, her fingers flying over the screen.

Every so often, it hits me that there are only two years between us, though Noemie's life is wildly different from mine. When The Catch laid me off five years ago and eventually folded, unable to keep up with BuzzFeed and Vice and HuffPost, she was buying a house. When I was struggling to sell freelance articles about new local musicians and the evolution of Seattle's downtown, she was juggling high-profile clients and contributing a respectable monthly amount to her 401(k). She's twenty-nine to my thirty-one, but it's almost shocking how much better at adulting she is.

Only two years, and yet sometimes it feels like I'll never catch up.

"Go," I say, nudging her with the book. "I get it."

If I told her I needed her, she'd probably find a way to do both: comfort me and save her client. But most of the time, when work and anything else are fighting for Noemie's attention, work wins.

"Only if you're sure," she says. "You want to go back home, fire up DoorDash, and save me a couple samosas for when I'm done?"

"I actually might stay out a bit longer."

She gives me a lingering glance, as though worried there's something I'm not telling her. It's the same way she looked at me when I learned about The Catch slashing its staff. My onetime dream job forcing me to find a new dream.

"Nome. I'm *fine*," I say, with so much emphasis that it sounds more threatening than reassuring.

She gives me a tight hug. "I'm proud of you," she says. "In case I didn't say it before." She did, when I turned in my draft and my revisions and then on the book's release day, when she had to go into work early but had a spread of donuts and bagels waiting for me when I woke up. "You wrote and published a *book*. Two of them, in fact, with another on the way. Don't let her take that away from you."

I'm not sure I can put into words how much I love her in this moment, so I just hug her back and hope she knows. Clearly, I'm not the best at words today.

One great thing about this bookstore is that it has a bar, and I hate that on my way over, I have visions of Maddy sitting down next to me. I'd offer to buy her a drink and then tell her something that only someone intimately acquainted with *Go Drink Some Water* would know. She'd gasp, apologize, gush about how happy she is with the book. She'd confirm that all those months weren't just a paycheck—they *mattered*.

Except this isn't really about Maddy DeMarco at all.

It's the bundle of self-worth tangled in the sheets on Wyatt's bed, in the paychecks that don't always arrive on time, in the lovely bedroom in my cousin's lovely house that I'd never be able to afford on my own. It's the persistent tapping at the back of my mind that sounds suspiciously like a clock, wondering if I picked the wrong career path and if it's too late to start over. And if I'd even know how.

It's that every time I try to move forward, something is waiting to tug me right back.

The two bartenders are immersed in what looks like a very serious conversation, so I have to clear my throat to get their attention. I order a hard cider that's much too sweet, and before slipping Maddy's book into my bag, I open it up to the title page.

If I weren't already gutter-adjacent, it would sink me even deeper.

For Chandler Cone, it says in magenta ink. *Drink up!*

EMERALD CITY COMIC CON

SEPTEMBER 8-10,
WASHINGTON STATE CONVENTION CENTER

Meet Finn Walsh, better known as Oliver Huxley from *The Nocturnals*! We're delighted to welcome everyone's favorite nerd to ECCC once again. Here's where you can spot him this weekend:

PANEL:
Every Hero Needs One: Familiars, Friends, and Sidekicks
Friday, September 8, 6 p.m., Room 3B

SIGNING BOOTH:
Saturday, September 9, 4 p.m., Hall C
AUTOGRAPHS: $75 · PHOTO OP: $125

chapter
TWO

At first, I intend to do exactly what the inscription tells me to: become heavily intoxicated, which is probably not what Maddy meant and also might not be possible with this too-sweet cider. I snap the traitorous book shut, letting out a sigh that draws the attention of the man a seat away from me.

I meet his gaze and give him an apologetic look, but instead of the judgmental frown I'm expecting, he nods toward my bottle of cider. "What are we celebrating?"

"The disintegration of my self-esteem, sponsored by my complete mistake of a career. And the funeral of a relationship that ended before it even began." I lift the bottle and take a sip, trying not to wince. "It's a wake, actually. I have a front-row seat to watch both those things implode. Spectacularly." Or at least, Chandler Cone does.

"Those aren't easy tickets to get." He holds his hands together, then bows his head as though paying his respects. "Dearly beloved, we're gathered here today to—"

In spite of everything, I burst out laughing. "I think that's what you say at a wedding. Or at the beginning of a Prince song."

"Ah shit, you're right." His mouth curves into a smile. "Good song, though."

"Great song."

In the most discreet way possible, I take a closer look at this stranger. I don't think he was at the signing, but then again, the room was packed. He looks older than me, though probably not by much—auburn hair, shorter on the sides and floppy on top, graying a bit at the temples, which I discover in this moment is something I find very attractive. He's in dark jeans and a casual black button-up, one sleeve unbuttoned at the wrist, as though he got distracted when he was putting it on, or maybe had a long day and the button simply gave up.

"I'm sorry, though," he says. "About your work, and your relationship."

I wave this off. "Thanks, but it'll be okay. I think." *I hope.*

I could easily turn away, tell him to have a nice evening. Down my drink in silence and stumble home to takeout, trashy TV, and wallowing. I've never chatted someone up at a bar before—I'm usually too busy avoiding eye contact with other humans—but something about him compels me to keep talking.

Because full honesty: maybe my ego needs a little boost tonight.

"What about you?" I say, picking up my bottle and gesturing toward his glass. "You're drinking alone because . . ."

When I trail off, I watch his face, catching a split-second flinch. It's so brief, I'm not sure he's aware he's doing it—maybe I even imagined it. But then he collects himself. Seems to relax.

"Same as you. Career-related existential dread." He motions to the pair of bartenders, dropping the volume of his voice. "I was going to head out twenty minutes ago, but then I got too invested in their personal lives."

He taps a finger to his lips, and I strain to hear what the bartenders are saying.

"Those guinea pigs are not my responsibility. If you're going to insist on keeping them in our apartment, you need to clean up after them."

"You could at least call them by their names."

"I refuse to call those little beasts Ricardo and Judith."

"Just like you refused to do the dishes after that party you threw last week? The one with a build-your-own-chili-dog bar?"

"I want to call you out for eavesdropping, but I can't blame you," I say. "This is quality entertainment."

"Right? Now I can't leave until I know how it ends." Then he raises an eyebrow, squinting at the water bottle I stupidly placed on the bar next to me. "Is there a reason your water bottle says . . . 'Live Laugh Girlboss'?" He holds up his hands. "Not judging, just curious."

"Oh, this? I'm part of a hydration-based MLM. I'm in really deep. They'll be running the docuseries any day now."

Without missing a beat, he calmly places his glass back down. Flicks his eyes around the bar. When he speaks again, it's in a whisper. "Do I need to call someone for you?"

"Afraid it's too late." I give the water bottle a shake. "But if I can sell you a thousand of these babies, I might be able to get off with minimal prison time."

"The thing is," he says, drumming a couple fingertips on the bar, "I could probably find a use for three hundred. Maybe four. But I don't know what I'd do with the rest of them."

"You'd just have to find other people to sell them to. I could hook you up, give you all the training you need to become your very own boss."

"I'm not falling for that one." He's grinning at me, his teeth a brilliant white. The longer I study him, the cuter he is. It's all in the details—a dusting of reddish facial hair, the warmth of his rich hazel eyes, the freckles spiraling across his knuckles, up onto his left wrist where his shirt is unbuttoned and bare skin peeks through. And the way he's looking at me might feel better than I've felt all day. All week. All month since Wyatt.

"I'm Drew," he says. "I completely understand if you can't tell me your name, though. For legal reasons. What with the show and all."

I try and fail to hold in another smile. God, he's charming. "Chandler," I say. "I was at the book signing over there." I drag out the book, as though the introduction necessitates some additional shred of truth. "What do you do? When you're not trying to rescue women from MLMs drinking at bookstore bars?"

"I mean, jeez, that's practically a full-time job." Then he takes another sip of his drink before tenting his fingers together. "I'm in sales. Not very interesting, unfortunately."

"I disagree. That depends entirely on what you're selling. For example, tiny rain boots for dogs? Fascinating, and I'll need to see photos immediately."

"Tech sales," he elaborates with a little sigh that makes him seem eager to change the subject. Which, fair—tech sales doesn't sound like the most edge-of-your-seat career. "What about you?"

If that isn't the million-dollar question. "I'm a writer. A journalist, I guess, but I haven't written anything I'm proud of in a while." I take a sip of my cider, remember it's too sweet, fight a grimace. "The whole capitalist machine really sold us lies about becoming an adult. I was under the impression that each of us was supposed to flourish into this perfectly well-adjusted, impressively accomplished person. That was what they told us all throughout school, right? That we could be anything we wanted. That we were special. But now I'm just . . ." *Writing books without my name on them. Struggling to pay my reduced rent. Floundering.* "Being a millennial in your thirties is a trip and a half," I finish.

"I'll drink to that."

He takes a long sip before setting down the empty glass, then splays a hand on the table, index finger tracing the wood grain. As though he's carefully considering what he wants to say next. A dim light bulb catches the swirl of freckles along his cheeks, down his neck, tucked into the hollow of his throat. Not the exact shade of his hair, I'm noticing—some darker, some lighter. A whole beautiful constellation.

"I've got to preface this by saying that I don't usually do this, but . . . Do you want to get out of here, Chandler?" At that, he winces. "Wow. That sounds like a really bad line. I swear, I'm genuinely wondering if you're interested in leaving this place and going to a different place. One that has more food, because I'm kind of starving and the 'loaded totchos' on the menu don't look very appetizing."

I could tell him I have plans. That the loaded totchos actually sound fantastic and I've been debating ordering a basket ever since I sat down. And yet.

Drew saying it sounds like a bad line could fully be a line, I realize that, but maybe I'm not ready to go back to Noemie's house and feel sorry for myself. This isn't something I'd ever do, and yet in this moment, that feels like exactly the reason to say yes. I could toss my half-empty cider and get drunk on his attention alone.

I grab my wallet, throwing a few dollars down on the bar. "Let's get out of here."

WE'RE ON A MISSION, DREW AND I: FIND THE PERFECT LATE-NIGHT slice of pizza. The first restaurant we tried was closed and the second only served full pies, and now we're on our way to a place I swear is right around here somewhere . . .

"There!" I point to a flashing green OPEN sign on the corner, the delicious savory scent tugging us closer.

It's almost ten p.m. and Capitol Hill is just waking up. So far on our walk, I've learned that Drew lives in Southern California and he's in town for work. He's been to Seattle a few times but never had the chance to really explore, so I've made it my unofficial goal to show him as much as I can.

I can't remember the last time I was out on a Friday night, and it suddenly feels so full of possibility that I'm a little dizzy. Uncertain on my feet, so much that when I stumble across the pizzeria's threshold, Drew steadies me with a hand to my lower back, that warm rush of contact going straight to my head.

"I'm relieved for you," he says as we take our place in line. "I was about to be very disappointed in Seattle."

The place is staffed by two aging punk rockers, Mudhoney playing over the sound system. I can always respect a Seattle establishment paying tribute to the Northwest's long history of excellent bands. We may not have an abundance of by-the-slice pizza joints, but we know our music. Everyone clustered inside is in various stages of their nights: a trio of girls with flawless makeup and matching jumpsuits, a couple on what appears to be a first date, a group of college kids looking absolutely trashed, a shocking number of empty bottles covering their table.

Drew gestures for me to go first, so I order a slice of pepperoni roughly the size of a YIELD sign while he asks for a garden veggie. A guy with a tattoo of what I think might be the old King-dome on his neck eyes the pie for a moment before selecting the largest slice, piled with green peppers, mushrooms, olives, and artichokes.

When the cashier gives us plastic cups for the soda we order, Drew spends a moment inspecting his before filling it up with Sprite.

"Just making sure it's clean," he says with this sheepish smile. It makes sense—this hole-in-the-wall's hygiene is questionable at best.

There are no chairs, only high tables with shakers of Parmesan and red pepper flakes. I dig into my pizza right away, feeling only a little barbaric when Drew opts for the more elegant fork-and-knife method. "God, *so good.* Their pepperoni is otherworldly—you want some? Just don't tell my Jewish parents."

"Oh—I'm a vegetarian," he says, not sounding at all offended. He chews, then cuts off another small triangle, popping it neatly into his mouth. "About eighteen years. And Jewish, too, actually."

I stare at him for a couple moments, because what are the odds that I'd meet a Jewish stranger in this way?

"No shit. I think the only thing I've done for eighteen years is manage to function with a consistently medium level of anxiety," I say. "What made you decide to become a vegetarian?"

"Is it cliché to say that I love animals?" Drew asks. I get a flash of him holding a lamb, a piglet, a baby goat. "If not: that, and I was traumatized by *The Jungle* in high school. Couldn't look at a hamburger the same way after that."

"If you have time, you should try Pear Bistro. It's this vegan restaurant downtown that's always packed. Expensive, but amazing food."

"One sec, I'm going to write that down." He pulls out his

phone, types it in, and slides it back into his pocket. Takes a sip of soda. "So you talk to strangers at bars, listen to Prince, and mysteriously came into possession of a self-help book written by an influencer. What else should I know about you?"

"I highly doubt she wrote it." I might say it a bit too quickly, so I tear off a piece of crust, dipping it into the sauce on the pizza, trying to act nonchalant. "I always assume anyone remotely famous has, you know, a ghostwriter or something. But in terms of fun facts . . ." I give him my most serious look and prepare my sole fun fact, the one I've spent much of my life saving for games of two truths and a lie, only to be sorely disappointed by how few opportunities there are for it outside of corporate America. "I'm only seven years old."

He just stares at me, a furrow appearing between his brows. "I . . . don't have a witty response to that. Only concern and confusion."

"I was born on a leap day," I say. "I'm thirty-one, but technically, I've only celebrated seven February twenty-ninths. I get another one next year, which is always exciting. And I'm a Pisces, so I love drama."

"I've never met a . . . leaper? Leapster? Do you have a name for yourselves?"

"Actually, yes. Leaper and leapster both work, but I've always preferred leapling." I aim my pizza crust at him. "Your turn. Fun fact me, please."

"Hmmm. I don't know if I can beat yours, but I do have an encyclopedic knowledge of *Lord of the Rings*. And not just the books or the movies—like, I actually studied the Elvish languages as a kid," he says. "As you can imagine, this made me very popular at parties."

"It should have! Say something in Elvish?"

His mouth quirks upward. "You have no idea how many times I lay awake at night, hoping one day a cute girl would ask me that." Then he schools his face into a more serene expression. "*Vandë omentaina*," he says, a smile sneaking back in. "Technically, Elvish is a language family, with multiple languages and dialects created not just by Tolkien but by fans, too. That was 'nice to meet you' in Quenya, which originated as the language of the High Elves, who left Middle-earth to live far west in the Blessed Realms."

"Holy shit." I flutter my lashes as I lean forward across the table. "You are . . . a *huge* nerd."

The groan and balled-up napkin he tosses my way are 100 percent worth it.

The doorbell jingles as another group pushes inside, and it takes me a moment to realize why they're all wearing costumes—Yoshi, Wonder Woman, and something I don't recognize—because in Capitol Hill, you never know. One of those comic book conventions is happening downtown this weekend, and I'm guessing they just came from it.

On the other side of the table, Drew stiffens, seeming to relax only once the group takes their pizza to go. Secondhand embarrassment, maybe? Residual childhood trauma involving *Mario Kart*? Whatever it is, he doesn't offer an explanation, and I don't ask for one.

"You're a journalist," he says, spearing a green pepper with his fork. "Did you study that in college?"

I nod. "It was a lot of doom and gloom. Newspapers had started folding all over the country, and it was made clear early on that none of us were going to be able to find jobs at a local paper working one specific beat, in part because some of those papers wouldn't exist, or they'd be online-only, and also because it was getting less and less common to even have a specific beat. We had to learn how to do everything—photography, video, basic coding. And then I minored in gender and sexuality studies."

At that, Drew coughs a little, then swallows. "*Really*," he says with a gentle thwack at his chest. Another cough. "That's . . . intriguing."

I roll my eyes. "I can never tell anyone without getting a completely pervy response. Like, 'What are the practical applications of that?' or 'Hey, you wanna show me what you learned?' Sure, I can give you my junior year textbook about data bias. Guaranteed to make anyone horny."

Drew laughs, but I don't miss the way his cheeks have turned pink. Even when he's trying to play it cool, his face gives him away. "It's not something you hear every day. What made you decide to go for that? And what are some of the practical applications?"

Groaning, I lean in and give him a nudge, a soft tap of my fingers against his sleeve. That's it—a split second of skin-to-sleeve contact, but it has deadly consequences. He glances down at the spot I've touched, his blush deepening, which makes my heart leap into the general location of my trachea. Immediately, I want to touch him again, and based on the lowering of his lashes, he might want the same thing.

"A horrible abstinence-only sex ed program in high school," I say, refocusing on his question, because it's something I feel strongly about. A program that didn't properly prepare me for what happened my sophomore year of college, but we're not talking about that right now. And since he doesn't live here, we probably won't talk about it ever. "Or at least, that was part of it. I'd never had a chance to learn about sexuality anywhere but the internet, and I barely even knew my own anatomy. It seemed like something I could use beyond an academic setting." I feel myself getting flustered, especially with the way he's watching me, so I pass the question back to him. "And you studied . . . business?"

"I didn't finish college."

"Oh—I'm sorry—I shouldn't have assumed," I say, stumbling over my words, but he holds up a hand.

"No, no, it's okay. I always meant to go back, but I'd been working since I was in high school, which led to a full-time opportunity I couldn't pass up. And then it just never happened."

"No shame in that." I take another bite of pizza. I can't decide if he's being purposefully vague about his job, or if it really is so dull that he can't bear to talk about it except in generalities. "If you're traveling for work, you must be good at what you do. Successful."

"Successful," he repeats, directing that word to the crust on his plate, which he's cutting into with his knife. "How do you even measure that?"

"Ah, so we're moving on to the philosophical portion of the night?" I gaze around the restaurant, wondering how I got here, spilling my career woes to a Jewish vegetarian stranger who works in sales. It's wild how easy it is to talk to him, this guy I didn't know only an hour and a half ago. "I guess I just thought I'd be . . . well, more successful by now," I say, brushing this off with a hollow laugh. "So there it is. It's not that I want to be famous or anything. I just want to create something I can be proud of. You know?"

"I do," he says quietly, his eyes heavy on mine, the soft creases on either side of them making him seem weary for the first time all evening.

We finish our pizza and continue wandering. As his self-appointed tour guide, I go deep into Seattle lore, pointing out the

Jimi Hendrix statue on the intersection of Broadway and Pine, the movie theater that used to be a Masonic temple.

At one point, he holds out his phone, beckoning me closer to see what's on the screen. "I googled 'dearly beloved.' You can say it at a funeral, too."

I exaggerate a groan. "I hate being wrong."

"Would a churro make it better?" he asks, gesturing to a food truck on the next block, and I instantly brighten.

We take our churros to a bench in Cal Anderson Park, which even this late is full of people picnicking, drinking, dancing to music blaring from phones and mini speakers.

"I'm kind of glad that bartender's guinea pigs were such agents of chaos," I say. "Or we might not have met."

"God bless Ricardo and Judith." Drew nudges his churro out of the paper to take a bite. As he does this, his jeans brush against mine, our hips just barely touching. My lungs catch on an inhale, and when I finally let out a breath, I can sense the heat of him not just along my thigh but in the tips of my toes, the back of my neck. He's half a foot taller than I am, but all night, he's carried his height with a quiet kind of grace I'm not used to. He doesn't slouch, but he doesn't lord it over those of us who are vertically challenged.

We could spread out if we wanted to; the bench is big enough.

It quickly becomes evident that neither of us wants to.

This whole thing is surreal. There's no desire to check my phone for the time or chart an escape route, the way I might if I'm at a gathering that's gotten too people-y. When I'm on deadline, I'm laser-focused, but I sent off a final revision of the personal trainer's book last week, and now I'm waiting for my agent to submit me to other gigs, browsing job websites, sitting in that strange void of *what's next*. This is the first time since that mistake with Wyatt that I've felt at home in my own skin. Maybe since before then, if I'm being honest.

"Seattle is winning me over," Drew says. "I might even be a little sad to leave tomorrow."

When he says it, there's an inexplicable twinge in my chest. Of course he's leaving—he's only here on a business trip.

"I can't imagine living anywhere else." I take a sugary nibble of churro. "Do you feel that way about SoCal?"

"Los Angeles," he specifies, and maybe he's realizing he can open up a bit more, too. "It's strange—it's a city where everyone cares about who you are and who you know, and yet it's so massive that it's easy to be anonymous. It makes me feel both like I'm living under a microscope and like this tiny speck in the universe at the same time." Then he shrugs. "But, you know, the weather. And the Mexican food. I'm not sure I could give up sunshine or burritos."

"Fair." And then, when he adjusts to reach for one of the napkins he shoved into his jeans pocket: "Only one of your sleeves is buttoned, by the way," I say, reaching out and tapping the sleeve lightly on the wrist. "Not sure if that was an intentional fashion choice, or . . ."

I'm aware I'm hard-core flirting, punctuating nearly all my sentences with a laugh. This version of myself—I don't hate her. She's carefree and laid-back, two adjectives I've never associated with myself. She's *fun*.

He glances down. "It's probably been that way for hours, huh?"

"I'll fix it for you." I lean in as he gamely holds out his arms, and now my knee is pressed against his, too. "Do you want them both up or both down?" I ask the question hoping for a specific answer. *Up* would give me more reasons to touch him.

"Up, please," he says, blushing again.

His skin is warm, his breath even. I take my time, making sure his sleeves are the same length, each roll of fabric revealing more freckles. When my thumb grazes the underside of his forearm, he twitches but doesn't move away. The next time I do it, it isn't an accident, and his eyes lock on mine with a steady intensity.

I didn't think rolling up the sleeves of a man's shirt could be erotic, but here we are. My heart is hammering against my rib cage and this close, I can see how long his lashes are. Those lines around his eyes, the graying of his hair. I wonder how he feels about it, if he's fighting it or if he's made his peace, or if it's something that's never bothered him at all. His scent, something woodsy that might be leftover cologne he wore to his sales conference or something purely *him*.

He's really lovely, this man, and suddenly it seems unfair that I have only one night with him. The mysterious Drew.

"Thank you," he says in a new kind of voice. Rougher. Richer.

My throat has gone dry, and when I reach into my bag for my entrepreneurial water bottle, my fingers skim the top of Maddy's book.

I fight back a laugh as I pull it out. "I—I accidentally stole this," I say. "I was supposed to pay for it after I got it signed, but then I went to the bar and forgot. We have to go back."

"All this time, I've been cavorting about with a common criminal?" he says, but the look on his face is sheer amusement.

"I could just as easily blame you!" I pat the book gently against his chest, and he clutches his heart, pretending I've wounded him. "If you hadn't been so charming, maybe I wouldn't have been cavorting about with you and forgotten to pay."

As though summoned, a dimple appears in one cheek. "You think I'm charming?"

"I think you're an accessory to petty theft," I say as we get to our feet. "And I also think I've never heard someone use the word 'cavorting' in casual conversation before. I kind of love it?"

"Ah, you see, that's what makes me so charming."

We haven't ventured too far from the bookstore, only about five blocks. Except now when we walk, I'm more aware of Drew's body than I have been all night. The way he makes his steps smaller to keep pace with me, his arm brushing mine.

Of course, when we get there, it's closed—lights off, parking lot empty. Something I did not, in my churro-and-lust-fueled haze, pause to consider.

"Shit," I say after trying the door anyway. "I could just slide some money under the door?" I open up my wallet, realizing I used the last of my cash on the churro. Drew reaches for his pocket, but I shake my head. "Or more logically, come back tomorrow, tell them I inadvertently stole a bestseller, and hope I won't be banned for life."

With a sigh, I drop the book back into my bag. More trouble than it's worth, that thing.

This part of the neighborhood is quieter, the sounds of nightlife echoing in the distance. I lean against the wall of the bookstore, right next to a sticker with a few sparse lines of poetry on it, no longer drunk on anything but adrenaline and staying up late with a handsome stranger.

One who can't seem to take his eyes off me.

"I like this," he says, touching the side of his nose, the same place where mine is pierced. "Suits you. How long have you had it?"

"Since I was seventeen. Or, you know, four and a quarter. My cousin found this place that didn't ID, and she's forever bitter because hers got infected and she had to take it out, and mine didn't."

There's no way discussing nose rings is a precursor to anything remotely romantic, and yet the way he's looking at me, you'd think I'd just said I wasn't wearing underwear.

"It's very cute on you," he says, the compliment landing low in my belly. It's refreshing, someone clearly letting you know they're into you, as opposed to all the back-and-forth with Wyatt. The years of overanalyzing, every brush of sleeve against sleeve necessitating an hour-long mental debrief.

"You, too," I blurt, and then try to laugh it off. "That was a weird reflex. You don't have a nose ring. I'm not even sure what I was trying to say. That you're cute, maybe? I mean—I don't usually do this, run around the city with guys who may or may not be cute—"

"Chandler," he says, that smile playing on his lips as he sways closer. I like the sound of my name in his voice. And the way his gaze keeps dropping to my mouth—I like that, too, though probably not as much as I'd like the scrape of his stubble against my face. Neck. Hips. "It's okay."

And then, as though letting me know how okay it is, he places a hand on my cheek, fingers skimming my ear and sliding into my short hair. Almost involuntarily, I close my eyes. He is so, so close—but I need him closer.

"I don't usually do this, either," I whisper, repeating what's become something of a refrain for us tonight.

"Then I'm glad you made an exception for me."

I open my eyes to find raw determination in his. One sharp inhale, and then I'm reaching up to his collar and pulling his mouth down to mine. The kiss isn't sweet or kind or polite—it's instantly rough, his lips moving against mine in a way that feels urgent. Desperate. A moan catches in my throat, one that he echoes when I slide my tongue against his, gripping his shoulders. It's an electric, intoxicating feeling, kissing this guy against the brick wall outside a bookstore, his hands traveling down to my hips, steadying me so he can kiss me harder. Back to the wall. Shoulder blades digging into brick. I feel drugged, drunk, utterly addicted. Disconnected from reality.

There's something about being anonymous with him that makes me do things I wouldn't normally do—not in public, not with someone I barely know. I scrape my nails along his back, not caring when he kisses my neck and tugs the moan free. It's nearly pornographic, the sound I make, and the way he hardens against me, I can tell exactly how he feels about it.

When we move apart for a breath of night air, his cheeks are an even deeper scarlet, his hair wild, and all I want is to see where else I can make him blush.

His mouth drops to my collarbone, pushing aside my jacket and Sleater-Kinney T-shirt. "Jesus," he murmurs against my skin. "It's ridiculous, how much I like you."

"I like you, too," I say, this innocent statement juxtaposed with the not-at-all-innocent way I arch my hips into his jeans, drawing out a low groan. "Where are you staying?" The street is still deserted, but I imagine it won't be for long. Capitol Hill never is.

There's that smile again, even as he rakes a hand through his make-out-mussed hair. "Not too far from here, actually. The Paramount."

"Solid choice. What with the rooms, and the elevators, and the . . . general Paramount-ness to it."

"Have you been?"

I shake my head, reaching out to roll up his sleeve that's started to fall down. "Maybe you could give me a tour?"

I'm only half-aware of what I'm asking when the question leaves my lips, heavy with suggestion. And once it's out there, I know, the way I haven't been sure of anything in a while, that this is what I want.

Tonight.

Him.

"It seems only fair, when you've been such a great tour guide," he says, eyes never leaving mine. Fierce and inviting, his pupils the deepest black. "But I should mention, I've really only been inside one room. I could show you around the hallway. The closets. The desk chair." A twitch of his mouth. "Or any other pieces of furniture you happen to be interested in."

"I love furniture." I kiss him with more weight this time, heart beating a frantic new rhythm. "Lead the way."

chapter

THREE

've never had a one-night stand. Maybe there's some truth to what Wyatt said about me being a Relationship Girl, but I think the more accurate statement is that I'm simply an Anxiety Girl. I've read too many murder mysteries to go home with a stranger.

So it's a bit of a surprise, then—an excellent one—that as soon as we turn onto the street the hotel is on, we stop at a drugstore for condoms. Before we check out, I add a small bottle of personal lubricant. There's no tiptoeing, no awkwardness, only the certainty of *more* as his hand finds mine, leading me through the hotel's revolving doors and down an ornately decorated hallway to the elevator.

"You know," I say as Drew hits the button marked 14, "just because there's no number thirteen doesn't mean you're not technically on the thirteenth floor."

"And yet I don't feel too unlucky."

There's a family inside, a man and woman and two kids looking like they just came up from the pool, hair dripping and towels wrapped around their shivering shoulders.

"Evening," the woman says to us as we step inside, pushing

into a corner to make room, and I offer the kids a smile. I'm half tempted to tell Drew we can wait for the next one, but I don't hate the way he runs a fingertip up my spine and then back down.

"Evening," Drew says back, voice perfectly solid.

I can't believe I'm doing this. It's an electric pulse of adrenaline that makes me squeeze my thighs together at the pressure starting to build there. I am going to have sex with this man I just met, whose last name I don't know, who I haven't stalked on Instagram or asked Noemie to check out on LinkedIn (because she has one of those accounts that doesn't show when you've looked at someone's profile), and then we'll part ways.

No phone numbers. No strings.

"Have a good night," Drew says to the family when the elevator opens on the fourteenth floor.

I'm all legs as I stumble into the hall with him, as though the slight press of his finger along my spine was what was holding me up. He stops in front of Room 1412, a lock of hair falling over his brow as he struggles with the key, like his nerves are getting in the way, which endears him to me even more. It strikes me that it could be an act, in which case I'm absolutely falling for it, but in this moment, I can't bring myself to care. All I want is his skin on mine as we erase the world outside. A sweaty, indulgent night and a polite goodbye the next morning.

The door's barely clicked shut before he has me pinned against it, mouth on my throat. Nothing polite about it. He's cinnamon sugar and that hint of cologne and something else, something that makes me dizzy when I drag my hands up his back and take a deep breath. My skin is buzzing, burning, *alive.*

It's not until he backs up to kick off his shoes, fisting a hand in his pocket to toss a conference badge onto a desk, that I get a peek at the room. He's kept it clean, or maybe the hotel staff already stopped by to tidy up. His suitcase is open on one of those luggage racks, a closet revealing another button-up shirt and blazer.

But my mind can focus on this for only a split second before he covers me again, freeing me of my denim jacket, which lands in a dark heap on the floor. I toss the bag of condoms somewhere next to it. Maybe because I'm entirely too eager, I go for his belt buckle first. A laugh slips past his lips as I yank it from his waist with a flourish. Our kisses turn deeper. Harder. He's solid heat as he runs his hands down the sides of my body, curving over my generous hips and ass. I give it all right back. A thrust against the bulge in his jeans. A hand palming his back pockets. A shove so that I can get him against the door this time, tasting his jaw, neck, throat, fingers working to undo the buttons at his collar.

Then he tugs me forward in a motion that propels us back, back, back—until my leg slams into hard, cold metal.

The luggage rack.

"*Shit*," I hiss out, clutching at my calf as I try to regain my balance.

He steadies me, eyes going wide, face gorgeously flushed. "You okay?"

"Yep. I'm good." That sting of pain doesn't stand a chance against my libido. I could be limping and I'd still need him on top of me. "And I should also say . . ." My anxiety intervenes, reminding me I've never done this before. "I tested a couple weeks ago, and I'm negative."

"Me, too. Sorry, I should have said something earlier—I don't know all the etiquette for this." There's a sheepishness to the way he says it.

"It's okay," I say, reaching for him again to finish his shirt.

He closes his eyes, lets me take control. "When you were doing that on the bench . . . I was so turned on."

I toss the shirt aside and drop kisses along his bare chest, dragging him down onto the bed with me. I'm too distracted by touching him to get anything more than flashes of what he looks like: the soft curve of his stomach, skin dotted with freckles. A trail of reddish hair disappearing into his boxer briefs. "Not going to lie, I was, too."

When I slip off my T-shirt, he spends a few moments taking in my breasts, spilling out of the bralette I dug from the back of my drawer this morning. My belly has a soft curve to it, too, faint pink stretch marks around my hips and waist, beneath my arms and along my breasts. I thought I'd be self-conscious with someone I met only a few hours ago, but the way he's gazing at me leaves little room for it.

"Your body is just . . ." He trails off with a ragged breath, tracing a reverent thumb down my bra straps. Along the thin cotton, where my nipples are tight and desperate for his touch. "Wish I could tell that Tolkien nerd that things'll really turn around for him one day."

"You're thinking about *Lord of the Rings* right now?" I say with a laugh, but I can't deny the boost he's giving my already inflated confidence. When I imagined casual hookups, I thought they'd be all sweat and gyrating bodies. I didn't realize they could have a sense of humor.

A lowering of his lashes to half-mast, grin turning wicked. "Not anymore." He turns his attention back to my bra, reaching an arm around to the back. "Elusive little thing, isn't it?" he says, fingers fumbling with the fabric, and it takes me a second to realize he's searching for a clasp.

"Oh—it's a bralette," I say. "I can help—"

"No, no, I can do it."

But he doesn't seem to get what I'm saying.

"No—there's no clasp." I twist around, trying to remove the bra. As he pulls it off, I feel a sharp yank around my neck and—

"*Ow*—"

"—oh fuck—"

"—I think your watch is caught in my necklace," I manage as the chain digs into my skin, drawing out a shaky breath. I'm naked from the waist up, my breasts bouncing as we try to untangle ourselves. Left. Right. Under. Through. I'm half trying to keep the necklace from cutting off my air supply, half trying not to laugh—because from any angle, these acrobatics have got to look hilarious.

"Shit, shit, shit, I'm sorry," Drew says when his watch steals a strand of my hair.

"This room is cursed," I mutter, holding a hand to my boobs to keep them from bouncing quite so enthusiastically.

Once he extricates his arm and places his watch safely on the bedside table, I rub at my throat, wondering just how many casualties I can sustain in one night and if this is the universe trying to send me a sign.

"Rule of three," Drew says. "It's got to be smooth sailing from here."

"Please." I reach for his jeans, giving him a lift of my eyebrows when this act does not end in anyone getting maimed. He repeats it with me and—success. "Curse broken?"

"I'd say so."

I tug him on top of me, his bare chest meeting mine, the weight of him allowing me to relax into the moment. Just like that, we're back on track, and the relief is instantaneous. He buries his face between my breasts, teasing a nipple with his thumb and sending a jolt of pleasure straight to my core. I arch my back, my hand drifting to the front of his navy boxers, tented with his desire. The sound he lets out when I palm his cock through the fabric is a work of art. A perfect little moan, a thrust of his hips. A tightening of his hands on my breasts.

Just when I'm starting to think I could lie here all night like this, he lifts up, starts kissing down my stomach. There's an impatience to him now—he doesn't linger. And maybe I can understand that, even if foreplay's always been my favorite part. He hooks his thumbs on either side of my panties and pauses, lifting an eyebrow at me, waiting for my nod before he slides them down. Then his hand is inching up one thigh, everything in me tensing, anticipating before he parts me with two fingers.

Oh. Yes. I sigh into his touch, wrapping my arms around his neck and fisting strands of his hair. And then . . . *yes?*

His technique isn't *bad*, exactly . . . it just lacks finesse. He pumps a finger in and out. In and out. And that's it. No variation. Surely he's just warming up. I refuse to believe that he thinks the key to a woman's pleasure is treating her body like one of those finger-trap toys he just—can't—escape from.

The bed squeaks as he shifts around, getting off to retrieve the drugstore bag. He drops the condoms on the nightstand and holds up the tiny bottle of lube, asking a silent question. *Yes.*

But then he squirts—

Too much.

Way too much.

It drips between my legs and onto the bed beneath me, my ass in a slippery puddle that smells like strawberry vanilla.

"Came out a little faster than I thought, sorry," he says sheepishly, grabbing a few tissues and doing his best to mop it up.

Bless the man, he's persistent. Even if he's not hitting the right spot, the lube makes everything better, slick and warm and sensitive.

"Does she like that?" he asks.

"She?"

A smirk as he uses his other hand to point between my legs. It takes me longer than it should to process what he's saying—and then it hits me.

He's talking about my vagina. Like we're two separate entities.

"Mm-hmm" is all I can say.

It's a relief when he dips his head, and I try my best to focus on what his tongue is doing instead of the wet patch of comforter beneath me.

At first, I think it's is a joke—that he can't really be this inept. But nope, he is entirely serious about what he's doing down there, and I'm worried that if I open my mouth to give him some direction, I'll start laughing. Because he's really just perched right there on the edge of the bed, licking my pubic bone like it's a firecracker Popsicle on the Fourth of July.

"You're doing amazing," he says. Amazing at . . . lying here? And then, as he continues to work his tongue around the same spot: "Oh yeah. Right there?"

Two things become instantly clear to me. One, that this man has no earthly idea where the clitoris is. And two, it's not the room that's cursed—it's *Drew*.

Drew, who blushed when I rolled up his sleeves. Who spoke in one of the Elvish languages in a way that was weirdly charming. Who kissed me like he couldn't wait to get my clothes off but is evidently mystified by oral. A night like this isn't supposed to come with instructions. At least, I don't think so.

"Could you—a little lower?" I finally manage.

He obliges, switching back to his fingers, which is better in the sense that I can feel *something*. "You feel so good," he says. "So hot. So *ready*. I love how hot and ready you are."

In the parts of my mind that aren't cringing, I remember that Little Caesars sells pizzas called Hot-N-Ready, a fact that does not make me any hornier.

His erection strains against his boxers. Gently, I push up on his chest so that I can flip us around. He is *extremely* Hot-N-Ready, and one additional benefit to all this lube is that when I slip my hand inside his boxers and wrap my fingers around him, his head falls back against the pillow, all his freckles giving the impression of filthy, sexy innocence. *Jesus.* The way he shuts his eyes, exposing his elegant neck . . . I don't hate the view. Not at all. And damn it—despite all our mishaps so far, I still want this to be good. Tonight was supposed to get me out of a rut, remind me I can be wild and carefree. I'm not ready to give up just yet.

"I need you," I say into his ear, wondering if there's more truth in those words than I care to admit. His groan and mumbled *please* bring me closer to orgasm than I've been all night.

With my remaining shards of hope, I reach for the box of condoms. He gives me a sly lift of his eyebrows as he takes one from me, and before I can tell him not to, sinks his teeth into it. When he removes it from his mouth, he frowns down at the torn wrapper. A Casanova, he is not.

I grab another one and open it myself this time, giving him a few hard tugs before I roll it on. His eyes flutter shut as he lets out a low hum, shifting me back against the bed with his cock poised at my entrance.

"Fuuuuuuck," he exhales as he pushes into me. "Fuck. Yes. Fuck. *Yes.*" He punctuates each sentence with a pump of his hips.

I try to meet his strokes, but he's going so fast, I can't keep up.

When I reach down to where our bodies are joined in a half-hearted attempt to get myself there, he interprets this as me reaching for his hand.

"*Oooh*, there it is," he pants out as he threads our fingers together. "There it is."

Rhythmically, it sounds like some porno version of "Whoomp! (There It Is)," which is if not the least sexy song in the world, at least in the top five.

"Oh my fucking god," I say out loud, because I can't contain it anymore.

Except he interprets it as a cry of ecstasy and only starts pumping harder. "Almost there," he says. "We can do this. Can you get there, baby?"

Baby. As though he's so lost in the moment, I could be absolutely anyone to him.

In that split second before he tumbles over the edge, I decide I have to fake it. Subtly, of course. A few shaky breaths, a clench of my teeth, and a moan before he collapses on top of me with a harsh, guttural sound.

He rolls to the side, chest heaving, face flushed. "That . . . was incredible," he slurs out.

I just blink up at the ceiling, too stunned to process how this sweet guy turned out to be such a disaster in bed.

After a few moments, he turns to me, placing a hand on my hip. All of a sudden, I feel too exposed. I draw the sheets up over my breasts, but what I'd really love is to bury myself under the whole bed. Maybe dig a grave in front of the hotel. DIED IN PURSUIT OF AN IMPOSSIBLE ORGASM, they'll write on my tombstone. May her memory be a blessing.

"Was it good for you?" he asks.

"Mmm," I say, wondering how obvious it would be if I checked the time on my phone, which is somewhere in the no-man's-land between the bed and the door. It's got to be past two a.m. by now.

I let my eyes fall shut, turning my body to his and letting out a sigh of contentment. And as a result, feel a bit like an asshole. If we were really together, I'd be honest with him. But in a few hours, I'm never going to see him again, a fact that now feels like the most beautiful flash of relief. I barely know anything about him—maybe he's a flat-earther or doesn't believe in vaccines—and I don't have to.

Maybe this is a sign from the universe. One-night stands: clearly not a Chandler Cohen kind of thing.

Relationship Girl, Wyatt's voice taunts.

"I don't have to be at the conference until tomorrow afternoon. Maybe we could sleep in? Order room service?" His mouth kicks upward as his hand dances along my hip. "Do this again?"

I'm too exhausted to come up with an excuse. "Definitely."

Drew yawns into his shoulder. "I'm really glad you sat down at that bar." It's the last thing he says to me before he drifts off, chest rising and falling with his steady breaths.

I can't stay here. If we wake up in the morning and he asks how "she" slept, I'm going to lose it. This was a bad idea, terrible idea, and the only hope I have for self-preservation is if I make a run for it.

Now.

As delicately as I can, I peel back the sheets and swing my legs out of bed, grimacing at the pain that shoots up my calf. We were messy, and my clothes are scattered across the floor. I tiptoe around the room before finding my phone beneath my T-shirt, using the light from the screen to collect the rest of my clothes.

It's okay, I tell myself as I shove on my pants. *I'm going to laugh about this tomorrow. Probably.*

Finally, I make it to the door, opening it up and shutting it with the quietest click, locking my bad decisions inside.

AFTER 4 SEASONS, IT'S LIGHTS OUT FOR 'THE NOCTURNALS'

BY TASHA KIM, *THE HOLLYWOOD REPORTER*

LOS ANGELES—In announcing its fall schedule yesterday, TBA Studios shocked many of its dedicated fans: *The Nocturnals*, a soapy drama following college-aged werewolf Caleb Rhodes and a ragtag group of friends navigating life, love, and the supernatural, has not been renewed for a fifth season.

Fans immediately took to Twitter, and a petition to revive the series amassed more than ten thousand signatures overnight. The show, which pulled in meager but consistent ratings for TBA, has gained quite a cult following since its 2008 premiere. Parties fans have dubbed all-nighters are common for season premieres and finales, and its stars are a staple at fan conventions nationwide.

"It's not going to be easy to say goodbye to these characters," said creator Zach Brayer, who admitted he was still reeling from the news. "But we're so grateful to the fans who've stuck with us for this long. That's the most any showrunner can ask for."

The Nocturnals stood out on a slate of shows marketed toward teens, largely because the main characters begin episode one already in college.

"College has killed so many shows," said Marion Welsh, head of series programming at TBA. "As soon as you split up the characters you've gotten to know throughout high school, the show loses some of what hooked you in the first place. That was what we loved about *The Nocturnals*—that they were doing something different."

Brayer says they prepared themselves for the possibility of cancellation, and that when the season 4 finale—now the series finale—airs in two weeks, he hopes it'll be satisfying for viewers. "We were able to end it the way we wanted to, with these characters graduating and heading out into the world, one they now know is full of danger and mystery but also love and hope. And that was really the crux of the show: that hope would always conquer all."

FOUR

The sound of Noemie's high-end espresso machine wakes me up too early, a whirring and grinding that sounds more like a Category 5 storm than a prelude to coffee.

When my pillow does nothing to drown it out, I heave a groan and slowly extricate myself from beneath the blankets, rolling over to check my phone.

Missed you last night.

With a start, I bolt upright in bed, wondering how the hell Drew got my number. I must have been careless and left something behind, or maybe he's just this side of creepy to manage to track me down. Oh god—I *cannot* see him again.

My heart starts back up with a new, less panicked rhythm when I blink my bleary eyes and see the name: Wyatt Torres.

Missed you last night. Just four words and he's able to take me back to that evening a few weeks ago, desperate kisses and twisted sheets and entry number one on my list of regrets. A list that only seems to keep growing.

I flop back onto the pillow, scrolling his social media for photos of the housewarming. There he is with some of our other friends from college, posing in front of an impressive charcuterie board. It looks like a proper, classy AF party for the gainfully employed, nary a Ping-Pong ball or Solo cup in sight. Wyatt, with his job as a reporter at the *Tacoma News Tribune*. Alyssa, an investigative reporter at a local TV station. Josh, the sole reporter for a twice-weekly newspaper on the Eastside, covering everything from city council meetings to high school football games.

We always joked in college that we couldn't wait to be the age where we could throw *mature* parties, the kind with hors d'oeuvres and cocktail napkins and wine we hadn't bought for two dollars at Trader Joe's. We'd all be award-winning journalists then, sharing anecdotes about our latest stories and bragging about who'd be the first to make the front page. If only we'd known that a digital front page was slightly less exciting.

It's easy to forget that even before that, I wanted to write books of my own, before I realized it was impractical to think I'd be one of the lucky ones who could survive on that alone. I wrote all the time as a kid, stapling together little books with haphazardly doodled covers. Mysteries were my favorite; I loved the thrill of being able to trick the reader (aka my parents or Noemie), dropping what I'm sure were very obvious red herrings and leading them to a conclusion they swore they never saw coming. In hindsight, they might have been lying to protect my fragile preteen self-esteem. Being able to create chaos and then wrap everything up soothed my anxious brain, and there was something innately satisfying about stringing sentences together, to the point where I could hear their rhythm in my head before I typed them out. Nothing beat the pure and utter joy of finding exactly the right word to mean exactly the right thing.

That was a long time ago, when you could tell adults you wanted to be an author when you grew up and they'd grin and tell you how creative you were, how smart! But then you got older. Closer to the age you'd need to be when a school printed on a piece of paper the thing you'd committed the last four years of your life to. *You have to be a little more realistic*, guidance counselors said. *Does anyone even make money doing that?* your parents asked, worried. So you started saying *journalist*, because that was writing, too, only you didn't get to make anything up. And they started smiling at you again, told you about all the interesting articles they'd read lately.

Sometimes on weekends, when I'm between deadlines, I open up the password-protected folder in the depths of my computer, My Documents / Personal / Other / Misc, just long enough to read what I wrote the last time I was between deadlines. Maybe I'll swap out a word or two, but I haven't made progress beyond that in months. Years.

Somehow, looking around my room, with its discounted Anthropologie duvet and candles burned down to stubs and stack of cozy mysteries I've read dozens of times but keep close for comfort, I don't feel nearly as settled as I hoped I'd be at this stage of my life. I'm still not entirely sure I'm doing my taxes right.

I throw off the sheets, noticing the violet bruise blooming on my calf. A lovely memento from last night. When I got home after an Uber ride with a too-chatty driver—I check my phone again—five hours ago, I grabbed for the first clean-ish pajamas and socks I saw. I almost never sleep without my feet covered, except on the two days of the year it hits eighty degrees. It's become something of a joke in my family that I ask for socks for every birthday or holiday, always seriously. I love wearing them, I'm always cold, and the occasional teasing is entirely worth it.

I can't think of anything charming or witty enough to text Wyatt, but there's a message from my mom from earlier this morning, a slightly blurry picture of Maddy's book with the caption, **I still don't know who she is bt u did a grt job! thirsty!!** And then a string of water droplet emojis. I don't have the heart to tell her what they really mean.

It always takes a moment to decipher my parents' texts. They're a bit older, and while I've taught my dad five times how to attach something to an email, they're trying, and I love them for it. This text, at least, is easy to reply to, so I send my mom a thank-you and pull on a robe, following the scent of Noemie's bean-of-the-month subscription box downstairs.

My room, a bathroom, and a guest room comprise the upstairs, and I pay a comically low rent compared to most Seattle apartments. This quaint Ballard neighborhood with its brightly painted houses and landscaped backyards might as well have a sign saying YOUR PAYCHECK MUST BE THIS BIG TO MOVE IN. Every time I try to tell my cousin I should pay more, she waves it off. "I like you here," she'll insist, as though the mere fact of my presence is worth a few hundred dollars a month.

"Morning!" Noemie chirps from the kitchen. "Just opened a new bag. From Maine."

Put something in a subscription box, and my cousin will lose her mind over it. Over the years, she's subscribed to products ranging from practical to bizarre: toilet paper, sheet masks, artisan hot sauces, even a box that mails monthly clues to solve a mystery. One Hanukkah, she got me a sock-of-the-month subscription, and it remains the best gift I've ever received.

I've lived here for three years, and it never fails to surprise me how she sticks to a schedule on the weekends. She's Saturday chic in a cropped sweatshirt and leggings, dark hair in a ponytail, wearing her tortoiseshell glasses and sipping coffee from a mug one of her publicist colleagues got her that says LIFE'S A PITCH, paging through the *Seattle Times* because we refuse to let it go the way of the *Post-Intelligencer*.

There's a pan of scrambled eggs on the stove, dotted with red peppers and onions and broccoli, a new loaf of sourdough next to the toaster: a pale pink one I fell in love with in the clearance section at Target that remains my sole contribution to the house's appliance collection. I take out my favorite mug, the one with a vintage typewriter on it, and fill it to the brim.

Noemie flicks to the arts and culture section as I sit down next to her. "You didn't have to make breakfast," I say, dabbing my scramble with some of July's prickly pear habanero hot sauce.

"It was the least I could do. The lights were off when I got home, so I figured you must have beaten me here."

"Is everything okay at work?"

She shrugs, not meeting my eyes. "Maaaaaybe."

"Nome. You cannot let them yank you around like that. You deserve to have a life outside of work."

"It's not my forever job," she reassures me, as though a career is something that can be permanent. "Once I finish this campaign, I'm out of there. I swear. I've been looking at other PR jobs."

I can't count how many times she's said this before. Even with the house and the steady paychecks and the subscription boxes, Noemie has precious little time left for friends or hobbies. Pivoting from journalism was maybe the right choice financially; publicist jobs are more stable and higher paid, but it's wreaked havoc on the rest of her life. More than a couple holidays with our family have been cut short because she had a client who needed something right that moment. Sometimes I think she did the smart thing, leaving journalism when she did, before she ventured out into the industry and it flattened her self-esteem. Other times, I wonder if she fast-tracked her life when she might have been happier slowing it down.

Noemie takes a sip of coffee, clearly eager to change the subject. "What time did you get home?"

"I didn't exactly beat you here." I nudge eggs around my plate, debating how much I want to share. It's a pointless thought process—I tell Noemie everything eventually. "I, um . . . went home with someone."

She nearly drops her mug, liquid splashing down the side. "Oh my god. *Who?*"

"A guy I met at the bookstore bar."

"I need more than that," she says. "The extent of my social life is one-sided flirting with the barista in my office lobby. I have to live vicariously through you."

"Well . . ." I decide to start with the positives. "At first, it was great. We were vibing, he was funny and a little nerdy in this supercute way. And you know me—as soon as I detect even the slightest hint of creepy, I'm gone."

"You do have an excellent creep detector."

"Thank you." A bite of toast, and then I keep going. "He was in town from LA for a conference. We got into this friendly argument about how Seattle doesn't have any good by-the-slice pizza places—"

"True—"

"—and we tried to find one. So we ate a bit, talked a bit, flirted a bit . . ." My face heats up as I remember the way he looked at me as I rolled up his sleeves. *It's ridiculous, how much I like you.* "Oh, and then I realized I forgot to buy Maddy's book. I still have to go back and pay, by the way. I don't want that on my conscience." As if it's a Pavlovian response, I reach for my glass of water. "Then we wound up back at his hotel. At which point we proceeded to have"—I lower my head to the table made from reclaimed wood, pausing for dramatic effect—"the worst sex of my life."

This time, my cousin drops her fork onto her plate with a sharp clang. "No, no, no—what? That's not where I thought this was going."

"Trust me, neither did I. It was the Murphy's Law of sex—everything that could go wrong, did. His watch got caught on my necklace, lube went everywhere, and then he just . . . jackhammered his way through the rest of it."

"And I'm guessing you were left slightly unsatisfied?"

I nod. "I don't even think a map would have saved him. Poor guy was clueless," I say. "If we'd been dating, I would have tried to help him out a bit more, but it felt so strange, giving instructions to someone I didn't know."

It strikes me again that I could have said something. Could have told him, *Hey, I'm not there yet* and showed him how to get me there. I've grown comfortable giving directions in bed, but I can't help thinking it wouldn't have been worth it during a one-night stand. Besides, I've learned that not everyone wants to be coached. Some past boyfriends took it as an insult, although with those who were open to it, we managed to have good, communicative relationships after some initial fumbling. But that definitely wasn't everyone, and I wasn't in the mood to do any ego soothing last night.

I imagine him waking up this morning, reaching to the other side of the bed only to find it empty. A slight pang of guilt settles in my stomach.

But I would have been gone at the end of today, anyway.

Noemie gets up and refills her mug, then takes a sip while she leans against the kitchen counter, looking pensive. "I want to ask how sex ed could have failed so many men in this way, but I didn't know where my clitoris was until I was twenty-five. So, it definitely failed me, too."

This I know, because when she told me a few years ago, I was all too happy to recommend a starter vibrator and a list of my favorite sex-positive influencers. And it wasn't the first time—I've had other friends ask me the same thing. Ever since the first intro course I took for my minor, it's felt completely natural to talk about. No shame or embarrassment. Or maybe it was always supposed to be natural, but society tried to convince me otherwise.

"He seemed to think mine was located in my kidneys."

"I'm sorry. I'm trying so hard not to laugh."

"And I'm trying to erase it from my memory, thanks," I say, but I can't help laughing, either. Surely, the more space I have from it, the funnier it'll be.

Noemie heads back to the kitchen table and lays a hand on my shoulder. "I have just the thing."

"THIS IS DOWNRIGHT INHUMANE," I MANAGE. I JUMP RIGHT, LEFT, throw my arms up and then back down. Above us, green and purple lights flash in time with the techno dance track. "You—are—a masochist."

"I prefer the term 'aerobic connoisseur.'" Noemie bounces on the trampoline next to me, her dark ponytail swinging from side to side. Her form is perfect as she launches into a set of ten jumping jacks. I can already feel myself lagging behind, muscles protesting.

"Knees up, punch it out!" the instructor shouts from the front of the room. "Beautiful! Double time!"

I force my legs to go faster, struggling to catch my breath. During her rare weekend free time, Noemie loves trying the latest exercise trends, and as a result she's dragged me to hot barre, aerial Pilates, and now, to Trampoline XXX—seriously, that's the name of the class, and when she texted me the link while I got dressed, I was very concerned about what I was about to click on. There are twenty of us in a dark room, sweating on top of mini trampolines while neon lights blink overhead. It's sensory overload, and maybe that's their tactic: distract you from the fact that you're exercising with blinding optics and terrible music.

The song changes, the instructor bounce-bounce-bouncing to a Jennifer Lopez remix. "Find that beat, press those heels down. Do it for J.Lo!"

The trampoline trembles beneath me as I work to keep my balance.

"At least you're not thinking about last night, right?" Noemie says.

"Shhh, I'm trying not to disappoint J.Lo."

On my trampoline, I bounce harder and harder, until the music ends and the instructor gives us all a round of applause.

"Fantastic work, tramps!" the instructor yells, and I turn to Noemie and mouth, *Tramps?* She just muffles a laugh as we head toward the gym's locker room, grabbing a couple towels to dry off. "See you next week!"

"How do you feel?" Noemie asks, flashing me a grin as she unlocks her locker.

I dab my face with a towel, readjusting some of the pins I haphazardly slid into my hair to keep it from flying everywhere. "Amazing, and I hate you for it."

Annoyingly, the trampoline workout has cleared my brain more than . . . well, more than I hoped the one-night stand would. Drew was a blip on my sexual timeline. And I'm sure I'll be able to see Wyatt again soon without wanting to crawl into a hole and embrace the darkness as my one true god.

Although deep down, a tiny part of me is worried something's wrong with me that Wyatt didn't want a relationship. In the past month, I've had two one-night stands—the first because I thought it was heading toward something more, and the second because I wanted to feel *good*, desired, beautiful. The things I thought I could feel with Wyatt, who already knew me.

Wyatt Torres: kind eyes, incredible hair, the source of my agony. We met freshman year in a journalism prereq, and while I'd always thought he was cute, there were so many breakup horror stories in our cohort that I was terrified of acting on it. So I convinced myself I was happy to stay friends with him, and for the most part, I was. We lived in the same dorm, took the same classes, got the same magazine internship, but we were never competitors. A win for one of us was a win for both of us, for the future of journalism itself! Wyatt wasn't picky about where he wanted to work; he'd go anywhere that wanted him. So we applied for the same fellowships. Were rejected from the same fellowships. Then, in a brilliant burst of journalistic hope, the two of us were hired at The Catch a year after we graduated. The online mag covered everything from politics to pop culture, hitting its stride with the kind of listicles that started popping up in the early 2010s. It was fresh and fun and felt so *current*, even though it wasn't groundbreaking journalism. I'd been an avid reader for years, and getting a job there, working alongside names I'd read in bylines, felt like meeting a celebrity.

We had all these shared experiences that it only made sense to share the rest of our lives. Before we saw each other naked and ruined everything.

I open up my locker, digging for my phone. Three missed calls from my agent, who generally does her best not to work on weekends, and a handful of texts with increasing levels of urgency. Chandler, hi, are you free? I know it's a Saturday, but I need to talk to you. Call me back asap!

"What is it?" Noemie asks, retying her ponytail.

"Stella." I grab my bag as quickly as I can, phone in a vise grip. "Meet you outside?"

Stella Rosenberg is one of the top nonfiction agents in the country. She's a fortyish mom of twins, living in Brooklyn, down-to-earth with her clients and an utter shark when she needs to be, and I still can't quite believe we work together. Though I've never met her, I owe her everything for turning my freelance articles into something resembling a career.

After I was laid off, I sold some pieces for pennies as the journalism world went up in flames. I applied to so many jobs that when I got the email from Stella, I had to peek back at the posting to remember what it was. *Looking for writing samples for a ghost-written book. Utmost discretion required.* Honestly, it had seemed like it might be a scam. I had to sign an NDA before I even learned the name of whom I'd be writing for.

At first, the fact that I was able to find something using my journalism degree—technically, communication with a concentration in journalism—felt like a good sign. Ghostwriting involved research, interviewing, deadlines, all things I'd had plenty of experience with. My parents always told me a college degree was a jumping-off point, that it didn't necessarily matter what I studied because my skills would be transferable. But I didn't want to transfer them anywhere. I wanted to write.

It isn't that I'm not grateful for the work—I am, tremendously. Maybe it was turning thirty last year that made me reassess my career, but I'd love to have something I could put my name on.

And maybe that thing is a book and maybe it isn't, but there has to be some kind of story I'm the right person to tell.

Stella picks up on the first ring. "Thank god I caught you," she says. In the background, I hear dogs barking, kids babbling. "Sorry, I'm at the park. It's a zoo on weekends."

I lean against the wall outside the gym. "No worries. What's going on?"

"So, you know we've been submitting you for a few new projects." Another thing about Stella: She doesn't waste time. Dives right in, no pleasantries. "There's an actor who just sold a memoir whose team is looking for a ghostwriter. And they loved your samples."

"An actor," I repeat with some trepidation. And, okay, maybe a little excitement. "Who is it?"

"Finnegan Walsh," she says. "Lola, you know you need to ask permission before petting a dog! My kids had too much sugar for breakfast. Anyway—he was on this werewolf show that ended about ten years ago. Four seasons. Really devoted fans."

The name doesn't ring a bell. Then again, I can't remember the last time I had cable, and I used my parents' Netflix account in college, so if it's not an early-2000s sitcom or Netflix original, odds are, I haven't seen it.

"I know you said you wanted to do something a bit more serious this time," Stella continues, "but I think this could be really exciting. He has a huge cult following, especially among millennials and Gen Z. And the team wants you two to work closely on this—it's not going to be another Maddy DeMarco." She curses under her breath. "I swear to god, they're lucky you were such a saint about it."

I can't deny that's appealing. "Okay, so what's the next step?" I ask. "Do they want to talk to me?"

"That's the best part. He's in town for Emerald City Comic Con until the end of the day, and he and his manager want to meet you for lunch. That's why I sounded so frantic—they're going to be at the restaurant at one thirty."

Lunch? It's almost too many things to process at once. I check the time on my phone—it's already ten past one.

And I'm wearing gym clothes, still dripping sweat from Trampoline XXX.

"I—I think I can make it."

"Excellent," she sings, just as there's a commotion in the background, before giving me the restaurant name. "Tell them you're there to see Joe—that's his manager. And call me after to let me know how it goes. Thanks, Chandler!"

With that, she hangs up.

I stare at my phone for a few moments, my brain whirring as Noemie approaches, her gym bag slung over one arm. "Can you drive me downtown so I can meet someone named Finnegan Walsh?"

Noemie blinks wide dark eyes at me. "Excuse me, I blacked out for a moment. What did you say?"

"Finnegan . . . Walsh? He's an actor?"

"No shit, he's an actor," she says. "Finn Walsh, of *The Nocturnals*, the most formative show of my teen years? I've only tried to get you to watch it a hundred times." She unzips her bag and unearths her keys. "Holy shit. Are you *writing a book* with Finn Walsh?"

"I might be," I say, and explain the call. And that I have to be at lunch with him in fifteen minutes.

On our drive downtown, Noemie does her best to fill me in on 2008's biggest paranormal teen drama while I shimmy out of my leggings in her backseat. Typically, I'd spend hours researching a potential new author, but this time, I'm going to have to rely on my cousin. And she might be better than Wikipedia.

By the time we hit the freeway, I know the following about Finnegan Walsh:

He starred on the TV show *The Nocturnals* from 2008 to 2012, about hot werewolves navigating college life (but he didn't even play one of the werewolves). Oliver Huxley was a biology major trying to find a cure for his werewolf crush, who Noemie explains he was adorably devoted to, even when she pushed him away because she thought he could never love a beast like her. As a result, he ranks high on Noemie's list of sexiest nerds, sandwiched between Adam Brody and Joseph Gordon-Levitt.

During filming, he kept a relatively low profile, i.e., no scandals or controversies ("that we know of," Noemie says). Since *The Nocturnals* went off the air, he's starred in some low-budget romantic comedies, and more recently, a couple of Hallmark Christmas movies, including one from a couple years ago called *Ms. Mistletoe* that Noemie admits she watched and unironically loved.

She opens up the glove compartment and hands me a bottle of dry shampoo as the car swerves. "Here. Put this on. And there should be some ballet flats in that Whole Foods bag."

"Be honest with me. Are you running an Ann Taylor outlet out of the back of your car?"

A glare in the mirror. "Don't knock Ann Taylor. She's gotten me through a lot of tough times."

Noemie and I are not the same size. Her black-and-white-checked blouse strains over my chest, but with a cardigan, it'll be okay. Some dry shampoo in my hair and I'm good to go.

"Are you sure I look presentable?" I ask, tugging at the skirt once she pulls into a loading zone downtown. It shows my bruise, but it's better than the threadbare leggings I wore to the gym. "My breasts aren't too breasty in this?"

Noemie assesses me, smooths a stubborn strand of hair back into place. "You look business-casual hot. I'd hire you to write a book for the horny werewolf fandom."

A quick hug and a promise to tell her everything, and then she's gone.

My heart roars in my ears. I've never met an author in person like this, not in what essentially sounds like an interview situation with two strangers I learned about less than a half hour ago. It's been cobbled together so last-minute, which cranks my anxiety up past eleven. Typically, I'd need at least a week to prepare for something like this—write practice questions, rehearse practice answers, try on a dozen outfits before settling on whichever one I hated the least. It's always been easier to let my writing do the talking.

They loved your samples, Stella said. I just have to be normal. I cling to that as I step inside Pear Bistro, funnily enough, the same vegan restaurant I recommended to Drew yesterday, although now is not the time to think about that. Hopefully I've learned enough from Noemie's Finnegan Walsh monologuing to fake my way through this meeting. *The Nocturnals. Lucky Us*, a direct-to-DVD romantic comedy about two people with winning lottery tickets who have to share their jackpot. *Ms. Mistletoe.*

When I tell the host the manager's name, he gives me a closed-lipped smile and says, "Right this way."

It's only when the table comes into view that I start to wonder if I passed out during Trampoline XXX and now I'm stuck inside a nightmare.

Because sitting at the table next to a middle-aged man in a

gray suit is someone a little too familiar. He's looking down at his phone, but the auburn hair, the freckles, the confident set of his shoulders—I'm positive it's him.

The guy who stumbled his way around my body and doused me with strawberry lube.

The guy whose room I snuck out of only nine hours ago—because I wasn't supposed to see him ever again.

THE NOCTURNALS

Season 1, Episode 7: "Revelations"

INT. OAKHURST LIBRARY—NIGHT

*ALICE CHEN enters and spots OLIVER HUXLEY at his
usual table, head bent over a book. She stalks
toward him, shoulders high, ready to give him a
piece of her mind.*

> ALICE
> You need to stop hanging around Meg
> if you know what's good for you. You
> might think she's a normal girl,
> but . . .

> HUX
> None of us are normal. In fact, I've
> always considered normal to be quite
> boring. I'd much rather be unusual.

> ALICE
> There's unusual, and then there's
> *this.* And she wouldn't want me to
> tell you *this.*

> HUX
> If you're messing with me, Alice, it
> isn't funny. I get enough of that
> from Caleb, and it's not exactly my
> favorite way to spend my time.

                    ALICE
          I'm serious. She's not just an
          experiment you can run again and
          again until you get the results you
          want. She's my best friend.

                    HUX
          I know that. And you have to believe
          that I care about her.

                    ALICE
          I—I do. God, I'm going to regret
          this . . .

*Alice walks to the edge of the room, glances out
the windows, and takes a deep breath.*

          That night you were in the dining hall
          and she suddenly had to run out? And
          you didn't hear from her for two days?

                    HUX
          I thought she was late to class. An
          evening class, she said later, one
          with a lot of homework.

                    ALICE
          Or when her clothes were covered in
          fur and you asked if she had a dog,
          and she couldn't give you a straight
          answer? Or when she got sick during
          the full moon? Or those scratches on
          her neck?

                    HUX
          There has to be a rational
          explanation for—

                    ALICE
          She's a werewolf, Hux.

                    HUX
          And how the hell do you know that?

Alice whirls around, eyes flashing.

                    ALICE
          Because I am, too.

chapter

FIVE

This has to be a mix-up. A mistake. The wrong table.

But his manager is getting to his feet, giving me a warm smile. "Chandler Cohen?" he asks, and somewhat mechanically, I feel myself nod.

Drew/Finnegan finally glances up, and when his gaze meets mine, he spills one of the restaurant's signature juices down the front of his unfortunately white shirt. Something with beets, from the look of it.

"Careful there!" his manager says, flagging down a server. "Could we get some more napkins?"

I just stand there, frozen, Noemie's skirt too tight around my hips and her shirt too tight around my breasts and that bruise far too noticeable and dear god *why*. And *how*. And *fuuuuuck*.

Finnegan/Drew is ashen, unsure whether to focus on the spreading fuchsia blotch or the sudden appearance of the one-night stand who wasn't there when he woke up this morning. He seems to settle for both and neither, mouth falling open while he dabs a napkin two inches to the left of where the stain starts.

"I'm so sorry," I sputter out, wondering if it would reflect poorly on Stella if I turned and made a run for it. "Your shirt, I—"

"Not your fault," Finnegan says to the stain. It's a different kind of voice than the one he used on me last night. Professional. Distant.

The server arrives with another glass of water and a stack of cloth napkins, which Finnegan uses to attack his shirt with a newfound gusto. His manager pulls out a chair for me, and I practically collapse into it, folding my legs to hide the bruise from view.

Slowly, the pieces come together. He lives in LA. He was here for a conference—that must have been Emerald City Comic Con. The way he spoke about his career, the vagueness . . . he must have been worried I'd recognize him. Hence the fake name. And when those costumed con-goers showed up, he'd acted strange, hadn't he?

"Well! What a way to break the ice," his manager says with a laugh. He extends a hand to me. "Joe Kowalczyk."

"Chandler. And you must be Finnegan." I place a distinct emphasis on his name.

"Finn," he says, and when he breaks from the stain long enough for a handshake, his eyes flash with suspicion. As though maybe I planned this all along. His freckles are even more pronounced in the daylight. At night, he seemed to have an air of mystery about him, but at one thirty, the September sun slanting through the greenhouse windows and turning his red hair golden, he looks every bit the Hollywood type. Defined cheekbones, microscopic pores, a my-aftershave-probably-cost-more-than-your-entire-outfit set of his jaw.

This isn't the first time I've touched him, of course, and it's much less intimate than anything we did in that hotel room. The handshake should be perfunctory. Awkward, maybe. And yet somehow, the way his fingers slide against mine, thumb briefly rubbing my wrist—so slight, I'd think nothing of it if we hadn't already met—manages to spark far more electricity than anything we did last night.

Last night. The way he kissed me up against the door of the hotel room before everything went so horribly wrong. The way I moaned into his mouth and—

—and faked an orgasm.

I cannot work on this book.

Joe sets down his menu. "Thanks for taking the time to meet with us on such short notice," he says. "Typically, we'd have arranged a video chat before flying you out to LA, but given you live here, it seemed a little like kismet."

Finn continues to scrub at his shirt. I can't look at him, because when I do, I'm going to imagine the guy who asked *Does she like that?* starring in a movie called *Ms. Mistletoe,* and I'll be forced to wonder whether it's about someone who literally has the last name Mistletoe or if there's some kind of Christmas-themed pageant where the woman with the most holiday spirit wins Finnegan's heart. And then I won't be able to stop laughing. And if I start laughing, I'm going to pop a button on Noemie's ruffled Ann Taylor blouse and treat Joe and Finn to a show of the five-dollar neon yellow sports bra from Ross Dress for Less I'm wearing underneath.

I do my best to match Joe's grin. Might as well make Finn as uncomfortable as possible. "I couldn't agree more."

Finn starts coughing. Violently.

"Food first, and then business," Joe says. "And Chandler—it's on me."

While both Joe and Finn order portobello burgers, the priciest item on the menu, I can't bring myself to ask for anything other than the soup of the day, which at $17 is one of the cheaper dishes. I don't belong here—not in my borrowed clothes, and not with the history I have with Finn. This isn't my world.

Once we've ordered, Joe folds his hands in front of him. With his immaculate suit and slicked-back salt-and-pepper hair, he's a little too polished for this Seattle weekend crowd. "I'm not sure if your agent told you, but we've fallen in love with your writing."

"She might have mentioned it, but I'd never turn down a compliment."

Joe laughs. "Then allow me to tell you again: You have a relatable, authentic style that we think would be perfect for Finn's book. You have this way of capturing even the most everyday details and making them seem significant."

Finn punctuates Joe's words with a slight motion of his chin.

I reach for my water, hoping it'll calm the blush on my cheeks. "I—thank you. I'm honored to hear that." Joe seems kind enough, but the little experience I've had with celebrities has taught me that they're often not who they appear to be. Knowing Finn's an actor, I shouldn't be surprised he gave a fake name or charmed me so easily, even though he's far from A-list. In fact, it's a relief I've never seen him in anything. I'd be too starstruck to string together a sentence.

Now that I'm sitting across from him in the daytime, there *is* something vaguely familiar about him, but that could also be simply that now that I know he's famous, my brain is working overtime to place him.

"We want someone young enough to appeal to the millennials who grew up with Finn on *The Nocturnals*, but with enough experience to handle a project of this magnitude. It's been a challenge, finding a writer with that unique combination of skills. Your second book just came out?"

I nod, wondering where I tossed Maddy's book after I got home last night. "And I just turned in a revision of my next one."

"Excellent," Joe says. "Your publishers all spoke very highly of you."

I'm about to reach my compliment threshold. "What exactly are you wanting this memoir to accomplish?" I ask, no longer physiologically capable of talking about myself. "I mean, obviously, you want it to sell well. But what kind of angle are you looking at for Dr—for Finn's story?"

"Great questions. There's a side to every actor that the public never sees, of course. We don't want this to be a typical memoir. Maybe the chapters aren't chronological, or it's a series of vignettes or anecdotes . . . something like that. Some kind of unique structure. Essentially, we know Finn has a story to tell, and this is our chance to rebrand him, while also capitalizing on what made him popular in the first place."

Strange that his manager would answer this instead of him. I glance over at Finn, waiting for him to add something, given this whole discussion hinges on a book that's, well, about *him*.

But he just nods, finally seeming to give up on the juice stain and adding one last napkin to the pile to his left. "Joe pretty much covered it."

Okay then.

Our food arrives, and I dig into my curried pumpkin soup like the lifeline it is, trying not to estimate the cost-per-spoonful. It doesn't escape my attention that Finn does the same thing with the utensils that he did at the pizza place. He inspects them in this surreptitious way, as though he doesn't want anyone to catch him doing it. Then he carefully saws off a hunk of bun and portobello with a knife and fork. Meanwhile, Joe grabs his burger and takes a huge bite, either used to Finn's habits or unaware.

"Let's talk logistics," Joe says, dipping a sweet potato fry into eggless aioli. "We've made arrangements with the publisher to accommodate Finn's schedule, so you'd be accompanying him around the country as he attends various conventions he's already committed to."

"Oh—I see. My agent didn't mention that. I . . . haven't really traveled much." This seems like the most professional way of saying that I can't afford it.

Joe waves this off. "The hotels, the flights—all of that's covered, along with what I think you'll find is a very reasonable per diem. And I spoke with your agent, and we'd be happy to negotiate a thirty percent increase on what you were paid for your last book."

I choke on a pomegranate seed, trying and failing to act as though it's normal to be receiving this kind of offer—if it's even an offer. I hate how appealing it sounds after the shit show with Maddy. Even with personal trainer Bronson's book, we were on such an accelerated schedule that our calls and meetings never left much room for the writing to breathe. I've never done anything like this: getting to know a subject on a level this deep before writing about them.

I try to imagine it, sitting in a corner with my notebook while people dressed as otherworldly creatures pose for photos with Finn.

Then I push it all out of my mind, out of the restaurant, into the compost bins outside. There's just no way that my next project is writing a memoir for my failed one-night stand. I'd laugh if I weren't *thisclose* to spontaneously combusting from the sheer embarrassment of it all.

"We expect the work to last up until the reunion," Joe continues.

"Reunion?" I repeat, hoping I haven't missed something else.

"For *The Nocturnals*," Finn says. It's the first time he's spoken directly to me in at least ten minutes. At this mention of the show, he seems to come back to himself, straightening in his chair as he continues to slice off sections of his burger. "They haven't officially announced it yet, but we've all signed on. A special to mark ten years since the finale aired. It'll be taped at the beginning of December."

"My cousin will be over the moon. She's a huge fan."

Joe smiles again. "And then you can finish writing on your own—of course, with Finn and the publisher's input, but that part can be done primarily remotely. You'll have all the access to him that you want."

Oh, I've already had plenty.

My traitorous body heats up. All of this is too much, and Noemie's business casual is nearly suffocating me. Death by ruffles. I tug at the collar of the blouse. Cross and uncross my legs, accidentally flashing my bruise.

"That looks painful," Finn says, and I can see it in his eyes: the chance to gain control over the situation. "How'd you get that?"

I do my best to send him a glare as I sink my spoon into the soup bowl, bright orange sloshing over the side.

A phone rings, and Joe reaches to pull it out of his pocket. "Would you two excuse me? I have to take this. It's Blake," he says with a knowing roll of his eyes, and I mouth, *Lively?* to Finn, whose mouth only twitches in response.

Once Joe leaves, all the questions and confusion about Finn rise to the surface. My grip tightens on my spoon. Because I'm not just confused—I'm *angry*. Angry he lied to me, angry I'm sitting here like a fucking idiot with my delicious pumpkin soup while his manager taunts me with an amazing job I absolutely cannot take. My mind was made up as soon as I saw him sitting here.

"You gave me a fake name." Somehow, this is the first thing that comes out.

Almost too calmly, Finn nudges a fry with his fork. "Typically not my opening line. 'Nice to meet you, I was on a TV show about werewolves in the early to mid-aughts, some weather we're having.'"

"You said you were here on 'business'"—I make a show of the most obnoxious air quotes to ever air quote—"and that you work in *tech sales*!" When a woman at the table next to us glances over, I lower my voice. "I bet you aren't even a *Lord of the Rings* fan."

"That one is real. You heard me speak Quenya." He crosses his arms over his chest, remembers the stain, and thinks better of it. "And I *am* here on business. I make money off sales of autographs and photos, so . . ." His gaze flicks around the room, and then, seeing everyone's immersed in their meals and his manager is still outside: "Besides, if I recall correctly, you were the one who snuck out of my room this morning. If anyone has the right to be upset here, I think it's me."

And yet he's so composed, so seemingly unbothered now that the initial shock has worn off, that it makes me even angrier.

"It doesn't matter," I hiss. I have no desire to litigate who has the right to be more offended, and definitely no desire to talk about why I left. "I'm not doing this."

He blinks at me. A lock of hair has fallen over one eyebrow in a way I'm sure his mid-aughts fangirls, Noemie included, would lose their minds over. Too bad I can't take him seriously when Bewitching Beet is spilled down the front of his shirt. "Just like that, huh? You're not even going to consider it?"

"I've heard enough. It's a conflict of interest." I purse my lips, hoping I appear decisive. Resolute. "I realize that maybe you're not used to not getting what you want, but there it is. You can find someone else to write what I'm sure is the riveting story of your life. Can't wait to find it in a bargain bin at Goodwill in two years."

The burn lands the way I want it to. Finn recoils for a moment, brows coming together to form an offended little wrinkle. I won't allow myself to feel sorry for him. Maybe I didn't watch his show, but I'm sure he makes enough on merchandising and reruns to fund a lifestyle that's far more lavish than mine. And now he's doing what every bored white guy of a certain age tries to do: write a book about himself.

Even as I say it, I think about my bank account and how my most recent advance barely paid off one of my credit cards. How I love living with Noemie but how incredible it would be to have a place of my own. Joe indicated I'd be paid far more generously than I have in the past. That kind of money would give me space to decide what's next. Freedom to figure out what, exactly, I'm meant to spend my life doing.

Although—*oh god*—I told Finn that my career was a mistake. If he remembers, he must not care to bring it up.

Then something else occurs to me. "You didn't know who *I* was when I sat down out at the bar, did you? You thought you could seek me out and—" *Seduce me* is how I was going to finish the sentence, but the horrified look on Finn's face stops me.

"*No*," he says firmly. "We read all the samples and résumés blind to avoid bias. I read some of that *Bachelor* book and a couple chapters of Maddy DeMarco's book earlier this week. I had no idea who you were."

Marginally reassuring.

I let out a groan, dragging my spoon through what remains of the soup. "I can't believe this is happening. We weren't supposed to see each other again."

Then his voice turns gentle, as though he's realized I really am opposed to taking the job. Or maybe it's genuine—I wouldn't know. "Can you at least hear me out?"

The look on his face is so pained, I give in. "Fine. Go ahead. Plead your case. Tell me why this book is so important."

Finn sets aside his silverware, clasping his hands together as he waits to come up with the right words. He did this yesterday, too, gave his mouth time to catch up to his brain. "Cons—conventions. That's the majority of what I do these days. I sit at a table so people can pay two hundred dollars for an autograph and photo. I sit on panels talking about this thing I starred in nearly fifteen years ago, as though nothing I've done since can even remotely measure up. Because it hasn't. And I love the fans of the show, I really do—but this isn't what I thought I'd be doing with my career when I was just starting out."

I can't deny that sounds a little familiar.

"I can't keep doing the con circuit forever," he continues. "Hollywood still thinks I'm that lovesick guy pining for his werewolf girlfriend. I want this book to mean something—for it to be even a fraction as meaningful as *The Nocturnals* was for some of our fans. I really think it could do that. If it has the right author." I don't bother pointing out that Finn is technically the author. I'd just be the one holding the pen. "There are things I want in the book that I've never really talked about before. And I just . . . I'd love for this book to be able to help someone, if they're in a similar place." He gives me a sheepish shrug. "Sorry—you can understand why I can't discuss the details without an NDA."

The vagueness is *mildly* intriguing, but . . .

"I feel for you. I do." If I can't convince him with the sheer awkwardness of the two of us working together, I'll use logic. "But I haven't seen a single episode. Which is probably pretty obvious, since I didn't recognize you."

"Doesn't matter. You'd research. And . . . I like that." His gaze settles on me with a renewed determination, his voice even softer now. "I like that you're not going in with some preconceived notions of who I am."

When he leans forward, I have to fight the urge to hold a hand to my heart to keep it from speeding up. There's a seriousness to him, one that seemed attractive yesterday and almost intimidating now. Twenty-four hours ago, we were strangers. Now, if Finn is to be believed, I might have the power to alter the trajectory of his career.

And he might be able to do the same with mine.

"I don't want to grovel. But I will if I have to, Chandler." The way he says my name—I try to ignore how it feels. How it reminds me of his voice wrapped about it last night. He does this professionally. Everything is an act, and there's a distinct possibility all of this is a performance. I can't let myself get steamrolled just because he's reading from a please-pity-me script. "I didn't want this process to be such a headache for everyone. I'd write the book myself, but all my attempts at even a paragraph are complete shit. We've had a few other phone calls, other meetings. Other writers. No one's been the right fit. What Joe said earlier—we've turned people down. And others, well . . ." He grits his teeth, glances down at the table. "I may not have been the easiest person to work with. On occasion."

"Shocker."

"The publisher isn't exactly thrilled about it."

I bark out a laugh. "So I'm your last choice, is what you're saying."

"Absolutely not." His voice is solid. "From the beginning, you were on our short list. The publisher just wanted to try some bigger names first."

"Bigger names in the ghostwriting industry."

He allows a half smile at this, as though realizing the irony. "People who'd written more books," he clarifies. "So, no. You're not my last choice, Chandler. But you might be my last hope."

Oh.

Turns out, I don't hate seeing a man grovel.

When I got the call from Stella, I assumed he was a C-lister desperate to extend his fifteen minutes of fame. And yet that's not the vibe I'm getting at all.

Somehow, I'm starting to believe that he might actually be genuine.

"And what about the king-sized elephant in the room?"

His expression remains serene. "I can forget about it if you can."

This hovers between us for a moment, until I'm the first to break eye contact. *Forget about it.* He makes it sound so easy, like I'm just one in a long line of women who've shared his bed and left unsatisfied.

We're still quiet when Joe reappears, chuckling to himself as he slides his phone back into his pocket.

"Sorry about that," he says, seeming not to notice the shift between Finn and me. He flashes yet another smile, picks up a fry as he turns his attention to me. "We realize this is a big ask, especially with all the travel. We just want to make this book stand out in a crowded market. And if you're on board, we think it has the best chance at making a splash."

Finn's gaze meets mine again, hazel eyes somehow both warm and inscrutable. And then, as though he remembers every word I said last night, he adds: "For both of us."

chapter

SIX

"Stay with me. Please," Oliver Huxley says onscreen to the stunning raven-haired girl in his arms. "Just once. Just for tonight."

Meg Lawson wrenches free of his grasp, the moonlight catching a tear slip down her face as she turns away from him. They're in a forest, snow falling all around them. "I can't. I want to, Hux, believe me—it's all I want. I think about it all the time, you and me falling asleep together. Waking up together. But the full moon . . . it's never much cared for what I want."

"Screw the full moon, Meg!" Hux sounds nearly out of breath. His hair is a mess, glasses askew, snowflakes dotting his charcoal peacoat. "I don't care if you have fangs and fur tomorrow. I don't care if you become a dangerous, terrifying beast, and I don't care if you're too lost inside yourself to remember who I am."

She looks back at him, gives him this sad, wistful smile. "But I do," she says softly.

I glance up from my laptop, where I've been reviewing the contract and itinerary. Phoenix and Memphis and Pittsburgh and a dozen cities in between, all places I've never been. I had no idea there were this many cons—I knew about Emerald City and San Diego, but there's at least one happening every weekend in some part of the country.

"Nome," I say from across the couch with as much respect as I can muster, "I'm starting to think this show is . . . bad."

"That's because you're watching it all out of order." She pauses YouTube a split second before a teary-eyed Meg kisses a decade-ago Finn in a video called *Mexley Best Moments, 4/10*. "This wasn't until the middle of season three. I know Caleb was the main character or whatever, but Hux and Meg are just . . . well, they set the bar *high* for future romance for me. I didn't want anyone who wasn't going to attempt to fight an evil supernatural corporation for me."

"I can't believe I didn't know how much you loved it." I'd been distantly aware that she was into some werewolf show, but maybe our two-year age difference had made me write it off as something childish.

"I guess it was a guilty pleasure back then, but now I'm like, fuck it. I'm Mexley trash, and I'm proud." She motions back toward the screen. "They dated in real life, too. Finn and Hallie."

This, I know from my research. Finn said he liked that I didn't have preconceived notions about his life and work, but I hate the idea of starting this knowing nothing. And, well, there's no shortage of information about Finnegan Walsh out there, from interviews to gossip to a behind-the-scenes *Entertainment Weekly* cover shoot he did with a dozen puppies that is unfairly cute.

I've learned that he's thirty-four, originally from Reno, and got his start on a family sitcom called *Dad in Training* that was canceled halfway through its first season. By that point, he'd already been cast in *The Nocturnals*. He dated Hallie Hendricks for a couple years, starting in season two and until after the show was off the air. I stared at the photos of the two of them together for a little longer than I'd like to admit, the red-carpet events where they looked almost inhuman in their attractiveness, the paparazzi photos of them at The Coffee Bean or hiking Runyon Canyon. One at a Teen Choice Awards with Hallie wearing a shirt that said CAREFUL, I BITE. Finn wore glasses back then, even on the red carpet, just like the ones he wore on the show.

It's bizarre, reconciling the gossip blogs with the person I've now met in real life. In two very different circumstances.

In the end, my thinking about it lasted only the rest of the weekend. I'm in a professional rut: that much is clear. I might be writing another book without my name on it, but the gig feels different enough to shake things up. Traveling with Finn will be new, unpredictable, out of my comfort zone. Even if I've loved being comfortable—or at the very least, I've gotten used to it—I need a change. I can't keep hunching over my laptop, unmoving for hours as I bite out paragraph after exhausting paragraph. Plus, the realist in me couldn't turn down the money, and the idealist couldn't stop thinking about what Finn had said. *This isn't what I thought I'd be doing with my career.* If he believes we can keep things strictly professional, forget about those cursed minutes in his hotel room, then so do I.

Less than an hour after I told Stella I was in, I was put on an email chain with everyone, and Finn emailed me separately.

Glad to have you on board, Chandler. I think we'll write an excellent book together.

Best,
Finn

Cordial. Brief. There was a measured, almost passive-aggressive distance in the *Best, Finn.*

I haven't told Noemie that Finn was my one-night stand, which feels strange as we watch him kiss Hallie Hendricks over and over and over. Maybe I'm taking to heart what he said on Saturday: *I can forget about it if you can.* And maybe I don't want to ruin her image of him, especially now that I know the depths of her adoration.

Because there's probably an ethical boundary here, and if we crossed it before we even started working together, well . . .

Noemie crosses her legs on the couch, flicks away a speck of lint from her sweatpants. "You realize we've never been apart for this long, right?"

It's true. In fact, I can count on one hand the number of times we've been apart for any significant length of time: the vacation I took with all four of our parents that overlapped with a week of sleepaway camp for her when we were in elementary school, and I refused to let myself have fun because if everyone else was paired up, it seemed unfair that I didn't have my person. Then there was the summer in college her moms, Aunt Sarah and Aunt Vivi, took her to Europe for two weeks, and though I wanted to go, my internship at *Seattle Met* magazine felt more important. So I settled for transcribing interviews and gushing over her photos, unsure if what I was feeling was jealousy or loneliness or both.

Again, I feel more than slightly shitty about keeping the truth from her.

"I miss you already," I say, meaning it. Moving in with her a few years ago didn't just save my mental health—it's a comfort I've needed more than I'd like to admit. It's felt, quite literally, like coming home. "And you'll look after my parents?"

Noemie knows how I worry. "I'll invite them over for a healthy, low-cholesterol dinner every Sunday night. It will be understated but elegant."

"Perfect, thanks. And . . ." I trail off, scratching at the lavender nail polish I applied a couple days ago. If I don't paint my nails, then I'll anxiety-pick them to mangled stumps. "If work gets awful and you need to talk, you know I'm just a few taps away. Even when I'm in Minnesota or Tennessee."

She nods, but I don't miss how she breaks eye contact. A classic Noemie deflection. In one swift motion, she turns off the TV and hops off the couch. "I should get the mini quiches in the oven."

"And I should probably finish packing. Unless you want some help?"

Tonight she's throwing me a casual wish-Chandler-good-luck party before I leave early tomorrow morning. A week ago, my life was entirely unremarkable, and now I'm about to spend most of my waking hours with a celebrity. Sometimes I'm excited and sometimes I'm terrified and usually, I just want to throw up.

Noemie waves me away. "Not a chance. This is *your* party." She squints at me. "You just really don't want to pack, do you?"

"I don't know how to pack for something like this!" I fake-whine. "How do you pack for ten cities and at least four different climates?"

"Layers?"

I roll my eyes and head up the stairs. My suitcase, the ancient black one I borrowed from my mom because at age thirty-one, I still don't own my own luggage, is open and overflowing in the middle of the room. Because my mom read one article one time about how black luggage is the likeliest to be stolen, it's covered with an array of peeling, faded hippie stickers: STAY GROOVY and FREE YOUR MIND, peace signs and retro flowers. I wasn't lying when I told Joe I haven't traveled much. My parents and aunts were always more fond of Oregon Coast road trips than plane travel, and Noemie and I were happy as long as we were together. I've been almost swayed by those sleek Instagram suitcases a number of times, the ones that come in colors like sea breeze and rose gold, but I've never had anywhere to take one and it's always seemed like a luxury. Something I'd be able to afford one day, when both my life status and paycheck merited it. My work has always been here, and so have all the people I love.

There's been no need to go anywhere else.

I put on my headphones and blast Bikini Kill while I pack—because even my taste in music is stuck in the Northwest.

AN HOUR PASSES IN A BLUR OF SWEATERS AND T-SHIRTS AND TOO many pairs of socks, plus an amazing moisturizer from Noemie's makeup subscription box. I toss in the latest book in my favorite series, about a bagel shop employee turned amateur detective, and it's only when I'm searching for my denim jacket that I realize I must have left it in Finn's hotel room. It was perfectly worn and buttery soft, and now I must take a moment to mourn.

"How many vibrators is too many?" I yell to Noemie, popping out an earbud. When I don't get a response, I put one of them back in the drawer. "If I have to ask, is it too many?"

"Uhh . . . Chandler? Wyatt's here!" Noemie says, rushing up the stairs, and I drop the LELO on top of a mound of clothes.

"Please tell me he didn't hear me shouting about my small army of self-pleasuring devices?"

"Oh, he definitely did." A frantic Noemie appears in my doorway, the hair on half her head straightened and the other a chaotic mass of curls.

Yes, I invited him. Yes, it was probably stupid. But if it's the last time I see him for a couple months, I want some closure—whatever that looks like.

On the way out of my room, I glance at my reflection in the mirror and quickly change into the black T-shirt dress I was planning to wear for the party, grimacing at the state of my hair and trying to finger-comb the short blond strands back into place.

Wyatt is in the kitchen, brandishing a container and calling out, "I brought hummus!" as though we didn't already have three half-open tubs of it in the fridge. "Hey," he says when he spots me, giving me a nudge of his chin in hello but never quite making eye contact. "Thanks for inviting me over."

I don't love the way my stomach swoops when I see him, with his shaggy black hair that hangs to his shoulders, full lips that are now intimately acquainted with my body. I spent so many years dreaming of him—this guy who was just as passionate about journalism as I was. Or at least, as I thought I was. He was even laid off from The Catch at the same time, then managed to snag a coveted reporter job at the *Tacoma News Tribune*. I thought that shared layoff would bring us closer together. And I guess it eventually did, before what happened in August pushed us all the way apart.

I can't deny that's some of the appeal of skipping town. Instead of confronting this mess of awkward, I'll simply put a couple thousand miles between us.

By the time I come back, I won't be hung up on him at all.

"Yeah, no, of course." I force a laugh as Wyatt scratches at his elbow. *Yeah, no*: the mantra of the chronically anxious. See also: *no, yeah*. "It's good to see you."

Noemie shoos us out of the kitchen, so we make our way to the living room, where Wyatt pretends to be deeply entranced by the gallery wall above the couch and I spend far too much time selecting carrots and celery sticks from the platter on the coffee table.

It feels like the night we slept together happened months ago with how much distance it's created. I was just so convinced we were a good fit. Sophomore year, when there was an outbreak of lice on my floor but he'd promised to quiz me for our journalism ethics class—I kept mixing up court cases—he told me he didn't care, that he'd come by my room to help anyway. Of course, he wound up infested, too. There is nothing that bonds you quite like having nits picked out of your hair together at a treatment center called Lice Knowing You, and maybe that shouldn't have made me like him more, listening to him crack jokes while we tried our best not to scratch at our scalps, but somehow it did. He was selfless and he was smart, and I dreamed of us becoming the next journalism power couple. An Ephron and Bernstein for the modern age. Minus the affair.

He knows my past, my whole past, and he's never judged me for it. When I had an abortion junior year, he dropped off a heating pad and takeout gift card at my apartment. I've never had to explain it to him, the way I want to in new relationships, which means no worrying over the right timing. Because even though it's a choice I'm glad I made, it doesn't make me any less anxious about telling someone for the first time.

Part of me has always been scared that I won't find someone who knows me as well as Wyatt does. Someone who accepts every piece of me.

Wyatt turns to me now, toying with a baked lentil cracker. "We're okay, right?" he asks. "I mean—you asked me to come, so I guess you don't completely hate me?" He follows this up with a wide-eyed pleading look, one that a traitorous part of me still finds adorable.

I dip a cucumber slice into sriracha hummus. "How could I

hate the one person who doesn't complain when I want to have a *Murder She Wrote* marathon?" He lets out a laugh, but I can't bring myself to join in. "We're fine." A lie. "I guess I'm just . . ." *Confused. Embarrassed. Desperate for answers.* "Processing," I finish, wondering if I've ever had a spine when it comes to Wyatt or if this is new for me.

He lets out a visible sigh of relief. "Good. Because I'd feel like shit if I knew you were mad at me. We've been friends for too long for something like this to come between us."

Great. Glad we cleared that up.

Still, I can't help wondering why, if we're such good friends, I didn't merit a better explanation than the one he gave me. I'd love some confirmation that the guy I've spent my whole adult life pining for has not, in fact, turned out to be a total fuckboy.

"So what's the deal with this Finn Walsh guy?" he asks while I crunch too loudly on a baby carrot.

Noemie swings through the living room, balancing a couple trays. "Baked brie, feta-stuffed tomatoes, and mini quiches." She sets everything down on the coffee table next to a trio of candles. "I guess the theme is cheese?"

"I can't imagine a better send-off," I say, reaching for a hunk of brie before settling back into my favorite teal armchair. The one that'll be empty for the next couple months.

"Were you asking about Finn Walsh?" Noemie asks, turning to Wyatt. "Because I could give a whole TED Talk about him, if you want."

She proceeds to do exactly this, and I'm grateful for her interference. I'm even more grateful when the doorbell rings again.

"Sorry we're late," my mom says, brushing some of her long gray hair off one shoulder. It's a sight to behold, and she gets constant compliments on it. "Dad had to finish today's crossword."

"And I knew Chandler would respect that." My dad pulls me in for a one-armed hug, a new thing since he started walking with a cane. I try not to think about how his frame feels a little smaller each time I hug him.

It's only when I see my parents through other people's eyes that I realize how old they are. Most of my friends haven't seen my dad with the cane yet, and I catch Wyatt's eyes widen for a split second as I scramble to take their jackets and generally make them more comfortable. Even as they tell me again and again that they've got it.

My parents still live in the house I grew up in, a cozy bungalow in North Seattle. They were free-spirited high school sweethearts who spent their twenties and thirties traveling the world, which is part of the reason I haven't traveled much with them—because they'd already done plenty of it on their own. They were in their midforties when I was born, and now they're approaching eighty. I got used to people asking *Is that your grandma?* when my mom picked me up from school, or gaping at the disabled parking permit in our car when my dad had knee surgery that took him out for months. Even as a kid, I spent a lot of time at Noemie's house, because her moms were able to do things that my parents didn't quite have the energy for.

I can't deny that going on this trip has me worried about them.

"It's been a while, Lev, Linda," Wyatt says to them, grinning. "Now it's a party!"

"You always know just how to boost an old man's ego." My dad gives Wyatt a pat on the shoulder, sparking this uncomfortable twinge in my heart. Another thing I always liked about him: he is great with my parents, and they love him right back. He was welcome at every birthday dinner throughout my twenties—always bringing me a big number-shaped candle with my "real" age—

and every Jewish holiday. My family's never gone to temple regularly, but we go all out for Passover with a huge seder potluck. My mom even shared her grandmother's prized matzo ball soup recipe with him last year.

Stop, I urge myself, because none of this is helping me get over him.

My mom reaches inside a canvas Trader Joe's bag. "We brought you some of those elote chips you like," she says to me. "Just in case you get hungry."

"I'm not going to be gone for that long." I accept the chips regardless, because I do love them. "And I'm pretty sure they have Trader Joe's in nearly every state. I'm worried Noemie made it sound like she was getting rid of me forever."

My dad asks if I'll join him in the backyard, and I reach for his arm to make sure he doesn't trip on the loose porch step. He holds up a hand, letting me know for the nine hundredth time that he's okay.

When he pulls out a joint, I hide a smile. My parents were no strangers to marijuana even before it was legalized in Washington. Now they use it mainly for medicinal purposes, but there's still something amusing about seeing my late-seventies father with his Coke bottle glasses and entirely white hair getting stoned.

I shake my head when he offers one to me. "Early flight. I won't want to wake up if I smoke."

A nod, a puff, that familiar earthy smell. "Now," my dad says as we sit down in a pair of wicker chairs on the patio, "I know you're old enough to handle yourself on this trip—"

"Are we having a birds-and-the-bees talk? Because it might be a little late for that."

My dad lifts his eyebrows at me. "You're not the only one in this family who worries, you know." Another puff. "I have to admit, we wound up watching his show a few years back. Thought it looked interesting, and by the end of the third episode, we got sucked in."

I just stare. "How much did you watch?"

"All of it," he says with a laugh. "Told you—it was addictive. Of course, we realize he's probably much different in real life than he was on TV. But you never know with these Hollywood types. This Hux—he's a decent young man?"

"Finn," I correct gently, still processing my parents knowing who he was before I did. "Well, aside from the weekly orgies, he seems to be pretty scandal-free." I shake my head. "Dad, I'll be fine. It's just part of the job."

"And you want to be doing this job?"

It's not a combative question—he just wants to know.

"I love writing," I say simply, because no matter what else is happening in my world, that's still true. "And I haven't done anything like this before. It's a good opportunity."

My mom opens the sliding door. "Noemie's getting out Cards Against Humanity," she says. "Didn't think you two would want to miss out."

"Never!" my dad says. "I hope you all don't mind losing."

And *this*, I realize when we go back inside and start playing, and my mom laughs with a hand over her mouth and my dad tries his hardest to be as crass as possible, isn't going to be easy to leave. Wyatt heads home early and Noemie's moms stop by with yet another bag of elote chips, and I realize all the people I love most are in this house right now. This is what's kept me here all these years, this little community I've had. I don't know how I'm going to live without it until December.

Noemie slings an arm around my back, rests her head against

my shoulder. My cousin, who seems to have cemented herself in adulthood while I can't seem to keep my balance. I try to imagine it, her coming home after her endless workdays to a quiet house, and I'm hit with a stab of loneliness.

But maybe this trip will be good for both of us.

If I think it enough times, hopefully I'll start to believe it.

UNKNOWN NUMBER
11:07 AM

Hi Chandler. I trust you arrived safely?

UNKNOWN NUMBER
11:09 AM

This is Finn Walsh, in case you haven't put my number in your phone yet. Not that there's any pressure to, or any assumption that you're going to. I just wanted to let you know. That this is my number. So you're not sitting there wondering who it is.

UNKNOWN NUMBER
11:12 AM

[message deleted]

UNKNOWN NUMBER
11:14 AM

Welcome to Portland?

chapter

SEVEN

PORTLAND, OR

I stare down at Finn's texts as the airplane taxis, saving his number to my phone. The flight from Seattle to Portland was so short, I barely had a chance to finish episode one of *The Nocturnals*, which introduces the small New England college town where spooky things start happening on the first day of classes—because, little do most of the students know, at least one freshman is a werewolf, and a centuries-old battle between good and evil is brewing in their backyard. Finn's character has only a few lines; we see him in the library, because what surer way to establish that he's a nerd, falling asleep in the middle of a book. When he wakes up after the library's closed, he's hit with a sudden chill. A sense of unease. Nothing around him appears to be wrong, though . . . until he heads out into the night and the audience sees paw prints tracking him down the library's dusty hallway. Roll credits.

The Finn on my phone seems to be going out of his way to be professional. Which, in theory, I shouldn't mind—it's just so clearly a concerted effort. I decided last night, in the middle of not being able to sleep because of airplane anxiety and not being able to sleep because of new-job anxiety, that this trip doesn't need to be uncomfortable. This is a rare, frankly incredible opportunity I've been given. And I'm going to do everything I can to enjoy it in all the ways I couldn't with Maddy's book.

That mood lasts about until I check into my hotel and open the door to my room. It's not that I was expecting lush digs or anything, but there's barely any space to walk around the bed, there's no shower curtain in the bathroom, and the room's single electrical outlet is, inexplicably, located inside the closet.

Stay positive, I urge myself, unplugging a lamp so I can charge my phone.

I'll be here only a couple nights, so I unpack my carry-on but leave my larger suitcase untouched. Then I put on a vintage Harley Quinn T-shirt I found in a thrift shop years ago and have only ever worn to sleep in because it's a little big, but today it seems perfect. I tuck it into high-waisted jeans and add a cotton blazer, which I swap for an oversize flannel, which I swap for the blazer again before lying down on the bed and forcing myself to breathe.

At these cons, I'm meant to essentially become Finn's shadow, tailing him from panel to signing and back again. Watching how he interacts with fans. Getting to know him—not just his personality, but his *voice*, his mannerisms and quirks and favorite turns of phrase, all of which will help me embody him when I start writing. He had a fan meet and greet earlier today, so I won't see him until his panel this afternoon. In theory, today is supposed to be low stress.

While I have a few pages full of research and links I compiled over the week, I'm not starting an outline of the book until we get a chance to discuss what he has in mind. Some of my authors have had clear ideas of format and narrative structure, or they'll have already worked with an editor on an outline, which Finn has not. This book is important to him, he assured me. I have to believe he'll have some sense of direction.

Even though I have enough per diem for an Uber and I've been urged to use it, I can't justify it for the twelve-minute walk to the convention center. Rose City Comic Con is smaller than ECCC, but that fact doesn't prepare me for the sheer chaos once I get inside—or the stormtrooper who nearly runs me over. After some profuse apologies from both of us, I pause for a few moments, gazing around and taking it all in. It's a swirl of color and noise, extreme sensory overload. Capes swish as attendees huddle over maps and swarm booths, waiting in line to buy merch and comics. And everywhere, *everywhere*, people are posing for photos. The celeb signings are in a different spot, but out here in the atrium, a drag queen Black Widow has amassed a huge crowd, along with a trio of cotton candy–colored Chewbaccas and at least two dogs dressed in *Star Trek* costumes, one of them complete with Spock ears. There are anime characters and video game characters and even a man whose entire body is painted silver wearing a *very* tiny Speedo.

There's a unique kind of energy here, one that I can sense right away. Everyone here has such a clear passion for their fandom, whether it's Marvel or *Doctor Who* or *The Nocturnals*. And it makes me wish, for much longer than I'd like to admit, that I loved anything this much. It used to be writing, and then more specifically journalism, and now that space in my heart I carved out years ago is as blank as a fresh Word document.

I head to the press area and collect my credentials, draping the lanyard around my neck and feeling very much like a Seasoned Professional—until I realize I have no idea where I'm going.

"Excuse me, do you know where Hall E is?" I ask a Dalek.

They point in the opposite direction, up an escalator. "Right down there. If you're going for the two o'clock panel, you probably want to get there early. Anything with *Nocturnals* cast fills up fast." And then, as they maneuver their blocky metallic costume into the crowd: "*Exterminate!*"

As it turns out, they're not wrong. I make it to the auditorium with five minutes to spare and only just manage to claim a seat in the back row. A hush falls over the crowd as a moderator with short lavender hair and a Rose City T-shirt steps up to the microphone.

"Good afternoon, PDX!" she yells. Cheers erupt from the audience. She tells everyone to save their questions for the Q & A after the panel, along with some general etiquette: photos are okay but no flash, anyone being disruptive will be asked to leave.

"And now, give a warm Rose City welcome to our panelists! You know him, you love him, you doodled his name in your teenage diaries—it's Finn Walsh!"

The way the audience reacts—I am not at all prepared. Finn struts onstage in dark jeans, a forest green cardigan, and graphic tee featuring some collection of symbols I'm not familiar with, a gleam in his eye as he gives the crowd a hearty wave. They *roar* back, a few people even jumping to their feet. The girl next to me might even be . . . crying? He carries himself differently than he did that first night in Seattle, and even the next day at lunch. There's almost a swagger to him, a confidence that only hundreds of screaming fans can buy. Is he taller, or am I just farther away? His face is clean-shaven, the bright overhead lights glinting off his auburn hair as he takes a seat in a plush pink chair, stretching out his long legs.

I may have watched those Mexley clips and one whole episode of *The Nocturnals*, but this is Finn performing right in front of me, or at least from a dozen yards away. And he's *good*.

The moderator introduces the other two panelists: Lizzy Woo, who starred as a government agent in a superhero TV adaptation, but who I'm more familiar with as a lovelorn barista in an ensemble romantic comedy Noemie and I were obsessed with a few years ago, and Jermaine Simmons, from a mermaid show on HBO we watched a season of before getting frustrated by how sexy it surprisingly wasn't. "It's HBO," Noemie had said. "Why is no one getting naked?"

Until this point, I've never considered myself someone who would get particularly starstruck. I was a little intimidated by Maddy, mainly because of how minimal our interactions were, but my *Bachelor* contestant, Amber Yanofky, who went professionally by Amber Y after being one of a record number of Ambers on her season, made me feel comfortable right away. And yet here, watching Lizzy and Jermaine, I'm struck by the fact that they are simply gorgeous human beings. Almost supernaturally so, which is fitting, given the panel is about the enduring power of the supernatural in pop culture.

Finn, Lizzy, and Jermaine are all properly charming, drawing numerous laughs from the audience. I open up a floral notebook, part of a Rifle Paper Co. set Noemie got me for my birthday last year and I haven't used yet because it's just too pretty. Since this trip is all about taking risks, it seemed right to bring it. As I drum the matching pen on the pages, I can't help wondering why this guy wants to write a memoir that he's not even technically writing. The reason he was so cryptic about during lunch.

Of course, everyone wants to believe they're special enough, that they've acquired enough life experience to fill a book. They assume their deeply profound story will fly off the shelves. In my experience, that's just not true. The publisher had too high of hopes for Amber's *Don't Ask Y: And Other Things I'm Sick of Talk-*

ing About. They printed too many copies, thousands of which wound up getting pulped.

"What is your story," I murmur to myself as I stare down at the blank page.

When the panel ends after a Q & A, I fight my way to the stage, where Finn disappeared through a red curtain.

"Hi, sorry—I'm press?" I hold up my badge.

A man in a security T-shirt leans in to scrutinize my badge. "Go right ahead," he says.

Backstage, Finn is leaning against a refreshments table with Jermaine and Lizzy, taking a long sip from a water bottle. The three are midconversation when I approach, offering up an awkward wave. For one horrible moment when Finn turns his gaze to me, I'm terrified he won't recognize me.

But then his mouth quirks upward and he beckons me over, and my shoulders release a tiny bit of the tension they've been holding on to all day.

"Chandler," he says. Warm. Friendly. "I was afraid you didn't make it. I didn't see you."

"I'm not sure I would have been very easy to spot from the back row."

Finn frowns. "You had a seat saved in the front. You didn't have to hide in the back."

"Oh—sorry," I say, my face heating up. Day one, and I'm already making mistakes. "I didn't know."

He's already moving on. "Jermaine, Lizzy, this is Chandler Cohen."

"A pleasure," Jermaine says in his posh British accent.

Lizzy flutters a wave as she reaches for a blueberry muffin with gemstone-studded nails.

"Hi, oh my god, I'm sure you get this all the time, but I loved

Arbor Day." I fully expected that I could remain a functioning person in the face of celebrity, and yet here I am, words sticking in my throat.

Next to me, Finn might be muffling a laugh.

Lizzy beams. "I actually don't! Thank you so much." Then she rolls her eyes. "Most people here just want to ask how my *Renegades* costume managed to stay up during filming."

Jermaine uses a tiny fork to dip a red pepper spear into ranch dressing. "The fandoms can be ruthless," he agrees, mouth full. "You don't want to know how many questions I get about mermaid anatomy."

I decide not to mention Noemie and I have had philosophical discussions about that exact topic.

"I've got a signing in five," Lizzy says with a flip of her sleek black hair. "Great panel—see you in Memphis?"

"Not me, but I'll be in Pittsburgh," Jermaine says.

"And I'll be at both," Finn says, accompanying this with a dramatic such-is-my-life shrug.

Jermaine chuckles. "You just can't quit the con circuit, huh?"

Finn tosses a look at me I can't quite interpret. "Nope," he says. "This is my job."

"I PROBABLY SHOULD HAVE MENTIONED THIS EARLIER," I SAY TO FINN at dinner, after a server drops off two falafel wraps sprinkled with feta and dripping tzatziki. We're at a Mediterranean restaurant in Portland's Hawthorne neighborhood, a place dotted with charming boutiques and hip eateries. Far enough away from the con madness to give Finn a bit of a break. "But this was actually my first con."

Finn just blinks at me. "Are you serious? You haven't even

been to Emerald City?" When I shake my head, he asks, "What was your favorite part?"

"I . . . only went to your panel. I got a bit lost and almost didn't make it in time."

It takes some mental gymnastics to process the fact that we're calmly sitting across from each other after our first and second meetings were so wildly different. Especially after seeing him in action only a few hours ago, animated and electro-charged—now his energy has dimmed, to the point where One-Night Stand Drew seems like a completely different person. Which, in a way, he was. His cardigan sleeves are pushed to his elbows and his posture is more relaxed, but I'm not sure yet whether this is Finn *actually* relaxed or if it's just another performance.

His signing and photo op aren't until tomorrow, so this is supposed to be prime getting-to-know-you time. The chance for me to fill in all the gaps on Wikipedia and IMDb and learn the real Finnegan Walsh, whoever he is.

He looks almost disappointed in me. "There's so much more to it than that," he says, excavating a piece of falafel with his fork. "Get there earlier tomorrow, if you can. Go check out Artist Alley. I know you're not a *Nocturnals* fan"—he says this with a wry twist of his mouth—"but there's got to be something you're really into."

I bite into my wrap. "I love riot grrrl bands from the nineties?"

"Believe it or not, there's a lot of music-related merch, too." He gives me a reassuring smile. Even in the half-light of the restaurant, he might be the loveliest person I've seen up close, and I wonder if I'll ever get used to it. "We'll find you something. A souvenir."

"Oh—okay. Sure. Thanks." Somehow, I have a hard time imagining it: Finn and I strolling through the con, picking out a sou-venir. He'd be mobbed. Surely he meant *we* in a figurative sense.

A silence falls between us. There's none of our easy conversa-tion from the night we were strangers, as though now both of us have masks on. I'm saved from further awkwardness by a couple of college-aged girls wearing homemade Mexley shirts who pause in front of our table.

"Hux? Oliver Huxley?" one of them says, and the other elbows her. "Oh my god, sorry. Finn! Hi! We were at your panel earlier. It was *amazing*."

"Could we get a photo?" the other girl asks. "I mean—I know you have to pay at the con, but it was a little out of our price range." She blushes. "But never in a million years did we think we'd run into you like this!"

"Sorry, sorry, we probably shouldn't ask . . ."

But Finn is already standing up. "Of course, I'm happy to. Love the shirts, by the way."

I practically leap out of the booth, desperate to feel useful. "I'll take it!"

And as I snap a picture of Hux aka Finn aka legit Rose City Con royalty with these sweet girls, I wonder if I'm slightly in over my head.

This is very much not my scene, and I even admitted it to Finn. Maybe he'd be better off with someone who followed at least half of what he said about *The Nocturnals* on his panel.

Someone who didn't sleep with him a week and a half ago.

Calm down, I urge myself, willing the anxiety not to get the better of me. *He picked you. Kind of.*

Once the girls leave, I decide to take control. "So. This book," I say, dipping a fry into harissa ketchup. "It might be helpful for me to get a sense of how you envision the structure. Are there other celebrity memoirs you've liked, anything that might have a similar vibe?"

He considers this for a moment. "I really liked Ali Wong's book."

"Ah yes, because you, too, would like to format this book as letters to your daughters about life as an Asian American comic?"

"Probably shouldn't. What about Judy Greer's memoir?" he asks, and I confirm that I've read and loved it. "I was listening to it on the plane. For research," he adds with a little wink. "I love the idea of making it a series of interconnected stories, not necessarily in chronological order. You know, not just—I was born, I went to school, I started acting."

I nod along with him, jotting this down, trying not to think about how that little wink sent a strange shiver through me. "We can absolutely do that. Maybe we could even take quotes from your past roles as a diving-off point for each chapter?"

"Yes!" He leans back in his chair, pleased. "I had a feeling you'd be exactly what I needed."

I try not to blush at the double meaning of those words because *this*, right here, is what I'm good at. The reason I'm here.

By the time we're halfway done with our food, we both feel confident about the structure, with Finn pinpointing a few topics we can devote chapters to, both personal and professional. His *Nocturnals* audition. His first Hollywood party, where he made the mistake of asking a very famous actor, *And who are you?* A failed attempt at a tofurkey that nearly burned his house down, which will include a deeper discussion of his vegetarianism. No dark secrets, but I wasn't expecting them yet—it's only our first real talk about the book.

Even though I should be in my element, I can't get over the fact that just a week ago, he was kissing me in front of a bookstore.

"That wouldn't be too much?" he's asking, after I mention that I should probably watch as much of his work as possible, including the entirety of *The Nocturnals*. "I don't want to work you too hard."

I quietly burst into flames. It's criminal that he's not seeing the innuendo.

And that's when I realize I cannot keep reacting to him like this.

Because even if Finn is acting perfectly professional, the history between us is a swath of cotton in my throat, a fist wrapped tight around my lungs. Every time his eyes meet mine, an electric current rushes up my spine and I remember how he pressed me against the door. How his frantic fingers searched and searched and searched.

Despite all the faux pas, he *knows me*, intimately, in a way only a few other people do. And now he's right in front of me, pretending he doesn't.

If I can't get past this anxiety, I'm not going to be able to write the book.

"Everything okay?" he asks. "You look a little queasy."

I blink myself back to reality. "I feel like . . . we might need to talk about the thing we said we weren't going to talk about?" I hate the way my voice tilts upward at the end, but I push forward. "I know we said we were going to forget about it, but I just want to make sure it's not going to be an issue. That both of us are on the same page." A nervous laugh slips out. "Literally, I guess."

I'm not prepared for the full force of his gaze, hazel eyes intently focused as he studies me. Cheekbones sharper than any of the swords I saw at the con today. I assume Finn wears contacts, but no wonder they had him wear glasses on *The Nocturnals*—otherwise, Caleb Rhodes, the werewolf protagonist played by former teen heartthrob Ethan Underwood, might have had some competition for leading man status. If my face is growing warm, it's only because Friday night is now playing on repeat in my head. The way he took in my body. The weight of him on top of me. All that lube and *oooh*, there it is.

"I don't see why it has to affect our working relationship," he finally says. "What's one night of mind-blowing sex between co-workers?"

A kalamata olive lodges itself in my windpipe as I lose myself to a coughing fit. In my rush to reach for my glass of water, I knock it over, sending ice cubes skidding across the table. Cold water floods Finn's plate, turning his falafel into a sad, soggy mess.

If this is how Finn and I are going to deal with our past, we're going to be banned from every restaurant on this tour.

A server swings by somewhere in the middle of my fiftieth apology, promising Finn she'll have a new plate as soon as possible, even as he assures her that it's fine and I contemplate launching myself into the sun.

When I finally regain my composure, it occurs to me that I have a chance to shut this conversation down again. Let it all go.

Instead, I make a thoughtless, fatal mistake. A silver bullet straight to my jugular.

"Mind-blowing," I repeat. "That really blew your mind?"

Finn's eyebrows push together in confusion. "It didn't blow yours?"

"We've got to stop saying the word 'blow.' "

"I'm serious, Chandler," he says, that seriousness painted all over his face. Thirty seconds ago, he didn't want to talk about it, but now his interest is piqued. "Is that—is that why you left? I wondered about that all day, even after I met with you and Joe for lunch." His voice is level. Quiet but concerned. Then he brings a hand to his throat and swallows hard. "If I did something to offend you, or god forbid, *hurt* you—"

"You didn't hurt me," I say quickly, cutting him off. *Fuck, fuck, fuck.* Heat rushes to my cheeks, and I stare down at my plate. I wanted only to clear the air between us. I didn't want the actual *truth.* "I—I'm sorry I left without saying anything. I'd never done that before, as you know, and I just didn't know how to navigate it, I guess."

Now this conversation is treading dangerously close to the truth, and while I haven't had much experience with actors, I have a feeling telling one that he's not very good in bed might spark a reaction I'm not entirely ready for.

At the very least, it's enough to get me booted from this assignment. Blacklisted from publishing.

The server returns with a new wrap, extra tzatziki. Finn barely glances at it, instead flicking his eyes around the restaurant to make sure no one's paying attention to us. Then he asks in this low, uncertain voice, "So was it . . . not good for you?"

A dozen lies wait on the tip of my tongue, but I can't pick a single one.

My silence gives me away.

"Holy shit." He leans back in the booth, running a hand down his face, along the reddish stubble that's just started to reappear. "It was that bad?"

"No, no, no," I rush to say. The restaurant isn't busy, and yet I'm suddenly certain everyone in here knows what we're talking about. A neon sign declaring THIS MERE MORTAL SLEPT WITH A BELOVED ACTOR AND HAD THE GALL TO INSINUATE HE WAS ANYTHING LESS THAN GODLIKE.

"But you sounded like . . ." Finn trails off, the pieces seeming to come together. My forced gasps. My faked orgasm. The escape.

I stare down at my nails, picking at the burnt-orange polish I applied the night before I left solely so I'd have something to keep the anxiety at bay. This is how I die, I think: confessing to Finnegan Walsh over falafel that he did not rock my world.

"I guess we could call it acting."

He has the nerve to look genuinely astonished. "I don't know if that's ever happened to me before."

"Right. Because most women dissolve into ecstasy the instant you touch them?"

A twitch of his mouth. "I'm sure sometimes it can take up to three whole instants." Despite the joke, I can see him deflating right in front of me, his cheeks turning crimson, his posture sagging. This is not the Finnegan Walsh from the panel—I'm not sure who this version is. "I'm so sorry, Chandler. I could have done something different. You could have told me."

As though it's that simple. "I tried."

Finn's blush deepens.

"Look—it's not a big deal," I say, desperate to salvage this. "People have bad sex all the time. It was a weird onetime thing, and it stays completely between us." Now that we're discussing it, I'm not sure I see a way out. But plenty went wrong that night unrelated to Finn's lackluster bedroom skills. So I decide to focus on that. "Maybe we were doomed the moment I smacked my leg on that luggage rack."

By some miracle, he plays along. "Almost certainly by the moment I couldn't get your bra off." A self-deprecating laugh, one that makes me realize it's okay to join in. For both of us to laugh about it. "Okay. Wow. I guess I was off my game or something. Because now I'm replaying everything and . . . it was kind of a disaster, wasn't it?"

"It absolutely was. And I have the bruise to prove it." I roll up my jeans to show him the violet patch of skin on my calf.

He mashes a hand into his forehead. "God, I'm so sorry. Not your fault at all. You were . . . you were amazing." His eyes meet mine as he says this, steady and unblinking, framed by ungodly long lashes. "Really."

I have to glance away, pressing a hand to my cold glass of water and then to my cheeks, hoping he doesn't catch me blushing. I get a flash of him before we kissed, before we went back to the bookstore. The easy way we talked to each other, flirted, danced around our vulnerabilities in a way I haven't done even with the people closest to me.

How I'd never clicked with someone so instantly.

"So . . . we're good?" I say, and he nods.

"I'm glad you mentioned it," he says. "Now we can move on and focus on the book."

"Great." I punctuate the word with the first full breath I've taken all night.

"Great," he echoes.

But if everything really is so great, he keeps our talk about the book surface-level for the rest of dinner, rehashing today's panel with slumped shoulders and forced laughter. All that confidence he had at the con—in a single conversation, I've put a dent in it.

Because I think he might be *embarrassed*.

"I'm beat," he says when the server swings by with the check. "Think I'm going to head back to the hotel, rest up for tomorrow. You want to share an Uber, or do you have other plans?"

"Oh—" I break off, trying to process this sudden tone shift. "Uh, no. I can go back."

I really couldn't have just laughed it off and continued forgetting about it, the way we decided to do in Seattle. Maybe he's putting on a brave face, but he's a white man who's had a modest level of fame—his ego is probably irrevocably shattered. Because I am a complete fucking idiot.

During our small talk–laden drive back to the hotel—"look, the moon"—"wow"—it hits me with a stark, painful clarity.

He's going to fire me.

WEEKEND HIGHLIGHTS

Finn Walsh, TV's sexiest nerd, celebrated his twenty-first birthday at The Spot in Hermosa Beach with onscreen love interest and off-screen girlfriend, Hallie Hendricks.

When asked about his plans for this milestone birthday, Walsh told us he probably wouldn't be out very late. "Nothing too wild," he said, grinning at Hendricks. "Just cozying up on the couch with a movie and my favorite person."

Hendricks, looking stunning in a deep green halter dress, kissed his cheek. "He's just too good for this world, isn't he?"

The two have been inseparable since season 2 started airing, rarely seen in public without the other. When asked if there might be wedding bells in their future, Walsh laughed.

"Nah, we're too young for that," he said. "Right now, we're just having fun."

chapter

EIGHT

PORTLAND, OR

The *Nocturnals* changed my life. *You* changed my life. I've seen the whole show nine times, and I have all the original DVDs. And I actually majored in biology because of you." The girl's shirt says I'D MUCH RATHER BE UNUSUAL, which, from what I can understand, became something of a catchphrase for the show. Hux said it for the first time in season one, and then later repeated it to Meg when she insisted he find someone else so he could have a chance at a normal relationship.

Finn smiles, swooping his signature over the photo while a staff member collects the girl's $125. "I'm honored," he says earnestly. "Thank you so much. Do you have a favorite season?"

"Three, definitely," she says. "When you and Meg were trapped in that snowstorm, and she had to protect you from that rival wolf pack . . . I rewatch that scene at least once a month."

"That might have been the coldest I've been in my entire life." He passes back the autograph, then gets up for the photo. "One hundred percent worth it, though."

"Thank you, thank you, thank you," she says, squealing as he poses next to her in front of the Rose City Comic Con backdrop.

I'm sitting behind Finn's table, notebook perched in my lap. Everything I've written so far is woefully banal. *Loves talking to fans. Smiles at everyone. Liked filming season 3.* Someone's going to show up to take away my journalism degree any moment.

Finn's level of fame clearly isn't the getting-constantly-recognized-on-the-street kind—that didn't happen to us in Seattle. I was surprised he chose somewhere so public for dinner last night, but aside from the girls who stopped by our table, no one seemed to bat an eye at him. And yet here, he's a god. The costumes, the shirts with quotes from the show and his ship name, the fans who burst into tears or suddenly turn shy upon meeting him—I've never seen anything like it.

I'm still a little starstruck by the whole thing, and I have to wonder if that'll ever wear off. How long it took Finn to get used to it, or if it's always seemed normal to him.

To my complete shock, he hasn't fired me yet. But there's something off about him today, or as off as I can tell from having known the guy for a week. Last night's conversation kept me awake, along with the too-loud humming of the HVAC in my room. At first, I was worried about feeling lonely in the hotel by myself, but my anxiety hasn't left much room for anything else.

How was your first day?! Noemie texted, and I didn't have the heart to tell her it might be my last day, too. Nothing from Wyatt, as committed as he is to our friendship. An email from my agent, a couple messages from my parents. **Is Finn just as nice as he is on television?** 🦊, my dad wants to know. **r you eating enough?** my mom asks. **dont forgt elote chips** 🌽 🤍

I don't want to disappoint any of them.

At one point, when I return from the bathroom while the signing wraps up, my jean jacket is draped over my chair. The one I left in Finn's hotel room in Seattle.

I throw him a questioning look.

"Chandler," he says, placing a hand on the back of my chair. It's the first time he's made eye contact with me all day. "Do you want to take a walk?"

——— ——— ———

WE END UP AT THE PORTLAND WATERFRONT, A TREE-LINED STRIP OF sidewalk that hugs the Willamette River. It's early evening, the sun hanging low in the sky and autumn leaves crisscrossed overhead. In a month, all of them will be on the ground.

"I love the Northwest," he says. "There's a rivalry there, right? Between Portland and Seattle?"

"I guess so?" The question catches me off guard. I tug my newly reclaimed denim jacket tighter across my chest. "With some of their sports teams, and maybe some people have a bit of a superiority complex about the city they live in. But they both have great food, nature, music scenes . . ."

"You're into Northwest music." It's a statement, not a question. "You were wearing that Sleater-Kinney T-shirt when we met."

"You're a fan?"

He shrugs. Today he's in a blue plaid flannel and nondescript gray sneakers, the kind that look like they were designed by an algorithm. "One of those heard *of* them but haven't *heard* them situations."

"You've got to listen to *All Hands on the Bad One*. Probably my favorite album of all time. I found it in a bargain bin in Olympia, and maybe I'm biased because it was the first album of theirs I ever heard, but it just felt so *special*." Then I pause. This is not the time, but I can't not wax poetic when Sleater-Kinney is involved.

"I do love how particular people are about their music up here."

"It's the perfect place to be a music snob." If he's going to drag this out, make me suffer, I'd rather he rip off the Band-Aid. This small talk feels excruciating when I know what's on the other side of it.

My room upstairs in my cousin's house. A depressing bank account. A future with a giant question mark.

A woman walks by pushing a stroller, a young Portland mom with an undercut and two sleeves of tattoos. Her gaze lingers on Finn before she abruptly looks away, either embarrassed to be caught staring or convincing herself that he's not who she thinks he is. Maybe she'll google him later, wonder if she really did spot him.

"It's not that I don't love discussing the merits of various Northwest cities," I say. "But if you're going to fire me, could you just get it over with?"

Finn stops walking. "Fire you? Why would I do that?" He glances around us, making sure we're alone, and I wonder if this is something he's gotten used to doing over the years. If he's simply accustomed to not having privacy, even with his relative low level of fame. Back when the show was on, though, it must have been relentless.

It strikes me that I'm deeply curious to hear what he'd have to say about that.

"The thing is," he says, voice low. "I'm actually kind of glad you told me the truth."

I'm too stunned to respond, certain I've misheard him.

"I mean, am I completely fucking embarrassed? Did I want to crawl into a hole last night? Yes, absolutely. But the honesty was . . . I don't know. Refreshing."

Huh.

That was not at all what I expected.

"We really can forget about it," I say, still unsure how to navigate this. "Like we said, it was just a onetime thing between semi-coworkers, and I didn't want to upset you—"

"I'm not upset," he says calmly. He lets out a long sigh. "After I got back to my room, I did something I'm not proud of. I . . . called one of my exes."

"I don't need to hear the graphic details of your booty call."

His eyes grow wide. "I called her to *talk*," he says, sounding horrified. "We're still close—we talk all the time. So I swallowed down whatever meager amount of pride I had left and asked her about it. What it had been like, when we were together. And Hallie"—he breaks off with a cough—"hadn't ever been one hundred percent happy in that department, either."

I'm speechless. He called his ex-girlfriend, Hallie Hendricks, who played his love interest on *The Nocturnals*, to ask if she was satisfied in bed.

And she told him *no*.

"That's—that's just two people," I manage, unsure why he's sharing this with me. We've crossed yet another boundary. "And she's an actor, in all fairness. She probably made it sound, um, more realistic than most."

"I may have texted a couple others, too." He rubs at the back of his neck, sheepish. "There also may have been alcohol involved. Not my finest hour, I'm sorry to say. And, well, it only got worse." He moves his eyes from the sidewalk up to me, that blush back on his cheeks. "The consensus seems to be that no matter who my partner is, I've never been able to make it . . . mind-blowing." It must be intentional, the way he borrows the word from yesterday.

Then he lets out a hollow, disbelieving laugh. "Christ, I can't believe I'm saying this out loud."

I would have assumed men would get aggro about this kind of blow to their ego, but Finn seems more perplexed than anything else.

"I'm not going to tell anyone," I say firmly. "Or put it in the book."

This only makes him laugh more, which turns into a groan. "I can see it now. *How to Make Your Girlfriend Howl with Laughter . . . In Bed.*"

"Instant bestseller."

More groaning, and it's easier for me to laugh this time—not at him, but at the absurdity of the whole situation.

"I'm sorry," he says, swiping a hand over his face, collecting himself. "I didn't want to drag you back into this. I'm just—I really am grateful. That you were honest with me. Is that bizarre?"

"You're welcome?" I match his questioning tone. "It's not something most people are instantly good at. It takes practice. And every time you have a new partner, you have to learn a whole new set of . . . well, everything."

"Right." He goes quiet for a moment, watching a boat in the water. "I might regret this . . . but do you think you could give me some specifics?" Then he grimaces, as though immediately regretting the question. "Only if you're comfortable with it."

I consider this. I suppose we're already in this deep, and if it helps the next girl he's with . . .

"Well . . ." I start, wondering how detailed I should get. "You already know I didn't—finish. The whole thing felt a bit rushed, I guess? Then there was the puddle of lube I was lying in for most of it. And the dirty talk could have used some work." Finn's grimace deepens. "Aside from that, I don't think either of us was paying attention to what the other liked."

"You were," he says softly, placing an emphasis on *you*. "I could tell."

My face warms as I remember the way his eyelids dropped shut when I wrapped my hand around him. *Please*, he'd said.

"Hallie said something similar," he continues, yanking me back to reality as he pulls his phone from his jeans pocket. "Actually, I believe her exact words were, 'Sometimes it seemed like you were trying to find something you lost in my vagina. All search and no rescue.' And then—well, this one's kind of funny. Another ex replied with a mouth zipped emoji. Followed by the emoji of the monkey covering its face."

"So what you're saying is that I had you on a good night."

He holds his arms wide, stopping short of flinging his phone into the Willamette. "I don't know! I have no idea what I'm doing!"

A guy biking past us holds up a fist. "None of us do, bro," he says, and Finn gives him a halfhearted fist pump in response.

"You're not hopeless," I tell Finn once the cyclist is out of earshot and we're relatively alone again. "I have plenty of awkwardness in my past, too. And the fact that you're not making this about your fragile, wounded masculinity is a huge plus."

"I want my partners to have a good time. Or at least, for us to be able to talk honestly about why someone isn't."

And it's ridiculous, isn't it, the way those words settle low in my belly after having had a decidedly not good time with him.

"A solid place to start." I lean back against the railing, draping my arms over it. "Women can just be . . . a little harder to please, and it's not always easy to express that. There isn't some button you can press and then voilà, instant orgasm."

I watch him swallow hard as he dips his head, inching closer.

The wind twirls his hair across his forehead, nudges open the collar of his flannel shirt.

"How would I do it, then?" he asks, curling a hand over the railing next to me. His voice is only a notch above a whisper, and though his body is at least a foot from mine, it feels like he's speaking right against my ear. I can practically feel the vibrations along my skin. "How would I make you come?"

My throat instantly goes dry. All the water in the Willamette couldn't rehydrate me at this point.

"This feels like the opposite of what we were saying last night." I try to laugh, but there isn't enough air in my lungs. Maybe even in the whole state of Oregon.

"I want to learn." He pushes a wayward strand of hair back into place, but it's no match for the wind. "I was up half the night googling, but it all started to blur together after a while. And I'm only a little scared of the targeted ads I'm going to get now."

I let out a deep, shaky breath, my heart turning wild in my chest. Because maybe the scariest thing about this conversation is that I *want* to tell him. The thrill racing up my spine is a foreign, delicious thing, impossible to ignore. Maybe it's the fact that we've already seen each other naked that makes talking about this easier. Maybe it's that I went on this walk thinking I was about to get fired, and any other outcome has me feeling like I've just cheated death.

Whatever it is, I run right toward it.

"Hypothetically . . . you'd want to start slowly." My voice takes on a huskiness that feels wholly out of place in a public setting, and when I get quieter, Finn leans in closer. "The more aroused she gets, the more likely she is to orgasm. It's crucial to spend time building up that tension, figuring out what she likes. Ask her. She might prefer your hands, or your mouth. She might have a specific way she likes being touched. Or, even better—have her show you."

At that, his mouth slides open, accompanied by the smallest hitch in his breath. I almost don't catch it, but that slight hint this conversation is as exciting for him as it is for me sends a shock straight to my core.

"You've done that?" he says. "Shown someone?"

"Yes," I say, as calmly as I can. "Masturbation doesn't always have to be a solo act. What about you?"

He shakes his head, that pesky lock of hair falling back across his forehead. "I'm usually fairly easy."

"I got that." This earns me a soft jab of his elbow against my shoulder. "You have to listen. Communication is probably the most important part of it, more important than the physical." Although I wouldn't hate his physical elbow touching my physical shoulder again. "You can't expect that what works for one person will work for everyone."

"I'm not asking about everyone." His gaze clings to mine. "I'm asking about you."

Jesus. I have to break eye contact or else I'll incinerate.

"I like when someone's clearly paying attention to my body," I say, dragging my fingertips out along the railing, and then back. His eyes follow them. "My breaths. My slightest movements. The places where I might be tighter, and the places where I open up."

A nod. Another step closer, a few inches separating his chest from mine.

"And I love when it's obvious that he's enjoying what he's doing to me. When getting me closer also gets him closer—there's something so incredibly sexy about that." My pulse is roaring in my ears, louder than the rush of the river. "I don't mind if it takes a while, and I want to know that the other person doesn't mind, either. Because the longer it takes, the more desperate I get for it, the more my body begs for it . . . the better it feels when I finally go over the edge."

Now I'm picturing it: the two of us in a different hotel room this time, his hand between my thighs while I narrate exactly what I want him to do to me. I'd draw it out, make it last as long as possible so he could wring every drop of pleasure from my body.

I watch the rise and fall of his chest, unsure how we got here. My own inhales are sharper, heavier.

"God," he breathes out. On the railing, his hand is an exhale away from mine. I'm not sure what would happen if we touched right now. If we'd cross a line that started wavering the night we met. "I wish—"

He cuts himself off, and I don't dare say anything. I'd do unforgivable things to know what's on the other side of that sentence.

Instead of finishing it, he straightens his posture, drops his hand, backs up a few steps. I can breathe a little easier—but not better.

"I don't know why it's so easy to talk to you about this, but it is," he continues, pressing his back to the railing, a healthy distance between us. "Maybe because you were the first person to say something. I guess I trust your opinion."

"What, should we leap back into bed so I can give you some pointers?"

In my head, it sounds exactly like the joke it is. A lighthearted quip in the middle of the strangest conversation. And yet the moment the words are out of my mouth, I feel something shift between us.

A tilt of the earth on its axis. A slow swivel of his head toward me. A blink of his eyes, thoroughly, intently intrigued.

The way this maybe-joke doesn't seem to register, given how he says, "You'd do that?"

My heart shudders in my chest. Both questions linger on the sidewalk with us like living, breathing things. Every rational answer waits on the tip of my tongue. *What of course not ridiculous why would we just kidding—*

The way he's looking at me, I'm no longer certain I was joking, either. Because when he broke off a minute ago: *God, I wish—* I could have sworn he was about to say he wished he could have another chance.

With *me*.

"Like . . . give you sex lessons?" I say, certain it'll sound ludicrous once the words leave my mouth.

He gives me this soft, sheepish shrug. "I don't know," he says, a rough quarter-laugh stuck to his voice. "Maybe that's what I need."

I am no longer tethered to reality. We tripped into a fantasy world back at the convention center, one populated by robots and demons and jokes that somehow aren't jokes.

"I—maybe we've had too much to drink, or we're getting too much sun, or . . ." I squint toward the sky, even though I'm shivering a little.

"Chandler. I'm dead sober. And it's barely sixty degrees."

I try to take a deep breath. Maybe I can convince him with logic. Maybe I can hurl myself into the river. Either sounds like a realistic way to end this conversation. "You really think I'm qualified for something like this? To—to help you get better in bed?"

"You're someone who slept with me, and it was bad. I want to be able to make it good for you." He clears his throat. "Future, hypothetical *yous*."

Sixty degrees must be the new ninety because I am goddamn feverish. "I got that."

"And, well . . ." The smallest quirk of his mouth. "You minored in human sexuality."

Oh my god. I did tell him that. Because, as has been recently established, I am a massive fucking idiot.

Again, I think back to that night a week ago, but not the way it ended—the excitement when he ran a finger up my spine while we waited for the elevator, or when we kissed for the first time in the parking lot. His groan in my ear, how unashamed he was of what he felt for me. There was a spark at first—sure, one that fizzled out, but it was there.

It's ridiculous, how much I like you.

I hardly think it's what my professors had in mind when they talked about how we could apply our studies outside the classroom. Maybe I could just recommend some podcasts and direct him toward some sex-positive videos, the kind I've used to get off plenty of times, searching for ones that look like the women are genuinely enjoying themselves. Because they're out there—they're just harder to find.

The fact that some of those videos are now parading through my mind makes me need to squeeze my thighs together, especially with Finn standing there, looking so earnest about this deeply outrageous thing.

"We're here to write a book," I say. One we've made little progress on so far.

He takes a couple steps backward, and it's incredible how I can still feel him right next to me. In the elevator. Against the hotel room door.

How would I make you come?

"I'm not going to push you." His words are gentle. "If you don't want this, I understand one hundred percent. Tell me that right now, and I'll never bring it up again. I swear."

I swallow hard, ready to tell him it's a bad idea on every single level. Unethical in about a hundred ways, practical application of my minor be damned.

And yet.

Here he is, this beautiful man I'm going to be stuck with for the next few months. It's a golden opportunity, really. I must be unhinged, given the fact that I'm still so attracted to the person responsible for the worst sex of my life. But maybe it's not something I need to keep pushing away.

Maybe I could embrace it.

The past few years have been a study in exposition, a whole lot of buildup that's led me absolutely nowhere. My life has been my laptop and me sunk deep in Seattle quicksand, with occasional breaks for friends and family. I've canceled dates and missed out on opportunities because I was too chained to work that wouldn't love me back. This bizarrely appealing idea of helping Finn in bed—it would be *fun*, the thing I've denied myself over and over because I didn't have the money or the energy or I was hung up on Wyatt.

I chose to study human sexuality because I was fascinated by it: history, policy, social and cultural expectations. On a basic physical level, I love what my body can do, and I love losing myself in someone else. Before I slept with Wyatt, it had been a few years since I'd connected with anyone, and maybe that was why it had felt so fantastic. Because I'd made myself stop thinking and given in to a decade of pining, even if it had disastrous results.

I think about the person I was the night I met Finn, how much

I loved that caution-to-the-wind version of myself. I was convinced that wasn't me at all. But maybe it can be.

My whole life, I've been the kind of person for whom "living in the moment" simply didn't exist.

Well, here's my moment.

"I guess—I guess I could give you a few pointers," I say. Maybe this will be the stupidest thing I've ever done, but at least I'll have done *something*. If it helps me forget about Wyatt, that'll just be an added benefit.

Plus, I'll be doing a mitzvah for the next woman he has in his bed. A double mitzvah if it's on Shabbat.

Finn's shock is etched into the soft curve of his mouth and the creases at the corners of his eyes. He recovers quickly, standing straighter and raking a hand through his hair. "Well. Uh. That's— wow. Okay. This isn't where I thought this conversation would go."

"Me, either," I say, laughing. "I have no idea what happens now."

"Should we . . . should we shake?" He extends a hand, but then immediately withdraws it. "Nope, that feels weird." A scratch at the back of his neck. It's similar to what Hux does in the clip of him and Meg at a campus formal Noemie showed me, right before he tells her he's never seen anyone as beautiful as she is and that he might die if she doesn't dance with him. Only in real life, it's even cuter—because it might be real.

"Maybe a hug?" I suggest, because at this moment in time, a hug seems innocent. Something you'd share with a friend or a professional collaborator-slash-sexual-experimenter.

His features relax as his arms fall open. The instant my chest meets his, something loosens inside me. Relief or anticipation or satisfaction, I'm not sure. Maybe it's just a reaction to his scent, that lovely mix of earth and spice. I knot my hands behind his neck, relishing the warmth of his skin against my fingertips. *You are so fucked*, the practical part of my brain tells me, the part I decide to ignore. His exhale hums through me as his hands settle against my lower back, thumb stroking shivers up my spine.

Whatever semiprofessional boundary we still had earlier today: it officially no longer exists.

JUST MY TYPE

INT. GO FONT YOURSELF OFFICE—DAY

EMMA is in the conference room with CHARLIE. She gazes at him, bewildered, while Charlie remains calm and clearheaded.

                    EMMA
          I don't get it. All these designs,
          all these amazing fonts . . . and you
          still don't want the promotion?

                    CHARLIE
He strides toward her, taking her hand in his. Both their hands are covered in ink.

          Because it was never about the
          promotion, Emma. Don't you get it?
          Every single font choice—every glyph,
          every stem, every serif—all of that
          was for *you*.

NINE

PHOENIX, AZ

I expect the regret to hit me hard the next morning, a torrential downpour of *what the fuck* and *there's just no way* and *this is absurd*. And yet when Finn calls a car and helps me with my suitcase, sliding me a half smile as I settle into the backseat, it doesn't.

It doesn't when we go through airport security and I fumble with my bag of three-ounce containers, a bottle of shampoo spilling everywhere and earning me a little one-on-one time with TSA.

It doesn't when our flight is delayed two hours and Finn guests me into the airport lounge, where he drops a cherry tomato while going through the salad bar, causing the woman next to him to trip and fall face-first into a bowl of spinach, prompting our immediate removal from the lounge.

It doesn't when our Uber driver drops us off at the charming house in a suburb of Phoenix, where we'll be spending the next few days until Canyon Con, Arizona's biggest comic book and pop culture convention.

And then, when we're finally alone after six hours of travel, really truly *alone* for the first time since that Seattle hotel room, I'm still not sure I regret it. I feel awkward as hell, that's for sure—but not regretful.

If the strained smile on Finn's face is any indication, he's feeling it, too. It's thoroughly unfair that after the car ride and the waiting at the airport and the flight, he looks disheveled in a rugged way, shirtsleeves wrinkled and eyes a bit droopy, which only accentuates his long russet lashes. In sharp contrast, my bangs started sticking to my forehead the moment we touched down in Arizona, as though immediately protesting the weather.

"So, uh," Finn says, gazing around the space. "I'm gonna go unpack."

I place my backpack on the floor. "Right. Me, too."

The Airbnb is a minimalist two-bed, two-bath with a shared kitchen and signs everywhere that say NO PETS, NO GUESTS, NO PARTIES. It was cheaper to put us up here than flying us back home and then out to the con. Oddly enough, this job is kind of the perfect scenario for the plan we devised in Portland. Well—as "perfect" as agreeing to hook up with an actor to help him hone his skills in the bedroom could possibly be. We're already on the road together, sharing hotels. Everyone to report to is back in New York or LA.

Last night before I fell asleep, I imagined a dozen different ways to tell Finn that my suggestion was a joke that should have never gone as far as it did, and we owed it to our careers and to this book to keep our hands to ourselves. Then, when that didn't sound appealing, I turned the ethics over and over in my head. Granted, journalism ethics wasn't my strongest course in college no matter how much Wyatt helped me study—or maybe I was too easily distracted. But this can't be any worse than what happened at that Seattle radio station a few years back, when two hosts pretended they used to have a relationship for the sake of their dating podcast.

And hey, it worked out okay in the end. Their sexist boss wound up getting fired, and I heard through the journalism grapevine that the two of them just got married.

Not that whatever I have with Finn is trending in that direction—just that these things don't always end in fire and ash. All of us can come out unscathed, with Finn more skilled in the art of pleasure and me allowing myself some fun for the first time in years.

Still, maybe I take my time unpacking, showering, even reading a chapter of the bagel shop mystery before throwing on leggings and a striped sweatshirt because the AC is making some strange noises. I go through the longest skincare routine my face has ever seen, and then scrunch some salt spray through my hair. I text Noemie a reminder to check on my parents, which she replies to right away with a thumbs-up emoji.

It's midafternoon when I emerge into the kitchen, where Finn is in the process of loading what looks like every dish and piece of silverware into the dishwasher.

"What are you doing?"

Finn whirls around, so startled he drops a plate.

"Shit, sorry. Didn't mean to scare you."

"No, no. It's fine. All good." He picks up the unharmed plate, presenting it to me with a flourish, face pale. "Just . . . making sure everything's clean. You never know."

In the silence, the clattering of the AC might as well be a fleet of helicopters overhead. I'm starting to think there's more to this than a simple desire to eat off clean plates, but I'm not going to say anything to him about it. If there's something Finn wants to share with me, something he wants to put in the book, then he'll tell me when he's ready. At least, I hope so.

Based on the way he quickly turns back to the dishwasher, shielding his face from me, I'm not sure he's ready.

"It's not a big deal," he rushes to say. "Is there something you need? I can hand-wash it for you, or—"

"Nope," I say, holding up my Nalgene. "Wash away. I was just coming to get some water. And maybe check on the AC, though I'm not sure I'd be able to diagnose what's wrong."

He finishes up, dropping in a dishwasher pod. The hum of the machine fills the space, creating an oddly soothing harmony with the AC.

"If you're ready to—" I start, just as he says, "I was thinking about—"

Both of us hurry to backtrack. He gestures for me to speak, and I force myself to take a deep breath. "I was just going to say, if you've settled in, maybe we could start in my bedroom?"

His eyebrows jump to his hairline. "To . . . work on the book?"

The book. Obviously. "No, uh—we can do that out here, of course," I say, my face flaming.

Finn has a call scheduled with his manager first, which ends right around when the dishes do, so I unload everything. It's still freezing in the house, and I've had to add another pair of socks.

When the doorbell rings, Finn slips by me to answer it. "Ordered some groceries," he explains.

"Oh. Thank you."

He brings the bags to the kitchen counter, the two of us stumbling around each other. "Thought I could whip something up if you're hungry. If you don't mind eating vegetarian." He has to speak loudly to be heard over the sound of the AC.

"I don't mind!" I shout back.

Then the house emits one final clatter as the air-conditioning breaks.

———   ———   ———

WE SCROUNGE UP SOME FANS FROM THE CLOSETS, OPEN ALL THE windows before realizing the air outside is too hot and then shutting them again. We debate leaving the house before realizing we're in the suburbs and the first five Ubers we try to get decline the trip. So we decide to tough it out.

I changed into cutoffs and a tank top, and even with my short hair, I'm still scraping sweat off the back of my neck. Finn's in a heather gray T-shirt and gym shorts, a bowl of fresh berries waiting on the counter for me. While he cooks, I pepper him with basic questions, the kind that are easy to answer in between chopping onions.

He talks me through his career before *The Nocturnals*, because his audition is widely documented online. The story goes, a nineteen-year-old Finn started talking about Middle-earth during a callback because one of the producers asked whether he could relate to the feeling of being an outcast, like Hux is at the beginning of the series. Finn rambled on and on about Elves and Orcs and Hobbits, unsure why it was relevant, and by the time he paused to take a breath, he was certain he'd fucked things up. But that was exactly it: he seemed so perfectly Oliver Huxley that they couldn't not cast him. In all the interviews, that's what they've said made the decision for them.

"I grew up in Reno," he says, salting tempeh sizzling in a pan. "Which you know. I drove myself into LA for auditions and got cast in a couple commercials at first. Then I played one of Bob Gaffney's kids on a sitcom that got canceled during season one, but it's what got me the audition with Zach." Bob Gaffney: a sort of everyman stand-up comic whose lowest-common-denominator jokes have somehow landed him three TV shows, all of which feature him playing some version of himself. I watched a couple clips of *Dad in Training*, the show Finn was on, and could barely make it five seconds without cringing.

"That's not a short drive."

Finn shrugs. "Eight hours, ten if there's traffic."

"What made it worth it for you?"

"I had a pretty meat-and-potatoes childhood," he says, sounding as though he's choosing his words carefully. He gives the veggies a stir. "Traditional. Or at least, my dad was, which didn't match up with how I felt about the world, and my mom just wanted to keep the peace. He moved out when I was sixteen, sent my mom divorce papers in the mail. All the fighting between them—in a strange way, that was how I got into acting. I wound up in a drama elective in middle school, thinking I'd hate it at first, but I got *obsessed*. It felt like I could escape into a different world, become someone else for a while. And even better if that someone else wasn't human, or lived on a different planet."

"I can understand that," I say softly. I try to imagine a teenage Finn, losing himself in theater because the reality of his home life was just too bleak.

"That was why I'd fallen in love with *Lord of the Rings* when I was a kid. Only I couldn't exactly live in Middle-earth, no matter how badly I used to want to, but I could *act*, and suddenly, that was all I wanted to do. So I commuted to LA from Reno for a while, and then when I turned eighteen, I moved out there on my own." He flashes me a goofy grin. "And then I became ridiculously, disgustingly famous. Can't even check my mail without getting attacked by paparazzi."

I laugh at this, but what I'm trying to figure out how to ask—without actually asking—is whether he's still chasing that high from when *The Nocturnals* was on the air, if he's eager to be relevant again.

And if that's even such a bad thing to want.

When we sit down to eat, the whole house smells heavenly.

"This is delicious," I say between bites. "I've never had tempeh like this." He's marinated and baked it, cooked it in a peanut sauce and served it with a zucchini-and-carrot salad.

"Ah, you thought I was just one of those Hollywood types with a private chef?" he says. "Well, one, I probably couldn't afford one. And two, I like cooking. It's soothing. My dad didn't really get being a vegetarian, so I had to learn how to cook for myself pretty early on. And . . . it's easier when I can control everything."

I'm deeply curious about his family, but it doesn't quite feel like the right time to ask.

"I can assemble, but I can't cook," I say. "I bet you'd never guess what I can do with a tortilla and a bag of shredded cheese."

Finn saws off a sliver of tempeh. Even with about a thousand fans going, his sideburns are damp, the neckline of his gray T-shirt a shade darker than the rest of the fabric. "I could teach you some basics. If you want. You're already doing so much for me." Then his eyes grow wide. "Not that this needs to be transactional. Unless that's what *you* want?"

I almost don't want to cut him off, just let him keep babbling while his cheeks turn a lovely shade of pink. It's the first real acknowledgment of our agreement all day, and it's almost a relief that he's the first to bring it up.

"I think I'm still deciding what I want."

He chews slowly. Thoughtfully. "Are you thinking of backing out?" he asks. "Because it's okay if you are. It's absolutely okay."

"No. Are you?"

His gaze drops to my mouth. "Not one bit."

When heat floods my cheeks, I'm not certain if it's the lack of AC or something else entirely.

It occurs to me that we still barely know each other—and that I'm getting paid to know him, and not the other way around. I take a bite of salad, the cool vinegar doing little to combat my rising body temperature. "Maybe it would be less weird if we talked about the logistics first?"

"Nothing sexier than logistics." When I lift my eyebrows at him, he backtracks, motioning with his fork. "Sorry. Please continue."

"No one can find out," I say as he nods vigorously. If we're really going to do this, I need to make sure we both know what to expect. And that means establishing all of this up front. "The book has to come first, of course. And I'm sure we'll be done before then, but when the trip is over, we are, too. We go our separate ways and never tell anyone." I swirl my fork through the extra peanut sauce. "Protection is nonnegotiable. And consent, obviously."

"No arguments from me there."

"If one of us ever wants to call the whole thing off, for any reason, they can," I continue. "And it's not going to happen every night. In fact, it's probably better if it doesn't, since the book needs to be our top priority. If one of us doesn't want to, that's it—they don't have to defend it or make excuses."

"Frankly, I'm not sure I could, uh, perform every single night," he says. "So that's a relief." Then he adds: "We should be able to feel like we can say something. If one of us is ever uncomfortable."

"A safe word?" I ask, and he nods. Glances down at his plate.

"How about 'tempeh'?"

I crack a smile. "Sure. Tempeh it is. And we should sleep in

our own rooms. Just to keep it from becoming . . . complicated."
I'm not sure it's the right word until it leaves my mouth. If I really
am a Relationship Girl, having sex and waking up with someone
I'm not in a relationship with is probably the kind of thing that
would confuse my heart, make me get overly attached. So I'll simply prevent that from happening.

Finn looks pensive, as though he hadn't considered this.
"Okay," he says. "Makes sense."

I stare down at my hands, picking at my nail polish, the burnt
orange hanging on by a few stubborn flecks. It's just casual sex.
People do this all time. I've done this, with this exact person.

"One more thing," I say. "I sort of made an outline? For the
lessons? On the plane?"

"While I was watching *Ted Lasso*?"

I press my lips together, nodding. "I know we said it would just
be 'a few pointers,' but I thought it might make things easier, and
we're doing the same for the memoir, so . . ."

He grins at this. "That's kind of amazing. I'm both impressed
and intrigued."

I swipe around on my phone before passing it to him. "It's a
work in progress. We can adjust it based on whatever you want to
work on or whatever we feel like needs more attention."

It all makes perfect logical sense—at least, I think so. We'll
start with kissing, then gradually add various forms of foreplay,
with roman numeral sections devoted specifically to topics like
oral sex and dirty talk. A sexual lesson plan.

"This is . . ." Finn starts, staring down at it.

The panic sets in. I went overboard, classic Chandler Cohen
overthinking.

". . . extremely thorough," he finishes. "Wow. I'm kind of
touched?"

Slow exhale. In part, this felt like a way to soften any lingering anxiety. Most of all, though, it just felt natural. I'm a writer—all my finished products start with an outline, and any good book needs proper buildup. You can't jump to the climax right away, and Finn especially needs some time with the early chapters.

"I'll send it to you," I say. "There are some links to diagrams, too, and a list of podcasts and sexfluencers I really like—and before you ask, yes, that's a thing. And I was thinking, each time, that we could have both a discussion and then a practical portion." It's possible I'm making it sound too structured. "I mean—if that doesn't seem overly formal. That way, we can talk through everything and really ease into it."

Finn doesn't protest. He just glances at the phone and then back at me, mouth quirking upward. "I didn't think I could be so turned on by a Google Doc."

We decide to meet in my room in half an hour, after we've cleaned up dinner and I've spent approximately seven minutes brushing my teeth. I'm not sure how one prepares for a scheduled make-out with a former TV star, but oral hygiene seems as good a place to start as any.

In a way, it's a chance to rewrite our history. If I ever feel like I'm floundering, I remind myself I have that outline for guidance. I can absolutely live in the moment—as long as I have a backup plan.

Because if I can do this, then I can march back to Seattle with my head high, shoulders unscrunched. I'll be a Woman Evolved, unafraid of taking chances and leaving my comfort zone in the dust.

A knock on the door interrupts my mental pep talk.

With a deep breath, I pull it open, and I'm immediately hit with the scent of Finn's aftershave, woodsy and warm, with a hint of spice. He's changed into a navy T-shirt, his freckled cheeks tinged pink and his hair damp from a shower. Instantly I feel less clean, running a hand through my hair and hoping I don't sweat through my extra layer of deodorant.

"Hi," he says, at least a hundred times sturdier than I feel.

"Hi. Welcome to this side of the house. It's unfortunately just as hot as the rest of the house."

"I don't mind."

A half smile as he follows me to the bed, where we proceed to sit in silence for a good ten seconds.

Until I burst out laughing. "Sorry. I swear, it's not you."

"We don't have to do this," he says. "Really. If you don't want to—"

Before I can overthink it, before my brain gets the better of me, I lean in and kiss him. As fearlessly as possible, just like I did that first night.

It's true, he's not a bad kisser. It feels clumsy only for the first few seconds, and then we exhale into it, deepening the kiss. The fresh mint of his toothpaste, the warmth of his mouth as it opens against mine. There's a familiarity to it, the two of us becoming reacquainted.

He's the first to draw back, with a force that leaves me slightly breathless.

"How was that?" he asks, smirking a little.

"Not bad." The room spins, and I have to blink a few times to settle back into my own skin.

The next time his mouth meets mine, his hands start to wander. One of them goes to my waist, curving around to my ass, while the other migrates up toward my breasts. Just like the first time, he's too eager for the next step. It's not unpleasant, exactly— it's just too soon for me.

Gently, I reach down and slide one hand back to my waist. He gets the message, dropping his other hand from my chest and into his lap. But I can tell he's not sure what to do with them.

"You can touch me," I say gently, realizing only when the words are out how desperate I am for it. "But let's make certain body parts off-limits."

"I feel like it's going to be all the fun ones."

I give him a grin. "When I'm with someone, I don't want to feel like I'm just a collection of body parts. And you might find that your partner really likes to be touched somewhere you didn't know," I say. "That's the most important part. You have to take your cues from what they're giving you. This"—I gesture between us—"doesn't work if we're not communicating."

He grimaces. "You were trying to. That first night. And on paper, I get it. It's just not always the easiest thing to do in the moment."

"But always worth it," I tell him. "I'm probably going to say this a hundred times, but the waiting builds up tension. I'm very rarely ready to just go all in right away, no matter how attracted I am to the person."

He nods as he takes all of this in. "All right," he says, with this chipper readiness that somehow manages to send a shiver up my spine when he utters his next sentence: "I'm going to figure out what you like."

He leans forward, but instead of kissing me, which I'm expecting him to do, he presses his mouth to my forehead. "How's that?"

"Sweet. Very sweet."

A kiss to my cheek. "This?"

"Are you just going to try every—"

I break off as his lips slide along my neck, a thumb tracing the shell of my ear, dragging out a shallow breath. *Oh.* Now the shiver is a full-on quake, and I can feel him grinning against my skin before he draws my earlobe into his mouth, tongue flicking the gold stud that I rarely take out.

Then he does something I'm not at all expecting, although I'm starting to think that with Finn, I should drop my expectations completely—he scrapes his teeth along the rim of my ear, sending a bolt of pleasure down my spine and straight to my core.

And I fucking *moan*.

"Well," he whispers into my ear, right before he does it again, "that's a nice surprise."

I clutch at him, trying to get closer, both wanting him to keep going and somehow, inexplicably, wishing he'd try something else because it's almost too good. There's no awkwardness, just the heat and scent of him and a lovely, fuzzy feeling of weightlessness.

Slowly, blessedly, he explores some more, giving me a chance to catch my breath. He trails his fingertips up and down my spine, across my shoulder blades, keeping everything above my T-shirt. When he accidentally grazes my ass, he whispers "sorry" and returns his attention to my back. I close my eyes and lean into his touch. It's been ages since I had anyone explore me like this: zero sense of urgency, just a quiet curiosity as he learns what I like.

His eyes snap to mine as he reaches for one of my hands. He brings it to his mouth, stamping a kiss to the inside of my wrist. Then the other. His movements are so delicate, drawn-out seconds punctuated by a strange tenderness that somehow manages to steal my breath.

"You're . . . really great at following directions," I say, because it's true. Maybe Finn will be a fast learner, and we'll be done with this before I finish writing the book.

"I've had a director say that once or twice." He readjusts on the bed, bending down to brush his mouth along my bare knees.

"Ahhh," I say, laughing, trying to pull them up onto the bed. "Ticklish?"

"No."

Eventually, he makes it back to my mouth as I reposition myself on top of him, legs on either side of his hips. His shorts do exactly nothing to hide his arousal, and the first time I push against him, I swear it's an accident.

"Is that okay?" he asks, as though worried he was the one who initiated it. He runs a hand up my back, tracing the strap of my tank top.

It wasn't in the outline for today, but . . .

I move his hands to my hips, telling him *yes* with another forward motion, the friction dragging a groan from my throat that he meets with one of his own. God bless gym shorts.

We alternate control; sometimes he guides me and sometimes I take the lead, grinding against his hard-on until he clutches me tighter and tighter, one hand at the nape of my neck and the other on the small of my back. Everything I'm wearing is damp, sweaty, but neither of us cares.

"See?" I pant out. "Look how much fun we can have without taking any of our clothes off."

From the half-lidded contentedness on his face, hair askew and cheeks flushed, it's obvious he's enjoying this, too. "The way you cried out when I was inside you," he says, mouth on my collarbone. "Back in Seattle. I can't wait to make you do that for real."

An ache settles low in my stomach. I'm about to tell him that maybe we won't need that dirty-talk lesson at all, and I can't help wondering what might have happened if he'd done these things that first night we were together.

Except this isn't a rewrite.

This is practice.

"That's probably good for today," I say, the suddenness of that realization shocking me back to reality. Because it's not me that Finn's here with—I'm just a stand-in for a future mystery woman. Waiting for someone real to take over the role.

Finn stops right away as I move off him. "Yeah?" he says.

"I think you've got this down. Top marks. Eleven out of ten."

His gaze lingers on me, but I focus instead on the rise and fall of his chest, and when even that makes my skin heat, I drag my eyes to the plain white duvet. I blink away the stars at the edges of my vision, trying not to think about how another minute of rubbing against him, and I probably would have come apart.

"Thank you," he says. "If that isn't weird to say?"

"I think all of this is weird," I manage. "But—you're welcome."

A few more strained seconds of silence. "I might go for a run," he finally says. "I think it's cooled off enough."

After he leaves, I lie there for moments, minutes, waiting for my breathing to return to normal. Distantly, I hear the AC kick back on, but my body refuses to cool down.

Lesson one was far more thrilling than I thought it would be. There's no doubt I'm attracted to him, given I went back to his hotel that first night. Maybe we should have kept going, finished everything in one day so we could focus on the real reason we're stuck in this Airbnb outside of Phoenix, Arizona.

But we're here to work.

So I open my laptop, pull up *The Nocturnals*, and hit play on episode two.

THE NOCTURNALS REUNION
SET FOR DECEMBER

Entertainment Weekly

The werewolves are back.

After ten years, *The Nocturnals*, the fan-favorite TBA Studios show, will return for a two-hour reunion special filmed in front of a studio audience. All principal cast members have been confirmed: Ethan Underwood, Juliana Guo, Finn Walsh, Hallie Hendricks, Bree Espinoza, and Cooper Jones.

For a list of our top ten best *Nocturnals* episodes, *click here*.

"It's a great feeling," said Underwood, who played Caleb Rhodes in the series, from the set of his new movie, *Deathrace*. "Can't wait to have the whole gang back together."

The reunion will be available to stream beginning December 10 at 9 p.m. Pacific Time.

chapter

TEN

ST. PAUL, MN

Hell is baggage claim and the endless, dizzying loop of suit-cases that does not include one's own. Or, more specifically, one's mother's.

"It's not here," I tell Finn. "I've seen that one wrapped in caution tape go around at least twenty times. Mine's not coming."

"It's got to be here." He frowns, sliding his phone into his pocket. The reunion announcement went live this morning, and his socials have been chaos. He did a couple interviews in the Airbnb this morning before we left for the airport. "It has all those stickers on it, right? The hippie ones?"

I nod. My voice cracks as I gesture to the screen above the belt. "It says they're about to unload bags for the next flight."

Finn must be able to tell I'm about to start panicking, because when he speaks again, his voice is level. Soothing. "We'll figure this out. It's happened to me dozens of times, and the airline's always been able to find it. Almost all bags eventually get returned to their owners."

I'm not sure if he's right and I don't love the *eventually*, but at least I don't have to deal with this alone. First, we check the other carousels to see if my bag somehow wound up there—no luck. Then we make our way to the airline desk, where I present my luggage ticket and a woman dressed in a bright blue skirt suit looks it up on her computer.

"Hmm," she says, typing away. "It says it left Phoenix, but I'm not seeing it show up in our system here yet. Might have been a scanning error . . ." A sheet of paper is shoved toward me. "You'll have to fill out this report."

I scribble down the bag's details.

The woman gives me a tight smile. "We'll call you. Most delayed luggage turns up within the next twenty-four hours. We hope it doesn't keep you from enjoying your trip to the Twin Cities!"

"Is there any way you can help her out in the meantime?" Finn asks.

"Yes, of course." She passes me an amenity kit with the airline logo stamped on it and packets of soap, shampoo, and toothpaste inside.

"Thank you. Thank you so much," I say, grasping the kit like a life preserver.

Fortunately, I kept my electronics in my carry-on, but there's a week's work of layers in that missing bag, all my favorite T-shirts and too many extra socks and hair products and that moisturizer I hate to admit I love so much. And—oh god, my vibrator is in there, too.

I know I shouldn't be this emotionally attached to T-shirts, but I can't shake the feeling that something's off-kilter, even as Finn steers me toward the airport shops to find some replacement clothes.

That's how I end up getting ready for Supercon, a convention dedicated entirely to the paranormal, in hastily applied werewolf makeup and a shirt that says SOMEONE IN MINNESOTA LOVES ME. Because after all the chaos of my lost luggage, Finn has the gall to tell me that I might feel out of place if I'm not dressed up for this one. At least he had the decency to look sheepish while doing it.

"I don't know about this," I say to Noemie on FaceTime, after I've checked into the hotel. I tilt my face one way and then the other, giving her a full view of the cheap paint and ears I found at a dollar store a couple blocks from the hotel. "I look like that old Snapchat dog filter."

"You look *adorable*." Noemie has the phone propped up on something, and in the background, she's rummaging around the kitchen. "Cuter than Meg did, even. Please tell me you've seen that episode?"

"Yesterday," I say. And I'll admit, it was a good one: the season one Halloween episode, where Meg dresses up as a werewolf as an inside joke, since only a couple people know she really is one.

"Ugh, I wish I could watch with you. I miss you."

It's strange, talking to her and not sharing everything going on with Finn. The rest of our time in Phoenix was uneventful. That single make-out session must have loosened both of us up, even if I blushed at least three times as much as normal the next morning. We made minimal progress on the book, focusing on the basics about his career. Still, I haven't made another move and neither has he. He seems to be very clearly giving me the reins, which I appreciate.

"By the way, that new murder mystery box came in the mail," Noemie says. "Do you want me to wait until you get here to open it?"

"You know that's my favorite one. Yes please, if you have the willpower."

A smirk. "I'll do my best."

After we hang up, I meet Finn in the lobby. When he spots me, he breaks into a grin, lighting up his face in this pure, genuine way I'm not sure I've seen on him yet. "Chandler Cohen," he says. "You look fantastic. Even with the Minnesota T-shirt."

Despite the compliment, I bring a hand to my face. Suddenly, it hits me that I'm dressed like the character played by Hallie Hendricks, Finn's ex-girlfriend. I don't want him to think I'm doing this because I'm playing a similar role—because everything with Hallie was real. What Finn and I are doing is not.

If I underestimated *Nocturnals* fans before, it's nothing compared to this afternoon, which helps to distract from my lost bag anxiety. Finn can barely move through the halls without being swarmed.

Backstage, he introduces me to Zach Brayer, the show's creator, and Bree Espinoza, who played Sofia, introduced in season two as a second love interest for Caleb, Hux's former bully turned good friend.

The rest of the cast is busy with media at other cons. Ethan Underwood was Caleb, the undisputed lead of the show. Juliana Guo: Alice Chen, a headstrong popular girl who doesn't take anyone's shit. Cooper Jones: comic relief Wesley Sinclair, a friend of Caleb's. And Hallie Hendricks, of course. They'll be together at Big Apple Con in New York in November, which their teams designed for maximum exposure.

"Looks like we're really doing this thing, huh?" Bree says backstage. She's tall, tan, with brilliant white teeth and a cute gingham dress. If Alice was Caleb's bad-girl love interest, Sofia was the girl next door, the one brought on board specifically to compete with Alice. Because it's not a teen show if young women aren't pitted against one another. The Calice fandom, sometimes called Callous because of how cruel Caleb and Alice could be—both to other people and to each other—is stronger than Caleb/Sofia, and I wonder if it's simply because their portmanteau is catchier.

"Guess so," Finn says, sipping from a bottle of water. "You handling everything okay?"

Bree shrugs. "My social media's a nightmare, but that's nothing new. Although I could really do without all the Sofia hate." A shake of her head. "Funny how Caleb's the one who cheated on Alice and *I'm* the one getting death threats for coming between them. Still. All these years later."

"Jesus," I say. "That's really fucked up."

"I hate to say I'm used to it, but . . ." She trails off with a wave of her hand.

Bree and Zach start talking about a new pilot they're working on. For some reason, I expected Zach to be some seasoned industry vet, but he's only a few years older than Finn, dressed in a canvas jacket and dark jeans, several days of stubble on his face.

A staff member approaches us. "It looks like we're down a mod for this panel," he says. "We accidentally overbooked. But not to worry, we're looking for a new one now."

Zach points to me. "What about her? What's she doing during the panel?"

I blanch, eyes going wide as I look to Finn.

A furrow appears between his brows. "She's not here to work the con. She's a journalist." The way he says this makes it sound like a much more serious career than it is. Makes me want to live up to it.

"That's perfect. She's got interviewing experience."

Finn holds my gaze. "You can say no, Chandler."

I remember him in bed a few days ago. The sweetness in the way he kissed my forehead, my cheek, the inside of my wrist. Even if it was fake, even if I'm never quite sure which version of Finn is the real one, there's some of that sweetness in him now. He's looking out for me, and though it's not something I've ever craved from a guy, it's a simple kindness.

"If they don't have anyone else . . ." Surely it won't be that bad. I don't love speaking in front of large groups, but none of these people are here to see me. "I can do it—I just haven't seen the full show."

"It's okay," Bree says. "The questions are all prewritten. You probably won't be able to get us to shut up."

In this moment, I become deeply grateful for my werewolf makeup, if only because it acts as another layer between me and the audience.

"Okay," I say, half-certain I'll end up regretting this. "I'll do it."

IT TAKES ABOUT THE LENGTH OF TIME OF THE WALK ONSTAGE FOR that regret to sink in.

The con staffer ran through what I'd need to do, which turned out to be slightly more complicated than reading questions off a piece of paper. I have to keep track of the time, watch for cues, transition to audience questions.

I squint at the lights, my stomach hovering somewhere in the vicinity of my throat.

"Um. Hi." The audience seems to grow antsier by the second. "How excited are you about the *Nocturnals* reunion, huh?"

The room erupts into cheers.

My hands tremble on the sheet of paper. My first task is easy: introducing everyone, which I do as the *Nocturnals* theme music plays, a spooky punk-rock instrumental.

Then we all take seats in the black leather chairs onstage.

The questions start basic enough. "What are you most looking forward to about the reunion?" I ask.

"Seeing how far back Ethan's hairline has receded, definitely," Bree says, and this gets a lot of laughs. "No, I mostly can't wait to be in the same room as everyone again. Being on this show was the most fun I've had in my career, and we just felt so lucky to be making it."

Finn crosses his legs, brings his mic up to his face. "Exactly. We were taking a chance because most teen shows took place in high school. Since *The Nocturnals* centered on college, I always feel like we were able to get a little darker, go a little deeper, while exploring themes that felt universal. Even when we were battling evil creatures."

"Like rising tuition costs," Zach puts in, getting another laugh.

I stare down at the sheet of questions, heart pounding when I read one I have no earthly idea how to pronounce. *What was it like battling the League Loup-Garou in season three?*

Scattered laughs from the audience as I botch it. "It's *loup-garou!*" someone yells out, correcting me, and my face flames.

"Took me forever to get that one right," Finn says, with the briefest eye contact. Even if he's just saying it to make me feel better, I appreciate it. "I know the league was a fan favorite in terms of villains, and it was just as exciting in front of the camera. We were only reading scripts a few episodes in advance, so we had no idea how that plotline was going to resolve. And I'm pretty sure I pulled a muscle during that chase scene in episode twenty-one."

We cycle through a few more questions until it's time for the audience Q & A. The first person who steps up to the microphone is wearing a Spider-Man mask that muffles his question.

"Sorry, can you repeat that?" Zach asks.

"I was saying," the guy starts, tugging off the mask, "what do you guys think about—"

The rest of his question gets lost in the collective shriek the audience lets out, because standing at the mic is none other than Ethan Underwood, Caleb Rhodes himself. Finn, Bree, and Zach are slack-jawed—no one knew this was happening.

"Ethan!" Bree says. "I can't believe you're here. And I also hope that mask prevented you from hearing what I said about your hair."

Ethan flashes a dimpled smile. There's something magnetic about him, a particular leading-man quality, and he knows it. He's in black jeans and a cream henley that appears to be a size too small, as though designed to show off his biceps. Lately he's starred in only mediocre action movies that made bank at the box office, enough to secure his next role in whatever men-battling-machines franchise comes next. I'm ashamed to admit I've seen a couple, and that I knew his name before I knew Finn's.

"This hairline?" he asks, fluttering his lashes at the audience as he tilts his head downward. "I've made my peace with the aging process. I've *matured*."

"I'll believe it when I see it," Finn says, a strange flatness in his voice.

Now Ethan's hopping up onstage, and a volunteer is bringing out another chair even as Bree offers half of hers to him and the two of them squish in there together, much to the audience's delight.

"Guess we have a lot of Team Sofia fans in here today!" Ethan says with a chuckle.

A muscle twitches in Finn's jaw. He doesn't like Ethan; that much is clear.

The same can't be said about the crowd. In the front row, one girl has started crying.

"Uh—" I fumble with my sheet of paper before remembering we'd moved on to audience questions.

Ethan already has it covered, pointing at the next person approaching the mic, a woman wearing an Oakhurst University sweatshirt.

"Yes, hi, um, wow," she stammers. "I can't believe you're here!"

"Was there a question somewhere in there?" Ethan asks, and though this gets a few laughs, something in it grates at me. Something like arrogance.

"Right, sorry!" The woman takes a few deep breaths. "This is actually a two-part question. The first is, I know some of you originally auditioned for different roles. If you had to play someone else, who do you think you'd have wanted to play? And then the second part is, who do you think would have been best suited to play you?"

Finn opens his mouth to speak, but it's Ethan who answers first. "For me, it was Caleb or bust. They had me read for Hux, but he didn't really feel like *me*, you know?" He turns to Finn. "But you read for Caleb too, right?" he asks, and Finn nods.

"It wasn't the right fit," he says. "I related much more to Hux."

"What do you guys think?" Ethan cups a hand over his ear. "You think we could have swapped roles? Would that have been a hit show?"

Uproarious laughter as scarlet creeps onto Finn's cheeks.

Ethan takes the remainder of questions from the audience, and I'm too intimidated to cut him off. It's not until a volunteer appears in front of the stage that Ethan says, "It seems we're being played off. Thanks for letting me crash your panel, and we hope everyone tunes in in December!"

I can still hear the crowd roaring even once we're safely backstage.

"Do you want to grab dinner and talk more about your post-*Nocturnals* roles?" I ask Finn after checking with the airline for an update on my suitcase. There isn't one. "Or if your mind is still on werewolves, we could just talk about that."

Finn's face falls. "Oh—I have plans with Bree and Zach. And Ethan, I guess."

"That's okay, maybe it'll be good for me to see you in your element. I could probably learn a lot from hearing you talk with them."

Then he gives me this odd, pained look.

"I'm not invited, am I." I don't even bother phrasing it as a question.

"It's Ethan, really. He's been burned by the press before."

"Right. Okay. Totally fine!" I say this with too much enthusiasm, and after we exchange goodbyes, I let him get absorbed by the mass of fans once again.

I've only spent a week with him—it's not as though he owes me anything. Definitely not a dinner invitation with his coworkers. It was ridiculous of me to think I'd automatically go.

I'm unsure how to explain the ache in my chest as I watch him leave, or maybe it's just misdirected stress over my missing suitcase. So I pull out my phone.

Tonight? After your dinner? I text him.

Maybe he won't be in the mood, or he'll be too tired. And that would be okay—we made those rules for a reason.

Still, I watch his face as he pauses halfway down the hall and reads the message, a soft flicker of understanding passing over his eyes. A little thrill sparks up my spine as his reply appears on my screen.

Tonight.

chapter

ELEVEN

ST. PAUL, MN

After a night of debauchery with his costars, Finn looks properly exhausted: hair disheveled, cheeks flushed, a soft slump to his shoulders. I wonder if it feels a bit like hanging out with friends from high school you haven't seen in forever, or if there's something deeper that bonds them after four years under the same microscope.

His hotel room is a mirror image of mine. Nondescript furniture, minimalist decor, a canvas print of a wheat field.

He reaches for a bottle of water on the nightstand, throat working as he swallows. "I feel too young to be this tired at ten o'clock," he says, running a hand through the graying hair at his temples. "Especially because we're an hour ahead of Arizona."

"There's really no order to these things, huh." I slip out of my shoes and shut the door behind me. "You're always just zigzagging across the country?"

"Pretty much."

"Must be hell on your circadian rhythm."

"Sometimes, but you get used to it."

I try to imagine that, spending the majority of the year getting used to waking up in a different hotel, in a different city, going to a different convention center and greeting a different set of fans, all of them there to see you for the same reason.

Then something catches my eye. "My suitcase!" I rush over to where it's propped up against an armchair, practically sparkling under the too-bright hotel room lights—as much as a beat-up suitcase with hippie stickers can sparkle. "Oh my god, she's so beautiful. Was she always this beautiful, what with the zippers and the pockets and everything? How did you—?"

"They brought it over about ten minutes ago," he says, trying to sound casual. "I had my manager make some calls. Turns out, one of the higher-ups at the airline is a big *Nocturnals* fan."

I run a hand along the suitcase. "You didn't have to do that. Thank you."

He waves this off. "All I did was send a few texts."

"Still. Between this and that jean jacket, I'm starting to think you're the patron saint of missing clothes."

He scratches at the back of his neck, which I've noticed he does when he's anxious. "I just don't want you to have a terrible time on the trip." When he says it, he doesn't quite meet my eyes.

You can say no, Chandler.

It's clear he feels some sense of responsibility since he's the one who begged me to write this book. And yet I can't explain why the sudden softness in his voice pricks at something deep inside me. Something that makes me eager to change the subject.

"How was dinner?" I ask. I'm also aware the small talk is delaying the inevitable. Sure, it's only the second time we've done this, but at some point, these clandestine meetings have to start feeling more natural, less "I'm here to writhe against you for a couple hours in an as-yet-undetermined state of undress."

"Ethan can be a little much," he says. "He insisted on a table in the front of the restaurant, even though the rest of us were hoping to go incognito. So naturally, it turned into the Ethan Underwood show." A low chuckle to himself, one that indicates he doesn't find it funny at all. "Haven't had anything like that happen in a while. Guess I didn't miss it."

"I can imagine." And I try to, picturing the four of them mobbed by adoring fans, Ethan shimmering in the spotlight the way only a leading man can. Again I wonder if Finn has ever wanted that for himself.

"Please tell me your evening was a little less self-indulgent?"

I shrug. "I video-chatted with my parents and read a bit." And the first half of the advance hit my bank account, which prompted a celebratory slice of cheesecake via room service.

"And how are your parents?"

I lift my eyebrows at him, because somehow it sounds like he's genuinely interested. "They're good. I swear, they've picked up five new hobbies each year since they've been retired. My mom just joined a pinochle league, and my dad is getting really into birds. And they're missing me desperately, of course, but they'll survive."

"Of course." And he gives me this little half smile as he unbuttons his black canvas jacket, folding it over the back of a chair. Then, it's as though he's unsure what to do with his body. He glances over at the bed before he settles for standing, crossing one leg over the other. "You did great today. By the way."

I exaggerate a groan. "Mood killer. If there was a mood left after talking about my parents."

"I'm serious! It's not easy to get up there and do that, especially if you haven't been prepped. And League Loup-Garou—that was a secret French werewolf-hunting agency from season three—that's a hard word."

"I have a feeling hard-core *Nocturnals* fans might feel differently, but thank you." I clear my throat, toying with a button on my cardigan. "So. Tonight's lesson."

"Ah yes. I see you called this one"—he pulls up his phone—"'Intermediate Foreplay: Turn a Touch into a Tingle.'"

"I was trying to be creative."

His eyes crinkle at the corners as he grins. "I'm just proud to be in the intermediate class."

I smirk at him as I move over to the bed. "Only because you're sleeping with the teacher." He sits down next to me, triangling an ankle on his knee. Then he laces his fingers together, the perfect image of an adult man waiting for sexual enlightenment. If he's nervous, he's great at hiding it. The next time I enter into an educational sex pact, I'm not doing it with an actor. Or at least, a much less talented actor.

Because that's one thing I've learned, watching *The Nocturnals* and *Lucky Us* and even his Hallmark Christmas movie.

Finnegan Walsh is a *good* actor.

It's the way he's aware of his scene partners, his body language attuned to everyone in the room. The subtleties of his expression, how he's able to convey joy or sadness or fear in a single tilt of his head or curve of his brows. And his eyes, those lovely hazel eyes the show hid behind glasses, always soft and sweet and inquisitive. I can see it now, how so many viewers fell for Hux.

"Before we go any further," I say. "I think we should talk about the clitoris."

Finn blushes. "Yeah, uh . . . that seems to be something of a problem area for me."

"You're not alone." I keep my tone light, wanting him to feel like this is a safe space to talk. To ask questions. Because it's kind of thrilling, getting to explain this to him, especially because of the way he listens. In any other circumstance, I'd be stumbling over my words, but something about his presence makes this feel much more comfortable than it has any right to be.

I take my laptop from my bag, where I already have a few diagrams waiting. In my spare time, I've been doing some of my own research—mostly refreshers, with some new information here and there. "The visible part of the clitoris is at the top of the vulva, right where the inner labia meet. There's a fold of skin that protects it, called the clitoral hood, which retracts to expose more of it when someone is aroused. But most of the clitoris is actually internal." I point this out on one of the diagrams. "And it's an amazing little piece of anatomy. It's the only part of the body meant solely for pleasure."

A nod as Finn takes this all in, eyes on the diagrams.

As a teenager dreaming of my first sexual experiences, I imagined someone would touch me and then—*magic*. But the gap between the expectation and reality can be vast. My first few partners were just as clueless as I was, and I wasn't sure yet how to vocalize what I wanted. How to show them.

I never quite pictured what I'm doing now, with Finn, but the longer we sit here, the more confident I feel.

"This might be shocking, given how society has historically treated women's bodies, but most of the research into women's pleasure is fairly recent," I say. "Like . . . I had no idea that when blood rushes to the clitoris and it swells during arousal, it essentially gets erect."

"Sounds familiar," he says with a laugh, and I can't help joining in. It must be because he's a redhead that his cheeks are still stained pink.

"All of this okay so far?" I ask, and he flashes me a thumbs-up.

"Oh, I'm just incapable of discussing anything remotely sexy without blushing," he says. "You wouldn't believe how much makeup they had to put on me during my scenes with Meg."

That makes me blush, too, thinking about their sex scene. I'm not there yet in the show, but it was part of one of those Mexley compilations, fade-to-black but beautifully shot, in a tent in the woods when the two of them were on a camping trip, tracking down a centaur. Flashes of her dark hair, his flaming auburn, glimpses of her upper thigh and the freckles on his stomach.

I force myself to think about something less sexy before realizing I'm literally giving him a lecture on the clitoris, a fact that makes me bite down on the inside of my cheek to keep from dissolving into laughter.

"Because of where the clit is located, it's difficult to come just from penetration," I continue. "It's not inside the vagina, which is why most people with clitorises need some other form of stimulation."

He waits several long moments before he speaks again. "I'm just thinking of every sex scene I've ever watched that makes it seem like the complete opposite."

"And that would be a little something called the male gaze." I move my finger along the screen. "You want to take your time. Maybe you don't go for the clit right away. Start with one finger and vary your technique: you can stroke slow circles around it, lightly tap it, rub it from side to side. You can gradually go faster depending on what reaction you're getting. Check in with her, see how she's feeling. Then you could add another finger. Or your mouth."

"That's what you like?"

"I love being teased," I admit, crossing my legs a little tighter.

A swallow. "Noted."

"And lube almost always makes it better. Everyone is going to be different, but usually, you want to be gentle. It's really sensitive, and sometimes direct stimulation can be a bit too intense." He presses his lips together, a muscle twitching in his jaw. My own breaths are coming faster, sharper, especially when I realize the way I've been caressing my laptop screen. "It doesn't have to be a mad dash for the finish line. I've been in some situations where the guy comes, and then he's just done for the night. Even when I'm not there yet."

"Jesus. Now I'm not entirely sure why I was so focused on something that would make the whole thing *shorter*." He readjusts on the bed, and it's only then that I realize our knees have been touching. "She should come first, then," he says. "Before we even have sex."

"Obviously, I'm on board with that. But I have a feeling when you say 'sex,' what you really mean is penetration." I wave a hand around the room. "Everything we do in here—all of it is sex, at least to me. There shouldn't be just one definition of it, and penetration shouldn't always be the endgame."

"No, you're right. That makes sense," he says. "So you don't enjoy it at all? Uh . . . penetration?" He runs a sheepish hand down his face. "Just going to put it out there, that's the most times I've heard that word in the course of a single conversation."

I bite back a smile. "I do, but it's not really the main event for me, the way it might be for you. Or the way I'm guessing it's been in the past." He gives me a guilty look. "It's not like how it is in porn, although there's some great feminist porn I'd be happy to show you. Or honestly, even in movies and TV. You can't just mindlessly thrust until both people come, and yet nearly everything you watch is trying its damnedest to convince you otherwise. There's more finesse to it."

"Not that I take all my sexual cues from porn, I just . . . well, you see it at a ripe-enough age, and some of it sticks with you. That's probably where my dirty talk came from, too." Then he looks at me with a new vulnerability. "What if I do all of this, and I still can't get her there?"

"That could very well happen."

"I thought you'd say something like, 'Absolutely not, Finn, you'll be a sexual virtuoso in no time.'"

I toss a pillow at him. "Fine, on the off chance that you're not—it doesn't mean your relationship is doomed. You just have to try other things. Toys can be great, and sex doesn't have to be the destination every time, let alone . . . penetration." This time I stumble over the word, laughing. There's no reason it can't be funny. My knee has fallen back against his, but neither of us moves apart. "There are plenty of fantastic stops along the way—there's no need to rush it. Or maybe those aren't stops—maybe those are the main event. It completely depends on the relationship. But the key is communication. That's the only way to know whether something is working for someone. If one person is unhappy, the other needs to know."

He takes this all in with a focused gaze. "I like that," he says, his voice dropping into a lower register. Now his hand falls to my knee, thumb rubbing a slow circle. "In fact, I like all of this. I think this was more informative than any health class I had in school."

"I'm glad," I say, "because I think we're ready for the practical part of the lesson."

I put my hand on top of his, and it just feels natural, leaning into him. I'm more than eager for him to touch me, which is encouraged in Intermediate Foreplay. This time when we kiss, it's soft at first. Exploratory. Finn runs a hand along the curve of my jaw, and when I shiver, he smiles and does it again. Then he bends to press his mouth to my ear, repeating what he did in Phoenix.

"Still good?" he asks, even as I'm shuddering against him.

I close my eyes, murmuring my agreement. It's as though our bodies are eager to pick up where they left off, and the kissing no longer feels like enough. *More*, I feel myself tell him with a slide of my hips against his. *More*, he agrees, coaxing me on top of him as our kisses turn deeper. Urgent.

It's *fun*, doing this with zero expectations, zero commitment. I'm not worried about what'll happen tomorrow morning or if one of us wants more out of this than the other. It's easier than I expected to turn off my brain.

There's also something about having him all to myself that stands in stark contrast to the Finn on his panels. I'm the only one who gets to see this side of him—for now, at least.

And despite the fact that none of this is real, the hard ridge in his jeans is immensely gratifying.

I rock against him, reaching down to fumble with his zipper, and once his jeans are puddled on the floor, he helps rid me of mine. Our shirts land on top of them.

"Slow," I remind him, even though my wandering hands are anything but. "Tease me."

He responds with a growl as he bends to fiddle with my bra. "I know how to do this now," he says, tugging it off with a satisfied smirk. "Jesus. Your tits are *phenomenal*. I don't think I gave them nearly enough attention in Seattle, and for that, I'm deeply sorry."

"Ah. You're learning." My laugh morphs into a moan as he flicks his tongue against a nipple. "More of that. Please," I say, and he's quick to oblige, teasing me with his teeth. I fist a hand in his hair, a warmth building low in my belly.

This time, he doesn't go too fast. He licks, sucks, gently bites until my nipples are hard peaks and I'm trembling beneath him. His hand drifts down, rubs against my hip bone. "Can I touch you?" he says into my ear, lips skating along my skin. Drawing another shiver, even though I'm warm everywhere.

I nod, and he lets out a low groan when he cups me through my panties.

"Clearly, I'm doing something right," he says, words rough as gravel as he runs a finger back and forth along the damp fabric. When his finger slips inside my underwear, I can sense him stumble, unsure where to start.

"Here," I say, reaching down to guide him until we both find that sensitive bundle of nerves. I graze it with the lightest touch. "Do you feel that?"

"I—I think so." He lets out a sharp breath. "*Oh.* Yeah, I feel it."

"You okay?"

"Just fifteen years of ineptitude crashing down around me."

I shed my underwear to give him easier access. A concentrated tension runs from his cheekbones down to his jaw. His touch is gentle, exactly the way I told him to be. Uncertain, and there's something undeniably sexy about that. I relax into it, letting him slowly, slowly take control.

"Yeah?" he says when my breathing quickens, and I pant out a *yes*.

But then he slows down too much and I lose the momentum, and I have to swallow down the frustration.

This must go on for at least fifteen minutes—getting close before the pleasure fades away.

"I—I'm sorry. I don't know what I'm doing wrong." With his other hand, he swipes at his brow.

"What if we tried something else?" We'd be deviating from the outline, but it might be necessary. "What if . . . what if I showed you how I make myself come?" The idea already has a new kind of pressure building in my core, my heart rate quickening. I hadn't planned on this, but suddenly it seems like not only a guaranteed orgasm but a perfect teaching opportunity.

And I really like the mental image of him watching me.

He tilts his head, curiosity piqued. "I would not be opposed to that."

I swat at his arm. "Teenage fantasy coming true?"

"Maybe if you were dressed like Galadriel." He glances around the room. "Should I turn the thermostat up? Or down?" he asks. "I don't want you to be too hot, or too cold. Since, uh, that's the function of a thermostat. To keep from getting too cold. Or too hot." He rakes a hand through his hair. "Am I being too awkward about this? Because I can guarantee you, I'm going to enjoy it."

"Yes," I say, laughing, even as heat rushes to my cheeks. "But it's very cute."

I sink back onto the bed, head pressed against the pillow. The temperature in the room jumps at least twenty degrees as electricity races through my veins. Maybe I should have asked him to turn down the thermostat after all. Yes, he's seen me naked, but that was back when I thought he was one-night-only. He wasn't taking in every detail of my body.

I let out a shaky breath and run a finger down my stomach. Past my navel. I start slowly, taking my time to find a rhythm, every ounce of awareness focused on the warmth beneath my hand. My body is tight, knees still nearly touching. With every rotation of my finger, I feel my legs loosen.

Finn's reactions spur me on, banishing any lingering self-consciousness. A flutter of his eyes when I slide my free hand upward, clutching at my breasts. A fist gripping the sheets, knuckles taut, when I finally part my legs completely, dropping my knees to the side of the bed, my heart pounding. I didn't think I'd be this turned on, simply having him next to me. Didn't realize how intense his reactions would be.

I let myself relax, reaching to the side table for a bead of lube, which somehow feels even better than I thought it would, and when I let out a low moan, he does, too.

Ever since we started, I've been attuned to his slightest movements, his softest sounds. He could half inhale and every cell in my body would feel it. Even if I move my eyes from him, he's so solidly *there* that I can't forget I'm being watched. And not just watched—*studied*, and Finn is an overachiever. The sound of his breaths and the rise of his chest and somehow, even, the physical *heat* of him from a couple feet away.

I slip a finger inside, dragging that wetness up to my clit. He swallows hard, Adam's apple trembling in his throat.

"You are really fucking sexy like this," he says. "If it's okay to say that."

"Yes. *God.*" I watch the way his forearm muscles contract, the way he barely blinks. The thought of him about to lose it because he's watching *me* about to lose it, forcing himself to hold back . . . it's unspeakably hot. The words tumble out before I have a chance to second-guess them: "Touch yourself with me?"

His gaze grips mine. "Yeah?"

I'm dying for it, I don't say. Instead, I just nod.

He shifts next to me. Swears under his breath. Then he drops one hand to the front of his boxers and rubs himself, letting out a low grumble as soon as he makes contact, shucking off his underwear as though he can't wait any longer.

When he wraps a hand around his cock, he lets out this ragged exhale that sounds like relief. Some of the tension eases from his face, his body, like he's been holding back ever since I knocked on his door. *Beautiful.* I let my gaze rove over him, the rhythmic pumps of his fist and the corded muscles in his neck and the triangle of sweat at the hollow of his throat. My fingers move faster, shoulder blades digging into the mattress.

A strangled sound slips from his mouth. "Fuck, I'm already so close."

"You can—" I start, wanting to tell him that it's okay, that he can let himself go.

"No. I want to wait for you."

"I—I'm almost there."

His movements turn sharper. A gnash of his teeth.

I throw my left arm over my face just as I feel my muscles contract. I need that release more than I need air. I'm only a few seconds away, everything in me tightly wound and ready to snap.

Then, all at once, both of us tip over the edge. Pleasure crashes through me, a brilliant neon tidal wave, and I cry out as a wild gasp tears from his throat. Everything else disappears. There is nothing but my body and this purest, desperate sensation, Finn falling apart right next to me, his free hand tightening on my thigh.

We breathe together, rough and recovering, for at least a whole minute. Faces flushed. Legs limp.

Then he turns to me, eyes heavy-lidded as he grazes my waist with a few fingertips.

"Holy shit," he says, a sweet, disbelieving laugh in his voice. "I've been doing all of this so, so wrong."

Twitter

@nocturnalsfanpage

It's official: The Nocturnals is NOT getting renewed for a season five. Sound off below, and just know that we're as heartbroken as you are. 😭 🌑 🦊

@mexley5ever

is there a petition anywhere? we can't let this happen! i've been watching since i was twelve, i literally grew up with hux and meg! #idratherbeunusual #savethenocturnals

@ultimate_caleb_rhodes_stan

I get that they said they're going to wrap it up with graduation butbutbut I HAVE SO MANY QUESTIONS. Do Caleb and Alice last? Does Hux's control serum really work? And WHAT was up with that wild boar in S3E17?? 🐺 🐺 🐺 🐺 🐺 #SaveTheNocturnals

@calicecalicecalice

i miss them already wtfffffff

@justiceforsofiaperez

Just posted a petition here. PLEASE sign!!! They can't ignore us, right?? 😔 #justiceforsofia

chapter

TWELVE

MEMPHIS, TN

"Print media is dying," one of my journalism professors told us on the first day of classes, and a rush of anxious whispers moved through the room faster than applications getting submitted for a *Seattle Times* internship. "You're not going to be able to graduate, instantly get a job at a local newspaper, and work there for thirty-five years until you retire."

That was, in fact, exactly what the professor had done.

A hand shot up. "I don't get it," said a guy two seats away from me. "Are you telling us to change our majors?"

The professor shook her head. "Not at all," she said, calmly but firmly. "You're just going to have to work a little harder. Be a little more versatile. You're going to have to *innovate*."

Somehow, I have a feeling when she said that, she was thinking more along the lines of learning how to use Photoshop and not fine-tuning X-rated lesson plans for Finnegan Walsh.

Two weeks, we've been on this trip, and I've been so wrapped up in our extracurriculars that I've almost neglected the whole reason we're here: to write Finn's book. Sure, I've spent some of our off days in cafés, trying to make sense of the notes I've taken so far, while Finn holes up in his hotel room reading a wholesome holiday rom-com script or doing . . . whatever else he does in his spare time. But once we land in Memphis for this weekend's con, I'm determined to get more material out of him.

To further ensure this, we're working from the least sexy place imaginable: a conference room in a Hilton DoubleTree.

Laptop and notebook open, voice recorder on. No prisoners.

"I listened to some Sleater-Kinney last night," Finn says from across the table before I can even get out my first question. He sets his phone in the middle of the table, and a familiar string of chords starts playing. The title track to *All Hands on the Bad One*, my favorite album. "You're right; they're pretty good."

It's so out of nowhere that it startles me. "You—oh. Cool," I say stupidly, unsure what to do with this. I clear my throat. "I mean, I'm glad. I was so beyond happy when they got back together, but they're just not the same without Janet Weiss."

"The drummer. She left in . . . 2019, I think it was?"

I lift an eyebrow at him. "Someone went down a Wikipedia rabbit hole."

He just shrugs, drumming one of the free hotel pens on the table to the beat. "You said you loved them. I was curious."

I'm not entirely sure how to name the way I react to this, so I decide to ignore it. "If you're trying to distract me with riot grrrl, it might actually work, so we should probably focus on the book."

He switches off the music. "I'm ready," he says, flicking hair out of his face, posture immediately straightening. "Hit me."

We start with a few softballs: behind-the-scenes *Nocturnals* antics, character research. After what we did in Minnesota a few days ago, I'm relieved we're able to slide right back into our professional roles.

"You were typecast as the nerd for a while," I say. "In *The Nocturnals*, of course, and in *Lucky Us*"—where he played a middle school science teacher who still lived with his parents—"and *Just My Type*"—his font designer character could barely speak to his love interest without breaking out in a cold sweat.

"There was a failed pilot, too," he says. "A sitcom about a group of socially inept accountants. Riveting television. And hilariously, it wasn't even typecasting so much as that was who I was. Hux wasn't that much of a stretch, although for me, it was Tolkien and mythology instead of science." Then he turns sheepish, tapping at the skin beneath his eyes. "My publicist even had me wear glasses with clear frames when we weren't filming, even though I don't need them."

"*No.* You're serious?"

He nods, laughing. "Isn't that ridiculous? I was just grateful to have the work. I probably should have been more grateful, now that I know it was about to dry up."

"We could probably do a whole chapter on that," I say. "The nerd stereotype, and how Hollywood has at turns degraded it and hypersexualized it."

I'm not expecting Finn to have such a strong reaction, but his eyes instantly light up. "Yes! I love that."

My fingers fly across the keyboard as we talk more about his transition from Reno to LA, and he tells me about the first time he got recognized in public.

"I was at a Ralphs in the Valley, waiting in line to buy an absolutely horrific array of groceries," he says. "Pop-Tarts, frozen Red

Robin onion rings, a whole tray of fancy cheeses I was going to eat by myself—that's what happens when you're twenty and living alone for the first time. These two girls who couldn't have been more than a few years younger than I was couldn't stop staring, and I was convinced they were judging me for what I was buying, so I kept trying to shield my basket from them. It wasn't until we were out in the parking lot that they asked if I was Finn Walsh, and I was so shocked that I forgot where I'd parked my car. Walked around in a daze for fifteen minutes, just trying to find it."

"What was that like?" I ask, grinning at the mental image. "The getting recognized, and the living alone for the first time."

"Surreal. To be honest, I'm still not used to it. And not just because it's less frequent these days. When the show was on, I had to go incognito just about everywhere—sunglasses, a hat, the works. Now I don't bother with any of it. The rare times it happens, I'm always convinced, like, one of the *Stranger Things* kids is behind me and that's who they're really staring at." That seems accurate, based on what I've observed so far. No one seems to know him unless they *know* him, unless they're in that world. "And I guess I should clarify—I had a couple roommates at first, but they worked restaurants in the evenings and auditioned during the day, so I almost never saw them. At the end of season one, I moved into my own apartment. And I loved it. I'd already been fairly self-sufficient for a while, so once I got all the Pop-Tarts out of my system, I was cooking pretty regularly. And I went back to Reno to see my mom whenever I could."

The sound of my keyboard continues to fill the space between us. "I'd love to hear more about your family," I say tentatively, because I haven't forgotten what he said about his dad, and the fact that he doesn't mention going back to see him.

Another few taps of his pen along the table. "Let's see . . . you already know they got divorced when I was in high school. My mom used to do hospital billing, but now she's a rabbi."

I gasp. "Are you serious? That's amazing. We can put that in the book, right? Please don't tell her I eat pork."

"She wouldn't judge," he says. "And you'll actually meet her in a few weeks. We'll spend some time at my old house in Reno when we're there for Biggest Little Comic Con."

"Sounds like a gold mine."

"I'm extremely proud of her. It was a massive career change and she had to go back to school for it, but she'd always wanted to do it, and she made it happen."

"And how does she feel about *Ms. Mistletoe*?"

He laughs, pretends to chuck the pen at me. "It was good money! And if you look closely in the Christmas Eve scene, there's actually a menorah in the background."

"Wow, the representation."

This makes him laugh harder, eyes crinkling at the edges. "I want that in the book. Not just the sad menorah, although that's a great image to open a chapter with, but my religion in general."

I nod, making a note of it. "And your dad?"

His mouth forms a grim line. "Not sure where he is these days. He tends to only pop up when he wants something from me."

"Oh—I'm sorry."

"Don't be," he says, waving this off, and I get the feeling there's much more to the story. "It's a relief, actually, not to need to worry about whether he's happy with what I'm doing or if he thinks it's a childish waste of time, which is what he said when I started auditioning." He presses his lips together. "We didn't agree on anything, really. Politics, money, what I wanted to spend my life doing. He was a bitter, unhappy person, and he seemed to make it his mission to ensure everyone around him felt the same way."

He talks more about his mom, telling me a story about how she convinced her synagogue's sisterhood to dress up as characters from *The Nocturnals* during one Purim. Naturally, I require photographic evidence.

"Somehow I get the feeling this isn't the reason you wanted to write this book," I say, passing his phone back to him. He is *so close* to telling me, I can sense it—I just need to give him the tiniest push.

He takes a few moments to consider what he wants to say, the way I'm realizing he tends to do before revealing something deeper. And I like that—that he needs time to collect the right words. Too many of us are too quick to fire off the first thing that comes to mind.

"The whole time I was on *The Nocturnals*," he finally says, "the media speculated on who I was dating. Who I wasn't dating. Whether I'd be as sweet and generous in bed as my character. They wanted to talk about what a dork I was in real life, too, and wasn't it hilarious, how much I knew about Tolkien? I was the ultimate nice guy, wasn't I? Wouldn't I make the best boyfriend, for all these readers who knew absolutely nothing about who I really was? The women on the show, it was even worse for them, being under that microscope. And it was fucking relentless."

"I—I hadn't thought of it that way," I admit. It doesn't feel right to stare at my laptop screen while he's speaking so candidly, so I push it to the side, letting my voice recorder take the reins.

Finn's breaths come faster as he gains steam, forearms on the table, leaning in to make sure the recorder is getting every word. "And then they loved to shit on the show itself. That's what Hollywood does, right? Anything meant for teens, even though none of us were teens, that was our primary demo. Any time I said something publicly, I had to think about all the ways it might be misinterpreted. The sound bites that would distill something I spent ages coming up with the right words for into a five-second clip. I couldn't speak my mind. I couldn't act out of character, even in my regular life, because no one wanted to see that. They wanted Hux, not me. This book is my chance to show them who I really am. Isn't that what we all want—to be able to talk, or create, and have other people listen?"

Oh. Wow. He might have me pegged.

"And then it was all just . . . gone. I love the show. I love the fans," he says. "But some of the actors were almost thirty and playing eighteen-year-olds. It's like we're trapped in this bizarre kind of extended adolescence, and the reunion . . ." He trails off, weighing his words again. "I don't want to be a household name, I really don't. I've seen what that level of fame does to people. Juliana— well, you probably read the stories."

I did. Paparazzi documenting her addictions and her time in rehab, photo galleries questioning whether she's too skinny or not skinny enough, and how long she'll be sober this time before another relapse. All of it horrifying.

"And that's just what makes it to the gossip sites," he says. "It can be fucking brutal."

"But it's worth it?" I ask. "It's worth all the bullshit?"

He considers this for a moment. "I don't know if it's that it's worth all the bullshit or that I don't have any other marketable skills. Well—maybe I don't. But there's truly nothing else like it. You get to create art that matters to other people, something that brings them joy or inspires them or helps them process, or something that just allows them to escape the real world for a while.

Maybe they'll find some connection with it that you never intended—that's part of the magic. When I'm in front of a camera, I don't have to worry about anything except making that performance as believable as possible, and it's an incredible release. And I hope to keep doing it as long as I can, even if I'm not getting huge roles. Even if those roles aren't 'prestige.' Maybe I'd like to produce or direct someday, but for now, I like my privacy. What I'm most passionate about, actually, is mental health."

This catches me off guard. I'd expected his reasons for the book to be tied with Hollywood somehow, maybe his relationship with his family. But I can't say this doesn't answer a few questions I haven't asked yet.

He stares down at his hands, weaving his fingers together. "I've been waiting for the right time to tell you, since I want this to be a focal point of the book, but maybe there isn't a singular right time." He cracks a half smile, one I can tell takes a tremendous amount of effort. "See? I'm stalling when what I want to do is just come right out and say it. Okay." A deep breath, and then: "I have pretty severe OCD."

"I thought it might be something like that," I say, as gently as I can. The inspection of his dishes. The way he opts for a fork and knife instead of using his hands.

"It's not always the easiest thing to discuss," he says. "I've had it since I was a kid, and before I started medication, before I met my current therapist, I was a fucking mess." He rubs at the back of his neck, eyes flicking around the room before landing back on me. "Most of my obsessions revolve around germs, contamination, mold, mostly food-related. If something's even mildly unclean, I can't be near it. Or at least, that's how I used to be. I wouldn't eat at restaurants because I could never be sure of how clean anything was and I'd worry about getting sick from it. I'd toss food. I'd throw clean sheets back in the washing machine if they smelled off in any way. It made me feel like shit because I was wasting all that water, which just ratcheted up my anxiety about it even more.

"I hid it from my parents for a long time," he continues. "Mostly my dad. It took me years of therapy to realize how emotionally abusive he was. I assumed because he never laid a hand on us that everything was fine, but he had an opinion on everything, and if you didn't have the same one, it would lead to a screaming match. He hated wasting food, so if something in the fridge was getting close to an expiration date or had the tiniest bit of discoloration that was most likely—fuck, I don't know. Some preservative. I'd wait until he was out of the house and hide it deep in the garbage can, and then when he asked later where it was, I'd say I ate it. Sometimes I'd even take a bunch of things to the dumpster at the end of the street, just because I was terrified of my parents finding out."

"Jesus," I say softly, because I hate the idea of a young Finn so scared, so uncertain. His brain working against him. "That can't have been easy. I'm so sorry."

"I got good at it." A rueful smile. "Of course, sometimes I'd have to wear gloves and shower immediately afterward. And of course, my parents eventually found out what I was doing. My dad was furious, and I think my mom was too scared of him to say anything otherwise. And he—he just told me to suck it up, that I was 'acting fucking insane.' And 'don't you dare let anyone see you doing that.'" Finn is breathing a little faster now, a fist clenching on top of the table. "So that's what I did. My compulsions morphed, and most of my free time was dedicated to figuring out how to make myself feel safe and comfortable without anyone finding out. If there was a speck of something strange on a plate, I'd say I wasn't hungry. I'd dispose of old sheets, old blankets at school and buy replacements with my Hanukkah money. I wanted to make my dad happy *so badly*, and that meant not being the fucked-up son he thought I was."

"Finn. You are absolutely *not*," I say firmly, wishing I could do more to reassure him.

He shakes his head. "It certainly felt that way, a lot of the time. I didn't even have much of a relationship with my mom until after he left—and good riddance. The worst of it, though, was actually the last season of *The Nocturnals*, when we knew we weren't getting renewed. I was so anxious about booking the next job because everyone else had things lined up and I didn't. I was putting so much pressure on myself, and I'd just bought a house I didn't know whether I'd be able to keep paying for, and the only thing it felt like I could control was how clean it was. I'd get stuck in these horrible cycles, scrubbing down the house, returning sets of dishes I'd just bought because I swore the box smelled weird when I opened it up, constantly running laundry because nothing ever seemed clean enough. And then my energy bill went way up and that only added to the stress. I knew I needed to do something, but I didn't know where to start. It wasn't until after the finale aired that I started getting help. Hallie was the one who suggested it, actually."

"That's great," I say, meaning it. "I've been in therapy, too. For generalized anxiety disorder. I think I've probably had it most of my life, but I didn't start seeing someone until my midtwenties. I haven't gone in a few months—though maybe I should?—but I fucking love therapy."

He nods. "So you get it."

"Not all of it—but some of it." Then something occurs to me. "What about sex? If that's okay to ask—since there's obviously, well, a lot of touching involved."

"Worked on that a lot in therapy, too," he says. "Oral sex was a bit of a hurdle at first, but I haven't had any issues with it for years."

"If you're not comfortable, we definitely don't have to—"

"No. I want to. Even if my skills are, uh, lacking at the moment . . . I love doing it." His voice is so earnest. I swallow hard, wondering if there really is something inherently horny about a Hilton DoubleTree that I failed to take into account. I know plenty of men enjoy going down on a woman, but to hear him admit it so casually . . .

Fortunately, he changes the subject before I can linger on it. "This is why it didn't work out with those other ghostwriters," he says. "I didn't feel entirely at ease with them—not to the point where I could open up about this. And I'm much better than I used to be. I can go to restaurants, though I never use my hands for anything—that's something I've been working on in therapy lately. I try to avoid public bathrooms, if I can help it, but I'm not running out to buy new sheets every other month like I used to. It's mostly low level, manageable, but sometimes high-anxiety situations . . . they exacerbate it." Then he lets out a laugh. "And lucky you, you seem to be nearby during most of them. It's not something I tell everyone," he says. "What about you?"

"Sometimes. Depends on how close we are." I regret the words immediately, worrying that by saying this, I've indicated we have some sort of closeness.

But he's just nodding. "I don't want it to be that way anymore. I've spent too much of my life hiding, lying, pretending. I want this book to be fun behind-the-scenes stories about *The Nocturnals*, sure. But more than that, I want to talk about OCD stigma and mental health in Hollywood." His voice gains confidence, his eyes meeting mine with the full passion of what he's saying. "I'm planning to put all proceeds of the book toward setting up a nonprofit to help actors with mental health challenges. Aspiring actors, established actors—anyone. I don't want anyone to feel like money or stigma is standing in the way of them getting the help they need."

I just stare at him. There's a shyness on his face now, replacing the confidence from just a moment ago.

"What?" he says, brows creased with worry. "What's that look? You think it's a bad idea?"

"No. Not at all." I reach for my laptop again, typing *NONPROFIT* in bold letters. "I . . . think that sounds incredible, Finn. Really."

A blush tinges his cheeks. "I haven't spoken about it much yet beyond with my team and some potential donors, but I could show you the business plan, if you want."

"More Google Docs? Yes, please."

A smirk, but I can tell he's pleased. I can see it on his face: this is his baby.

"I don't just want to be that guy from the werewolf show anymore," he says defiantly. "I've done everything I can to change that, but I've started to realize that unless something big happens, I'm just . . . stuck."

Stuck.

"I get the feeling," I say quietly, because even if I haven't experienced it, I understand what it's like to be trapped. "Maybe this is the something big for both of us."

▬▬ ▬▬ ▬▬

BY THE TIME I WRAP MYSELF IN A TOWEL AND MEET FINN AT THE HOTEL pool, where he's suggested we take a break, I'm no longer sure if

I'm doing it begrudgingly. Somehow, I thought to bring a swimsuit at the last minute, a black two-piece I bought five years ago in that dreamy way people in the Pacific Northwest buy swimsuits and hope for sunshine.

Finn's already there in deep blue swim trunks, stretching on the side as though he's preparing for a 200-meter backstroke. I've never seen him shirtless in decent lighting. He's not ripped, which I already knew. Though he was skinny in *The Nocturnals*, now he's filled out a bit more. Freckles dot his shoulders, his spine, his hips, little swirls of color.

"Are you wearing *socks*?" he asks, incredulous.

I glance down at where I shoved my socked feet into Birks. And not just any socks: my favorite pair, with grumpy faces all over them. "Okay, look. I didn't want us to have this conversation this early, maybe not ever. But I'm always cold, and I just hate the feeling of bare feet. I'm not going to swim in them or anything."

Finn shakes his head. "I'm sorry, I don't understand. Why are we writing a book about me when you're clearly an alien masquerading as a human?" He steps closer, giving me a serious look as he drops a hand to my shoulder. "Are you lonely here? Are they worried about you on your home planet?"

I try to smack him with my towel, but he darts out of the way. "We all have our weird shit, okay?"

"As long as you don't put them on afterward, we're good."

"I'm not a monster." He doesn't need to know about the extra pair in my tote bag for exactly that reason.

He heads toward the pool, throwing me an exaggerated lift of his eyebrows before he dives confidently into the deep end. He pops back up with a grin, swiping water out of his eyes and slicking back his hair.

"Let me guess, you learned how to swim for some daring

underwater rescue scene in *The Nocturnals*," I say as his arms slice through the water. I'm no expert, but his form looks pretty perfect.

He shakes his head. "*Aquamarine 2: Boy Out of Water.*"

"I didn't know that movie had a sequel."

"Yeah, it probably shouldn't have. It was both a critical and commercial failure, but the swimming lessons were legit."

I place my phone next to the edge of the pool, checking it for messages from my parents before dipping into the water.

"Just an FYI," I call out to Finn, who's now moved into an easy butterfly. "I haven't gone swimming in probably ten years." I nod my head toward the NO LIFEGUARD ON DUTY sign.

"Lucky for you, I've taken multiple CPR courses. Not sure how much I remember, but I can definitely *look* like I'm saving your life." He gazes around the pool. "None of these hotels have any personality, do they? How much more time do we have in Memphis? Maybe we could get out a bit tomorrow. Explore."

"We should be working. We're here two more days, and then we're off to Denver on Thursday."

"We can do both." He swims up next to me, water droplets lining his eyebrows and clinging to his lashes. "We're in a place you've never been. Aren't you curious? And hey, maybe it'll jog our creativity."

Because this is the trip of going outside my comfort zone, I give in. And check my phone one more time.

"Everything okay?" he asks.

"Oh—yeah, sorry. My mom had a colonoscopy last week, so I'm just waiting to hear how it went."

"I have to say, I'm curious about the kind of people who raised someone who insists on wearing socks down to a hotel pool."

"They're amazing. Kind of crunchy hippies—they smoke pot,

and my mom even had a phase when she followed around the Grateful Dead for a while, way before I was born," I say. "Before they retired, my dad worked as a sustainability consultant for big corporations and my mom was an elementary school music teacher. But they're a bit older. I probably worry about them too much, definitely more than they'd like me to. I can't help it."

"When you say older . . ."

I purse my lips, preparing for his reaction. "Pushing eighty. When I was in school, kids would always assume they were my grandparents. And now that I'm an adult, it's only occasionally hitting me that they're really, really different from how they used to be. And that terrifies me sometimes." My voice goes soft, the hum of the pool filters filling the space.

"I'd be doing the same thing," he says. "That can't be easy."

There's something new in his voice, a gentleness that makes me keep talking.

"It's like—each year brings me new and additional ways to worry about them. Is it going to get below freezing? Then I'm worried about them getting out of a car when it's icy. How's their eyesight, their reflexes? Is it safe for them to drive? And—" I break off, wondering if I'm telling him too much. It's definitely more than I've talked about to anyone except Noemie. "Even if they did need help, I feel like they'd go out of their way to prevent me from finding out. Because they wouldn't want to inconvenience me."

One time, they didn't tell me about a skin biopsy my dad had because they didn't want me to get anxious about it. Which was probably the right call, because when my mom let it slip over text that the results had fortunately been benign, I called her five times in rapid succession when she didn't answer. When she finally called me back, she didn't understand why I was so worried about it.

"They're good people," he says. "I can tell."

"Because they put up with me and my alien tendencies?"

"No. It's in the way you talk about them. There are so many parent horror stories in the industry, people who forced their kids to grow up too fast. I guess it's been a while since I heard about someone genuinely loving and getting along with their parents."

The message from my mom finally shows up, giving my shoulders a chance to relax: all nrml 👍 dad & I going to clbrate w 🌿 🦝

I push my phone away from the pool—but not too far. "Anyway, you don't need a whole history about my parents."

"What if I want to hear about Mr. and Mrs. Cohen?" He maneuvers into a back float, flashing me a Cheshire cat grin. "It's going to get pretty boring if I'm the only one who has to talk. I want to know things about you, too."

And then he swims off, sending a splash in my direction.

THIRTEEN

MEMPHIS, TN

Memphis is an easy city to fall in love with, which I do almost instantly. It's rich with history and culture, *alive*. The sun seems to follow us down streets of brick buildings, warming our necks and washing the whole place in amber hues.

We take a tour of Sun Studio, where Finn insists on snapping a photo of me holding the microphone Elvis supposedly used to record his first song. I roll my eyes when he shows it to me. I'm glaring at the camera, looking altogether too serious: shoulders hitched, jaw set, my free hand in a tight fist at my hip. "Future album art for your solo riot grrrl revival act," he says, grinning at it.

Then we go to the Civil Rights Museum and stroll along Beale Street, which strikes me as a bit of a tourist trap with its flashing neon signs and endless souvenir shops—but then again, that's exactly what we are. By the time we sit down for authentic Memphis barbecue—jackfruit for Finn—he's more relaxed than I've ever seen him. His freckles are sun-warmed, eyes bright, and he's casual in worn jeans and a T-shirt that says MORDOR FUN RUN, and in small letters beneath it: ONE DOES NOT SIMPLY WALK.

The restaurant is cozy, wooden tables and walls covered with vintage posters of country music stars, Johnny Cash playing from the staticky speakers, and all of it makes me feel like I might be able to relax a little, too. Finn was right about those hotels feeling stifling. We sent our teams an outline yesterday, so it feels like we've earned this time to explore. Now we're just waiting for their approval before we start writing.

I reach across the checked tablecloth for a bottle of barbecue sauce. "I thought this looked familiar. My cousin got this in a barbecue sauce subscription box once." When Finn gives me a quizzical look, I elaborate. "She's a little obsessed with getting surprises in the mail each month. It almost doesn't matter what they are, as long as there's a box to open. She loved this one—I'll have to grab a bottle for her before we leave."

"You and your cousin are close," he muses. "You talk about her a lot."

I nod. "Noemie and I—we grew up together. Went to the same schools, same college, even same major, before she decided on the more pragmatic and more financially stable path of public relations. And I live with her. We might as well be sisters, honestly."

"I used to want a sibling." He digs a fork into his coleslaw. "But I had Krishanu at least, and we were pretty inseparable for a while." He mentioned him a couple days ago: Krishanu Pradhan, his childhood best friend, who still lives in Reno and teaches high school English. "You'll meet him in a few weeks, too."

"I can't wait. I hope he has embarrassing stories."

"Too many, probably."

"What does Finnegan Walsh do when he's not filming or on the road?" I ask. "What's real life like for you?"

"This is my real life," he says, matter-of-fact.

I shake my head. "No, no, no. Real life is when you're at home and no one else is around, so you lick the sauce off a plate of spaghetti or walk around naked or pee in the shower. That's what readers want."

"They want me to pee in the shower?"

"Metaphorically, yes."

Finn takes a moment to consider this as the music changes to Dolly Parton. "It's very boring, actually. A lot of cooking. A lot of reading. Sometimes I'll video-chat with my mom or Krishanu." He shrugs. "I shot another Hallmark movie that'll be out in December, but I wanted to focus on the book, so I don't have anything else in development right now. It's funny—when I'm home, I miss being on the road. And of course, when I'm on the circuit, all I want is to go home."

There's a heartbreak carved into those words, intentional or not. Both options seem deeply lonely: at home by himself or on the road surrounded by people who know his character but not him.

"That's exactly why I took this job." I take the most heavenly bite of pulled pork. "Because I've never really left Seattle."

"Ah, so you'd have said yes to anyone who asked you to write a book for them if it meant following them around the country." He slices off a piece of corn bread, and now that I know the reason for it, I do my best not to stare. "How'd you get into ghostwriting?"

"Sort of stumbled into it, really," I say, explaining the job posting, finding Stella, writing Amber Y's book, and the other two that were less than satisfying. How, because of the secrecy surrounding it, I was worried at the beginning that someone might discover who I was and I'd get in trouble, somehow. My anxiety wouldn't let me exhale until I was halfway through my second book. Once I even found a Reddit thread where people were trying to unmask the identity of Amber Y's ghostwriter and I spent a solid hour raking through my social media, even though I was certain nothing could trace her book back to me. No stray pieces of paper or corners of my laptop screen where someone could zoom in and find a paragraph from *Don't Ask Y*. Still, even looking at the thread felt like hovering over a paper shredder with my NDA.

"When I first met you," he says, as though it's just occurring to him, "you said you were having some kind of career crisis. This isn't your dream job, I'm guessing?"

I'd kind of been hoping he'd forget about that. "That night . . . well, I was there for Maddy DeMarco's book, which I'm guessing you know now. I went up to have her sign my copy, told her my full name . . . and she didn't even know who I was." I stare down at my nails, repainted last night with a pale blue I brought with me, picking at my thumb as I recall the way my heart sank to my toes. "That's why I was so miserable when you met me."

Finn just blinks, trying to comprehend it. "You wrote that whole book for her, and she didn't have a clue who you were?"

"I barely talked to her during the writing process. That's part of why I said yes to this—because I'd actually get to work with you." My cheeks turn warm, even though he must know I mean it on a purely professional level.

"You should have said something. Made her feel like shit about it."

I shrug this off. "Maybe. I sort of just wanted to get out of there." At that, I can't help laughing. "And because of you, I guess I did. In more ways than one." Coincidence, fate, a cosmic joke— whatever it was, in this moment I'm radically grateful for it. This job has been unlike any of my others, which was exactly what I needed. "I'm starting to think there's no such thing as a dream job. I sort of hoped I'd start out with these lighter assignments—influencers, reality stars. And then I could move on to something deeper. Something with a little more . . . substance."

"Where do I fall on that spectrum?" He draws a fingertip along the table. "You assumed I wouldn't have any substance because I'm an actor?"

"I—no." I'm not used to being put on the spot like this, and maybe it should give me a little more empathy for him. I'm fully aware he probably has enough for at least a couple chapters on me at this point. "Well—maybe at first. You probably have to have some semblance of ego to see yourself onscreen, right?"

Finn shrugs. "Sure, it's an ego trip for plenty of people, but I've loved acting since I was a kid. A lot of us do it for the pure love of the art form."

"I've been wrong before," I continue. "That reality star had a lot more to say than I initially gave her credit for. But then I'm also like, who decides what's substance and what isn't? Maybe what doesn't matter to me is substance for someone else."

"And you're trying to find my hidden depth."

When his eyes flick to mine, I get a flash of us in bed back in Minnesota, shoulder to shoulder. Finn's throat pointed toward the ceiling, telling me in that rough voice that he was so close.

"For what it's worth," he says, pushing his empty red basket of food off to the side. "You're doing a fantastic job." Then something seems to occur to him. "All the ghostwriting . . . you don't ever want to write a book of your own?"

My face absolutely ignites, and I reach for my empty glass of water, then glance around anxiously for the server.

"*Oh*. You do."

"I mean. Doesn't everyone want to? The great American novel and all that?" I try my best to laugh it off. I haven't vocalized it to anyone in a long, long time. That dream died before I gave it enough space to breathe, and it's barely a hobby anymore. In fact, I haven't opened that document since we left Seattle.

"I used to," I clarify. "But not anymore. Now . . ." I gesture around us. "I do things like this."

He must be able to tell that it's not something I want to linger on because he doesn't push it. Still, it's almost like yesterday in the pool was a promise. *I want to know things about you, too.*

Except with me, there are limits.

And those conversations don't end with both of us getting a paycheck.

"THERE'S SOMETHING ELSE I'VE BEEN WONDERING," FINN SAYS AS WE step into the bright midafternoon, as he slides on a pair of sunglasses. An hour later, and it still feels a little like his cursor is hovering over that file folder on my computer. When I nod, he does that thing again where he pauses to summon his words, rubbing at his stubbled chin for a moment. "What's in this for you? The 'few pointers' you've been giving me." Those words freeze me in place right on the sidewalk. "I've been thinking about it, and I figure you can't possibly be doing it out of the goodness of your heart."

I wish I could see his face, especially as the sun burns a blush onto my cheeks. It's a much easier conversation than the one about my writing. "I guess I've had my reasons. For years, I was in love with one of my closest friends," I start, and strangely, it's not too difficult to admit. "Wyatt. I'd had a bit of a crush since college, and it never fully went away. I'd date someone else, we'd break up, and the crush would come back with a vengeance."

Finn nods, doesn't interrupt.

"A few weeks before I met you . . . he and I slept together. And I had all these delusions—of course, I didn't realize that's what they were back then—that we'd instantly become this perfect couple. I liked him so, so much, and I'd been patient, and it just felt like everything was falling into place." It's not some dark secret, and yet it's not the most fun to relive. "Until he told me that wasn't going to happen. That I was a 'relationship girl,' and he wasn't looking for a relationship."

"What does that even mean?" Finn asks. "A relationship girl?"

I think back through my dating history. Justin, my high school boyfriend and the first person I slept with, an act that lasted a total of six minutes. David, who I dated sophomore year of college, who'd been so supportive when I got pregnant and decided to get an abortion. We only broke up because he left to study abroad for a semester and neither of us wanted to do long-distance. Then there was Knox, the first guy I had an orgasm with, which made me bolder with the rest: a handful of other guys throughout my twenties from a handful of different dating apps, relationships lasting from four to eighteen months, until they ended and I went back to pining for Wyatt.

"I guess I haven't ever done the casual thing. Until now." I scrape at my thumb again, loosening a little stripe of blue. "In a way, he's right. It just felt like the worst dig, coming from him— from someone who knew me that well, and who I liked so much. I was a relationship girl . . . but he didn't want to be in a relationship with me."

It's the first time I've put those exact words together. Because that's the truth, isn't it? If he'd wanted to be with me, it wouldn't have mattered, what kind of girl I am.

I glance back up at Finn, intent on brushing all of this away if he thinks it's too normal-person trivial. I'm not sure why that's my first inclination. But when he speaks again, his voice is serious.

"There's nothing wrong with being a relationship person. Or not being one," Finn says softly. "I've done casual—the first year the show was on. I'm not proud of all of it. Even more so, imagining how terrible that sex probably was. But I was young and inexperienced and entirely out of my depth." He tries a grin. "Maybe my enthusiasm made up for it."

I have to laugh at that. "Have you only dated within Hollywood?"

A nod. "I've found that no one else really seems to *get* the industry," he says. "Sure, it can be stressful, but it's easier when both people understand that very unique kind of stress."

What he's saying makes perfect sense—and yet I can't explain why it lands in a strange place in my stomach.

"You still have feelings for him? Wyatt?" Finn's tone is tinged with a guarded curiosity, like he doesn't think he should care about the answer but still really wants to know.

"I'm not sure," I say honestly. It's true that I haven't thought about him in at least a week, which is a welcome realization, and I'm no longer checking my phone for messages that aren't coming. "It's not that I still think we can be something—I know we can't. But those feelings didn't exactly vanish overnight. And, well, I'd be lying if I said that wasn't also part of the reason I said yes to this job."

"I'm sorry. I'm sorry it didn't go the way you wanted." He sounds genuine, a kind of sympathy I'm not used to hearing from him. He slips his sunglasses to the top of his head, and I can see that sympathy painted in the soft angle of his eyebrows, the set of his jaw. Suddenly, the way he's looking at me is too focused, taking me out of this city and into a hotel room.

I still haven't answered his question, but I'm getting there.

"Then I went to Maddy's event, and my career seemed like it was going in the wrong direction, too. Like I couldn't win at anything. So that's about where I was when you met me—not quite rock bottom, but an all-time low. I'd been focused on my career for forever, and that wasn't going anywhere I wanted it to. And my romantic life was completely wrapped up in Wyatt. So I guess I thought, when we first started joking about those lessons, that maybe I'd allow myself the chance to have a little fun."

His eyes haven't moved from mine "And has it been?" he asks. "Fun?"

The memory of Minnesota sends another wave of heat through me. Minnesota, and Phoenix, and maybe tonight, with no impending deadline and no early wake-up. I'm certain I don't imagine the way he shifts closer to me.

I press my lips together, giving him a nod. "And I think it's about to get even better."

Because we're standing in front of a shop with MEMPHIS EROTIC BOUTIQUE spelled out in neon pink letters.

"Why do I get the feeling you planned this," Finn says with a laugh. "It must be somewhere on that Google Doc. In very tiny letters."

I lift my eyebrows at him as he readjusts his baseball cap, slips on his sunglasses. Disguising himself. "Seriously? You're worried the employees of a sex shop in Memphis, Tennessee, are going to recognize Oliver Huxley?"

"Hey. Our fans are diverse and hopefully sex-positive."

"There's no shame in this." I make a swipe for his hat, but he ducks out of the way. "Come on."

Begrudgingly, he takes off his hat and sunglasses. Still, I catch him averting his eyes as we walk inside, pretending to focus on the displays of toys modeled after parts of porn stars' anatomy. Finnegan Walsh, in a sex shop, in his Mordor T-shirt. His cheeks turn pink in this adorable way as we pass the more risqué products, the BDSM section, the blow-up dolls. Meanwhile, I let myself look everywhere, half keeping an eye out for anything we could use in our lessons, half because it's just interesting. The best sex shops are open, inclusive spaces, and it took me far too long to enter one.

I pluck a bottle of lube from a shelf. "Always good to have."

"Mm-hmm." Finn nods toward another display. I can see him slowly starting to relax. "What are those for?"

"Vibrating nipple clamps? It's kind of in the name."

"Ah. I think I'll have to work up to that." He motions to a tube of warming lube. "I could get into something like this, though."

A jolt of sensation sparks low in my belly. "Yeah? Let's get it."

He's watching me, an interesting expression on his face. "You're so comfortable with it," he says, sounding almost impressed as he rakes a hand through his hair. "Talking about all these things. Being here."

"I guess part of it was school," I say. "And the rest . . . I guess you could say that I practiced. I knew that if I couldn't be comfortable with it, then there was no way I could tell someone else what I wanted." I give him a sly smile. "It's empowering, telling a partner what you want. And just because it's comfortable doesn't mean it can't be hot, too."

"Oh, I absolutely know that now."

I had this thought yesterday, and today confirms it: we've become more open with each other. Against all odds, Finn and I might be turning out to be more than sexual partners or ghostwriter and author: we might be something close to *friends*.

When we get to the shelf of vibrators, I spend a couple minutes browsing before picking up a clitoral massager not unlike one I have at home. "What about this?"

"I am . . . looking respectfully."

"I was thinking we could use it together."

"And now I am looking *very* respectfully."

We make our way to the front with the vibrator, lube, and an array of condoms: flavored, ribbed, ultra-sensitive. The middle-aged woman at the cash register gives us a warm hello as she starts ringing things up, then drops her scanner as she makes eye contact with Finn.

"Oh my god, Finn? Finn Walsh?" she asks in a lilting Southern accent. "I thought my eyes were playing tricks on me when you walked in, but it's you, isn't it?"

Finn's posture goes ramrod straight next to me. He glances to the door, as though debating how quickly he can make it there, then seems to realize there's no chance at escape.

He lifts a hand in a halfhearted wave. "Hi. Nice to meet you."

Her hands fly to her mouth. "Goodness, it *is* you! I'm Tamara—I'm the owner here, welcome! Anything I can help you find? Or"—she cranes her neck to see what I'm carrying—"looks like your girlfriend already picked out some of our bestsellers!"

"Oh—she's not—"

"I'm not—"

Tamara gives us a wink. "Don't worry, I won't tell." Then she lets out another gasp. "You must be so busy with the reunion coming up! I *screamed* when I heard the news, scared my husband half to death."

"We're really excited about it."

I beam, loving every second of this.

"Can I get a photo? I've always wanted to have one of those

celebrity walls, but, well, we don't get quite as many famous people in here as I'd have hoped. You might be the first!"

"How lucky," Finn says in a flat voice. "Of course."

A gleeful Tamara whips out her phone.

"I'm going to kill you," Finn says through gritted teeth.

"With the spiked dildo or the leather flogger?"

"Whatever's the slowest and most painful."

"Sounds kinky." I nudge him as the shop owner aims her phone at him. "Now *smile*."

<u>THE NOCTURNALS</u>

Season 2, Episode 18:
"Something Wicked, Something Wild"

INT. OAKHURST BIOLOGY LAB—DAY

PROFESSOR DONOVAN sits at a lab table behind a microscope, surrounded by test tubes, beakers, and X-rays. CALEB RHODES leans casually against the table while OLIVER HUXLEY waits nervously next to him.

> PROFESSOR DONOVAN
> As all of my experiments have shown,
> there's nothing that could alter her
> DNA and completely erase the canine
> part of herself. It's simply an
> irreversible process, I'm sorry to
> say.

> CALEB
> That's what I've been telling him.
> I'm just not the best with all the
> sciency stuff. And I don't mind being
> a werewolf. In fact, I think I kind
> of kick ass at it?

Caleb attempts to howl, then dissolves into a coughing fit.

> Well. Most of the time.

HUX

It's not for him. It's . . . for
someone else.

CALEB

Have you even asked her, Hux? Maybe
you should start there, huh?

HUX

Well, no. But you think if she had
a choice, this is really what she'd
pick?

CALEB

*He moves closer to Hux, jabbing a finger at his
chest.*

We have super strength, super speed,
and night vision. I can hear
conversations happening a mile away.
I can heal myself if I get hurt.
And not to brag, but it's just a
fact—we're more beautiful than the
rest of you. Shinier hair, perfect
skin, bigger muscles. Who wouldn't
want that?

HUX

How would you know what she wants?

CALEB

Because I'm the one who turned her.

chapter

FOURTEEN

MEMPHIS, TN

The energy between us is different as dusk falls. Kinetic. My sleeve brushes Finn's at least a half dozen times, and he forgets to drop his palm when it lands on my lower back for a few extra moments. After a walk to the waterfront, I ask if he's ready to go back to the hotel and his breathy *yes* jolts my heart into a new rhythm. The evening is unseasonably warm for late September, the humid air filling my lungs and making me a little unsteady on my feet. No alcohol, just a steady shot of lust straight to my brain.

I switch on the lights in my room and empty the bag from the sex shop onto the bed. As nonchalantly as I can, I flip over the mystery novel on my nightstand. I'm not embarrassed of it; *The Sourdough Slayer* just isn't the sexiest title.

Our next lesson was supposed to be oral sex, but there's no reason we can't spice it up. Another deviation from my outline, but an essential one.

Based on the way Finn's eyeing our stash, he's thinking the same thing. "It would be a shame if we didn't test all these out," he says, turning over a textured condom. "Make sure everything works."

"I couldn't agree more."

He reaches for the vibrator, pulling open the packaging. "Anything I should know before using this?"

"Start slow," I say, even though I'm already eager to get his hands on me. "But otherwise . . . feel free to play around with it."

"I fully intend to." Then he places it on the nightstand, turning his attention back to me. "Soon," he promises, sitting down on the bed, patting the spot next to him. It's a small amount of direction, but my body thrills at the thought of him taking control—and knowing what to do.

"I liked today," he continues, lifting a hand to run through my hair. My eyes slide shut at the gentle press of his fingertips. His other hand comes up to cup my jaw, tracing the curve of it before his thumb lands on my lower lip. "Thank you. For indulging me. Maybe I'd forgotten that I could have some fun, too."

"This isn't fun for you?" I part my lips to taste the salt of his skin. Give his thumb a few flicks of my tongue before I draw it into my mouth.

He groans as he watches me suck his thumb deeper, fist tightening in my hair. "I think you know exactly how this feels for me." With a breathless urgency, he pulls his thumb from my mouth and covers my lips with his. "But tonight is about you."

And I'm entirely too aroused to argue.

I love seeing him gain more confidence. We shed our clothes even quicker than that first night in Seattle; shirts, jeans, belts, underwear piling onto the floor. I discover a mole between his shoulder blades, just slightly off-center, before he props himself on his side, facing me, looking beautifully, intensely determined as he rakes his gaze over my body.

I love this, too, the hungry way he takes me in. So I tell him. Because this is all about communication.

"Yeah? Because I could do this all night, if you prefer," he says, a lazy smile appearing on his face.

I shake my head, laughing, but by the time he runs his hand up my thigh and closer to where I want him, my breath stills in my lungs.

If this were our first time, I might be embarrassed by how needy I am, evidenced by the slickness he finds when his finger slides between my folds. I could get addicted to the way he reacts to the sounds of my body. The low scrape of his breath. The press of his face against my neck.

But in his enthusiasm, he goes a bit too fast, too soon.

"Gentler," I say, nudging his arm with a few fingertips. "Softer."

"Right, right, right. Sorry." His touch turns featherlight, and I close my eyes, grip his shoulders. There.

He was clearly paying attention the other night, because now I can tell he's mimicking my movements, sweeping his finger in an agonizing circle. He's focused, waiting for my reactions before he changes his speed or pressure.

"Good?" he asks when he grazes my clit and draws out a shudder. I nod and rasp out a *yes*, rocking my hips to encourage him. He does it again and again, the briefest taunts of pleasure. Then he reaches for the warming lube, rubbing it between his fingertips before slipping them between my thighs. I cry out when he makes contact with my skin, all that heat nudging me closer and closer.

"You feel amazing," he murmurs against my chest, capturing a nipple with his tongue. Sucking lightly, and then harder as he fills me with a finger. After a few pumps, he slides upward again, stroking and rubbing and tracing and *Jesus. Christ.* I clutch him tighter because it's all so good, even when he stumbles. Especially when he hears my breath catch and starts moving faster.

Especially when he reaches over to the nightstand for the vibrator.

But he doesn't place it between my thighs right away. Instead, he flicks the ON switch and gives me a wicked smile. He leans in, lowering it to my mouth, holding it there for a few moments. The vibrations humming through me are a pleasant sensation, if a little ticklish. Then he sweeps it down to my neck. The silicone pulses across my skin in slow, increasingly satisfying bursts.

"That's—that's really nice," I say, and he grins like he knew just how nice it would feel.

When he reaches my breasts, he teases them for a few moments before pressing the vibrator hard against one nipple, and then the other. My back arches, every muscle in my core clenching. *Lower. Please.*

There's a slight tickle as he moves the vibrator along my stomach, but it's not nearly as strong as the anticipation. My body wants pleasure from him so badly, wants to shiver and tighten against him before exploding.

My hips thrust forward, trying my best to urge him a little farther south. He sees exactly what I'm doing but doesn't take the bait.

"You said to go slow," he whispers, drawing it upward, away from the one place I want it.

A whine slips from my throat. "Fuck slow. Don't make me beg you."

He just laughs, continuing his teasing. My stomach. Back up to my breasts. Down to my navel. I love it. I hate it. I want to throttle him and push his head between my thighs at the same time.

"I might like to hear you beg," he says.

Finally, *finally*, he takes a break only to slick the vibe with lube, and when he settles it between my legs, I let out a sigh of relief. Followed immediately by a gasp.

He kicks the speed up a notch.

A stream of obscenities falls from my mouth as he alternates speed, pressure, location. All of it incredible.

"Don't stop," I say when he finds exactly the right spot. "*God*— please—"

"No way in hell," he's quick to reassure me, his own breaths coming faster. Shallower.

I feel it, the heat building at the base of my spine. It's going to happen this time, with him—I'm certain of it. I bury a fist in the sheets. He seems to read my mind and ups the speed once more, until nothing exists except my body and this feeling and the way his brow furrows with determination as he adjusts his weight so he can lean into me harder. Faster. *Yes.*

Something rips open inside me, a moan tearing from my chest. It's an exquisite release, one that makes me shake and whimper and clutch his hair. He loosens his grip on the vibrator, riding out the aftershocks with me.

I'm utterly spent. Speechless. And maybe he's not sure what to say, either, because his mouth tips upward into this lazy smile and he reaches for my face again, just like he did before. This time, there's almost a reverence in the way he cradles my jaw, something I'm certain I must be imagining. It's natural to feel closer after orgasm. He may have just made a woman come for the first time—with a little help from the Memphis Erotic Boutique.

"Chandler," he says quietly. Only, I never get to hear what's on the other side of my name. He blinks a few times and I'm close enough to see the pattern of freckles on his eyelids. After weeks of watching Oliver Huxley, I find that Finnegan Walsh still has some expressions I can't read.

He crooks a finger under my chin, bringing me closer. When our mouths meet, I'm surprised by the sudden softness in the way he kisses me. The gentleness in the way he brushes his lips against mine, so slowly before he draws away.

And then, from somewhere beneath our mountain of clothes, a phone rings.

Finn's.

He doesn't make a move to answer it. "They'll leave a message," he says. Still, it's jolted us apart, my lips still tingling with the memory of his.

The phone stops—only for mine to start buzzing immediately afterward.

"I should—" I say, and he nods his agreement. I stumble out of bed, riffling through our shirts and belts and underwear. Did I really have to wedge it into my pocket that tightly, and it's a crime that women's jeans are made with pockets that can feasibly fit only one-third of a cell phone and—

"It's our editor," I say. Finn scurries to the edge of the bed, racing to tug on his boxers while I put the phone on speaker, pulling my shirt on backward. I cannot have a business call in the nude, and if they called both of us, then it must be important.

"Hi, Nina," I say when I answer, and Finn calls out a hello in the background.

"Oh good—you're together!"

I press my lips together. Hard. "Mm-hmm."

Finn has readjusted on the bed, sitting up with one leg half inside a pair of jeans, the other tucked beneath him.

"Sorry to call so late," she says breezily. "But I was just too excited. I finished your outline this evening and absolutely loved it. I think you two are on exactly the right track."

The tension eases in my shoulders as Finn flashes a thumbs-up.

"We're thrilled to hear that," I say.

"Chandler's really been working overtime. Long hours." He gives me a lift of his eyebrows. "Late nights."

I hold a fist to my mouth as I nudge him.

"Consider this your official green light," Nina says. "I can't wait to read the draft."

"Thank you so much," I say, and Finn echoes me. "We'll dive right in."

When I end the call, the room goes silent. It occurs to me that it isn't too late. That we could keep going.

"We should get some sleep," I say instead of beckoning him closer. "So we can start drafting first thing in the morning."

"Right. Of course." Finn rummages around for his shirt, his cheeks coloring when they land on the discarded vibrator. "Great work, by the way. I had a feeling we'd nailed it." Then he catches the double meaning. Grimaces. "Why are there so many writing-related innuendos," he mutters, and when I laugh at this, it sounds hollow.

He only dates within Hollywood, I remind myself, because it seems worth remembering. If I ever feel myself wavering on the wrong side of casual, I'll simply replay that conversation. I'm not in the industry. End of story.

Still, I'm not sure why, but as I walk him to the door, I feel oddly grateful for the interruption.

Or why, when we've already made substantial progress on both our outlines, I can't stop thinking about that tender press of his lips on mine.

FINN WALSH:
YOUR ULTIMATE NERD CRUSH

BuzzFeed

Somehow, we kept watching *The Nocturnals* not for the gratu-
itous shirtless shots of Ethan Underwood, who plays alpha
werewolf Caleb Rhodes, but for the sweet, determined, adorably geeky Oliver Huxley, aka Hux. And it turns out, he's not too
different from his real-life counterpart, Finn Walsh.

As the story goes, Finn got the part because he actually
spoke in Elvish during his audition—yes, the made-up language
from *Lord of the Rings*. If that weren't enough, we have it on
good authority that he read from his character's biology textbook between takes, and even consulted a real scientist to
make sure Hux would sound as authentic as possible. Swoon!

What do you think about Finn Walsh? Glasses or no glasses?
And with all that red hair, do you think he blushes *everywhere*?

chapter

FIFTEEN

DENVER, CO

Finn with you? Just got a call from con staff and he
was supposed to check in twenty minutes ago. Not
picking up his phone, either.

I frown down at the text from Joe Kowalczyk, Finn's manager.
I'm in the hotel lobby, waiting for Finn to come downstairs so we
can head to the convention center for Rocky Mountain Expo. He
hasn't answered the text I sent earlier this morning, either, the
one about how apparently at this hotel, continental breakfast
means plain yogurt and an unripe banana. I just assumed he ignored it because it wasn't exactly thrilling commentary.

Despite my debilitating millennial fear of phone calls, I call
him. No answer.

That's odd.

When we checked in last night, his room was right across the
hall from mine. He seemed tired, which was fair, given we'd opted

to go up five flights of stairs to our floor. A reasonable trade-off for waiting behind a family getting onto the elevator with their eight suitcases. He said he was turning in early, and I guess it wouldn't be strange if he slept in, even unintentionally. Although my anxiety helpfully informs me there are a number of accidents that could befall him alone in a hotel room, several of which are now parading through my mind.

The elevator isn't fast enough, so I take the stairs again.

Out of breath, I knock on the door gently at first. Probably too gently. "Finn?" I say, and then wait. Nothing. Surely, he's just in the bathroom. Or still sleeping. Definitely not lying on the floor unconscious. No need to panic. Except the not-panic pitches my voice even higher as I start banging on the door. "Finn? Are you in there?"

I must be knocking so loudly that I don't hear anyone come to the door, and when it gives beneath me, I stumble forward. It takes a few moments for me to regain my balance as I bring my eyes up to his.

And there he is, face half-hidden by the comforter he's draped around himself like some kind of sad wizard.

"Just need a few more minutes," he rasps out before turning around and plodding back to the bed. The room is a mess, his suitcases spilling over in the middle of it.

"Oh—you're sick," I say quietly.

"I'm fine. Like I said, I just need a few more minutes." At that, he lets out a full-body shiver. "Is it cold in here, or is it just me?"

A laugh gets stuck in my throat because he is very much *not* fine. "Yeah, no. We're going to cancel. You should get some rest."

He glances back at me, hair askew, face ashen. He really does look miserable. Stars: they're just like us! "But all those people . . . they're counting on me. I made a commitment."

"They'll understand," I say. "These things happen. Don't tell me you've never taken a sick day before."

The way he looks at me, I wonder if maybe he really hasn't. He and Noemie have that in common.

"Get back in bed." I gesture to the tangle of sheets. "I'll let the con know."

I swipe the key card on the nightstand before stepping into the hall to message Joe and call our Rocky Mountain contact, telling them that Finn sends his apologies but he's too sick to attend today. Once I'm done, I let myself back into Finn's room.

"Hey," I say, approaching the bed. "It's all taken care of. Is there anything I can get you? What are your symptoms?"

"Mmmf," he says, clutching the comforter tighter around himself. "Everything. Hurts."

"Might be the flu. I'll go downstairs and grab some things, okay?"

Finn opens his mouth as though to object, but must realize it'll take too much energy and decides not to. "If you must."

A half hour and $50 later, I unpack my haul on the desk in Finn's room.

"Did you rob the hotel?" he asks.

I open up a box of meds, unscrew the cap from a bottle of water. Tip in a neon packet of Emergen-C. "The sooner you're better, the sooner we can get back to work. That thing you're so upset to miss."

"Right." He takes the medicine from me and swallows it down with another little twitch. "You should probably go," he says. "Sightsee. I don't want to get you sick."

I wave this off. "I have a strong immune system. Besides, we've been in such close proximity that if it's going to happen, you've probably already infected me." I'm not sure if this is scientifically true, but it sounds like it is, and it's enough to make Finn stop protesting.

Because the thing is, the thought of leaving him alone in here while I explored Denver never once occurred to me.

"If you're sure . . . then I guess I wouldn't hate the company. Thank you." It's almost cute, the way he resigns himself to this—a forced kind of resignation, as though he was hoping I wouldn't leave. "We could at least work on the book, or—"

I let out a laugh-groan. Two days ago I started drafting, playing back our recorded conversations to find the rhythm of his voice. I'm not sure I'm there yet, so spending more time with him can only be a good thing. For the book. "Finn. No. You're taking a sick day, and that's final. Can't you just watch some mindless TV like the rest of us?"

"You pick," he says as I grab the remote and flick it on. "I'm too disillusioned to mindlessly enjoy TV these days."

"Well . . . I've been watching this show about werewolves."

A groan. "What episode?"

"Just got to the season one finale."

He's quiet for a moment. And then: "That's a really good episode."

"We're watching it. But I fully expect behind-the-scenes commentary."

I eye the empty space on the bed next to him, and then the armchair across the room. I could drag it over, or—

Finn's at least lucid enough to surmise what I'm currently debating. "You can sit here," he says, patting the bed. "If you don't mind my germs."

Gingerly, I arrange myself next to him, on top of the covers, in my high-waisted jeans and socks dotted with tiny lemons. Then I get the show set up and settle in for the ridiculousness of watching *The Nocturnals* with one of its stars. There's something oddly domestic about it, to the point where I can almost forget the person onscreen is the one in bed hacking into a tissue.

When the season one finale ends in a battle that pits werewolves against the humans trying to wipe them out and the season two premiere autoplays, he doesn't say anything. We watch Caleb, fresh off having confessed his love for Alice in the season one finale, find himself tempted by new girl Sofia. And Hux, settling into a friendship with Meg, consults cool-guy Wesley on how to get out of the friend zone, a term he's just learned the meaning of.

"In retrospect, it was a little problematic," Finn says as Wesley tells a horrified Hux that he needs to take action, let the girl know his feelings, and not to take no for an answer. We both wince at that last piece of advice. "Well, maybe more than a little. It was the late 2000s, after all. And thank god, I don't listen to him."

Hux continues to fumble around Meg, inviting her on a study date that proceeds to go hilariously wrong: toppled book stacks, spilled coffee, Meg's long hair getting stuck in the back of a chair. Until it's interrupted by a girl in a vampire coven Meg has a longstanding rivalry with. Meg doesn't know at this point that Hux knows she's a werewolf, and when she saves Hux from vampires at the end of the episode, the two share a lingering look—*now* she knows, and she manages to communicate both relief and trepidation in the episode's final shot.

"This scene—we had to shoot it close to thirty times because Hallie and I wouldn't stop laughing," he says. "Even though it's supposed to be a serious moment. I honestly thought Zach was going to fire us right there on the spot."

And I have to admit, based on how eager I am to see what happens next, that I've gotten just a little invested in these characters.

HUX AND MEG CONTINUE TO DANCE AROUND THEIR FEELINGS UNTIL two more episodes have passed, and Finn's starting to fall asleep. I wince when there's a knock at the door, even though I've been expecting it. As quietly as I can, I fetch the delivery and bring it back to the desk.

"What's that?" a groggy Finn asks from the bed.

"Sorry—you can go back to sleep," I say. "Matzo ball soup. My parents used to make it whenever I was sick. My mom swears by it."

"You ordered matzo ball soup?"

"It's vegetarian," I assure him. "No chicken broth."

I'm not expecting his reaction, the slow smile that starts at one corner of his mouth as he attempts to bite it back. "You're too nice to me," he says, quirking an eyebrow. "Why are you being so nice to me? You could have just let me wither away."

"There will be no withering." I remove the lids from twin cartons of soup.

"I think that's enough of me," he says as I bring them over. He gestures to the TV currently frozen on his face. "I can only handle so much of it."

I switch it off and cozy up in the bed again, spooning soup into my mouth. Amazing that it tastes just as comforting in Colorado as it does in Washington State.

For a few minutes, we sit in the relative quiet with our matzo balls. It's midafternoon, the chilly October sun splashing our shadows across the bed. This is good, spending time with him like this. Surely, seeing him pale and congested will obliterate whatever I thought I felt in Memphis, before the phone call from our editor interrupted that strange kiss.

"What did teen Chandler watch?" Finn asks, nudging his head toward the TV.

"Hmm. Teen Chandler's tastes were varied and slightly anachronistic. I went through an Agatha Christie phase that started with the books, of course, so then I had to watch all the adaptations, too. But nothing could beat the books for me."

"I haven't read any," he admits. "Tell me about your favorites?"

So I do. I tell him about Miss Marple and about Hercule Poirot, who I had a bit of a crush on when I read about him as a kid. I tell him about *And Then There Were None*, my favorite Agatha Christie, making sure not to spoil any of the plot points. Slowly, slowly, we step closer to that document on my computer.

"I tried to imitate her, growing up," I say, because this truth doesn't feel like it's been yanked from too deep inside my heart. "Write like her, I mean."

"Yeah? Chandler Cohen, killing off fictional people?" He's smiling, head propped up with one elbow as he turns to face me. His hair is sticking up in the back from where it was pressed against the pillow. "You know what, I can see it. That's how you get out all your aggression. Someone wrongs you in real life? You just murder them on the page."

"You're not *completely* wrong," I say. It's possible a drowning victim in one of my earliest preteen attempts, *Watery Graves*, was based on a girl who'd copied off one of my tests in fifth grade math. "In the wrong hands, my preteen diaries would probably be very concerning. But I'm not a huge fan of all the blood and gore. Do you know what a cozy mystery is?"

"A mystery you read by the fireplace with a mug of hot cocoa?"

"Ideally. But no, it's a book where the mystery is solved by someone who isn't a professional detective. Everything's wrapped up by the end and none of the main characters die. It was great for my anxiety. There's no violence on the page—or sex, actually, which is kind of a bummer—and they usually take place in a small town or quaint seaside village. And they have these fantastic titles. Like *The Quiche of Death*, where a baking contest judge gets poisoned, or *Live and Let Chai*, about a tea shop owner framed for the murder of a customer." I think about this for a moment. "They're not *all* food puns, but a lot of them are."

He's just watching me, an unreadable expression on his face. "What is it?"

"I haven't seen you light up like this in a while," he says. "You really love them."

Suddenly self-conscious, I turn my head away from him slightly. "They're comforting, and they're fun, and they're absurdly addictive. You always know the villain's going to get caught in the end. But you know. I mostly just read them now."

"Why'd you stop writing?" he asks. "Fiction, I mean."

A deep breath—because I had a feeling this was coming. "I haven't stopped, exactly. I'm just on a very long break." I knot my fingers together, play with the bedspread, fluff my pillow. All while he waits for me to continue. "It's the same old story, the same reason most people stop doing something they love—it wasn't practical. Trying to get published would have meant leaving so much up to chance. It made better sense as a hobby, but once I decided to focus on journalism . . . that hobby sort of faded away." I shake my head, because I let it go a long time ago. "But that was okay. Because I could do what I loved and still get a steady paycheck."

Except the paychecks are rarely steady, and I've been stuck telling other people's stories instead of my own for so long.

"Besides," I continue. "I feel like I know too much about publishing at this point, and it's all about living at least a year in the future. You're always looking at the endgame and not the process. It can be easy to forget to enjoy writing."

As I say it, I realize it's true. That it used to be a passion, but now it's simply a job.

His face falls. "You're not enjoying this?"

"No, no, no," I rush to say. "This is actually the first time I've enjoyed it in a couple years." When his features soften, that concerning feeling from our night with the vibrator comes back, full force. The way he tucked a finger beneath my chin and kissed me so gently—in that moment, it was almost too easy to forget that what we're doing isn't real.

"I can honestly say," he starts, placing his bowl of soup on the nightstand and fidgeting with the sheets, "that this is the most fun I've had on tour in a while."

"I'm guessing that might have something to do with what's been happening in our hotel rooms?"

Finn laughs, this open, brassy sound that I've come to learn is his true laugh. Not the one he reserves for panels, the one with slightly sharper edges. This one is smoother. Softer. "Sure, I won't discount that. But I might have been talking about myself when I was saying that I haven't gotten out much lately. It's usually me and the hotel and maybe some room service, if I'm feeling adventurous."

His eyes have started drooping, his words coming out more slurred. The medication is doing its job. "That's the way it is," he says with an uncoordinated flick of his hand. "And I know this book might come out and nothing will change, but . . ."

"It will," I say firmly, believing not just in the quality of my writing but in the story he has to tell. Because I really, truly do.

"Sometimes I wonder. After all these years, if I'm clinging to relevance just like everyone else. I'm just doing it a slightly different way." Now he's sinking back into the pillow, no longer able to hold his head up. "Is anyone even gonna care about that nonprofit? Because . . . I'm kind of a nobody."

"That's just patently untrue. We spent three hours watching nobody defend Oakhurst University. Which has a shockingly high number of student deaths for such a small school." My attempt at levity earns me a small quirk of his mouth. "Look, I've already learned more about OCD than I ever thought I would. You have something important to say, and for a lot of people, this is going to be the first time they read about it. For others, maybe it'll be the first time someone's given words to something they're going through. And maybe that'll be the push they need to get help—the knowledge that they're not alone."

He nods slowly, taking all of this in. "Thank you. For all of this," he says, reaching to give my arm a haphazard pat, not quite making it. "I mean it. I'd probably be a husk of a human being by now if it weren't for you."

The way he says it makes me wonder whether anyone else has taken care of him like this before.

Whether he's let them.

"Of course," I say, my throat suddenly dry.

His head lolls to one side of the pillow, and it's clear those meds are stronger than either of us thought. "Chandler, Chandler, Chandler. I must be hell to work with. I can hardly believe you're putting up with me."

"It's the paycheck, mostly."

His eyes open wider and he looks at me hard, the weight of his gaze pinning me in place. "I reeeeeally shouldn't tell you this, but . . . I know someone who has a crush on you."

He says this in a singsong, like we're at fourth grade recess and he's relaying a message from a friend.

"Ha, ha," I say. "Well, we don't have many mutual friends, so—"

"It's me," he clarifies, holding up his thumb and forefinger. "Just an itty bitty crush when we first met."

"I did, too. That's kind of why I went back to your hotel room."

His grin deepens, and he wags that finger back and forth. "After that," he says. "Not just that first time. A little bit in Portland, too, and maybe also Arizona." A wrinkle of his nose. "I know we're supposed to be professionals, but maybe . . . maybe also right now, too."

I crane my neck to look over at the desk, hoping he won't notice the way my cheeks are heating up. "How much of that medicine did you take?"

"I'm serious, Chandler Cohen." He rolls closer to me in bed, his long lashes and freckles and mess of hair. Even with his eyes beginning to droop, he's still stunning.

"But—but you *can't*," I say, as though simply denying it will make it untrue. *You can't* and we'll rewind to thirty seconds ago, back when our relationship still made sense. Because that wasn't how this was supposed to work.

It takes every ounce of strength in me to scoot to the edge of the bed, so violently that I nearly fall off. It's not real. It's purely chemical, his brain convincing him that he feels something for the person he's sleeping with. There should have been a warning on those meds: DO NOT MIX WITH OXYTOCIN.

Despite the fact that we've seen each other naked a handful of times now, his words linger, wrapping around my heart and setting down roots there, where they could grow into something even more invasive. There's a terrifying sweetness to them, an innocence that isn't always there when our hotel room doors are locked.

Maybe also right now, too.

"Can't, schmant." He seems to get another burst of energy, sitting up in bed. "You're just . . . so smart. So nice. And you wear socks when you shouldn't and take me to sex shops and read books about people killing each other with poisoned pastries." He looks up at me with this fierce vulnerability, one that makes my heart swell in my chest. "And you're beautiful and adorable and cute, and I guess some of those mean the same thing, but I stand by it. I have this monster crush on you, and there it is." He flings his arms out, punctuating the whole thing with a wide, loopy grin.

Then he yawns, drops back to the pillow, and immediately falls asleep.

Well . . . fuck.

chapter

SIXTEEN

MIAMI, FL

Maddy DeMarco's face grins back at me from a Staff Picks table at the airport bookstore. Taunting me. *New York Times Bestseller!* declares the new gold sticker on the cover.

"Chandler?" Finn calls.

With a sigh, I leave Maddy behind and hurry to catch our flight.

The Miami con is massive, but I have to admit, they're starting to blur together a bit. More autographs, another panel, another line of fans waiting to meet their favorite fictional biology major unequivocally devoted to his werewolf girlfriend.

Any moment I'm not scribbling away at our first draft, I'm frantically refreshing the Alaska Airlines flight tracker. Because last night, I beamed out an SOS to Noemie before I even made it back to my room, Finn's confession doing acrobatics in my chest.

"I know it's a six-hour flight and you have a million things to do and—"

"Chandler," she said calmly, a welcome contrast to the chaos in my brain. "It doesn't matter. I'm coming. First thing tomorrow morning." This was PR problem-solving Noemie, and maybe that's the version of her I need.

All morning, I've tried to explain it away. It was the medication messing with him, or maybe he meant it in a different way—like, *You're crushing it!* Or he was just being polite. Everyone knows you tell someone you have a crush on them when they take care of you while you're sick. That's just etiquette.

One small blessing is that Finn doesn't seem to remember much of what we talked about after my cozy mystery diatribe, or if he does, he's doing an incredible job hiding it. I, on the other hand, am an absolute mess, made all the messier by the fact that our next stop is Reno, where I'll be meeting his mother and his childhood best friend.

Nothing about last night made sense. If anything, I should find him *less* attractive today, but that's unfortunately not true. I shouldn't have blushed this morning when he knocked on my hotel room door with a cup of coffee as a thank-you for taking care of him.

Because either of us having feelings for each other would be nothing short of disastrous.

Crushes fade, I remind myself as Finn poses for photos, grinning and generally being charming as hell. Crushes fade, and we already cemented this as a casual relationship. If it became anything more and ended badly, it might harm our working relationship, too, and I'd never forgive myself for jeopardizing a job like that.

We'll go our separate ways when the book is done, anyway. No attachments. No feelings.

"Could you make it out to Noemie? That's N-o-e—"

"Nome?" The sound that comes out of my mouth can only be

compared to a pterodactyl screech. I leap out of my chair, its legs squealing against the linoleum floor. There she is, the last person in the signing line, grinning back at me. "You made it!"

I nearly knock over a stack of Finnegan Walsh headshots in my attempt to hug her. No shock, she looks extremely put together even after a six-hour flight, dark hair in a low ponytail and not a single crease in her linen pants. "Thank you, thank you, thank you. I love you." When I release her, she's gazing at Finn with what might as well be heart-eyes.

"This is the famous Noemie," Finn says, and my cousin looks like she might faint.

"You told him about me?" she stage-whispers.

"Only the embarrassing things." And I mentioned she was flying in, of course, white-lying that she had some spontaneous time off and wanted some sun.

Finn extends a hand. "Pleasure to meet you. I've heard a lot about you."

"Icantbelieveyourereal," she says in one breath. "I was trying to play it cool when I was in line just now, but . . . oh my god. You're *him*. I mean, he's you. And you're about a hundred times cuter in person. Not that you aren't cute on TV. I mean—" She inhales, trying to collect herself, a blush tingeing her cheeks. "Wow. This is why I shouldn't be let out of the house."

Finn laughs. "Thank you. I'm actually quite glad you left the house."

"I've been trying to get Chandler to watch *The Nocturnals* for *years*," Noemie continues, straightening her posture to her full height. "When she told me she was meeting you, I nearly died. I've always felt that Hollywood never properly recognized you. You should have been getting better roles. More challenging, more interesting roles."

Finn throws a pointed look my way. "It's so nice to finally be around someone who appreciates my talent." It's a testament to said talent that he's able to say this with a straight face.

"Oh please," I say with a roll of my eyes, waving an arm around the room. "What do you think all of this is?"

Finn bites back a grin before he returns his attention to my slowly melting cousin. "Chandler told me you're really into subscription boxes," he says, and Noemie bobs her head in a nod. He takes out his phone, swipes through some photos. "I did one of those for cocktails a few years ago. That's the only reason I have a somewhat decent cart."

"I've gotten that one! It's great."

The two of them start comparing their monthly boxes, chattering away. This whole thing is surreal, my best friend and my . . . whatever Finn is. *Collaborator* doesn't sound quite right, and yet neither does anything else. Everything Noemie doesn't know about the two of us.

Because this SOS also means I need to tell Noemie what's really happening on this trip.

"They're doing a private screening of the finale tomorrow, two parts back-to-back, with commentary from me and Cooper," Finn is saying. "If you're still in town, I have VIP tickets . . ."

Noemie gapes at him. "Are you serious? That would be amazing. More than amazing. Thank you!"

This shouldn't surprise me—Finn is a kind person. Generous. And yet this offer sparks a strange tug in my chest.

One that makes me even more grateful she's here.

━━━ ━━━ ━━━

NOEMIE AND I SPEND THE EVENING AT THE BEACH, SQUINTING AT THE sun and drinking watery cocktails. The space away from Finn helps me breathe a little easier, but it hasn't brought me any more clarity.

"I can't believe you were able to get the time off," I say as I put on the hat I bought for five dollars on the boardwalk. Back in Seattle, I'd be wearing at least five layers. "Unless . . ." I break off with a gasp. "Does this mean you finally quit?"

She pretends to be very interested in adjusting her sunbed. "Not exactly," she says. "I, um, took on two new clients?"

"Noemie."

Her sad smile reminds me of how she looked when she told me she wasn't going to study journalism anymore. That public relations was a better fit for her, and the journalism job market terrified her. "I know. I'm going to do it. After this project. I swear." She takes a sip of her margarita. "So. Spill it. I know you didn't ask me to fly out here just because you miss me."

I wait a moment, worrying the frayed edge of my towel before dropping it in the sand beneath us. The beach has emptied out a bit, families collecting their sunburned children and twentysomethings trading the ocean for Miami nightlife. "It's complicated." All day, this secret has felt too heavy, and suddenly I feel like I might collapse with the weight of it. A few deep, cleansing breaths, the kind we learned how to do when Noemie dragged me to aerial yoga last year. "Do you remember the guy I hooked up with in September? Right before I met Finn and took this job?"

"The worst sex of your life."

"Right. And remember how I had no idea who Finn was at first . . ." I trail off, hoping she'll connect the dots so I don't have to say it out loud.

Her eyes grow wide as she twists in her chair. "No. No. That's not—tell me they weren't the same person, Chandler."

I drape my towel over my head. "He gave me a fake name. Neither of us knew who the other was until that lunch in Seattle."

"You slept with Oliver Huxley," she says slowly. "Holy. Shit."

"There was absolutely nothing holy about it," I say, my voice half muffled by the towel.

She reaches forward, snatching the towel away and shaking her head in disbelief. "I'm sorry, my brain is rewriting everything it's ever assumed about Finn Walsh, cinnamon roll nerd of my dreams. This is absolutely devastating."

"It's been killing me, not telling anyone."

"And you still wanted to work on this book? It's been okay? Because as much as I've missed you, I've been really, really happy that you're doing this."

I chew on my straw, wondering what that means specifically. "We agreed we weren't going to talk about it, that it was firmly in the past. But then I wound up telling him what that night was like for me, and it evolved into this joke that maybe wasn't a joke at all, about me helping him improve his technique in bed. And, well . . ."

"*You're giving Finnegan Walsh sex tips?*" Noemie nearly falls off her sunbed. "I've never been happier or more shocked to be related to you."

"And I've never been thirstier in my entire life. It's like the more we're together, the more I want to be with him. It's a terrible, horny paradox. Is this the stupidest thing I've ever done?"

"Aside from the questionable ethics of the two of you working together . . . I don't know. I'd never judge you, except when you were going through your JNCO jeans phase."

"And I deserved that."

Her voice turns gentle, none of that frantic energy from a few minutes ago. "You're being safe, right?" she asks, and I nod. "I'm sorry, I'm never recovering from this."

"You're going to have to, because I need advice." I give the dregs of my piña colada a poke with my straw, summoning all my courage again. I didn't realize how badly I needed this. "A couple nights ago, he told me he had a crush on me. While high on cold meds. And he doesn't seem to remember saying it, so I don't know if that means I should just forget about it, too? Because I seem physiologically incapable of doing that."

Noemie's quiet for a few moments. "Do *you* have feelings for him?" There's no judgment there, only a gentle curiosity.

I think back to that first night in Seattle. How I hadn't had that kind of immediate spark with someone . . . well, ever.

"It almost doesn't matter," I say quietly, "because it's not like this can go anywhere in the long term. He doesn't date outside the industry, and the book has to be our first priority."

Plus, the sting from Wyatt's rejection is still a little too fresh. Even if it's a relief that I haven't thought about him in a while—at least, not in the lying-awake-at-night kind of way—I don't know if my heart is ready to go through that again.

"I'm going to say something, and I don't want you to get mad about it." She examines a sunburn blooming on her forearm. "I'm sure I could say the same thing about myself, but I think sometimes you avoid taking risks."

I expected her to give me some kind of encouragement, like *But you're* kind of *in the industry,* or press me for not actually answering her question, so it takes me a few moments to come up with a response.

"That's valid. It's part of the reason I took this project. My parents were worried about this trip. You were worried about this trip.

And yeah, maybe I've lived in the same place my whole life, with the same people. Maybe I tried to have a relationship with one of my best friends and it massively backfired. But this is the longest I've been away from home, pretty much on my own, and I'm *happy*, Nome. No anxiety attacks, no existential loneliness. I even do my full skincare routine on most days." With a flutter of my lashes, I place my hands beneath my chin, showing off my almost-blemish-free face. "I'm functioning. *Thriving*, one could say."

"All of that's great," she says. "But that's not entirely what I meant. Ever since your layoff, things have been hard. I get it. You're spending your career writing under other people's names instead of your own. I'm sure some people love ghostwriting, but I *know* you're not happy. When was the last time you opened up your book?"

I know she doesn't mean it to, but the question strikes a nerve. One that's been frayed and worn thin over the years. "I open up the document plenty."

She lifts her eyebrows. "Then when was the last time you worked on it?"

I go quiet, eyes trained on the dusky blue strip of horizon.

"When we were little, I just remember that being the happiest you ever were," she continues, and I get a flash of memory. Noemie was always my first reader, and I loved printing out a chapter, running across the street to show her. She'd never edit me, never critique—she'd just tell me she wanted *more*. "I love seeing you out here, and I know you're going to write a fantastic book. I just wonder if sometimes you hold yourself back from things you know you want. That's all."

I'm not sure why everyone in my life is intent on bringing up my past. I've moved on from it—Noemie should be able to do the same. Maybe ghostwriting isn't the dream job, but it's much less scary than trying to pivot to something I have no clue whether I can be successful at.

Still, I allow myself to imagine what it might look like, that career for a different version of myself. Just for a moment. Hours spent brainstorming plot points and building character arcs. Getting lost in my own mystery. A cover. A book signing.

Holding those pages in my hands and finally feeling *proud* of something I've created.

How hard it would be to just take that risk, close my eyes, and leap.

"I get it," I say, even if I'm saying it through slightly gritted teeth. "I'm glad you're here. Love you."

She throws her arm around my shoulders. "Love you even more now that I know your deep, dark secret."

As we pack our bags and head back to the hotel, I can't stop thinking about how Noemie's right: my collaboration with Finn has an expiration date, and the painful truth is that I have absolutely no idea what to do when I get there. This project was supposed to help me figure it out.

If that's true, then I'm not sure why I feel further away from an answer than ever before.

5 COZY MYSTERIES TO READ THIS SEASON

by Chandler Cohen

I love a cozy mystery. A regular person gets to solve a crime, be a badass, and maybe fall in love by the end. The best part is that you can feel like you're unraveling the mystery right alongside the main character, which leads to a supremely satisfying ending for both of you. Whether you're new to the genre or a seasoned reader, here are five of my faves—perfect to curl up with this winter!

KNIT ONE, KILL TWO BY C.B. MARQUEZ
The first in the Briar Beach Knitting Club mystery series finds one of the shop's most valued customers strangled by a skein of yarn.

SCHMEARED TO DEATH BY ROSE RUBIN
In a small New England town, a cook is poisoned when someone tampers with his world-famous cream cheese. Bagel puns abound.

OVERDUE AND UNDERGROUND BY TOYA LEGRAND
A librarian finds a dead body in her library basement, a nearby open book containing clues to the murder, which she solves with the help of a charming patron.

BERRIED ALIVE BY NATALIE CHANG

A pastry chef investigates a murder at her small town's annual strawberry festival. Bonus jam recipes included.

MURDER, SHE WROTE STARRING THE ONE AND ONLY ANGELA LANSBURY

I'm cheating a little here because it's a TV show, but you know what, there was a spin-off book series, and the protagonist is a mystery writer, so I say it counts. Jessica Fletcher is an icon and I will hear no arguments against her.

chapter
SEVENTEEN

RENO, NV

I thought it would be warmer."

"Common misconception about Reno," Finn says as we get out of the car in front of his mom's house. I pull my jacket tighter. "It's not Vegas. We're in the desert right up against the Sierra Nevadas. Summers are scorching and winters are cold and snowy." He peeks down at my feet. "Cactus socks today?"

"I wanted to be on theme."

Noemie stayed for a couple more days, working remote, through the VIP screening and another panel. Yesterday afternoon, I said goodbye to her before we flew to Nevada, and Finn humored her by taking no fewer than a thousand selfies and then made her the happiest I've ever seen by giving her a ticket to December's reunion taping.

"Noemie's really great," he said this morning on the plane. "I can see why you two are close."

"She was definitely more excited to see you than me. But I forgive you."

A pause, and then he asked: "You told her, didn't you?" The look I gave him must have communicated my shock. "I'm not mad," he clarified, holding up a hand. "I kind of figured you would."

"She won't say a word. I swear to god."

"I trust you," he said, and for some reason, those three words sent an odd shiver up my spine. We haven't hooked up since Memphis, and I'm no longer sure whether I'm missing it or grateful for the distance. Probably both.

After the conversation with Noemie, I've decided to try my best to forget Finn's drugged confession. It's simply safer for all of us.

I see the Chihuahuas first, a whole pack of them on the front porch, as a middle-aged woman with chin-length dark hair approaches the car.

"Finnegan!" she calls, the dogs trotting along behind her, tails going wild, a tornado of black and white and tan.

Finn scoops up one of the dogs as he gives his mom a hug and a kiss on the cheek. "Mom, hi. How many did you adopt since I last saw you?"

She makes an exaggerated pout. "Only one," she says before stage-whispering to me, "*Two*."

A white one is at my heels, and I bend down to give him some love. "This is, um, a lot of dogs," I say stupidly.

"They're all rescues," Finn's mom says. "I started with one, and then I thought it might be nice if she had someone to play with and, well, it kind of spiraled from there. Now I can't imagine life without them." She picks up two of them. "Isn't that right? You manipulated me with your tiny noses and perfect little paws." Then she extends a hand to me. "Sondra. Pleasure to meet you."

"Chandler. Thanks so much for having us."

Finn is scratching his dog under the chin, dropping kisses onto its head. "That's it. I'm really not going back to LA this time."

"Tell me that again when they wake you up at six in the morning for breakfast." Sondra fusses with his hair for a moment. "Did you pay someone to make it look like this?"

"Yes. Probably too much," he says, and then to me: "She gave me bowl cuts at home for a solid two years, so I can't fully trust her opinion."

"And every little old lady at synagogue complimented you," she says, patting his cheek.

"Please tell me you have pictures," I say, and Sondra assures me she does.

After his mom introduces the dogs, Freddie and Waffles and Moose and Galileo and Duchess, we make our way into the house. It's a homey one-story ranch style with bright patterned curtains and plush, cozy furniture. His mom flits about the kitchen, getting out glasses of water and arranging a plate of cookies on the table. They're not normal cookies, though—they're an absolute monstrosity of dough, chocolate chunks, M&M's, nuts, and marshmallows. I try to mentally capture every detail, wanting to do this place justice in our chapters about Finn's childhood.

His eyes light up. "You remembered."

"Of course. Every time," she says, looking pleased. I sense there's some kind of inside joke here.

"We made these all the time when I was a kid," Finn explains. "Kitchen sink cookies. As in, everything but the. To this day, they're my favorite cookie. Favorite dessert, period." He picks up a napkin, uses it to reach for the cookie. His mom doesn't even blink at this.

To his credit, the cookies are excellent. "Is that a potato chip?" I ask between bites.

"For extra crunch," Sondra says. "What are you two planning to do the rest of the day?"

"I was hoping to show Chandler the lay of the land. My old stomping grounds, and all that. For the book," Finn clarifies. "And we can't miss your Shabbat service Saturday morning."

"Perfect. I'll try to be on my best behavior. How's the book coming along?"

Finn and I trade a glance. "Chandler's making me seem much more fascinating than I actually am."

"You're plenty fascinating," I insist, unsure why his gaze on me in this moment, in this house, is bringing heat to my cheeks. I turn to Sondra, which seems much safer, and while I have a hundred questions for her about the man I've spent the last month on the road with, I suddenly have no idea where to start. "Were you surprised when he decided he wanted to be an actor?"

After taking another cookie, Sondra leans back against the kitchen counter. "A little, mostly because I was worried about how unstable it might be. But he always had a flair for the dramatic. Even before he took theater in school, sometimes he'd act out scenes in his favorite books over dinner."

Finn runs a hand down his face, groaning. "I'd completely forgotten about that."

"Then you also must have forgotten that I filmed some of them."

Even more groaning.

"That's adorable," I say. "Did you use the salt and pepper shakers as props? Or maybe you did voices for your silverware?"

"Now you're just being cruel. And yes. Yes, I did." Then he turns back to his mom, who's smiling at this exchange in a way that makes me want to assure her nothing is happening between her son and me. Nothing that isn't casual, at least. "You'll be the first to read it, I promise. After our editor."

Sondra places an arm on his shoulder. "You know you can write anything you want about me. I just . . . well, I worry. Once it's out there, it's out there. You want to make sure you're comfortable with what you're telling people—you don't get to take it back."

Finn swallows a bite of cookie. "I know," he says quietly, eyes flashing to mine for one brief moment. "That's what I'm figuring out."

He gives me a tour of the house, and I linger on the family photographs. His dad is notoriously absent; instead there are photos of Finn as a toddler, elementary schooler, teenager. There is the promised bowl cut, which is somehow more adorable than it has any right to be. Those little old Jewish ladies were right. I watch him get braces and have them taken off, endure poor fashion choices, and pose with his costars. Then there are photos of his mom with her friends, with her dogs—all of which have their own bed with their name embroidered on it.

Then he pauses outside his room. "Before we go inside," he says, voice serious. "I need you to know that I was deeply obsessed with *Lord of the Rings* as a child."

"I already know that. In fact, it was one of the first things you told me."

"Yes, but *knowing it* and *seeing it* are two very different things." His face has turned grim. "You're at the foot of Mount Doom. It's not too late to turn back."

Gently, I push at his chest. "You're being melodramatic—I'm sure it's not that bad."

With a defeated shrug, he reaches for the doorknob. "Remember, you asked for this."

My mouth falls open.

"Please just tell me what's going through your head right now," Finn says from behind me. "I'm not sure I can handle the silence."

"Well, to start, I'm thinking we have to rewrite the whole book. Scrap everything we have."

He hangs his head, faux somber. "I was afraid of that."

It is an absolute *shrine* to Middle-earth. Movie posters cover the walls, along with handwritten scrolls of paper with Elvish translations. A shelf of action figures, a miniature Orc army. I stride through the room, walking toward his Tolkien-stuffed bookshelf. As much as I'm teasing him about this, I also truly love it. That passion, the one he has, the one I've been chasing. There's something so meaningful about being able to see someone in their element. I imagine a young Finn running lines, dreaming of living among Elves and then later of Hollywood.

Hiding from his father.

Plotting his escape.

Then I spot a pair of fuzzy brown slippers peeking out from the closet.

"Oh my god. Is that a Hobbit costume?"

"Aaaaaand we're leaving," he says, doing his best to shoulder me toward the hall.

"Does it still fit? Can you try it on? I promise I'll never ask for anything ever again—"

I'm still laughing when he shuts the door behind us.

THE OFFICIAL FINNEGAN WALSH TOUR OF RENO TAKES US PAST HIS elementary, middle, and high schools and through the casino-dotted downtown, with a stop at what he declares is the good Taco Bell.

"Used to hang out here on weekends all the time," he says when we park at a strip mall. He points at a Barnes & Noble. Next to it is a game shop with a GOING OUT OF BUSINESS SALE sign hung across the windows. "There, too. Typical suburban kid in the late nineties/early aughts."

"Not a terrible way to grow up." I take a bite of my bean burrito, then tear open a hot sauce packet and drizzle on some more.

"It wasn't," he agrees. "Everyone was nice enough, and I never really felt a pull toward Vegas. Plus, we're less than an hour from Lake Tahoe."

"You come out here often?"

"Not often enough," he says. "Every few months or so. And I always do the Reno con—it's the first one I ever went to as a fan." He gazes out at the parking lot. "There are good memories here, but some not-so-great ones, too. I can't erase my dad completely."

"I'm so sorry. You deserved so much better than that."

If we were different people, I'd reach over and place a hand on his. Reassure him more than I can do in my capacity as ghostwriter.

Because that's all I am, I unwrap another burrito.

By the time we make it back to Finn's mom's, it's nearly nine o'clock and my body's stuck in another time zone. Sondra's at the kitchen table, fine-tuning her address for Saturday's Shabbat service, Galileo in her lap and the others perched on blankets and dog beds in the adjacent living room. Tomorrow will be a writing day, and then Saturday will be packed: services, con, meeting up with Finn's friends.

My eyes are heavy, but I don't want to assume I'm sleeping here just because Finn is, so I left my suitcase in the hallway. "Sorry, could I get the address for an Uber?" I ask.

Finn pauses at the kitchen sink, where he's been inspecting a glass of water before filling it. "What do you need an Uber for?"

"Oh—a hotel?"

"Don't be silly," Sondra says. "You'll stay here with us. We have a guest room made up already."

"I don't want to intrude."

Sondra gives me her best mom-side-eye. "Honey. You're not intruding. Besides, isn't this better than a cold, soulless hotel?"

"Stay," Finn says, and then adds, "please," with a heart-melting smile all his directors must have loved.

It's strange, how sweet the word *stay* sounds in his voice. The way it makes those roots deepen in my chest.

Just as quickly as the thought occurred to me, I brush it off. Hux must have said it in one of his scenes, and that's why it's making me react this way—I'm certain of it.

I'M LESS CERTAIN SATURDAY MORNING, AFTER A FULL DAY OF WRITING during which we finish rough drafts of two chapters, when Finn dons a yarmulke at the synagogue entrance and it's unfairly attractive. I have to bite back a smile, half because I'm not used to seeing him in one and half because I don't think a kippah should inspire these kinds of feelings.

Sondra told me yesterday that the congregation skews older and the temple is very bare bones, without much funding, but it has a charm to it. As a kid, I went with my parents to temple only for the High Holidays, a tradition Noemie and I have tried to maintain as adults. But I haven't been to services in a few years, mostly because my deadlines always felt more important. Now I can't remember why I thought I couldn't put aside my work for just a couple hours every week.

There's nothing like feeling at home inside a synagogue, this immediate sense of belonging. As Rabbi Zlotnick, Sondra has a natural magnetism in the way she speaks. I've found that no matter how long I'm away from temple, the prayers come back to me with almost no effort, as if they were imprinted on me a long time ago.

What strikes me the most, though, is when I glance next to me and find Finn's lips moving along—because of course they are. He grew up with this the way I did.

We were raised on these same songs, spoke this same language. It's like discovering we have the same favorite book, and not only that, but that we love all the same parts—that we've highlighted and underlined them and folded over pages when we probably should have been using bookmarks.

When we retreat to the foyer for snacks, Finn introduces me around.

"Is that Finnegan?" asks an elderly woman in a mauve floral dress.

He shines a genuine smile on her. "Hi, Mrs. Haberman. Shabbat shalom."

"Shabbat shalom," she says, giving him a hug. "All of us were whispering before the service, wondering who your lovely companion is."

"This is my friend Chandler Cohen. Chandler, this is Ruth Haberman."

"Your friend," Mrs. Haberman says, a glint in her eyes as I shake her hand.

Some version of this repeats a few more times, with Mr. Barr, Mr. Lowenstein, and Mrs. Frankel, a woman who tells me she taped every episode of *The Nocturnals* on her old VHS player.

"Going to be worth a lot of money someday," she says, and he just shakes his head, giving me the impression they've had this joke for years.

"Everyone here really loves you," I say once we have a few moments to ourselves. We've filled small paper plates with carrots and hummus, challah and jam.

"Don't sound so surprised. I'm very lovable."

I roll my eyes. "You know what I mean. You have this whole community here."

He pierces a grape with a plastic fork. "I'm lucky," he says simply. "I grew up going here, and when my mother decided to go to rabbinical school, this was the only congregation she wanted to lead. Even though it's not as swanky as the new temple on the other side of town. So I really have known all these people forever."

"I had no idea," I say, taking a bite of challah. "There isn't much online about your religion."

"Ah. It's strange, having a name that isn't Jewish coded."

"Walsh is your dad's name?"

And he gives me this look, like he can't believe he hasn't explained this to me yet. "No—it's a stage name. Finn has always been real, but I legally changed my last name in my twenties. My dad's last name, the one I grew up with, was Callahan, and my first manager told me Finnegan Callahan was too much of a mouthful to be booking anything. Too many consonants." A grimace. "But I haven't been Finn Callahan in years. I have about zero attachment to it. I've been waiting, actually, to be Finn Walsh longer than I was Finn Callahan, and it's coming up. A few more years. One less connection to my dad."

"I'm glad."

"When I decided to change my name, I spent a lot of time thinking about whether I wanted one that was visibly Jewish or not. And every so often, I wonder if I made the right choice," he says. "I've been pretty safe from antisemitism, but now . . . I don't know."

Without my voice recorder, I try to commit his words to

memory. His Judaism is important to him: the community, the traditions, the history. The chapter that starts with an image of that menorah in the background of *Ms. Mistletoe* is going to be an absolute knockout—I'll settle for nothing less.

"Speaking as someone with a name that's instantly recognizable as Jewish, it's a mixed bag. I love that immediate connection I can have with someone because of it, but on the other hand . . ."

I think back to a listicle I wrote back at The Catch, "Eight Unexpectedly Jewish Movies to Watch This Hanukkah"—a fluff piece, really, something that should have been innocent—where the comments had to be turned off when they veered antisemitic, which usually doesn't take too long when you're visibly Jewish online. Horrifying images started showing up in my DMs and I had to lock my social media accounts for weeks. I tell him this, and he shakes his head, disgusted.

"Fucking horrible," he mutters. "I'm sorry you had to go through that."

I attempt to shrug it off, because I accepted it long ago as a side effect of moving through the world with my last name. But then I stop myself. "Yeah," I say. Firmly. Solidly. "It was fucked up."

An older man stops by our table, asks if he can take a photo for his granddaughter.

Before we get up, Finn places a hand on my wrist again, a whisper of contact before he drops his arm back to his side. "Chandler? In case I haven't said it lately, I'm really glad you're the one writing this book."

chapter

EIGHTEEN

RENO, NV

The con that afternoon passes in a blur of capes and Sharpie ink. Afterward, we wind up at a karaoke bar where the bouncer scrutinizes my ID with its February 29 birth date for a few extra moments, something I got used to years ago and that Finn finds hilarious. It's a dive with neon signs and crackly speakers and, most important, Finn's best friend from high school. Krishanu is tall, Indian American, with wavy dark hair beneath a Reno Aces cap. He's a high school English teacher, and his boyfriend, Derek, a white guy wearing a college sweatshirt and easy grin, coaches the school's football, swimming, and baseball teams. "Budget cuts," he explains with a shrug.

Finn seems to relax the instant we slide into a vinyl booth across from them, his shoulders softening. I've never seen him this light, this unburdened.

"It's been too long," Krishanu says as a server drops off a foamy pitcher of beer.

"What, three months?" Finn says. "You really missed me that much?"

"Nah, I was just being nice. I barely think about you."

I learn that Krishanu was also a huge LOTR fan as a kid, one of the things that bonded him and Finn early on, and the most popular part of his class is a unit on Middle-earth.

"Is he making you regret taking this job yet?" Krishanu asks.

Finn crosses his arms over his chest with a practiced defiance. "I'll have you know, I am an utter delight to work with."

When I let out a snort, Finn holds a hand to his heart. "No, no, you're great. Obviously. It's the best job I've ever had."

"The sarcasm. It hurts."

"The way I'm dying for this book," Derek says, taking a sip of beer. "When Krish told me he not only knew you but that you'd survived puberty together, I told myself I couldn't screw things up with us or I'd never get to meet you."

I tilt my head toward Finn. "I'm sure Krishanu could write a much more fascinating, scandalous book."

"I'd definitely have to go into witness protection if he did that."

"You have to tell me what he was like as an awkward teenager," I say to Krishanu. "Don't leave out a single pimple."

"Unfortunately for you, I've always been blessed with flawless skin."

"He probably hasn't told you about the first show he performed in, has he? Eighth grade?" When I shake my head, Krishanu's smile turns wicked. "Our school was putting on *Beauty and the Beast*, and he was Cogsworth."

"Never mind the fact that I can't sing," Finn puts in and I assume he's just being modest.

"Anyway, we didn't have a huge budget, so his costume was

essentially just this big, kind of flimsy piece of cardboard painted like a clock that he wore. And during the last performance, right in the middle of 'Be Our Guest,' a dancing napkin stumbled into him and tore it right off."

"Oh no," I say. "Please tell me he was wearing something underneath."

"Just a pair of boxer briefs with elves on them."

"That definitely doesn't need to go in the book," Finn says with a groan, dropping his head to the table.

"Oh, it's already there. It's chapter one."

Krishanu meets Finn's gaze with a quirk of one eyebrow. Finn gives a slight but firm shake of his head, and I get the feeling I know exactly what conversation I've just witnessed. *Are you two—?* And Finn immediately shutting it down.

I'm not sure why it makes a pit settle in my stomach. We're not a couple. We're colleagues who are also sleeping together, which is a bit more difficult to communicate with eyebrow twitches.

"Enough about me," Finn says. "You two just closed on a house?"

Derek nods. "It's a bit of a fixer-upper, but we're excited about it."

"We'll see if we still feel that way after we knock out the attic to add a second bedroom," Krishanu says.

When his name is called for karaoke, Krishanu gets up to sing "Werewolves of London," much to Finn's horror, really going hard on the howls. Derek and I chime in on a few, Finn burying his head in his hands and swearing that he'll never speak to any of us again. Derek goes next with a solid rendition of No Doubt's "Don't Speak." Then Finn looks at me, a challenge in his eyes.

"I'll do it if you do," he says.

I glance at the stage. I don't have nearly enough alcohol in me for this to be a comfortable proposition. "That's not fair, you're . . . confident. You do this professionally."

"Sing? Absolutely not."

"And with good reason," Krishanu puts in.

Finn's gaze is still hard on mine. Insistent.

"Fine," I relent. "But you're going first."

Krishanu flexes his hands behind his head as Finn gets up and heads toward the stage. "This'll be good."

With that, I expect Finn to have the voice of an angel, or at least, like, Art Garfunkel. But when he steps up to the microphone, throws us a wink, and starts singing "Come On Eileen," I have to press my lips together to keep from laughing, though Krishanu and Derek don't even try to hide it. Because Krishanu was right: Finnegan Walsh is a dreadful singer, and he knows it.

And he doesn't seem to care.

He cradles the microphone like it's a precious, delicate thing, before whipping it off the stand and strutting across the stage. He's all in on this song, the audience singing along with him.

I lean across the table to Krishanu, thinking back to what Finn's mom said about his dining-table performances. "Was he always like this?"

He shakes his head. "Not at all. One-on-one, sure, he could be pretty animated. But most of the time when we were kids, he'd be a thousand times more likely to have his head in a book than on-stage. It's been such a trip, watching him become this completely different person." Then he considers this for a moment, takes a sip of beer. "Although every time he's back here, it's like he never left. So maybe he hasn't changed that much—not in the ways that matter, at least."

"How so?"

"He's not someone who opens up very easily," Krishanu explains. "He's always kept his private life very private. So the fact that he's doing it with you, letting you see this side of himself . . ."

"It's for the book." I'm almost surprised by how defensive the words sound, especially after that eyebrow quirk Krishanu gave Finn. The one Finn was so quick to shut down.

Krishanu and Derek exchange an odd glance, the kind honed by couples who've been together long enough to communicate without a single word. "Right."

Now Finn's dragging the mic stand across the stage, flicking his hair back, belting the chorus. The audience sings along with him.

He makes eye contact with me. *My thoughts, I confess, verge on dirty. Come on, Eileen.*

A shiver runs through me.

I like this side of him.

I might like it a lot.

The audience goes wild, and Finn dramatically collapses back into the booth, as though the performance simply took all the energy out of him. His hair is askew, body warm. I'm both desperate to get out of the booth and curious what would happen if I inched closer.

No, no, no, I remind myself, trying to forget about his DayQuil-induced confession. Besides, even if he did have a crush, it's very possible it's faded by now. Just because I spent years swooning over Wyatt doesn't mean Finn's feelings aren't mercurial.

And *crush* is such an innocent word, isn't it? It doesn't have to mean that he spends all his free time thinking about me. It could simply mean that he finds me attractive, which I already know from the time we've spent in bed.

So really, maybe it wasn't a revelation at all.

"Remember, you asked for this," I tell Finn as I head toward the stage, gripping the microphone with trembling hands.

The last thing I'm expecting when the chords of the Dandy Warhols' "Bohemian Like You" start—they're from Portland, I have range—is for my table to let out a whoop. It emboldens me, makes my voice come out slightly less shaky than I'm anticipating.

It's not a difficult song, easy enough for my limited vocal range, aside from what I realize is quite an absurd number of *woo-ooh-ooh*s, which my voice cracks on at first. I white-knuckle the microphone, watching Finn and his friends. His eyes barely leave mine, except for when he leans across the table to say something to Krishanu and Derek. When I nail the second chorus, his mouth quirks upward, and it gives me even more confidence.

When I return to the table and he lassos me for a hug, I'm unsure why my heart is thumping faster than it did while I was onstage.

I down a few sips of beer as the notes of a Frank Sinatra song start up, and when the elderly man onstage opens his mouth, the whole bar goes quiet.

"Holy shit," Krishanu says, because the guy is *good*. "Putting us all to shame."

Finn holds out his hand, and it takes me an extra second to realize he's holding it out to me. "This feels like the kind of song we can't not dance to."

All around us, that's what people are doing, including Krishanu and Derek. So I give Finn my hand and let him lead me to the dance floor.

"This has been really great," I tell him as his other hand finds the small of my back and I rest my palm on his shoulder. There's a healthy amount of space between our chests, as though both of us are worried what it might mean if we stood too close. "Meeting your mom. Your friends. I don't care if it's recency bias—I think I'm in love with this city."

Finn gives me a grin. "That might be the nicest thing someone's ever said about Reno. And I'm half sure all the little old ladies at synagogue are ready to adopt you."

"My parents might take issue with that, but I wouldn't mind."

The older guy croons through a chorus. Another verse.

"Speaking of . . . how are they? Your parents?"

I lift my eyebrows at him. "My mom's starting to get upset with my dad for how many birding books he's ordered, but they're doing fine."

"Good. Just checking. And now I'm curious how many birding books is too many." His palm is warm as we sway back and forth, and when he spins me, my face does little to hide my shock. He lowers his voice, his mouth right against my ear. "I may not have moves in the bedroom," he says, "but on the dance floor . . ."

"Your bedroom moves are improving."

Another spin. "What's next on the lesson plan?"

I think back to it, even though I had the thing memorized the night I made it. "It's more of an elective than core curriculum, but I thought we could work on your dirty talk."

"Mine was pretty abysmal, wasn't it," he says with a soft groan. "Out with it. I can take it."

"It was just . . ." I fumble for the right words. "It didn't feel personal. Part of it is what you say, and the other is how you say it. Most of it didn't feel like you were talking directly to *me*, if that makes sense? You kept saying, 'Oooh, there it is. Oooh, there it is.' And it kind of had the same rhythm as—"

His mouth drops. "That eighties song? 'Whoomp! (There It Is)'?" When I'm quiet: "Your face says it all."

"There was also the part where you referred to my vagina as a separate entity," I say, working to keep my voice down. "And that doesn't mean someone else wouldn't enjoy that kind of dirty talk—with the right person, after the right length of time."

"Then teach me," he says. "Teach me how to dirty talk."

I give him an incredulous look. "Here?"

"I can be quiet if you can." A quirk of his eyebrow. A challenge.

The song ends, but before the guy can leave the stage, the audience begs him to do another.

Neither one of us moves.

Krishanu and Derek appear next to us, jackets and scarves back on.

"We're gonna head out," Krishanu says, nudging his boyfriend. "This one has swim team practice early tomorrow."

"So great to meet you. Truly." We all exchange hugs, and Finn promises he'll be back in town as soon as he can. Thanksgiving, he hopes, if he has enough of a break from the circuit.

All of this dulls my libido, but only slightly. I don't register the song as we start dancing again, Finn steering us farther from the stage to where the bar is less crowded. It might be another Sinatra or it might be Harry Styles—that's how distracted I am.

"Well," I start, aware of how he's holding me a little closer than before, his grip on my lower back a little tighter. "As we've established, the most important thing is communication. If your partner isn't into it, you probably want to change things up. Or maybe she won't be a fan of it at all, and that's okay, too. You'd talk about that."

"Right."

"A good place to start is building anticipation. Tell her how you're feeling about her, what you want to do to her." This is perfectly fine. Clinical, even. Completely safe. "And you can say actual body parts. Get specific. And when in doubt, there are always some choice words that never really fail."

"Which would be . . ."

"Hard. Tight. Deep. Wet." Ironically, my throat goes dry, my face heating up. "And so on. A good 'fuck' or 'fucking' never hurts, either."

He nods, silently taking all of this in. "So . . ." His thumb brushes along my spine as he drops his voice. "I'm so fucking hard for you? Something that basic?"

"Basic, but effective." And if it really is so basic, I'm not sure why it turns me instantly light-headed, the bar around us blurring while Finn remains in sharp focus.

"I'm going to make you so fucking wet?"

Yes. Yes, you are. "That—that works."

It feels illicit, talking about this in public, even though no one can hear us. We've kept our lessons entirely in the bedroom until now, and I don't know what it means that they're spilling over into real life.

"What would you say to that?" he asks, and then he has the nerve to spin me again. When he brings me back against his chest, his grip is even tighter, breathing shallower.

Whatever I'm feeling has to be purely scientific, nothing else. The attraction is the simple chemistry of our cells, combined with the fact that we've seen each other out of clothes almost as frequently as we have with them on.

I try to gain back control, rocking my hips against his, savoring this power I have. Digging my nails into his shoulders. "That my panties are damp, and my nipples are aching, and I need to feel you inside me." I drag out each sentence, speaking as slowly as I can. He's hard against my stomach, so I press in even closer. "That I've been waiting for it all day, dying to take care of myself but knowing you'll feel even better. But I'm worried I might come too fast when you finally touch me, so you're going to have to tease me."

He swallows down a growl.

"I'll want you to go deep," I continue, not fully recognizing the sound of my voice, "because that's how I like being fucked. But you can't start that way. You're going to have to be gentle with me, even though I'll be begging you. You think you can handle that?"

"*Chandler.*"

"Then you could tell her how she feels." I'm certain he can hear my heart thudding against his. "How she tastes."

"Mmm." He seems to collect himself, his face millimeters from mine as his breath whispers across my skin. "I bet you taste so fucking sweet," he says, mouth grazing my ear. His scent, that mix of earth and spice, utterly jamming my senses. "Ever since Seattle, I've been dying to lick you again."

The room tilts. My entire body goes weightless. If he weren't holding me up, I'm not sure I'd trust my legs.

Suddenly, the audience breaks into applause, and it takes me a few seconds to realize the song has ended.

I glance back up at Finn. "Should we get out of here?" I ask, and the fierceness in his gaze tells me exactly how he's feeling.

He grabs my hand, leading me through the maze of people on the dance floor. As soon as he pays for our drinks, leaving a sizable tip, we trip out into the night, into the skinny alleyway next to the bar. Before I can ask if he wants to find a hotel somewhere, he has me pinned against the wall, chest to chest, hips to hips. Close enough to kiss.

But he doesn't. Not yet.

"I thought I was gonna detonate in there," he says against my neck, mouth burning a path along my jawline.

I wrap my arms around his shoulders, holding him closer. Briefly, I'm reminded of our first night in Seattle, outside the bookstore. Only this time, I don't want to move from this spot.

"Then we were doing it right." I scrape my fingers along the back of his neck, up into his hair. "Tell me what else you want to do to me." I have to make sure he has this down—for the sake of his education.

He gives me this look that turns me entirely liquid. "Whatever you say, professor."

I drag his mouth down to mine, that dirty perfect mouth, swirling my tongue with his. It's been too long since we kissed, even longer since it felt this desperate.

"I want to make you come so hard, you beg me to do it again," he says, kissing my neck. My throat. "I think about it all the time."

Fucking hell.

"Are you going to fuck me with your fingers? Your mouth?"

"Both," he says against my skin. "Repeatedly. And often."

He slides a knee between my legs, his hands dropping to my hips. An "oh" falls from my mouth as he guides me against his jeans, the seam in mine creating an exquisite kind of friction. Torturous and decadent all at once.

A sly smile. "Huh. Can't say I've imagined this exact scenario."

I laugh, despite how frenzied all of this feels. Then all humor leaves me as the sensation starts to build. I move against him faster, hooking my leg around his hips while he grips my thigh, pressing deeper into me.

The bulge in his jeans only makes me needier. I tighten my grip around the back of his neck, clutching at his hair, damp with exertion. His warm skin. His scent. He tilts me against him, fingers digging into my ass as we keep up this relentless rhythm.

Determination is painted on his face, like not even an apocalypse could break his concentration.

He must notice my breaths coming quicker because he hoists me higher on his thigh. "That's it," he says. "*God*, I've missed you."

He doesn't actually mean he's missed me—just that he's missed *this*. I'd correct him, only I'm no longer able to form words.

I forget that we're in public. I forget that I'm working for him and that all of this is starting to get a little confusing. I forget everything except the rush of pleasure between my legs and the adrenaline racing through my veins.

Then I'm coming apart, everything in me clenching and then bursting with a sudden flash of heat. I turn my face to the side, gasping into the night as he tugs me forward again, mouth working to capture my moan.

A door opens with a loud creak, and Finn cages my body with his, as though we've been caught doing something we shouldn't. I feel myself shake with silent laughter, grateful he's holding me up.

"Shhhh," he says, right before he dissolves into giggles of his own.

There's a thud as someone tosses a bag into a dumpster across the alley, and once the door to the bar swings shut, Finn takes my hand, the two of us panting, laughing, running toward the car as fast as we can.

I'm worried the drive back to his mom's place will be full of awkward silence. But as soon as we get into the rental car, Finn rests his hand on my thigh, grinning, like he's so damn proud of himself he just can't contain it.

"You live here," I whisper as we tiptoe from the car to his front door. "Or *lived* here. You don't have to sneak in."

"The dogs," he explains. "Better than any security system."

Once we get inside, I brace for a symphony of barking. But it's just Duchess, an affectionate Chihuahua with three tan paws and one white one, who trots up to us, allows herself to receive some love, and then disappears back down the hall.

Finn tosses me a wicked, playful look. "Good night," he says sweetly.

I just shake my head, biting back a smile. "Good night," I echo before we turn our separate ways at the end of the hall.

DAD IN TRAINING

Season 1, Episode 3:
"Dad the Babysitter"

INT. WILKINS FAMILY LIVING ROOM—DAY

CHERYL WILKINS arrives home after a weekend away. BOB WILKINS is asleep on the couch, BABY WILL in his lap. ANDY WILKINS rides his scooter around the messy living room while JENNA WILKINS applies makeup to her sleeping father's face.

>   CHERYL
>   Honey? Kids? What's all this?

>   BOB
> *He wakes with a start, gazing around at the chaos.*

>   What in the—oh! Why, Cheryl, I have
>   no idea what you mean. And might I
>   say, you are absolutely *glowing*?

Break for laugh track.

>   ANDY
>   *In a mechanical voice.*
>   Dad did a great job watching us. He
>   served us perfectly balanced meals
>   and put us to bed at nine o'clock
>   every night.

                    CHERYL
          And how much did he pay you to say
          that?

                    ANDY
          Twenty bucks.

                    CHERYL
She scoops up the baby, who's started to cry.

             Sweetie, it's okay, Mommy's here.
             Wait. Where's Laurie? You were
             supposed to pick her up from dance
             team practice!

*BOB looks at the camera with an exaggerated
guilty shrug.*

                    ALL
             Daaaaaaad!

NINETEEN

COLUMBUS, OH

Wolfing it Down: Vegetarian Cooking with Finnegan Walsh."

Finn shakes his head. "Absolutely not."

"Big Bad Wolf? The Story of the Least Villainous Man on TV."

"I think you're forgetting I didn't play one of the werewolves."

"But it's much easier to come up with a pun that way." I tap my fingers on the upright tray table. "I've got it. *Howl-arious: 101 Finn Walsh–Approved Nerd Jokes.*"

"You're banned. Banned from making jokes for the next twenty-four hours. At least."

I twist in my window seat to take a look up the aisle, toward the front of the plane. "Is it weird that we haven't left yet?"

As though I've summoned it, a loudspeaker announcement comes on. "Good afternoon, this is your captain speaking. We're experiencing some weather-related delays, but we should be taking off as soon as we get the signal from air traffic control."

I open up my bag and pull out an applesauce pouch. I couldn't take any more greasy airport food, and this seemed the least likely to make my stomach revolt.

"I think those are for children," Finn says. "But I guess it's fitting, since you're only seven. Is that what you got at Starbucks when I was in the bathroom?"

"This is my emotional support applesauce," I say. "Nowhere on this pouch does it say that it's for children."

"There's a drawing of a *child* on it!"

"Ohhhhh, no, no, that's actually just a very small adult. But I can see how you would get confused." I lean into his face and suck hard on the applesauce pouch until he breaks and starts laughing.

He removes a thick book from his carry-on bag, a Tolkien biography. "Holler if you need me."

I might as well take advantage of the delay, so I take out my laptop. Since we left Reno on Monday, the week has been nonstop work. Finn had an overnight trip to LA for some *Nocturnals* reunion press, while I holed up in Columbus, turning outlines into sketches of chapters. Whenever I struggled with his voice, I played back my recordings, or I texted him a question. He flew back for Comic Expo Ohio, and now we're on our way to Pittsburgh.

Slowly, slowly, it's becoming a book. I've always loved this part, watching as a flurry of notes and detached phrases become sentences, paragraphs. It feels a little like magic, expanding on his anecdotes, giving them a narrative structure.

Our editor has asked for the first five chapters as a status report, due tomorrow, and while I have three nearly complete, we might have to pull an all-nighter to finish the rest.

An hour later, it's begun to snow and we're still on the tarmac.

"We're sorry, folks, but there's a storm coming in from the

west, and it doesn't look like it'll let up anytime soon," says the pilot over the loudspeaker. "All planes are being grounded for tonight." A wave of frustrated chatter rushes through the aisles as they go on to talk about booking people on the next flights out tomorrow.

"Shit." I haul my laptop bag over my shoulder, picking at my black nail polish as we wait to deplane. I'm starting to feel bad about the specks of it I've left across the country, a colorful little trail of anxiety-confetti. "We have to turn this in tonight, and then the welcome dinner at the con tomorrow . . . maybe if we get out tomorrow morning, we can make it in time?"

Finn takes a few moments to think. "We'll rent a car. It's only three hours away. The storm is blowing in from the opposite direction of where we're heading." He tilts his phone toward me, showing me the forecast.

"In this weather?"

"I'm from the mountains," he says, waving this off as we head toward baggage claim to collect our luggage. "We learn how to drive in this before we learn our ABCs. Besides, they're always overly cautious about this kind of thing." He gives me a broad, nonchalant smile. "I'm sure it's nowhere near as bad as they're saying it is."

─── ─── ───

THE STORM IS, IN FACT, WORSE.

"What was that you said?" I ask as the rental sputters to a stop on an icy two-lane road an hour outside of Columbus. Stalled cars dot the street, drivers far smarter than us who've already given up. "You learned how to drive in this weather when you were how old?"

Finn wrestles with the steering wheel, pumps the gas. No luck. "I guess—it's entirely possible it's been a while since I drove in weather like this."

Snow batters the windshield. This was very obviously a bad idea, and even if we could get the car to start, I'm not sure we'd be able to make it back to the city. Deadline panic creeps in, tightening my grip on my bag. All I want is my hands on the keyboard and maybe a space heater.

"We can't just stay out here," I say. "We'll freeze to death."

Finn's already checking his phone, swearing at it when he can't get a signal. "There was a sign for lodging about a mile back."

Theoretically, a mile doesn't sound like too long a walk. A mile in the snow when you can't feel your hands and your mother's suitcase wheels slip all over the ice: less than ideal. Finn tries his best to help, dragging both my suitcase and his while I take his backpack, promising that "We're almost there—almost there," his teeth chattering.

By the time we make it to the bed-and-breakfast, a charming, snow-dusted building surrounded by oak trees, nearly all the stickers on my mom's suitcase have peeled off and I estimate I'm minutes away from succumbing to frostbite. THE DOLLHOUSE INN is written on a sign out front in swirly script.

"Hello there!" says the woman behind the front desk, petite and middle-aged, with a gray bob and knitted turtleneck. "Chilly out there, isn't it?"

"You could say that." Finn brushes snow off his jacket with a trembling hand while I work to catch my breath. "We don't have a reservation, but do you by any chance have a room available tonight?"

"Hmm, let's see. We usually book pretty far in advance . . ."

She opens up an honest-to-god reservation book, and it's then that I notice two things.

One: there are no computers in the lobby.

And two: the place is *swarming* with dolls.

Antique dolls on shelves, dolls at tiny tables drinking imaginary tea, dolls dressed in Christmas sweaters, and dolls carrying tinier dolls. Every single one of them staring right at me with glassy, dead-eyed stares.

Guess the name of the inn was literal.

"It looks like we've got just one left! It's the Victorian Room—lucky you. That's my favorite."

"We'll take it," I say, trying to avoid the gaze of a particularly haunted baby doll as she passes us an old-fashioned key that looks more likely to open a seventeenth-century cottage than a modern B and B. "Thank you so much. This is maybe a dumb question, but do you have Wi-Fi?"

A chuckle. "Of course we do!" she says. I feel my shoulders relax. "But it just went out. Sorry about that. We have someone coming out tomorrow to take a look—if they can make it."

We haul our suitcases up a flight of stairs, and I swallow down a gasp when I open our room. It's gorgeous, with a real wood-burning fireplace and luxe velvet wallpaper. There's only one doll in here, wearing a blue-and-white-checked pinafore and a bow in her hair. She is missing an eye. I make the executive decision to hide her in a drawer, and Finn flashes me a thumbs-up.

Then I examine the rest of the room, something I probably should have done right away. Because right in the middle is an upholstered, rich emerald queen-sized bed.

Just one.

"Oh," I say, dropping my backpack to the floor. "I could sleep in the chair, or on the floor, or—"

"Don't be ridiculous," Finn says. "*I'll* sleep in the chair."

I make my way over to the bed, as though it needs inspecting. As though up close, it'll somehow turn out to be two beds. "There's plenty of room for both of us."

This shouldn't feel weird. We've had sex but haven't slept together, and yet the idea of sleeping beside him is strangely intimate—getting to see him the moment he wakes up, still drowsy, his hair rumpled and eyes half-closed and does he sleep in a T-shirt or just boxers or—

I push this aside for now. We have bigger things to worry about.

We unpack a little, and I manage to set up my phone as a hotspot.

"I knew you liked socks, but how many pairs are in that suitc—" Finn starts.

"It doesn't matter!" I say it too sharply, but this isn't about the socks at all. Those chapters need to get done. I change my damp socks and then sit down with my laptop in one of two armchairs next to the fireplace, the anxiety keeping me warmer than the flames. I try to tell myself things will be okay. It's only five o'clock, we don't have anything else to do, and there are no dolls that may or may not be possessed by evil spirits currently watching me.

Finn must be able to tell I'm nervous, because after he pulls on a painfully soft-looking sweater, he kneels at my armchair, laying a hand on mine.

"Hey," he says, and I take it back—his voice is the warmest of all. "It's going to be okay. We'll make it."

But my body refuses to believe him. It's not just the flight delay or the chapters—it's all of it, all at once. My lungs are tight, throat thick, mouth dry, limbs heavy—

No. Not now. Not here.

I try to nod, but that doesn't seem to work, either. The panic is set deep in my muscles, racing through my veins and pinning me in place.

"Chandler?" he says. I can barely hear him over my labored inhales, rushed exhales. *Fuck.* I can't control the sounds spilling out of me.

This hasn't happened in a long time, and the last thing I want is to break down in front of him, with our deadline so close . . .

"Every—everything's going wrong," I manage between guttural breaths. My sentence ends in a hiccup, and Finn catches my laptop before it falls to the floor.

His brows draw together in concern as he gently places the laptop on the rug next to him. "I know it's been a weird day. A rough day. But we're going to figure it out. You don't have to do this alone, sweetheart. I'm here."

Sweetheart.

The unexpectedness of that word only pulls my pulse into a more frantic rhythm. He doesn't even seem to realize what he's said.

A vigorous shake of my head. "I don't want to fuck this up for you. It's important. And I just—I want to do it justice."

"You're not fucking anything up." His voice is firm but kind, and now he's stroking up my arms, this soothing motion that helps anchor me to the room. *Up*, and I can feel the chair beneath me. *Down*, and I can hear the flickering of the fireplace. "Listen to me. There is *no one* I'd trust to do this justice more than you. I've probably told you that a few dozen times at this point, so I'm a little worried that you're going to get a big head about it."

A laugh slips out.

"Is there anything I can do for you right now? Anything you need?"

His questions are too earnest. Because what I'm not sure I can tell him is that it's not just right now, this deadline. It's all the things I can't say yet, the questions I packed in my suitcase next to my favorite jeans and electric toothbrush. I've been running for so long that I'm no longer sure where the finish line is, or if there's a finish line at all. And sometimes that terrifies the shit out of me.

My whole life, I've been working myself to the bone, chasing something that's always just out of reach.

"Just this," I say, my voice coming out a little scratchy. But my breathing slows, shoulders starting to relax.

His thumb brushes my knuckles before he drops his hands, and I stare down at the space he touched for longer than I probably should. In the firelight, his hair is the richest gold, strands of gray turning silver. The lovely angles of his face, half cast in shadow. He has never once doubted me, not even during that first meeting with his manager.

"Okay. I—I think I'm okay. Let's do this." I make a move to reach for my laptop. "And—thank you."

Finn's gaze doesn't leave mine for a few more seconds. With the fire crackling next to us and the storm raging outside, there's something almost . . . *romantic* about this moment, an adjective I regret as soon as it enters my mind.

If we were two other people, it would be so easy to abandon my laptop, crawl onto his lap, and turn this into some idyllic winter escape.

But we're Chandler and Finn, and we're here to work.

It's as though Finn blinks out of a daze at the same time I do. I force my eyes back to my laptop screen while he takes the other chair, clearing his throat and stretching out his legs.

We work through the evening as quickly as we can, with Finn reading sections as soon as I finish drafting them, offering notes and corrections.

Around seven thirty, Maude from the front desk knocks on the door with a tray of food. "Dinner," she says sweetly. "Thought you two could use a hot meal."

We thank her profusely.

"How about this?" I ask an hour later, stomach full of mushroom risotto, turning the laptop to him. It's a section about his first day on set for *Dad in Training*. The show was seemingly made solely to enforce gender roles, plotlines revolving around questions like, How on earth will this blue-collar father watch his own kids for a full weekend while his wife's away? Can he really handle making brownies for his daughter's bake sale while helping his son with his science fair project? Not to mention the baby—and we all know he can barely change a diaper! Cue laugh track.

Finn reads what I've written, about how he was so nervous, he read the stage directions, not just his lines, and how his character, who was initially supposed to skateboard on and off set, much to the annoyance of his TV parents, couldn't manage to stay upright, so they changed it to a scooter. "This is perfect. You manage to perfectly capture what the show was about without insulting anyone too much. Although I'm not sure I'd mind—Bob Gaffney was an asshole."

"I watched a couple episodes and I was frankly appalled, if I'm being honest."

A grimace. "Yeah, if I'd been smarter, I never would have done it. But some part of me craved that nuclear family that I didn't have. And I guess it led to *The Nocturnals*, so . . ." He keeps reading, pointing to one paragraph. "I don't think I'd use the word 'ostentatious,' but aside from that—I love it. And you sound just like me." His eyes leap to mine. "It's kind of unfair that you don't get to have your name on it, after all of this."

I shrug, swapping out *ostentatious* for *extravagant*, forcing myself not to linger on the compliment. "It's the job. That's why you hired a ghostwriter."

"I know," he says softly. "I just wish . . ." Then he trails off with a shake of his head, and I bury myself back in the chapter.

It's almost one in the morning when our sample is polished to the point where both of us feel good about it. This is also around the time my hotspot gives up.

"We have to have service somewhere in here," I say, waving my phone around.

Finn's on the other side of the room, doing the same. "Not getting anything."

I hop up onto a chair and then onto the desk, hold my phone as high as it'll go, hit send—

"It went through!" I yelp, the desk creaking beneath me.

Finn strides over, holding out his hand for a high five. Except that's when I lose my balance, stumbling over my own feet and into his arms.

And there's this moment when he's holding me, when our eyes are locked and his expression is warm, open, victorious, that I'm almost certain is real. I swear I stop breathing as he slips his fingers into my short hair. I only start back up again to inhale him, that comforting, intoxicating scent that's been screwing with my brain for weeks.

Then he slides me down his body, solid and firm, so slowly that I have to wonder if it's deliberate, before gently placing me on the ground. Helping smooth my clothes.

It's not just the hug. I've genuinely enjoyed this collaboration, and turning in those chapters reminds me that sometime in the not-too-distant future, all of this will be over.

Although the reality is that sometimes I get the feeling I could write an entire trilogy about Finn Walsh and barely scratch the surface.

"We should get ready for bed," I say quickly, grabbing my stuff and racing to the bathroom. He's already neatly unpacked his toiletry kit, razor, and travel-sized shaving cream next to the sink. An orange Rx bottle stands there without shame, exactly the way it should.

We switch so he can do the same, and then both of us sit down on opposite sides of the bed. Most of the time I sleep in an oversize T-shirt, but tonight my pajamas are the single matching striped set I own. He's in plaid shorts and a thin white T-shirt, and it strikes me that while I've seen him without clothes on, I've never seen him this casual. The clothes immediately soften him, especially when I notice a small hole in his left sleeve.

I find myself wanting to get even closer. To tell him things I haven't shared with anyone in a long time. He already knows so much about me, and yet I've felt I can never be truly close to someone until they know about my abortion.

I can't think about what it means that I want to tell him.

"Tired?" he asks, and the bed might as well have a heart-shaped headboard and rose petals scattered across it. If that hug impacted me as much as it did, I'm only mildly concerned about how I'll feel with his sleeping body a couple feet from mine.

I shake my head. "Must be all the adrenaline."

I should be exhausted. The trip has been jarring—one day, we're in the middle of a desert, and the next, in the middle of a blizzard. We've experienced all four seasons in the span of a month and a half.

"You okay?" Finn asks when he catches me moving my hands and wrists back and forth.

"Yeah, they just get a little stiff after typing for so long. A little sore." I flex my fingers.

"Come here," he says, patting the bed next to him, and I scoot closer. He reaches out his hands, and I don't even pause to think about it before giving him mine.

"I can't believe we're here," he says, beginning to massage one hand with both of his. "Not just in a B and B in the middle of Ohio with dolls that are definitely going to come to life in the middle of the night, although that, too, but . . . together." He winces at that. "Not *together*—you know what I mean. I guess I've just gotten so used to doing these things on my own that I forgot what it was like, traveling with someone else. It's not the worst thing to have some company."

"I can't imagine doing all of this alone."

My eyes fall shut. The way he's touching me, fingertips moving in circles—it's not dissimilar from the way I've taught him to *touch* me.

And are we just . . . not going to acknowledge sweetheartgate?

"You know, you're kind of an enigma," he says, switching to my other hand. "Or at least, you were at first. Are you any closer to figuring out what you want to do with the rest of your life, Chandler Cohen?"

"I'd like to go to the grave without ever having learned what an NFT is."

"Wouldn't we all." Finn taps my knuckles. "I'm serious."

"The rest of my life," I repeat. "That's too much pressure. Can anyone really say, definitively, what they want to be doing for the rest of their life in their twenties or thirties?" He moves to my wrists, thumbs dipping into my skin. "I like this. Working on the book with you, actually feeling like we're collaborating. It's different from the others."

A grin. "Are you saying I'm your favorite?"

"Only if you promise not to get a complex about it." I shift my weight underneath me, half hoping this massage ends soon while also wishing he'd never stop. "Even when I was enjoying this work, it wasn't fulfilling, not in the way I thought it would be when I started out in journalism. Even when I was at The Catch, I don't know if I felt fulfilled every day. I've probably built it up in my mind because the layoff really sank my mental health, but creatively, professionally, fill in the blank—I didn't want to write listicles for the rest of my life. I want to love what I'm doing with my whole heart. Or is that just a lie that society sold millennials when we were young, and none of us really love our jobs?"

"Some of us do," he says. "But I see what you're saying. It reminds me of those posters every teacher had in their classrooms. Shoot for the moon—"

"—and even if you miss, you'll land among the stars," I finish with him. That bullshit kind of encapsulates the millennial experience. Because the thing is, some of the stars are really fucking far away from the moon. And maybe you don't want one of those distant stars at all. Maybe you never wanted the moon in the first place, you don't know if you even want to go to space, but you've got to make a decision soon. And it better be something you can see yourself doing *for the rest of your life*.

There's just no room for uncertainty, the place I seem to live these days.

"Before this trip, I felt completely trapped," I continue. "They told us we could have it all but that's just not true. We could do something creative, but also something stable. Something fulfilling, but that doesn't turn you into a workaholic. Something good for the planet, but that also makes money. I grew up with everyone telling me how *special* I was, which was amplified by being born on Leap Day. It was always, 'You're going to do something great' and 'You can do whatever you want' and never 'It's okay if you don't figure it out right away.' But I'm starting to wonder if none of that is true."

"Maybe ghostwriting isn't too different from acting." Finn drops my hands, and maybe worse than the massage is the way his face is inches from mine, his eyes sincere. "You're assuming someone's voice and identity for a little while, promising to take good care of it." He rubs at the back of his neck. "I feel that way, too," he says. "Trapped. By my brain sometimes, when I wish I could stop the obsessive thoughts but I'm too deep in a spiral. Or when I think about the general perception of OCD being connected to cleanliness, which is true for some people but not for everyone. And then I start worrying I fall into that stereotype, even though it's not about things being neat and tidy for me. It's, if this food has gone bad, it's going to poison me or someone I love. I have impostor syndrome about my OCD. Isn't that ridiculous?"

"No," I say. "I have impostor syndrome about nearly every facet of my identity."

"Our brains are cruel, cruel organs."

We're quiet for a few moments while snow flurries paint the night sky and the fire slowly turns to ash. Our relationship has been a strange journey, the physical and emotional pieces coming together at different times. I haven't been this vulnerable with someone in a long time, and it feels freeing. Comfortable. *Safe.*

"There's something I've been wanting to tell you," I start. "About my past. If that's okay?"

Finn's brow furrows. "Of course. You can tell me anything."

Right. I already knew that, really, but hearing it makes the words come even easier. If I'm going to be truly open with him, I can't go back—and maybe I don't want to.

Maybe I have always been able to trust him like this.

"I had an abortion," I say. Not looking away. Not avoiding eye contact. "My sophomore year of college."

Finn nods slowly, letting me decide how much I want to share.

"I'd been seeing this guy for a few months. David. I wasn't always the best at taking birth control pills, and we just kind of assumed since we were using condoms, we were being safe. But I missed a period, and then I started feeling nauseous, like, all the time, so I took a test. And it was positive." David had been sweet, equally happy to go to an off-campus party or watch a movie on the threadbare couch in the house he shared with eight other roommates. We'd met sitting next to each other in a physics class we were both taking for a science credit. "He told me that it was my decision, that he'd support whatever I wanted to do. I could see my whole career stretched out in front of me, or at least my vision of what I wanted it to be, and when I saw those two lines on the stick, it just . . . completely changed.

"I didn't have the money to raise a kid," I continue, running a fingertip along the floral comforter. "I didn't *want* to raise a kid, not when I had so many other plans for my future. So I think I knew, the moment I first thought I might be pregnant, what I was going to do. It's not this deep, dark secret, but I wanted to tell you because it's part of me. Part of my history."

Finn takes another few moments to collect himself, the way he always does when he isn't sure what to say. He's looking at me with a careful intensity, one that sets every anxious cell in my body at ease. "I'm so glad you could make that choice. And I'm not judging you. At all," he says, voice ever steady. "I've never had anyone tell me that before. Maybe you could tell me if I'm fuck-ing up this reaction?"

"No," I say. The relief is instantaneous. "You're not."

"You can tell me anything you want about it. Or nothing. Whatever you feel comfortable saying."

When I think about that day, what I remember most is the way my mom gripped my hand in the waiting room, told me she was there for whatever I needed. How fast and relatively painless the procedure itself was, a little discomfort and then some cramping afterward. I'd never known whether I wanted kids someday, not really—it was always something I thought I'd figure out when I was older. And maybe I do, one day, but I'm still not sure. I only knew I didn't want one when I was nineteen.

As it turns out, there's nothing about it that I feel uncomfort-able telling him. "I was lucky that in Washington State, it wasn't too difficult to find a clinic, and I was ten weeks along, still in the first trimester. There were protestors outside, just a few, but once I got inside, everyone was so kind. My mom went with me, and it was really just . . . a medical procedure. It was just a thing that happened, and it was the right choice for me," I say. "I know I had a much easier time than a lot of people—because of how early it was, how supportive my parents were, because I could afford it. And I'm grateful for all of that." I take what feels like my seventh deep breath in the past few minutes. "I don't regret my abortion. I don't even think about it very often, if I'm being honest."

The look on his face—I can't describe it in any other way ex-cept genuinely *affected*.

"Thank you," he says, voice solid and true. "For telling me. For trusting me with this."

"If someone's going to be part of my life, I need them to know this about me. And I need them to accept it. Otherwise . . . either we won't be close, I guess, or we won't be in each other's lives for very long."

Too late, I realize I've indicated some closeness between us that extends beyond this trip, beyond this book. But Finn doesn't even flinch.

"I'd like to be in your life for a while," he says. "If you'll let me."

He raises an arm, glancing at me, eyes asking a silent question. When I nod, he drapes it across my shoulders. Rubs my back. I drop my chin to his shoulder, letting myself exhale into him.

It's too nice, being held like this.

I try not to think about whether that niceness has an expiration date, if we'll still talk once he goes back to Hollywood and I go back to Seattle. If the extent of our friendship at that point will be me watching him on a TV screen, him no longer answering my texts because he's surrounded by more interesting people.

"Jesus, it's almost three in the morning," I say when I catch sight of the clock on the nightstand. "We should get some sleep."

He seems a bit jarred by the way I suddenly push away, but he doesn't argue. "Just don't touch me with your weird socked feet."

Of course, I can't resist doing exactly this. "At least I'll be warm."

TWENTY

I wake to the scent of maple syrup.

"Hope you don't mind that I made you a plate," Finn says from across the room. "I was up at an ungodly hour, and the good stuff was going fast. Didn't want you to miss out."

"Oh—thank you." I drag a palm across my face, smoothing the last blurred edges of sleep. It's the first time he's seen me in the morning, and I have to fight the urge to rush to the bathroom to make myself look presentable, raking a hand through my hair and scrubbing at my teeth with an index finger.

The aforementioned plate waits on the table in front of the fireplace, and *plate* is too tame a term. *Epic brunch feast* is more like it, piled high with pancakes and waffles, potato wedges, scrambled eggs, crispy peppered bacon, and at least five kinds of cheese.

"I also wasn't sure what you might want, so I just got a bit of everything."

"It's perfect." My growling stomach answers in kind. "They really don't skimp on the 'breakfast' part of B and B, huh?"

The storm hasn't let up, and after breakfast, when we call a tow truck for the rental car, we're told they probably can't dig it out until tomorrow. I've always loved the snow and we don't get nearly enough of it in Seattle, and now that we're no longer stuck driving in it, I seize the opportunity to go for a walk. Finn has a virtual therapy appointment and some email to catch up on and promises he'll meet up with me later.

Probably for the best. It'll give me a chance to clear my head, untangle some of these feelings. Because even if Finn and I haven't been together 24/7, I haven't felt truly *alone* in a while. If we're not in the same room, then I'm usually working on his book. Whether he's next to me or not, he's always in my head.

That has to be the explanation for why I'm feeling this odd attachment to him. I simply haven't talked to another single guy in weeks.

When he doesn't join me and doesn't send any texts, I head back, picking up two mugs of hot cocoa in the lobby before going up to our room. I knock once, just to make sure he knows I'm coming in.

And nothing in the world could prepare me for what I see next.

Finn's sitting in one of the armchairs, grinning into his laptop camera and holding up a peace sign. "What up, Mason, this is Finn Walsh, and I just wanted to say that you're going to absolutely *crush* your Spanish exam next week, just like Caleb, Meg, Alice, and I crushed that horde of banshees that—"

"What are you doing?"

I've never seen a grown man look so frightened. He jumps a

literal half foot before smashing his laptop shut with more force than is necessary. "Oh god," he says, burying his head in his hands. "You weren't supposed to see that."

My eyes flick between him and the closed laptop. Trying to hold back a laugh, I ask, "Are you filming a Cameo?"

Finn nods miserably. "It's embarrassing. I don't get that many requests, but I try to do a decent job with the ones that do come in."

"I'm sure they're great."

"You're trying really hard not to laugh right now, aren't you?"

"So hard."

When he opens his laptop back up, I notice he's wearing gray sweatpants. I don't know what it is about them, but they can instantly take a guy from a six to a ten, and Finn was already far beyond a six.

"Come out in the snow with me," I say. "We can at least take some cute photos of you hauling firewood for your Instagram to fawn over."

We bundle in the warmest coats we brought, Finn's red hair spiking out from beneath a wool beanie.

"This is *real* snow." There's some amount of awe in my voice as we traipse through it. The inn is surrounded by a forest, the snow still mostly untouched by footsteps. It's too beautiful to mind the cold.

"As opposed to?"

"We don't get this in the Northwest," I explain. "One year, I went up to Whistler with an ex, and I spent all this time planning the perfect winter outfits. Then we got there and . . . nothing. It was, like, a low of fifty-two. I was devastated."

"An ex." Finn sounds intrigued. "Tell me more about Chandler Cohen's dating history."

"As you know, it's been mostly defined by all the pining." I hug my coat tighter. "I had my first boyfriend in high school—we broke up after graduation because we were going to different schools. Then in college, there was David, who I mentioned last night. A guy I dated my senior year and after graduation, but the immediate unemployment was too much of a shock for us to last," I say. "A couple others, but there hasn't really been anyone serious for a few years." Because I put my career first. Because I assumed everything would fall into place with Wyatt. "I know you dated Hallie for a while, but I don't know much about your other relationships, aside from . . . what didn't happen in the bedroom and that they've all been with Hollywood people. All actors?" Of course I'm not asking about it because I'm wondering if he'll suddenly say, *You know what? It's time for a change—I'm done with Hollywood dating. Thanks so much for bringing it up again, Chandler!*

And of course, he doesn't. "Mostly. I dated a costume designer on *Just My Type*, but we were only together for a few months. Hallie was the most serious one. And we broke up . . . six years ago? Jesus, I feel old."

"What happened?" I ask. "Why did it end?"

He rubs his chin. "I think we just grew apart, although maybe the sex was part of it. Both of us had periods where we were struggling to find work, and I was still pretty new to therapy, so it was just a lot at once."

"She's on that medical show now, though."

"*Boise Med.* She's amazing in it," he says. "I was serious; we really are still good friends. And we work much better that way. It's hard to find people who understand exactly what we went through on the show, and even if I see the others from time to time, we've never been as close."

I nod, because even if I can't relate, I understand.

"Please don't take this the wrong way, because I mean it sincerely. It's a tragedy that you're still single. Wyatt's going to realize his mistake one of these days and won't be able to forgive himself."

I can't help it—I let out a snort. "I think I'm doing okay. Lately, I've been very busy in a casual physical relationship with one of the golden boys of comic con."

He stops walking, mouth quirking upward. "Ah. Have you now?"

Blame the siren song of the gray sweatpants, but I move closer, reaching for the fringe of his scarf.

I'm certain he's going to kiss me, but instead he says, "I read your books."

I back up, this revelation a shock to my system.

"I wanted to tell you earlier," he continues, "but I thought it might be too nerve-racking if you knew I was reading them on the flight."

"You mean, you read Maddy and Amber's books."

"Sure," he says. "Their names are on the covers, I guess. Maybe it's because I was looking for you, but I could hear you, even in their voices."

I open my mouth to argue, but nothing comes out. The fact that I was that visible in those books, enough for this person who's known me for only seven weeks to see me there . . .

"Then I screwed up," I say simply.

He inches closer, not seeming to care that his sneakers are wet. "I don't see it that way at all. Maybe you were trying to hide yourself in their stories, but you were still *there*. That's how talented you are. That's how vibrant your writing is—you can't remove yourself from it completely, even if you try." I swallow hard, unsure how to process all of this. "I know it would be a risk, and I know it wouldn't be easy. But you could write for yourself if you wanted to. What you said that night I barely survived a debilitating illness"—this earns him a jab in the ribs—"about not being able to enjoy writing for a while . . . it just made me so sad. Because even in those books you were just doing for a paycheck, I could feel how much you loved it."

"You remember that?" I ask, wondering just how much he remembers. Just the heart-to-heart about my writing, or the crush confession, too.

When he blushes, it ignites something deep inside me that I've spent ages trying to ignore. "All of it."

Everything he's saying, the compliments and the subtext, it's too overwhelming. My coat is too tight and the wind is too brutal and my socks are drenched. This whole moment is a symphony of Too Much. If I allow myself to think that I could make it as a writer, by myself, then that means opening myself up to the possibility of failure. It means leaving behind the security blanket of names that mean far more than my own.

So I bend down, scoop up some snow, and hit him with a snowball, because that's easier than thinking.

He holds a hand to where his chest is flecked with white. "Oh, you're in trouble now," he says, scrambling to make one of his own while I race off into the snowy woods.

EVENTUALLY, WHEN WE CAN'T FEEL OUR FINGERS OR TOES, WE shiver our way back to the inn. Our clothes are soaked from the snowball fight, so we peel them off and lay them to dry by the fireplace while we drag pillows and blankets onto the floor next to the flames.

"Any more Cameos to shoot?" I ask, toying with the edge of a blanket.

He gives me a sly look. "Nope. I'm completely free the rest of the day." Then he lowers his voice, even though we're the only two people in the room. "I can't stop thinking about what happened in Reno. Outside the bar. It nearly killed me, how quiet you had to be."

The memory tugs a groan from my throat. I need him on top of me, his weight pressing me back into the rug. There are still two major topics we haven't broached yet on the lesson plan, and I'm certain that if I don't get his mouth between my legs tonight, I might die. I need the reminder that this is just physical.

"The next lesson," I say with a rush of breath, my mouth an inch from his. "Do you remember—"

His eyes go dark. "As though I didn't memorize the whole thing the night you sent it to me. *Yes*, I remember." He grazes my lips with his. "I thought I told you how badly I wanted to lick you."

I squeeze my eyes shut, my muscles already tightening. Waiting. *Wanting*. The last couple times we were together, I was the only one who finished. I want to hear him fall apart and know that I'm the one who unstitched him. Suddenly I'm craving it.

We kiss on top of the blanket, in front of the fireplace, and there's no going slowly this time. I slide out from under him so I can get on top, rubbing his erection with my palm, then lowering myself down his body so I can kiss him through his boxers. He fists a hand in my hair, swears under his breath. I love him like this: completely surrendered to his own pleasure. Unashamed. I haven't seen enough of it.

But when I reach for the waistband, he shakes his head. "You first," he says, and because I don't know how to argue with that, I pin my shoulder blades to the blanket.

"Tell me what you said in Reno." Because there was no romance there, only pure physical need.

He blows out a breath when he leans over me, slips his hand inside my underwear. "About how wet I wanted to make you?" An amused chuckle. "I think you're already there."

I practically tear my panties in my rush to get them down my legs. "More."

A hum against my mouth as he parts me with his fingers. "I want you to be loud," he says, timing his words with his strokes. He draws a circle. A square. A shape that mathematicians haven't discovered yet. "I want to feel your body tremble, until you just can't keep it in any longer, and then I want you to come on my tongue."

I'm gasping now, clutching his shoulders. His finger isn't enough. I need more.

He lowers his head to my chest, dropping kisses to my abdomen, my thighs. My lips. Then, when I'm squirming and shaking and more than ready for him, he gives me a long, slow lick. I let out a moan at the contact, the hot, slick feel of his mouth on me.

"God, you taste so good." He keeps teasing, alternating quick strokes with longer, torturous ones. Only when I'm aching for it does he finally take his tongue to my clit, quickly learning that the softest little flicks are enough to drive me wild.

"Finn," I murmur as he falls into a steady rhythm. "*Finn.*"

He pauses for a moment. Glances up at me.

"What?" I ask.

"I think that's the first time you've said my name. When we're like this."

He's right—I've avoided it. Now I say it again, which makes him sigh and press his mouth against me harder.

For a moment, I can almost forget that he's Finnegan Walsh and I'm the nameless person writing his book. For a moment, we are just two people with a desperate attraction warming up on a snowy day.

Except, of course, this isn't real. He's not doing any of these things because he's madly in love with me—he's trying to learn.

So he can eventually please someone who isn't me.

I still my hand in his hair. "Hold on." Immediately he stops, glancing up at me. "Sorry, I—I have to pee."

I haul myself off the floor, untangling myself from the blankets, slipping on a T-shirt—I don't stop to check whether it's his or mine—on my way to the bathroom.

Of course it's his. Of course it fits the way a boyfriend's shirt should fit, baggy and sexy and perfect.

Get a grip, I tell my reflection once I've locked myself inside. My face is flushed, hair wild. *You are not having feelings for him.*

Two months, and it already feels like I'm deeper than I ever was with Wyatt. It doesn't make sense. My feelings for Wyatt grew over the course of ten years of friendship, classes and parties and late nights talking about our futures. I tended to that crush like a fussy succulent, giving it all the sunshine it needed to become a full-on invasive species.

With Finn, the way I feel is a fierce and foreign thing.

And that's fucking terrifying.

I force myself to think about when he was sick and burrowed in his sheets with a pyramid of Kleenex. Nothing about that should be appealing—and yet.

Probably very soon, he's going to be amazing in bed. With the next woman, and the one after that.

You don't have to do this alone, sweetheart.

Yes, I think. Yes, I do.

One last look at my face in the mirror, blotting away any evidence that I was having a crisis, and then I can leave.

Finn's sitting in one of the armchairs, shirt buttons undone, hair unkempt. When he sees me, his expression instantly changes.

"Hey," he says, nudging my arm. "You okay?"

I nod, unsure why it suddenly feels like I'm about to cry.

"Is it anything you want to talk about?"

"My mind is just elsewhere, I guess. I'm sorry."

"You don't have anything to apologize for." The concern on his face is almost too much, given what his mouth was doing to me ten minutes ago. "Our relationship is more than these lessons. I thought that should have been obvious by now."

I want to believe you, I think. Except once this tour is over, once I go back to Seattle and finish up the book, what relationship is left?

I tell him I'm going to sleep early. That way, I don't have to slide beneath the covers next to him, see his hair feathered across the pillow, hear his soothing, steady breaths as we drift off.

Because then I'd have to think about how desperately I want to wake up in the same bed for real.

ENTERTAINMENT WEEKLY COVER SHOOT

BEHIND-THE-SCENES VIDEO

FINN WALSH: Are they supposed to be—is it okay if they're—

OFF-CAMERA: Yeah, yeah, just let them run around. We'll be shooting the whole time.

FINN WALSH, TO PUPPIES: Hiiiiii. You're perfect, aren't you? Yes you are. Oh! And you're perfect, too.

OFF-CAMERA: If you could pick up one of the puppies and smile for us—great. That's great. Keep doing what you're doing.

FINN WALSH: Hello. Hello. I love you. Ahhhh, you're chewing on my shoes, but that's okay. You can chew on anything you want. Because I love you.

OFF-CAMERA: Does anyone have a poop bag?

FINN WALSH: Look how little you are. How did you get to be so little?

Finn tries to hold as many puppies in his arms as possible.

FINN WALSH: Can I take all of them home with me?

TWENTY-ONE

NEW YORK CITY

By the time we get to Big Apple Con in mid-November, the week after we're stranded in Ohio, the *Nocturnals* reunion hype is impossible to miss. Nearly every day, Finn's doing an interview, talking to a producer, or posting promo material on social media. THE NOCTURNALS: THE REUNION, screams a massive billboard in the middle of Times Square, with an old cast photo morphing into one they shot when Finn was in LA last month. He was stopped by no fewer than a half dozen people on our way to the Javits Center, posing good-naturedly for pictures, swearing he can't tell them any secrets about the reunion and that they'll just have to watch for themselves. Then he slipped into incognito mode and donned a pair of sunglasses.

Rehearsals start next week in LA, coinciding with Thanksgiving, giving me a chance to fly home to see my family before heading back to LA in early December. Reunion, finishing Finn's book, and returning to normal life. That's what the next couple months will look like, and yet despite missing my family—Noemie sent a photo of her cooking dinner with my parents last night—I can't bring myself to accept that this trip is coming to an end quite yet. That I'm not scheduled at any more cons after this one.

One great thing about New York is that it's so instantly overwhelming, so cramped and crowded that it's easy to disappear. I went here once for a journalism conference in college, but I must have barely skimmed the surface of the city because everything seems brand-new. New York means I don't have to think about Ohio. It means I can put some distance between Finn and me to keep my heart on track.

It also means, though, that I'm not ready to tell him what I did on the plane. When we were finally able to get back to Columbus and on a flight to Pittsburgh, just in time for Finn to make his last panel of the con, I did something I haven't done since before I left Seattle: I opened up my old cozy mystery manuscript. Just for a few minutes. Just to read through some of the setting details, since now I'd been to Florida—for a reason I can no longer remember, I'd decided it would take place at a tiny fictional beach town on the southern tip of the state—and could make it seem a bit more authentic.

In the book, a customer drops dead on the opening day of my main character's stationery store—coincidentally named The Poisoned Pen, a choice she regrets when she's implicated in the crime. But something about it still didn't feel quite right, and those setting details didn't seem to fix it.

So I switched over to the memoir and started work on a chapter about Finn's search for a therapist and how he loves therapy more than he ever thought possible.

Big Apple Con is also when I meet Hallie Hendricks for the first time. I've been worried it might be awkward, in part because

I've spent most of my free time watching her decade-ago self fall in love with Oliver Huxley, and because I'm sleeping with her ex—though of course, she doesn't know that—but she shines a genuine smile on me after Finn introduces us in one of the con's green rooms.

"It's so fantastic to finally meet you!" she says, holding her hand out to shake and then withdrawing it, pulling me in for a hug instead. "Finn's told me so much about you."

"He . . . has?" I glance over at him. Finn gives me a sheepish shrug.

"Only good things. I cannot *wait* to read the book."

Hallie's even more captivating in person, having traded her long Meg Lawson hair for a choppy bob that perfectly frames her face. She wears thin-rimmed oval glasses over striking blue eyes, and a patterned jumpsuit and satin Chanel bag. That *Boise Med* money must be pretty great, because everything about her gleams, from her hair to the buckles on her heeled booties.

"I'm sure you've heard this a thousand times," I tell her, "but I've been watching *The Nocturnals* for—well, for the first time, and I really love it. You're actually my favorite character."

I'm certain Hallie will wave this off, a compliment on something she did ten years ago. "Thank you. Meg's always been my favorite, too. No matter how many scripts I read, I can never fully get her out of my head."

"I can imagine," I say, liking her instantly. "It's like how they say the music we listen to when we're teens continues to resonate with us the most, even as adults, because we heard it when our brains were still developing, or whatever."

"Ah, is that why I still get emotional over Avril Lavigne?"

I grin back at her. "No judgment."

Finn seems pleased that we're getting along. I can't help imagining the two of them together, the relationship that ended six years ago.

Six years, and nothing serious since.

I thought the panels might feel repetitive, but Finn is completely in his element here with the rest of the cast, and it's impossible not to admire the way he interacts with the fans, all of them sharing this pure love for a show I'm starting to fall for, too. I can understand now why he hasn't given all of this up, why his first instinct was to soldier through it even when he was sick. Each fan, he treats like they're the first person asking that question or paying him that compliment. He makes each person feel special, and it's an incredible talent. He makes you believe he cares about each of them—because I truly think he does.

Somewhere between Tennessee and Ohio, I started seeing the appeal of Finnegan Walsh, too.

━━ ━━ ━━

AFTER A JOINT PHOTO OP WITH HALLIE AND BEFORE WE MEET UP with the rest of the cast for dinner, Finn takes a detour through some back streets.

"Where are we going?"

"You'll see," he calls back, leading me through a maze of shops and hole-in-the-wall restaurants. When he finally stops in front of a luggage store, I give him a quizzical look.

"I've asked around," he says, "and it turns out, it's customary to get your ghostwriter a gift when you finish working together. In fact, it's pretty nonnegotiable. Written into our contract in tiny print."

I lift my eyebrows at him, biting back a smile.

"I know we're not done yet, and I would have loved to surprise you, but I think it's really important you pick this out for yourself." He opens the door, gestures to all the stacks and stacks of bags and suitcases inside. "You've already traveled more over the past couple months than you ever thought you would. So . . . pick a suitcase. Consider it an investment in your future, and all the traveling you haven't done yet."

For a few moments, I just stare at him helplessly, unable to comprehend the generosity of such a gesture. "I couldn't. It's too expensive."

"I told you, it's in the contract. Paragraph 12, clause B, subsection 7C. That's why you always read the fine print." He bumps my hip with his. "I have a feeling you don't want to keep borrowing your parents' luggage for the rest of your life."

He's not wrong. My mom's suitcase, with its glue residue and battered stickers that now halfheartedly declare AY GROO, isn't lasting much longer. And some of these are really quite lovely. I'm already gravitating toward a sleek mauve.

"Then I think I'm out of excuses."

THE RESTAURANT IS TRENDY, DIMLY LIT, AND ENTIRELY OUT OF MY price range. Upscale tapas, the kind of place where you pay $18 per plate to share five roasted balsamic-glazed carrots and a few spears of artisan bread and leave hungry. And maybe they're the best carrots you've ever tasted in your life, but you refuse on principle to spend that much.

When we dropped the suitcase off at the hotel, I told Finn that maybe I should skip the dinner—I remembered what Ethan said a while back about not trusting the press. "If it's just cast," I said,

"I should probably stay behind." Finn just looked at me in this way I couldn't interpret. "I want you there." Then he straightened his spine, collected himself. "If you want to be there, that is."

After dodging some paparazzi hoping to catch a glimpse of post-con celebrities, we settle into a booth with Hallie, Ethan Underwood, Bree Espinoza, Juliana Guo, and Cooper Jones. I'm a little starstruck after watching *The Nocturnals* in most of my spare time over the past couple months. Finn introduces me as someone on his team, and no one asks any other questions about it.

"It's been ages since we did something like this," Cooper says, reaching for a slice of bread. At forty, he's the oldest of the group, mostly retired from acting to focus on the farm he runs with his wife in Northern California. A much quieter life.

"Because Ethan's usually too busy jumping out of an airplane just so he can say he does his own stunts." Juliana gives him a tight smile that makes me think pretending she was in love with him for four seasons required some top-notch acting. She's a little sharp-tongued, not unlike Alice, and dressed in corduroy overalls and a floral sweatshirt. Overalls have never looked cooler. "Where were you last month? I can't keep track."

"Fiji," Ethan says. "But that was just for vacation. I start shooting the *Indiana Jones* reboot in Majorca after the reunion."

"Rough life," Finn says.

Ethan raises his glass of bourbon, flashes his glimmering white teeth. "That's why they shell out the big bucks."

I have to fight rolling my eyes. Next to me, Finn is inspecting his water glass, and when the server swings by with another tray of appetizers, he quietly, politely asks for a new one. And I don't miss the way Ethan watches the whole interaction.

"What do you hate more?" Bree's asking. " 'This is more of a comment than a question,' or 'I have a two-part question'?"

Cooper runs a hand across his salt-and-pepper beard. "I don't think I do enough of these to get too bothered by any of it."

"More of a comment, definitely." Juliana takes a sip of wine and blots her red lipstick with a napkin. "That one, they always want to bring up some super specific detail, just to make it seem like they know the show better than anyone else."

Ethan shakes his head. "No, no, no. The two-parters are the worst."

"I don't mind them," Finn puts in.

"Well of course *you* don't," Ethan says. "You practically live at these things. When was the last time you were on a channel that isn't exclusively watched by grandparents?"

With the exception of Hallie, the rest of them laugh, and even in the dim light, I watch Finn's cheeks turn pink.

The conversation moves on to everyone's current projects. "I'm working on an indie film right now," Hallie says from across the table. "I've been dying to do something with A24, and it's been an absolute dream."

"What's it about?" I ask.

"It's about . . . well, there's this woman, and she feels sort of directionless in her job and her love life." Hallie frowns for a moment. "I guess there isn't really that much emphasis on the plot. It's mostly just vibes."

Bree laughs. "Oh my god, Hallie *hates* plot."

"It's true. Give me interesting characters over explosions any day of the week," she says. "*Boise Med* is a great paycheck, but it's not high art, by any means."

Finn gives me an apologetic look, I'm guessing for all the industry talk. And then beneath the table, his hand lands on my leg.

Everything in me tightens up.

I expect him to move it after a few seconds, for it to be a gentle pat, a *hi, I see you* kind of gesture. But he doesn't. And I find myself inching my leg toward him, just as his thumb starts stroking a slow circle on top of the corduroy fabric.

"Have you tried the carrots?" Hallie asks, passing me the plate. I decide not to tell her I've calculated the price per carrot and that it's exorbitant. Instead, I smile and take one, and it does, in fact, turn out to be the most delicious thing I've ever tasted.

After another round of drinks, Ethan snaps a finger, points it at me. "I just realized where I've seen you before. One of the cons."

"Twin Cities," I put in. "Supercon."

"Right, right," he says, eyeing me quizzically. "What do you do for Finn, exactly?"

"I'm working on a memoir," Finn says. "Chandler's ghostwriting it."

At that, Ethan bursts out laughing, silencing every side conversation at the table. "You have a ghostwriter? What, you can't find time to write your own book with your busy schedule?"

And now everyone's listening to us.

"You're working with a ghostwriter?" Cooper asks. "On . . . a book?"

"Plenty of people use ghostwriters," I say. "There's no shame in it."

"Oh, I completely agree with you," Ethan says, nodding in this horribly condescending way. "I'm just wondering what it is you've done that's worth putting in a book. All the character research you did for *The Nocturnals*? Scintillating."

The whole table seems to grow uncomfortable, most people staring down at their food or taking sips of their drinks. Ethan's full-on season one Caleb right now. On my leg, Finn's grip tightens, not to a painful degree, but enough for me to notice.

Hallie throws him a glare. "Don't be a dick, Ethan. When was the last time you did research for any of your big-car-go-boom movies?"

"For the last one that was number one at the box office opening weekend? Or hmm, let's see, the one before that—you know, I think that was number one, too." Ethan gestures for a server to refill his glass.

"It's not all about money," I say, with more sharpness than I intend.

"No, I guess it isn't." Ethan's eyes flick back to Finn. "I suppose some of us do it just for the love of acting, right? Guess you'd have to."

Bree coughs loudly into her elbow. "So, uh, anyone have any plans for Thanksgiving?"

It doesn't escape my notice that Finn is quiet the rest of dinner.

"We should really do this more often," Juliana says at the end, as sleeves are shoved back into coats and scarves are wrapped around necks. "I can't believe it's been so long."

Finn digs his hands into his pockets. "Definitely," he says. "See you all in December."

chapter

TWENTY-TWO

NEW YORK CITY

Finn remains quiet on the subway back to the hotel, and the trio of twentysomething girls who recognize him must be able to tell that he's deep in his head because all they do is whisper and point at him in the most subtle way they can. He's too busy staring down at his shoelaces to notice.

When we get up to our floor after he shrugs off my suggestion for late-night drinks or dessert, I follow him to his room. Without questioning it, he lets us both inside, and there's something so natural about the gesture, it freezes me in place. For a split second, I get a glimpse of a different kind of life. An alternate universe.

We're a couple returning home from dinner, and something's happened to upset my boyfriend. All I want is to pour a couple glasses of wine and cozy up on a couch together, let him tell me what's wrong so we can work through it together. We'd stay up late talking, and he'd surprise himself by laughing, and we'd realize we could figure it out. We might turn on Netflix or we might drink more wine or we might sleepily unbutton our clothes and let our bodies snap together. Or we might doze off right there on the couch, my legs in his lap, his head on top of mine.

The vision startles me, if only because it seems so *real*.

That alternate universe doesn't care about logic. Even if Finn felt the same way, he's said it himself more than once: he's only dated within Hollywood. There's an intrinsic incompatibility in our lives. He lives on the road; I live at Noemie's. We're at vastly different income levels. I have no idea what I'll be doing a few months from now, while he'll be starting to promote his book and his nonprofit.

The guy I'd been friends with for years only wanted to sleep with me and move on. Finn's known me just a couple months—I have no idea whether that's long enough to deem someone worthy of a relationship, or how I can hope to get there with anyone else. Wyatt screwed with all my timelines, snipped the edges of my confidence.

While I'd love to think Finn and I will remain friends after this, I can't imagine him calling me up just to talk. Grabbing a bite to eat the next time he's in Seattle. I know there's more to us than the book and the lessons, but without those things to anchor our relationship, I can't accept that cozying-on-a-couch visual as anything but what it is: a fantasy.

I shut the door to his room, shoving it all out of my mind.

He kicks off one shoe halfheartedly before sitting down on the bed, balancing his elbows on his knees. When he finally glances up at me, his eyes heavy, I'm not at all expecting what he says.

"I'm sorry."

I unbutton my jacket, take a seat next to him. "You don't have anything to be sorry for."

He runs a hand down his face, and maybe it's the shitty hotel room lighting, but those early signs of age are more apparent than they usually are. The creases around his mouth, between his brows. On his forehead, when his hair is less artistically styled. I have to fight the urge to trace them, because if I started, I have a feeling I wouldn't be able to stop. I'd need to run my fingertips across every mark and line and freckle on his body, and even then, I wouldn't be satisfied.

"For being a mopey sack of shit for the past hour? Yeah, I do. And for that dinner . . . not being what either of us expected," he says. "Embarrassing, for you to find out that I'm hardly accomplished enough to be publishing a memoir."

"Well that's just false." I tap his knee with mine. "And Ethan's a scumbag."

"I hate that I've never been able to stand up to him. Thank you—for what you said. Really."

"I wasn't saying anything that isn't true."

"Still. That meant a lot to me." More warmth creeps into his voice. "They're not all bad. Some of them are good people. Good friends."

"Good friends who didn't stick up for you."

The weight of his pause lets me know exactly how much it hurt. "It's hard, in this industry. We're pitted against each other from the very beginning—the whole audition process is a competition. Everyone always wants something they don't have, and when they get it, they're happy with it for maybe a second before setting their sights on something else. Something loftier. Sometimes Hollywood friends feel . . . there's a lack of permanence there. You never know what they really think about you. Or maybe you wrap and never see each other again."

That seems to be the truth about Hollywood in general, that lack of permanence. So many people are clinging to relevance, unsure when their fans will move on. The cons seem to safeguard the things we love, preserve them in amber so that we can always find those who share that love.

"You'd be honest with me if you thought I was a complete loser," he says. "If I was a talentless idiot who's just kidding himself that he has any kind of future in this industry."

I've never seen him like this. Over the past couple months, he's given me access to the version of himself that no one else sees, and it suddenly feels like such a privilege, I'm not sure how to handle it. His vulnerability cracks my heart wide open and lays it at his feet, bright and still beating. It makes me do things I might not otherwise do.

"Finn." I reach for his hands, and I'm relieved when he lets me take them, when he doesn't bat an eye at my abstract mess of nail polish. I think back to his hand beneath the table, rubbing circles along my thigh. There was a sensuality to that gesture, maybe, but more than that, touching him makes me feel calm. I can't help wondering whether he feels it, too. "I'm on the season two finale, and if Hux and Meg don't kiss soon, I *will* lose my mind. And I've watched your other movies, too, the more recent ones." It's true, even the Christmas movies. I hope he knows this is genuine, not an ego stroke. "I know they didn't make the same kind of impact as *The Nocturnals*, but you're *fantastic* in them. All of them. And it's not just your performances. You're a decent person, and you truly care about your work. It's impossible not to admire."

Finn looks deeply struck by this, blinking a few times before he gets his bearings. "How do you always manage to make me feel like every insignificant thing about me matters?"

"Because that's my job." *It all matters. So much.* "That's why you hired me, isn't it?"

He shakes his head. "Part of it, maybe. But it's more than that."

"You do the same." My voice is quiet but steady. The fear is still there, but it's smaller than it's been in a while. "I haven't taken my own writing seriously in a long time. But . . . I opened it up on the plane yesterday and fiddled around a little. I'm still not sure what I did was the right direction for it, and it wasn't a ton, but it was *something*."

"I can't wait to read it."

"Let's not get ahead of ourselves."

He turns toward the desk, picking up a paper bag. "I have something to show you. To give you, actually," he says. "Please don't refuse it because of the suitcase. Because I found these in Artist Alley today and couldn't resist."

Giving him a lift of my eyebrows, I open up the bag, my heart leaping into my throat. "You got me socks?"

"Your feet are always cold, and you said you never have enough. And they reminded me of you." He brushes this off, as though socks are a perfectly normal present for someone you're educationally sleeping with. A three-pack of adorable, detective-themed socks: one patterned with tiny daggers, another with magnifying glasses, the third with a skull and crossbones.

And then I do something else I'm not expecting until that moment: I lean forward and kiss him. Not because I think we can make a lesson out of it—because I want to. He seems shocked at first, even though we've done this too many times to count, but a split second later, he kisses me back, hands tangling in my hair as I drop the socks to the bed.

It's gentle for maybe half a minute. Then it turns desperate, hungry. I pour everything about tonight into that kiss, everything I've held back over the past few days or weeks or since we started this trip. I let it all out, and he gives it right back. I clutch him close, hands beneath his shirt, thumb grazing that mole on his back. Every detail about him has become impossibly lovely to me, and there are too many I haven't memorized yet.

I'll be flying home to Seattle tomorrow, but tonight, I'm not holding back. No hiding in the bathroom if I can't control my emotions.

This is what our "few pointers" have become: a blazing, painful desire for the one person I can't have. We built two separate sides of a relationship and drew a line between them, and I thought we used permanent ink. Now that line is blurred, thinner than it's ever been. I want this, *him*, and right now that's the only thing that matters. Maybe my heart will suffer for it later, but that's a risk I'm going to have to take.

If this is the only way someone can want me, so be it.

He's folded me into his lap, a hand splayed on my lower back while the other cradles my jaw. "So gorgeous," he says, and it's criminal, how just those few words can drag out a moan. His voice turns low. Rough. "Do you know what I'm thinking?" he asks, and I shake my head. "I'm thinking about how pink your pretty pussy is right now." A knuckle comes up to my face, tracing my blush. "Pinker than your cheeks?"

"You've gotten good at this."

This earns me a disarmingly sexy smirk. "If I fucked you with my hand," he continues, "I wonder how wet you'd be. Would my finger just . . . slide right in?" He lifts a hand, his middle finger turning a slow, lazy circle in the air. "Yeah," he says. "Yeah, I think so. Hot and slick and fucking perfect."

A whimper escapes me.

"You like that?"

I nod.

"Should I keep going?"

No.

"Yes."

He leans closer, mouth up against my neck. "I'd go so slow, because I want to savor you. I'd keep teasing you, exactly the way you like. I might want to spread you wide and rub your clit right away, but I'd make myself wait for it. I'd make *you* wait for it."

I clutch at him, trying to drag his mouth back to mine.

But then he pauses. Pulls away, arching an eyebrow. "You gotta give me something," he says. "I kind of feel like I'm doing the heavy lifting here."

Somehow, I manage to come up with the words. "I—I always get so wet for you," I say, and that makes him hold me tighter. "Not just when we're like this. I could be sitting next to you at a con and thinking about what we did the previous night. Or what I'd want to do the next night. I'll get so turned on I can barely stand it, but I can't do anything about it."

His head rolls back, and he lets out this fantastic groan. "That's not just part of all this? You're serious?"

"Yes," I exhale, wondering if I'm signing my own death warrant. If so, it'll be a wonderful death. "Sometimes I'd have to get myself off before we met up to work, too, just to clear my head."

"What would you think about?"

"The way your breath hitches when you touch me for the first time." This is it. No inhibitions. "You, talking to me exactly like this. Whether you'd want me to ride you, or if you'd want to fuck me from behind, or against a wall."

His eyes flutter shut, a low hum slipping from his mouth. "All of it." A fingertip glides up my spine. "I can't tell you how many times I've done the same. Imagined your hand or your mouth instead of my fist." My own hand drifts down to the front of his jeans. It's been too long since I watched him come apart. I want to see him needy, desperate. Begging. "We'd be together one night, and the next day, all I'd want was to touch you again. I felt so fucking depraved—like I'd never be able to get enough of you."

It sounds so real that I need to hear him say it again. "Really?"

He gives me this furrow of his brows. "You don't think you're irresistible?" he says. "I've always been attracted to you. Since we first met at that bookstore bar. When you were a petty thief."

I swat at his chest with my free hand. "I'll have you know that I returned the book and felt so bad about it, I bought two more."

He grabs my hand, bringing it to his mouth. Presses kisses to my knuckles. "A real stand-up person. A Good Samaritan." A little growl. "How does every part of you taste so good," he says. "No one's hands should taste this good."

He maneuvers me flat onto the bed, taking his time as he kisses down my body. Helping me out of my bra, sucking one nipple into his mouth while he thumbs the other, making me arch up off the bed. He doesn't let up, tongue dipping into my navel and then dropping kisses along my waist, before he skips my hips entirely and lowers his mouth to my knees. Calves. He lifts one foot into the air, planting a kiss on my ankle, before placing it down on the bed and repeating it with the other.

When he brings himself over my body again, there's a dark, greedy hunger in his eyes. "Here," he says. "Here is where you taste the best. So *sweet*." He kisses me through my panties, a deep inhale and a slow flick of his tongue. The sound he makes when he does this is absolutely unreal. I tilt my hips, urging him closer. "I want to bury my tongue inside you the rest of the night. But not just inside. Your clit, too. Because I now know where it is."

I choke on a laugh, even as the pleasure settles low at the base of my spine. "Please." It's the only word I'm capable of when his gorgeous dirty mouth is this close to where I need him. "*Please.*"

I don't have to keep begging. In an instant, my panties are off and he's lifting me to his face, until I'm spread against his mouth. I arch my back, grip the headboard to steady myself.

I feel everything—the swirls of his tongue, the rhythm of his breaths. Even a smile. My thighs tighten around his head as I ride him, rubbing myself against his mouth while he gives me both soft, quick strokes and broader ones that make me grasp at the silken strands of his hair, my other hand tightening on the headboard. I no longer feel in control, like I did during our earlier lessons, when I told him what to do. Now he knows what I want, and he knows how to give it to me.

He hooks his arms around my thighs, stretching me wider.

"*Finn,*" I manage, remembering how much he liked it when I said his name.

He moves his tongue faster, grazing the spot I want him most until I think I might scream if he doesn't lick me there. And then he does—a sweep of his tongue before he sucks on my clit for just a moment.

"Oh my god. Do that again."

I can feel him laugh as he obeys, sucking me longer this time before letting go. My thighs start shaking, and he keeps up a relentless rhythm, licking and sucking and anchoring me to his face with his hands squeezing my ass, until I throw an arm over my eyes, my body finally clenching tight—and then let it all go.

I incinerate.

We both go quiet afterward, breathing in sync as the ceiling above continues to spin.

I settle back onto the bed and he tucks me against him, finger-tips sliding into my hair. "I love your hair."

"Yeah?" We've never done this, been so generous with compliments.

He nods. "One, it's adorable," he says, and despite what just happened with his mouth between my legs, I feel my face grow warm. "And two . . ." The rest of the sentence fades out as he seems to weigh what he wants to say next. "I get to see your whole face. And whatever you're feeling—well, you're not the best at hiding it. It's right there." He tilts my face toward him, tapping my nose ring for a moment before drawing a fingertip along my eyebrows, resting right in the middle. "When you're angry, you get this little furrow right here. When you're horny, you blush . . . here." That finger lands on my collarbone. Dips lower. "And here. And here."

I swipe his hand away, and while he's laughing, I couldn't be further from it. Everything he's saying makes my heart twist in the way I've tried to avoid since the night we met.

That feeling I've been running from, finally catching up with me.

And yet: "What about when I'm happy?" I can't help asking.

An easy smile. "That's the best one. One of your eyes gets squinty. Just one."

"Sounds charming."

"It is," he insists, moving forward to drop a kiss onto each eyelid as I let out a yelp.

It's probably a good thing that I'm leaving tomorrow and won't see him for a few days. In Ohio, I wanted to send him away to protect my heart, but maybe the fact of it is that my body is stronger than my mind.

Right now, he is mine, and I'm going to show him just how proud I am of his progress.

I beckon him closer. I want to tell him everything I like about his face, too, his freckles and the angle of his cheekbones and most of all, the lovely warmth in his eyes when we're talking like this. How the shade of his hair has quickly become my favorite color.

"Come here" is what comes out instead.

"Insatiable," he says, and it's true, because I'm already greedy for another orgasm: *his*.

"Do you have the condoms?" I ask.

"You think I'm ready for that?"

"As long as you don't use your teeth to open it."

He lifts his eyebrows at me. A challenge. "Look, I'm sure with a little practice, I could get it right." He moves off the bed, returning with the condoms and lube we bought in Memphis. I take one from him, moving down his body, wrapping a hand around his hard length. He doesn't need it—he's been ready since we shed our clothes—but I give him a few strokes anyway. I've missed what this does to him. The way his eyes roll shut, a fist clutching my shoulder. A little lube, and the condom slides on easily. "That said . . . *god*, Chandler. I love the way you do it."

The way he says my name echoes somewhere in the vicinity of my heart.

"Now I just have to hope I don't get stage fright," he says with a self-deprecating laugh.

I straddle him, knees pressed into the mattress. "You know what to do."

We both do.

And then in one swift motion, I lower my hips, savoring the feeling of him filling me. Slowly, slowly, inch by incredible inch, as he holds me against him with a hand on my waist. I have to catch my breath the moment he settles inside me.

"Okay?" he asks when I let out a sharp gasp. His hands come up to grasp my hips, but he doesn't start moving just yet.

I nod, biting down hard on my lower lip. "I just—really like the way you feel."

As though encouraged by my words, he thrusts upward in slow, delicious strokes. I lift my hips to match his rhythm before picking up speed, urging him to go a little faster. My eyes flutter shut, the sensation already verging on too much. Too good. I've wanted him like this for weeks, and it's somehow even better than I imagined—the way his fingers dig into my ass, his cock pulsing inside me. The rough, desperate sounds that fall from his mouth.

"*Christ.*" A shaky exhale as he throws his head backward. "I didn't appreciate this nearly enough our first time."

Soon we're both panting, and I'm certain neither of us will last long, especially when his thumb lands where our bodies are joined. Everything in me tightens as he strokes, rubs, then licks his own fingers before sliding them back to my clit. *Jesus.* Now that he knows what I like, he's almost too powerful. With a gnash of my teeth, I ride him harder, his other hand anchoring me at the waist.

"You always turn your face away when you come," he says. "Can I watch you?"

"Oh—I do?" As soon as I say it, I realize he's right. That maybe, after all my bravado, there are still some things I've held close.

"I want to see everything," he says, his fingers circling and circling.

So I let him, because I think I've started learning from these lessons, too. I don't hold anything back, my moans and the way my body shakes, and when it's enough to send him over the edge, too, I wrap my arms around his neck to bring us closer.

It's not like our first time. It's not like anything I've had before, and whether that's because we've both spent weeks aching for it or something else entirely, I'm not sure I want to know.

It's just practice, I tell myself when we wake up in the middle of the night and reach for each other again. *Casual*, I remind myself when he whispers honeyed words into my skin. *No emotions*, I think as his fingers curl between my legs and I cry out against his throat, repeating his name like it's something sacred.

I am a huge fucking liar.

MS. MISTLETOE

EXT. CHRISTMAS TREE FARM—NIGHT

Ms. Mistletoe pageant has just ended. DYLAN emerges through a patch of trees and finds HOLLY, sitting alone on a tree stump.

> DYLAN
> Holly? I was hoping I'd find you here.

> HOLLY
> *Quickly wiping the tears from her eyes.*
>
> Oh—hi. Don't mind me. I'm just feeling sorry for myself.

She lets out a hollow laugh.

> It was silly, thinking I had a chance at winning Ms. Mistletoe, but my mom won, and my grandma . . . and I guess I just wanted to make them proud. But it's obvious I haven't been feeling the Christmas cheer as much as I usually do.

> DYLAN
> Well, that's just not true.

He inches closer to her on the tree stump.

You *always* cheer me up. No one makes
me laugh as much as you do. Every
time you come into my hot cocoa shop,
you put a smile on my face. And my
son loves you to pieces.

                    HOLLY
He does, doesn't he?

                    DYLAN
He said you're much better at bedtime
stories than I am, and I wasn't even
offended. Maybe you're not feeling the
Christmas cheer . . . but *I* do. For
you.

chapter
TWENTY-THREE

SEATTLE, WA

My cousin stares at me, eyes narrowed. "Something's different about you," she accuses me.

"I own a suitcase now? Maybe that's it."

Noemie shakes her head. "No, no. It's not that. Although that *is* a lovely suitcase."

I continue unpacking, Noemie leaning against the doorframe of my room. Returning to Seattle after two months away is a bit surreal. Everything is familiar, of course, but the house has a new scent to it, and I'm not sure whether it's been there the whole time and I just got used to it or Noemie switched fragrances or cleaning products.

Fortunately, I manage to avoid interrogation the rest of the day, and early the next morning, we have to start prepping for Thanksgiving dinner at my parents' place in North Seattle. Even though we grew up on the same street—though Noemie's moms bought a condo in Bellevue a few years ago—our parents always prioritized family time during this holiday, a tradition that's carried into our adulthood. Plus, Noemie's mom Sarah, my dad's sister, makes the most heavenly mashed potatoes known to humankind.

While Noemie and I work on the homemade cranberry sauce in my parents' kitchen, feigning innocence when my mom asks how much we've tasted, I do my best to put Finn out of my mind. What happened the night before I left wasn't like any of our past lessons, and I will not allow myself to wonder whether he felt it, too.

I will not wonder what he's doing right now. I will definitely not watch the puppy video.

Unfortunately, my parents and aunts are eager to hear about what Oliver Huxley is like in real life, even though I've kept them updated throughout the trip.

"Were there paparazzi following you around?" my dad asks when we sit down to dinner, and I have to shatter his illusions and tell him no, there were not.

"Did you meet other famous people?" Aunt Vivi wants to know as she spoons gravy onto her plate.

Aunt Sarah rolls her eyes. "What she's really asking is if you met Dakota Johnson."

"What? She's a really talented actor!"

Everyone around the table laughs at this, fully aware of Aunt Vivi's long-standing crush.

I tell them about the rest of the *Nocturnals* cast, the other actors I saw in passing at the cons. But I hate that my voice sounds strained, my smiles forced. Because the whole time, my idiot brain can't help imagining Finn here with us, charming my parents and making everyone fall a little bit in love with him.

When it's time to clear the table, I rush to intercept my dad before he picks up the heavy serving dish with the leftover stuffing.

"I'll get that," I tell him, and he levels me with a stern look.

"I can manage, Chandler." There's a slight thread of annoyance in his voice, enough to make me defensive.

"Okay, okay." I hold up my arms, placing the dish back on the table. "Sorry."

* * *

AFTER DINNER, I RETREAT INTO MY CHILDHOOD BEDROOM. I HAVEN'T lived in this house for over a decade, and yet this space still feels like a perfectly preserved museum of my adolescence. The mysteries stuffed onto the bookshelf, the Agatha Christie collection I hunted down at every Half Price Books location in Seattle. The Bed Bath & Beyond comforter set with an ice cream stain on one corner. The walls, collaged with photos of Noemie and me in our backyards, at the mall, leaning against bus stop shelters and trying to look cool.

When I imagined coming back home as an adult, I thought it would feel different. I'm almost ashamed to admit that I thought I'd have a book of my own to add to this shelf, one I'd display face-out and make my parents do the same in our living room.

My phone buzzes in the pocket of my jeans. Two texts, one right after the other.

Reno misses you.

So do the dogs.

This is accompanied by a photo of Finn's mom's Chihuahuas, two of them lounging on the couch together and three eagerly waiting for table scraps.

> Those chihuahuas are angels on earth, but
> I fully believe they'd eat one of their own
> if it meant ensuring their survival.

Probably, Finn writes back. **How's your Thanksgiving?**

The way my body relaxes, hearing from him like this—it's the loveliest relief. I slide backward onto my bed, settling against the daisy-patterned pillows. Like I'm in high school and texting a boy I have a crush on.

> **Good. My aunts are disappointed**
> **I didn't meet anyone famous.**

Don't they know you've met ME????

I can't help it—I laugh out loud.

How's your tofurkey? I ask, rightfully assuming that's what Finn's eating tonight. He sends back a photo of his mom's dining table: stuffing dotted with cranberries, glazed vegetables, flour-dusted rolls, and what looks like a lentil loaf drizzled with mushroom gravy.

> **Too many leftovers, though. I'm a little**
> **heartbroken I won't be able to finish it**
> **all before I have to go back to LA.**

And there I go, overanalyzing again. Does his talking about too many leftovers mean he wishes I were there to help reduce the amount? Or is he simply telling me they made too much food?

When Noemie knocks on the door, I realize that as much as I've tried to push it away, I think I need to talk it out with my best friend.

"I have a minor problem," I say, and when I attempt to laugh it off, it comes out strangled, high-pitched. "It's about Finn, and my sudden inability to stop thinking about him. And how we slept together before I left and it felt different from all the other times and I think I'm truly, deeply fucked."

I let this all out in one breath, chest heaving when I finish.

"Okay. Slow down." She joins me on the bed, tucking her legs beneath her. I'm amazed she made it through dinner with her taupe wool sweater unharmed; I spent ten minutes in the bathroom scrubbing at a cranberry smudge on my jeans.

"You have a crush."

"I'm afraid it's a more than a crush." I hug one of the daisy pillows to my chest. "And it's not just physical, either. I like spending time with him. I like talking to him. He's sweet, and he's funny, and he's just . . . really *good*." I think about the way he stayed with me during my panic attack. The way he massaged my hands and tracked down my mom's suitcase and defended me when I filled in on that panel at a con that now seems like it happened a lifetime ago. "Nome . . . I told him about my abortion."

Her eyes grow wide. "*Oh.*" And in that single word, she understands exactly what it would take for me to open up like that to someone. She places a hand on my knee. "You really, really like him."

I give her a miserable nod. "This whole thing was a terrible idea. I should have known it, too—I *did* know it, but I guess I liked the idea of being someone who could casually do something like this. And then move on emotionally unscathed."

"Have you ever considered that maybe none of this is casual for him, either?"

Of course I have. The thought has been running on a constant loop in my mind since New York, since he mapped out everything he loved about my face and held me against him until we both fell asleep. I can't even think about it without a terrifying tenderness rushing toward my heart.

"Maybe it isn't," I say. "But it doesn't change the fact that we live in completely different worlds."

She's quiet for a moment, taking this in. "Even after having met him, it's hard to disconnect him from *The Nocturnals*," she says, "but honestly, he seems like a pretty wonderful guy." That's the worst of it. That on paper, he's exactly the kind of person I'd want to be with. "I can't even believe I'm saying this, but is there any reason a real relationship between you and Finnegan Walsh, star of the font-based romantic comedy *Just My Type*, wouldn't work?" She tries for lightness, and I crack a smile to placate her. "Aside from the fact that you're still working with him, but you're just about done, right?"

Even though she doesn't mean it to, it twists a knife just beneath my heart. *Just about done.* And then he'll move on to new projects. New people.

"We don't live in the same place," I offer stupidly.

A flick of her fingernails against my knee. "Because no long-distance relationship has ever succeeded before. Next."

"Our lives are incompatible. He's always on the road, and I'm sure he'll be touring once the memoir comes out, too, and I'm . . ." I grasp for the right word, not finding one. "And he's obviously way more financially stable than I am."

"You're worried he doesn't think you're good enough? Successful enough?"

I hide my head in the pillow. *I don't know, I don't know, I don't know.* "Maybe that's the reason Wyatt didn't want me," I say quietly. "He had his thriving journalism career, and I had . . . I don't know, not that many inhibitions in bed?"

Noemie's expression turns dark. "I think Wyatt really messed you up." She moves closer to drape her hand along my forearm, giving it a squeeze. "Because you are *brilliant* and caring and funny and weird—I mean that as a compliment—and you're a million times more than your sexuality." Her eyes cling to mine, unblinking. "Especially with what you've been doing with Finn, I need you to know that isn't all you have to offer someone. Not by a long shot."

I want to believe her. I keep trying to connect the dots, but I might as well be using invisible ink. "I guess I'll find out next week in LA. I'm not sure how long I'll be able to keep hiding it." Or maybe he already knows, and he's using this time to figure out how to let me down easy. "You've been okay, though? While I've been gone?"

Her brow furrows. "Why wouldn't I be?"

"Everything we talked about before I left. About how this was the longest we'd be apart."

"Sure," she says. "But I've been trying some new recipes, taking some new classes—you've got to try modern hula hooping with me. I've missed you, of course, but I haven't minded being on my own. Not as much as I thought I would, at least."

"That's great. I'm glad." I'm not sure what I expected—that she'd be falling over herself, begging me to never leave again?

Maybe it's a sign things really are changing.

"I've got to help my moms with cleanup at their place," she says. "The kitchen is a disaster zone. See you back at home?"

She slips outside after a hug, leaving me alone in my childhood bedroom with too many magazine cutouts of people I can't remember the names of and a swirl of anxious thoughts.

But instead of letting them get too loud, I open up my bag and head over to my desk. Position my laptop there, exactly the way my ancient desktop was propped up through elementary and middle school, until I got a laptop my freshman year of high school and it seemed so sleek and cutting-edge.

The desk chair isn't anything I'd pick out for myself these days; it's light pink and covered with some of my mom's extra hippie stickers. But as I sit down, I remember all the hours I spent here, doing homework and typing away at stories. How happy I was, before I decided it wasn't a realistic career path.

I can't just keep opening and rereading my book. I have to make some progress.

So even though I'm scared, I scroll to the end of the document and highlight a section that I know won't work for the new direction I've decided on. Then I type a sentence. Not a good sentence, nothing profound, just a transition to move the plot forward.

There.

But something's not right. I frown at it, picking it apart until I like it a little more, until it sounds better to my ear. It grows into a paragraph. And then another. I change the setting to Seattle, because that's the place I know best, and when my parents call out that they're going to bed, I wish them good night and keep writing.

Maybe cozy mystery won't be the right genre anymore, because I want this book to be sexy, too. I make my protagonist's love interest, a graphic designer whose work she sells at her stationery shop, even more irresistible, and I build more tension between them. I give him a mane of hair that's always a little unkempt. Blots of ink on his palms and wrists, a detail she never fails to notice about him.

It's cozy to *me*, and that's what matters most.

Journalism let me forget that I once dreamed of this, and the deeper I got, the less it mattered. I went years without writing fiction, without writing anything for myself, and I convinced myself I didn't miss it. Until the layoff, which might have been the best thing that's ever happened to me. Until I opened a blank document and realized . . . this has always felt right. Not easy, necessarily, or at least not always, but *right*, like the words have just been waiting for their time to spill out and scatter across the page.

chapter
TWENTY-FOUR

LOS ANGELES, CA

When Finn meets me at the airport with a sign that says CHANDLER LEIGH COHEN, the first thing that occurs to me is that I've seen his handwriting a hundred times, scrawled in autographs across the country. But for some reason, seeing the way he printed my name strikes me as this personal, intimate thing. No two letters are quite the same size, his Sharpie having tilted slightly upward. I can tell he spent time on it, not a dashed off *I'd rather be unusual* on a photograph before the next fan in line.

His hair is a little longer and probably in need of a trim, eyes turning bright when he spots me, sliding off his sunglasses for a brief moment before putting them back in place. I don't blame him—an airport seems like the worst place to get recognized. I wonder if he'll need to keep doing it after the reunion airs. He's wearing a shirt I've seen before, blue plaid, and something about that familiarity has me urging my knees to stay solid as I make my way over to him in baggage claim.

"You didn't have to meet me in here. I know LAX is a hell-scape."

"Exactly. It didn't feel right for you to go through it alone." Then there's this moment where we're not sure how to greet each other. I see it play across his face—hug or handshake? I stick out my own hand, and he slides his palm into mine. "Good to see you again," he says.

And then I burst out laughing. "That was weird, wasn't it? The handshake?"

Finn looks visibly relieved. "Extremely. I missed you," he says, a little shyly. "I know it's only been a few days, but—I missed you. It's probably also weird to say that, huh?"

"You probably just missed having someone to tease about sleeping with socks on," I say, trying not to think about what *I missed you* does to me. Because *god*, it's such a lovely, almost painful thing, to be missed.

After Thanksgiving, I made a decision. I need to know if this is real, which means telling him my feelings are no longer solely professional. And the thought of doing that, the fear of rejection, makes me want to throw up right onto the baggage belt.

Unfortunately, things don't get any less awkward on the drive to his house, especially because I want to reach over the console and sink my teeth into his upper arm. Drag my mouth along his neck and down his chest. I have a hotel room in LA, but I wanted to see his place, get some time in to talk about the next section of the book. The last few chapters.

Finn starts waxing poetic about his Prius while we're stuck in traffic, and I nod and mm-hmm along. "You, uh, don't really care about cars, do you?" he says after a while, and I give him a guilty smile. "Me, either. I don't even know why I felt compelled to say all that."

When we pull up to his place in Los Feliz, I can't help it—I gasp. "Excuse me," I say as the house comes into view, an elegant Craftsman painted light green, with a neatly manicured lawn framed by rose bushes. "I think you neglected to mention when you were filming Cameos to make a few extra bucks that you live in a *mansion*?"

Finn runs a sheepish hand down his face, the auburn stubble there. "I've had it since season three—that was the height of it for us. My agent cut me a great deal, and I just lucked out and bought at the right time."

"The rest of us could use some of that luck, please."

At that, he laughs. "I know I could sell and make a profit, but I can't see myself getting rid of it anytime soon. And I guess I just thought . . ." He trails off, tapping the steering wheel as he pulls into the garage. "That I might raise a family here some-day."

The way that tugs at my heart.

The way that, just for a split second, my horrid brain conjures images of myself as part of that family.

"I have to admit, I'm a little shocked," I say.

"The Hollywood culture isn't for me, but I love this house. I wanted a place that would feel like a little oasis away from it, with-out being too disconnected."

I wheel my new suitcase inside, marveling at his vaulted ceil-ings and exposed beams. It's full-on *Architectural Digest* porn, down to a bowl of limes and gorgeous built-in bookshelves. The taste is more mature than his childhood bedroom, but because it wouldn't be Finn otherwise: in the living room, an actual *sword* is mounted on the wall in a glass case.

"We have to talk about this," I say after kicking off my shoes, worried about tracking dirt onto his cherrywood floors.

"So, you have to keep in mind that I was in my early twenties when we were filming *The Nocturnals*. And aside from this place, I didn't have a strong sense of the value of money." He dusts an imaginary speck from the glass. "It's Gandalf's sword from the movies—this one was used in *Return of the King*. I won it at auction with a few of my first paychecks."

"You won a *sword*."

"Glamdring," he says, biting his lip to hold back a smile. "That's its name."

And why does that make me fall even harder?

Then there's another strange moment. A silence. I don't know what happens here, what to do with my hands now that I'm no longer holding on to my bags. If we were a real couple, I'd be tugging him down the hall to his bedroom.

Finn clears his throat. "Can I get you anything to eat or drink?"

I tell him some sparkling water would be great, and we make our way into the kitchen. A rack of cast-iron pans hangs from the ceiling; a trio of succulents perch on the marble countertops. As he hands me a can of LaCroix and I catch sight of his pantry, my heart swoops low in my chest.

A Costco-sized box of those applesauce pouches. No—two of them.

"I, uh, didn't know how long you'd be here, or if you'd get hungry," he says, following my gaze. "Those are okay, right? You like that flavor?"

Slowly, I nod, all words leaving my vocabulary.

No. I won't do it. I will not allow myself to get weepy over applesauce.

The whole flight, I rehearsed what I was going to say. How I'd explain that I've grown to care about him and sure, this situation is a little messy, but I want to know if we could really be something. I'd put it all out there, calmly and rationally, and I'd wait to hear what he had to say.

Instead, when I open my mouth after an agonizing silence, what comes out is: "I think we should stop the lessons."

Shit.

It comes out so abruptly that it startles Finn, who nearly chokes on a sip of grapefruit seltzer. "Oh . . . okay?" Then he steadies himself, as though remembering what we decided at the beginning. That either of us could end it whenever we wanted to. "Yeah. Of course. We can do that. Can I just . . . Is it okay to ask why?"

I can't look at him. *Because I like you too much* and *because sleeping with you is just making it worse* and *why did you have to get me that fucking applesauce.*

"I think I've taught you all I can." I will my voice not to shake. "So I don't really see a point in continuing. You can go off and have fun with whoever else you want."

"I haven't been seeing anyone else," he says, still sounding confused. "If that's what you're worried about."

"But you will eventually."

He inches closer. Even with a couple feet of space between us, I can feel his body heat.

I try to summon all my courage. I'll say it as fast as I can, go to my hotel, conduct the rest of this relationship with two screens between us as a buffer.

"I feel like there's something else," he says. "Something you're not telling me."

I whirl around, meeting his eyes, increasingly frustrated by how casual he sounds. If he knows I have feelings for him, he's apparently going to make me spell them out. "You want to know what I'm not telling you? Fine. I hate thinking about you with someone else, even though that's the whole point of this—so you can be good for the next person. And I just . . ." *Want to be the next person so badly.* "Forget it. It's stupid."

He's just looking at me, features inscrutable. "I agree. We should stop the lessons."

I'm not expecting him to acquiesce so quickly. To just sever this connection between us. The shock of it is an instant gust of cold air, a painful clenching of my heart.

But then he steps closer, a hip pressing against mine. "Because those lessons imply that what's happening between us isn't real. That it's just practice. And that's not true." A soft smile, his expression changing into one I've seen on TV but never directed at me. "It's felt real to me for a while now."

"It—has?"

His eyes crinkle at the edges. "Chandler. Were you not there when I was waxing poetic about all the different expressions your face makes? Haven't you realized that I want to touch you . . . pretty much all the time? I've tried a hundred times to give you a hundred different hints."

And he has, hasn't he? I've been too stuck in my head to see them for what they are. "But you don't date outside of Hollywood," I say dumbly, as though this will negate everything he's confessed so far.

"Yeah. Until now." A slow shake of his head. "I haven't stopped thinking about you since we left New York. You're one of the most interesting people I've ever met, and I'm not sure you realize it. You're driven and loyal and compassionate, and Jesus—you're so beautiful, it makes my heart hurt to look at you sometimes." He pauses, swallows hard, and even though I'm not the one talking, I'm left struggling to catch my breath. I want so badly to reach out and touch his face, to see if his reddened cheeks would be warm against my fingertips. "We could have spent this entire trip in bed, and it wouldn't have been enough. We could have spent it just talking, twenty-four hours a day, and I'd still want to hear your voice," he says. "I've felt this way for a while. At least since Memphis." A laugh slips out as he mashes a fist on the countertop. "Hell, I *told you* I had a crush on you!"

"While you were high on DayQuil!" I say, and then more softly: "You remember that?"

He steps closer, a whisper of space between us. "I remember everything," he says, rich hazel eyes never leaving mine. He is so open, so vulnerable, and it's making me fall even harder. "I thought it would pass. I hoped it would, at first. But spending so much time with you only dug me deeper. Every night we were together, I only wanted you more. But even if we hadn't been physical, I think I still would have developed feelings for you. Honestly, I could never touch you again—and let's face it, I'd be devastated, and I'm obviously hoping it doesn't come to that—and I'd still be utterly wrecked over you."

There are no words in the English language lovelier than these.

Finn Walsh. Is utterly wrecked. Over *me*.

"I kept worrying I was being too obvious about it," he continues, "and I was going to scare you off."

I just stare at him, unable to process that we might want the exact same thing. *Even if we hadn't been physical.* I'm not sure I knew how badly I needed to hear that.

"I'm not scared off." My voice is a small, fragile thing. "Scared, maybe. But not scared off. Finn . . ." I have to take a few more moments to collect myself, wanting the words to come out exactly right. "I know it's only been a few months, but you've become so important to me. Every time we're not together, I miss you, and every time we are, I feel like I have to hold on tight to make it last as long as possible. I've been so uncertain about everything in my life, but the way I want you is crystal clear." I place a hand on the right side of his chest, thumb stroking upward and then back down. As though I could hold his heartbeat right in my palm—and maybe I already do. "Because I do. Badly."

His whole face changes, softens in a way I've never seen before. "Come here," he says, bringing up a hand to clasp mine. "Come here, sweetheart."

That's all it takes for me to melt against him, for all of my resolve to crumble. A single word, the same one he spoke in the snowy Midwest that I now know he meant earnestly. Wholeheartedly.

I wrap my arms around him just as he circles my waist, drawing me close, my cheek pressed against his flannel shirt. I don't want to think about what comes next or what we'll do when I'm back in Seattle and he's in LA. I just want to breathe him in.

Fingertips run through my hair. A kiss to the top of my head. "This is real?" I whisper. "Because I'm kind of wrecked for you, too."

He nods, tilting my chin upward to kiss me. "I want to be with you," he says, touching his forehead to mine. "Whatever that looks like. However you'll let me."

When we move apart, I change my mind. This face isn't one I've seen on *The Nocturnals* or any of his other shows or movies. I haven't seen this expression before, his features painted with the gentlest brush, eyes lit by the setting sun—because I think this one is solely for me.

━━ ━━ ━━

THE REST OF THE NIGHT IS AS NORMAL AS NORMAL CAN GET. FINN ANnounces he'll cook dinner, and I attempt to help him, despite not knowing where anything is. We wind up getting so distracted kissing on the kitchen counter that we burn the tofu and set off the fire alarm. So we decide on takeout burritos with tiny containers of salsa. And in the middle of it all, I sneak away and message Noemie, who seems to break her phone given the sheer number of emojis she texts back. Finn does the same with Krishanu, laughing when he shows me his response: **FINALLY!!!**

"He could tell I had it bad for you in Reno," he explains. "I broke down and told him everything once we got to Ohio, when you were out of the room."

"Did he have any advice?"

"Just to not fuck it up, which I worried I nearly did a couple times. He said it was the happiest he'd seen me in a while." Finn leans closer. "And it's true."

We carry glasses of wine into his backyard, stumbling over cobblestones because we can't stop touching each other. It really does feel like an oasis out here, peaceful and secluded, the tall hedges providing a considerable amount of privacy. The only sounds are the birds and the hum of the pool. At dusk in December, it's still sixty degrees out.

"I wrote over Thanksgiving," I tell him, settling onto a chaise longue next to his, beneath a heat lamp. *Bliss.*

"You cheated on our book?" he says, mock-offended.

I take a sip of wine. "Just a little. And . . . it felt *great*. Like I hadn't flexed those muscles in a long time, but it was so natural to finally stretch them out."

"You have no idea how happy I am to hear that it made you happy. Truly."

We kiss slowly as the moon beams down on us. Tonight, there are no deadlines.

"You're really beautiful, too," I tell him, all the compliments

I've held in beginning to spill out. I haven't wanted him to take anything the wrong way. "Your eyes, your freckles, the gray in your hair. It's kind of a crime, how lovely your face is."

His mouth turns greedy against mine, each brush of his lips a small thank-you. "I've been thinking about you all day," he says into my ear, pulling me onto his chair.

I let out a nervous laugh. "It sort of feels like we're about to have sex for the first time."

"We've been doing it for a couple months. Pretty successfully, I might add."

"But this is going to be different."

And he nods, because I know he understands. Because this time, it's *real*.

There are no instructions or how-tos, and there's something new and strange and thrilling about that. Even if both of us have felt like it was real for a while, this time, there's no doubt. Not in the way he tugs at my hair or swipes a thumb along my cheek, or the way I clutch at the fabric of his shirt because I can't get him close enough.

"You've been so generous," he says when we're still lazily kissing, my body splayed on top of his. "I want to do something for you." He pulls back for a moment, meets my gaze. "Do you have any fantasies? Something you've always wanted in bed but never told anyone?"

"We don't have to—"

"I know we don't have to. I want to." A sly grin. "And I've hoped I could fulfill them for you, now that I've graduated from the Chandler Cohen Academy of Sex."

"Valedictorian, no less." I let this hang between us for a few long seconds, my heart racing. Because yes, I have fantasies, some I've vocalized in past relationships and others I've held on to, as though saving them for some future perfect guy or maybe just locking them in my imagination forever. With Finn, I could let them all out—that's how comfortable I've become with him.

I decide to start with just one. "Could you . . . could you spank me?"

The moment I say it, I worry he'll laugh. Take back the offer. That it'll instantly turn the night awkward.

Instead his grin turns devious, eyes dark. "There's nothing in the world I'd like more."

He helps me out of my jeans before asking how I want to position myself, and I give his knees a shy nod. I want to be in his lap, as close to him as possible. Before we start, he runs inside to grab a pillow, and there's something about that sweet gesture contrasted with what we're about to do that sets me on fire. And the fact that we're outside—surrounded by tall hedges, sure, but still, anyone could hear us.

Maybe I don't mind.

I lower myself onto his lap, resting my upper body on the pillow while he pulls my panties tight. At first he merely teases, running his palm along my lower back before swooping lower. My pulse is in my throat, my veins filled with reckless anticipation.

"How wet are your panties?" he asks, a finger trailing along the fabric. "Because I think you must have gotten even wetter as soon as you asked to be spanked." When his hand settles between my thighs, he groans, taking his time sliding down my underwear. "Christ, your ass. It's perfect." He bends down, feathering kisses along each cheek. A few circles of his palm. "You'll tell me what you want? If I'm not doing it the way you imagined?"

I let out a deep breath, finding it difficult to believe this might be anything less than what I imagined. "You know I will."

He starts slowly, stroking me in agonizing circles. Then he

pulls his hand back, pausing for a breathless moment before delivering a tight smack that I feel in every cell of my body.

A moan slips from my lips as I clutch the pillow beneath me.

"You like that?"

"*Yes.*"

The next one, he moans right along with me. And *god*, that's even better, knowing he's loving this, too. "Harder? Softer?"

"Harder," I beg, and the next time he spanks me, I gasp out, my legs turning liquid, pleasure curling hot and low in my core. I'm certain sex has never been this freeing.

In between spanks, he smooths circles on my cheeks while filth falls from his mouth. "Lift up. I want to see that gorgeous pussy."

I lean forward, pushing up on my elbows, raising my hips.

"Jesus, this view."

He slides a finger beneath me, runs it through my slickness. Drops a few taps where I'm most sensitive. I'm no longer sure I'm breathing. Then he repositions my hips, the night breeze blowing against my dampest parts as he gives my pussy a gentle spank.

"Fucking hell," I manage through gritted teeth. "I'm gonna die."

He alternates between my pussy and my ass, each spank stealing more air from my lungs. "Let it out, sweetheart," he says when I'm moments from shattering, his fingers relentless and greedy and perfect. "Be loud."

The orgasm crashes through me, a shivering, shuddering earthquake that leaves me weightless, his name on my tongue as he wraps his arms around me, his mouth pressed to the nape of my neck.

Once I recover, I shift so I can see his face, the heat in his gaze.

"That was—fucking incredible," I manage.

His cock is straining against his boxers and I need to see him lose control, need to be the reason he cries out into the night.

"What do you want?" I ask.

"Your mouth. Please." The urgency in his voice is a delicious, decadent thing.

I shove down his boxers, overcome with the desire to taste him. He's already rock hard, hot velvet as I wrap my lips around him, holding him steady with my fist, swirling my tongue across the tip. He whispers my name like a curse. Like a promise. His fingertips are soft but desperate in my hair, and I suck him deeper as he drags his hand lower to cup my breast, thumb rubbing my nipple.

"I want to come on your tits," he says on a growl. "If that's—"

"Please. Yes."

I remove my mouth just as he starts to tremble, and he gives one more thrust against my chest before he falls apart, warmth slicking my breasts. He reaches beneath the chair for a towel before he draws me back on top of him, and I'm limp and spent and indescribably happy.

Several minutes pass before he rolls over to get his phone. When the familiar opening of "Whoomp! (There It Is)" starts up, I can't help laughing.

"I'm sorry," he says, laughing along with me as he smooths my hair. "I had to."

"Can we stay here forever?" I murmur against his chest. Because despite having sex in our real relationship for the first time, it still feels like we're living in this dreamworld of unreality. A place where the outside cannot touch us.

"I hope so." A pause, the way he always does when he's carefully choosing his words. "Because, Chandler . . . I'm pretty sure I'm falling for you."

And even though I'm worried about the future, about how tightly I've clung to my career in the past when it's just as nebulous right now—

"I am, too," I say, and the fear is worth it for the way he holds me tighter.

If anything could scare me off, it's how new and fragile and precious this feels. How badly I want this to last beyond the reunion, beyond the book. Tonight feels so beautifully normal that I think I might be able to live in these moments forever.

"So this is what life is like with Finnegan Walsh?" I ask.

He shakes his head, tightens his grip on my waist. "No. This is better."

chapter

TWENTY-FIVE

LOS ANGELES, CA

Ethan, Finn, Cooper . . . you three over there. Ladies—Juliana, Hallie, Bree—can I get you on the other couch?"

Bree lifts one perfectly penciled eyebrow in exactly the way Sofia was known to do on the show, especially whenever she was pissed at Caleb. "You're really going to have the guys on one side and the girls on the other?"

The director considers this. "New plan," he says, exasperated. "Everyone sit where they want."

But this doesn't work, because he wants Juliana and Bree next to each other, since a good chunk of the reunion will focus on their characters' rivalry. But Ethan and Juliana *have* to be next to each other, as the show's central couple, and since Cooper's Wesley eventually ends up with Bree's Sofia, they should probably be next to each other, too. Cooper is just standing there grinning at all of it, like as the show's comic relief, he's just along for the ride.

It goes on like this for twenty more minutes, just configuring the proper seating. Twin black leather couches are posed onstage, an Oakhurst University banner in the school's colors, silver and deep blue, draped behind them. On my way into the studio, I may have gawked a little at the signs indicating where a number of familiar shows are being filmed, but Finn just strolled right inside with a coffee cup in hand, like this is something he does every day. And I guess it used to be.

"Hopefully this won't be too boring for you," he said this morning.

"Going to a rehearsal for my boyfriend's show? Not at all."

And he grinned at that, *boyfriend*. I thought it might be strange, slipping into this domestic moment with him, but what's strangest is that it felt so incredibly natural: our lazy breakfast, showering together, getting back into his Prius and laughing about how he was so nervous yesterday, he thought his car was the best conversation topic.

I assured him I couldn't possibly be bored by anything *Nocturnals*-related, but now that I'm here, sitting where the live studio audience will be on the day of the taping, I'm starting to reconsider that statement.

Although truthfully, I'd have followed him just about anywhere today.

Hallie and Bree greeted me with hugs, though Juliana was still a little distant. I remember what Finn said about her rehab and more than understood why she'd be wary of press.

Ethan, though . . . Ethan is slightly less present than the others. From the first time I saw him at Supercon, dressed like a fan before revealing himself at the panel, he struck me as someone who loves the spotlight and who'd do anything to keep it from shining on someone else for too long. Ethan was fully aware that *The Nocturnals* was designed to revolve around him, even if it eventually grew into more of an ensemble show.

And I'm guessing he didn't love that.

There are two sets: the couches for the live Q & A, and the re-created library of Oakhurst University where they'll pretape material for the show. After they finish staging the Q & A, we all move on to the next set, overstuffed wooden bookshelves and flickering chandeliers and a long spiral staircase that I can now see leads absolutely nowhere. TV magic, and all that. The cast walks through the library, gazing at the remnants of their time together.

Hallie nudges Finn, points to a spot on the floor. "They even added back those paw prints from episode one," she says.

Finn drags a hand along the library table. "It's just like I remember."

I love watching him take it all in. Every so often, he glances out toward the audience, where I'm seated with a handful of managers and agents and publicists, a couple other journalists working on pieces in advance of the reunion. And every time he does, his whole face seems to change, eyes crinkling at the corners as his stage smile turns real.

I'm not sure when that won't feel like a novelty.

———

THE TAPED CAST INTERVIEWS LAST THROUGH THE AFTERNOON. THEY talk about how the show changed them, their favorite memories, juicy behind-the-scenes moments. Ethan's in an especially obstinate mood, which seems like par for the course for him, but he ends up having to do far more takes than anyone else.

"Some things never change," Hallie mutters, and I decide she and I could probably be friends. Even if the main things we have in common are saltiness and Finnegan Walsh.

This hits me in a strange place. Because in any relationship, the sharing of friends is a natural, expected thing. And yet . . .

Finn's friends, beyond Krishanu and Derek in Reno, are entrenched in the Hollywood world, too. That might be an adjustment, but surely not anything we can't figure out.

All of that is forgotten when the cast and crew break for a late lunch, Finn immediately heading for me.

"I'm shocked you've lasted this long," he says.

I pack up my bag. "I'll have you know that was fascinating. What Cooper said about adopting one of the dogs that played a wolf extra? Precious. Or how Hallie was so convinced Caleb would turn out to be the show's ultimate villain that the writers gave her a script with a different ending for the finale, one that had him betraying everyone?" It might have been cruel if it hadn't been so terribly written—she'd known right away that it was a prank, one they can all still laugh about.

When I slip my bag over my shoulder and follow him outside onto the studio lot, I don't miss the way Ethan walks a few paces behind us, like he doesn't want to have to speak to anyone. I give him a forced smile, hope it seems authentic, and don my sunglasses.

"See you back here," Finn calls out, holding open the door for him.

Ethan gives him an easy grin. A pat on the shoulder. "Sure, bud. If you can make it there on time."

Finn stiffens next to me.

My eyebrows crease together. "What was that about?"

"Nothing," Finn says, trying to brush it off. His hand tightens on my lower back. "Just something he used to do when we were filming. A joke."

I decide not to press it, but it seems as much like a joke as Los Angeles seems like a charming small town.

We have lunch at a café on the lot, taking a seat in a shady corner outside. It's relatively late in the day, not too busy, and now that he's no longer under the studio lights, I can see the powder on Finn's face and a bronze liner on his lower lids. A hint of color on his cheeks that's just the slightest shade cooler than his natural blush.

I try to ask Finn more about how it feels to be back at Oakhurst, and while he gives me some answers I might be able to use in the reunion chapter, he pokes his quinoa salad around his compostable bowl, barely eating.

"Something's bothering you." I give his leg a gentle tap with my sneaker. "Hey. You know you can talk to me about it, right? If you want to?"

A long, slow sigh as he reaches his hand toward mine, threading our fingers together. "I know. Thank you. It's just not the easiest thing to do." He lets out a rough laugh. "I guess that's been the thesis statement of this whole memoir."

I allow a small smile at that, but I remain quiet, giving him the space he needs to elaborate.

He takes that time, rubbing his fingertips along my knuckles, then glancing around to make sure we're alone enough to have this kind of conversation.

The glancing around: I wonder if that's something he ever stops doing. If it's something I'll start doing when we're in public, too.

"Ethan and I . . . haven't always gotten along," he starts. "I've never known why, exactly. Maybe he felt threatened because he was supposed to be the main character, and the Mexley shippers were more enthusiastic than the Calice ones. I don't know. Maybe he's just an asshole."

"He definitely is," I agree, giving my own salad a pointed stab.

A deep breath as Finn stares down at his salad. "He used to mess with me during filming. Little things—he'd drink from a glass of water and then pass it to me, ask if I wanted any. Laugh when I said no. Or he'd go through craft services and touch all the sandwiches when I was looking—real gross, immature shit. He loved trying to set me off between takes, just to see how far he could push me, and if any of my compulsions made me the tiniest bit late, he made sure the higher-ups knew I hadn't gotten there on time. And bad habits die hard, I guess, because he's a thirty-five-year-old man who derives joy from trying to trigger someone's OCD."

"What the fuck? That's *sick*." My stomach rolls over, imagining a twenty-year-old Finn, unable to manage his OCD on his own quite yet and dealing with a bully who thought the whole thing was a joke.

"Guess it's not enough that he has this great movie career. He has to make the rest of us feel like ants." A harsh laugh. "It's almost funny—he was so horrible to Hux in season one, and he's just as bad in real life. Some acting."

"The book isn't done yet," I say. "We could put this in the memoir. In fact—I think we should. These are exactly the kind of microaggressions people should hear about. You want the book to shed light on mental illness, to destigmatize it . . . here's how we show how *not* to act." I don't just want to bring Ethan down, although that would be deeply satisfying. I know enough about him to make the judgment that he's simply not a good person, and I want any other Ethans who pick up Finn's book to know that it's not okay.

Finn's expression changes, eyes flicking up to mine. "Yeah . . . I'd rather not."

"Are you sure? Because I'm positive you're not the only one who's dealt with something like this."

"Look—it's my name." He says it gently, but it hits me square in the chest. "It's my book."

"Right." How could I forget? As much as this has felt like a partnership, in the most basic contractual terms, it isn't. "Of course it's your book. I'm just the one getting paid to write it."

Finn softens. "Shit—Chandler. I'm sorry. I didn't mean for it to sound that way." He reaches for me, running a hand along my forearm. I let him. "I just don't want to feel like I have to tear anyone else down to make myself look better, even if they deserve it. Especially if they're bigger than I am. I'd hate for anyone to think I'm name-dropping for the sake of sales."

"I understand." I force a smile, halfheartedly pierce a hunk of romaine. This salad cost $14 and it tastes like absolutely nothing. We've had far more uncomfortable conversations over the past few months, so I'm not sure why this one stings so much. I try to put myself in his position, and I do understand, even if I disagree.

But like he said: His name. His book.

I'm just the nobody who's following him around, a little lost puppy. The person whose career cannot possibly compete with his. The ghost girlfriend.

"Let's just forget about it," he says. "I have to be back at set in twenty and I'd much rather talk about you."

Still, it refuses to leave my mind the rest of the day.

poisonedpen-real-REAL.docx

The shop was a mess.

Pens were uncapped and paper was strewn everywhere, inkblots bleeding into the new carpets. And the journal section, which Penelope had lovingly, painstakingly arranged the previous day, appeared as though someone had fed those gorgeous bound planners through a shredder. January-February-March confetti.

Of course, all of that was nothing when she took into account the body in the middle of the room, just under the banner declaring, BUY ONE, GET ONE FREE.

chapter
TWENTY-SIX

LOS ANGELES, CA

This is the way books were meant to be written: a café on a tree-lined street, chai latte and blackberry-lemon scone on the table in front of me. Sunlight pouring in, washing the whole place in golden light.

When I was a kid, imagining growing up to be a novelist, this was *almost* what I pictured—though there was a lot more rain. And people wearing Patagonia.

Last night when we got home, Finn was so exhausted, we fell right into bed. All the traveling must be catching up with me, because I slept in much later than usual. A kiss on my forehead, "No, no, don't get up," and he was gone.

So I made myself at home in this café while he went to set, my denim jacket draped over the back of the chair, intent on polishing the middle chapters of the memoir and, if I have time, sketching out the reunion. That'll be the last chapter I write before turning in this draft.

After that . . . maybe I'll open up *The Poisoned Pen* again.

I'm fine-tuning a chapter on Finn's bar mitzvah when my phone rings. It was the first time he experienced one of his compulsions, though he didn't have the words for it then—he refused to eat because so many people had touched the challah, and his dad yelled at him for being *an entitled brat*. Writing it in Finn's voice breaks my heart all over again.

"Don't you check your email?" Stella says when I pick up the phone. "Also, hello. How's LA, how's the book going, how are *you*?"

I hit save and navigate over to my email. "Sorry, I was in a writing trance. Had the Wi-Fi turned off. I'm good, book's good—it's all going well."

"Ah. I thought you'd be chomping at the bit to get started, once you see it . . ." She trails off, giving me time to read through the email that's at the top of my inbox.

It's a new offer—another ghostwriting gig. Another actor, Michael Thiessen, a midfifties guy who's been on some iteration of *CSI* for the past twenty years. I'm pretty sure my dad is a huge fan.

The money is double what I'm making on Finn's book.

"It doesn't sound like you're jumping for joy."

"I'm in public," I say, forcing a little laugh. I hate needing to spontaneously react to this. Ideally, I'd have had a moment to process by myself first.

And this is what the processing looks like:

I've never been outright offered a job like this before. There's always been a call or interview beforehand, either with the writer themselves or with their team. Even with Finn, I'm sure they wouldn't have offered the book to me if I'd massively bungled that lunch. This is a clear sign of success in my field, and yet I can't shake the feeling that if I take it, I may never write something just for myself, whether that project lasts two months or twenty. I am always going to have an excuse.

I love what we're doing with Finn's book, but I don't know if I can keep disappearing into the work like this. I don't know how much of myself will be left at the end of it.

Even if he said he could hear me in those books—I don't know if *I* can.

"It—it sounds great," I manage, the words like chalk in my throat.

"The timing couldn't be better. Finnegan's book is due soon, and you could jump right into a new project. It's exactly what we've wanted for you."

Exactly what we've wanted.

What *do* I want?

"We can get you on the phone with Michael's people, if you like. He's wonderful, really lovely guy. *Lots* of inside-Hollywood info—he's been in the business for so long. And while I love their initial offer, I think we could get them to go even higher."

"Great." I am capable of only one adjective. A skill befitting a writer. "My mind is still pretty wrapped up in Finn's book, so . . . do they need an answer right away?"

A pause. "These kinds of offers don't just wait, Chandler." She says it gently. And I know she's not wrong. Stella's been nothing but good for my career, and I trust her.

"By the *Nocturnals* reunion. I promise."

"Excellent. I'll let them know."

When we hang up, I sit there for a few moments, blinking out into the café. I should be flooded with relief that another gig is waiting for me. The money from Finn's book was going to act as a cushion, keep me from needing to rush into the next project. Now I could even move out of Noemie's. Get a place of my own.

And yet . . . all I feel is *heavy*, as though there's something physical yanking me toward the table. Chaining me to my laptop.

Telling me how soul-sucking this project sounds, the way it was with Maddy and Bronson, the personal trainer. Because even if Michael Thiessen has some fascinating hidden depth, I'm not sure I want to be the person to unearth it.

I open up Instagram and swipe over to Maddy DeMarco's profile, trying to remember if I felt anything but agony when I was working on her book. I scroll back, back, back to when I was drafting. There's a photo of her at some upscale cabin, a mug of coffee beside her on the table, where she sits with her laptop, next to a window with a stunning mountain landscape.

Hard at work on edits! I can actually hear myself think out here, says the caption.

I'm not sure how much longer I can be invisible.

FINN HAS A LATE-AFTERNOON MEDIA BLITZ, A HANDFUL OF PODCAST and YouTube interviews, and doesn't get home until after dinner, after a dozen apology texts and a dozen replies assuring him that it's fine, that I can fend for myself.

And it *is* fine, but it's also given me too much to think about.

About the job.

About the future.

About *us*.

Because that's a fun side effect of Stella's call: now that we're officially together, I have to wonder what happens to us when the book is done, when I go back to Seattle and he prepares for the next round of cons.

I save some veggie Thai takeout for him, pouring some wine and managing to figure out his sound system only to discover it's set to a jazz playlist. Finn likes jazz—something I didn't know about him until just now. I shouldn't have a strong reaction to this, since we've only barely talked about music, but still, it makes me realize I only met him a few months ago. There is still so much I don't know.

When he tosses his bag into his office and spots the wine and food on the dining room table, the grin on his face is enough to take those worries down from an eleven to a four. There's a coziness here, a domesticity that's almost a bit too comfortable. I could just slide right into his life, the way I'm doing now, and maybe my career would matter a little less.

And the anxiety is back. My cuticles are a war zone.

"So . . . I got an interesting job offer today," I say, after he tells me about rehearsals, about the YouTube interview that had him respond to the most popular Google search queries about himself.

"Oh yeah?" he asks between spoonfuls of tom yum soup.

I explain it to him, laying out as many details as Stella gave me. "And apparently he's like, really nice? So that's a plus."

"Hmm." More soup. More silence.

"I told my agent I'd think about it," I say, because something about his silence sounds like disappointment, and I don't want him to be disappointed in me. "But . . . it's really good money."

"You'd be ghostwriting again, though."

"Well, yes. That's my job."

Another bout of quiet. At the beginning, I used to love how Finn took his time to answer questions, but now all I want is to shake his shoulders until the words spill out. Finally, he says, "I thought you didn't want to do that anymore. I thought that's why you were working on your mystery."

"That's hardly a sure thing. Even if I sell that book, I'd probably still need another part-time job. I have some savings now, but I can't live on that forever."

"What about how much you loved getting back into writing?

Your writing." His gaze is hard on mine. "And how you always wanted to become a novelist."

"I can still do it." My voice is thin. Even my vocal cords know I'm lying. "I'd have free time."

"Bullshit. We both know the other book would come first. And you were burned out even before you took on my book." He moves his bowl toward the center of the table, gives me his full focus. "Chandler. How many times have you told me this isn't what you want to be doing with your life? You've been using someone else's name to guarantee a certain level of success—and that's okay. That's exactly what you've been hired to do. But that's just it: it's what you were hired to do, instead of standing on your own. You can hide behind someone else's fame without risking a goddamn thing. Ghostwriting is your crutch—a way to keep yourself from getting out of your comfort zone."

Even if that's true, hasn't he been with me this whole trip? Hasn't he seen me out of my comfort zone, again and again and again?

"That's not fair." It's too difficult, having this conversation while sitting so close to him. He said it himself—he can read me, and I don't want my face to give away anything I haven't found the right words for. I get to my feet, striding into the living room, over to his *Return of the King* sword. "You don't think journalism itself is a risk? Newspapers started folding before I even declared my major. My career has always been a risk. And forget health insurance—I abandoned that dream a long time ago."

"I know there isn't a guarantee your fiction would lead to a stable career, even if I think it should. I know it's just as much of a gamble as Hollywood. But if you don't *try*, you're always going to wonder, what if. What if I took that chance." He stands, too, stepping closer. "The way you did with me."

The way he's pushing me—now that he's my boyfriend, is it just something I'll have to accept?

"It's not the same thing," I protest, though every word of his slips between my ribs and stays there. "If I did this, I'd almost certainly be making less money. I'd probably have to take another part-time job to pay my bills. It's easy for you to tell me to just go do what I'm passionate about—you did it, and you succeeded. You wanted to be an actor, and you are."

"Sure, I got lucky early on. But you forget, I didn't have a safety net, either. My mom was back in school, and my dad was gone. I was taking a huge risk, too," he says. "And you wouldn't be able to write full-time? Isn't that what you're doing now?"

I let out a snort. "I can guarantee I'd be making a lot less for my original books than for what I'm doing for you." Then, realizing the way it sounds, I try to backtrack. "I mean—not just you. All of you, all the books I've written so far."

He props a shoulder against the wall, mouth forming a grim line. "Glad to hear I'm lumped together with the rest of them."

"You know you're different," I say. "In a million ways. But at the most basic level, I'm still doing the same thing. I'm writing for someone else—not for myself. And even if I took all of that out of the equation . . ." Then I ask in a tiny voice: "What if I fail?"

"What if you don't?" he counters.

We're quiet for a moment, breathing hard.

"So that's what I should do then—write my book, and what? Keep following you around from con to con, city to city? Or just visit you when you're back home? Would that even be enough?"

Even as I say it, I know it wouldn't be. The idea of that much time away from him after this trip makes me miss him already. The jazz was completely new to me. What else would I miss out on learning?

"I can cut down on the cons. I wouldn't have to be traveling all the time."

"I don't want you to do that just for me."

He gives me this lingering look, a thumb grazing my wrist. "Chandler," he says in this gentle, measured way. "You're the only thing that's made it bearable this time around."

It's nearly impossible to ignore what those words do to my heart. Even in the midst of a conversation about things I don't want to hear, I'm falling for him. Over and over and over.

I just wish it could erase all my uncertainties.

"What did you really think was going to happen when the book was done?" I ask. "Be honest with me."

A deep breath, a rake of his hands through his hair. "Hopefully my whole life won't be the con circuit at that point, but yes, there will be some traveling. It's unavoidable, especially when promo starts for the book and the nonprofit is launched. But I don't know why we can't try a long-distance relationship," he says, sounding more hopeful. "It's not that far. We'd see each other all the time."

"Those flights would get expensive."

He frowns, as though this would never have occurred to him. "I could pay for them." Before I can protest, he adds, "Or I'll move to Seattle and commute down to LA. Because I'd do it, if that's what you want. Or you could move in with me here."

"I—hold on a second."

My head is spinning, and I have to sit back down, dropping onto his couch with a soft thud. *Moving to Seattle. Moving in with him in LA.* It's all too much, too fast. I've only ever lived in Seattle, and the thought of suddenly uprooting my entire life is terrifying.

Two nights ago, he said he wanted to be with me—whatever that looked like.

Why is that image suddenly so unrealistic?

"I don't know if I'm ready for that," I say honestly. "Moving in together."

"Just throwing out ideas." He lifts his eyebrows at the couch, as though asking my permission for him to join me. When I give him a nod, he sits down, cupping my shoulder with his palm. "I haven't been this close to anyone in a while. So I don't know if I'm doing any of this right, but I care about you so much. Can't you trust me that we'll figure it out?"

"I want to. I do."

"Then why does it sound like this is something you're trying to talk yourself into?"

"Because it's fucking *hard*, okay?" Tears sting the corners of my eyes, unbidden, and I swipe them away as quickly as I can. I didn't expect the conversation to spiral like this, but I also hadn't realized just how many unanswered questions exist between us. "I don't know how to take two huge gambles at once. My career, whatever it turns out to be, and this relationship—"

"You think our relationship is a gamble?"

"I just—I'm still trying to figure out who I am." I'm reaching into the most vulnerable space now, letting him see what I sometimes refuse to show myself. "And you've had it figured out for so long."

"What other people think of me, maybe. But not who I really am." As his face softens, he cracks a smile. "In fact, I think we wrote a whole book about that."

I don't laugh. "That's the whole point."

Because he is someone worthy of a memoir, and in my lowest moments, sometimes I feel like a blank page.

I don't want to squeeze myself into the nooks and crannies of someone else's life. Have I been so wrapped up in the fantasy of him that I've forgotten how difficult this relationship will be? The past few days, we've just been playing house. Pretending that this is our real life, the same way we've been pretending the whole trip. Because now when I picture my relationship with Finn, I can see myself flying to LA every other weekend, feeling guilty if he paid for the flight and putting myself on a budget if not, the two of us arguing about what to watch that night or which new vegetarian restaurant to try. I can see him at benefits and events for his non-profit, taking the occasional role in a holiday movie with a meno-rah hiding in the background. I'll be the nameless person on his arm at premieres and events. The supportive girlfriend.

I can fit into his life, sure. I can be in that relationship.

But what about him fitting into mine?

"I admire you *so much*," I whisper, reaching for his hand and giving it a squeeze. "I just wish I felt the same way about myself." Slowly, I stand up, retrieve my bag from the hallway. "And I think I need a little time to figure that out."

Finn gets to his feet, looking torn between going after me and giving me space. "You could stay," he says. This time, he doesn't sound at all like he did when he begged Meg Lawson not to leave him. His chin is wobbling, eyes wide and glassy. "We can keep talking about it. Please, Chandler. We could figure it out together."

If he really could categorize every expression my face makes, then he'd know I'm serious. Terrified of what might happen if I leave this house but serious nonetheless.

I shake my head, adamant now. "I'm sorry. I think I have to do it alone."

And with trembling footsteps, I head for the door.

chapter
TWENTY-SEVEN

LOS ANGELES

In the backseat of an Uber, I try my best to act like I haven't made the single stupidest decision of my life. This translates into some truly terrible small talk. "Some traffic, huh?" I ask the driver, who just rolls her eyes.

I end up at the hotel the publisher originally booked for me, since they obviously weren't planning on me shacking up with Finn. It's in downtown LA, a gritty section of the city with none of the charm of Los Feliz. And then, because it's my go-to coping mechanism, I call Noemie.

She listens as I explain everything, recounting some of my argument with Finn almost word for word. And when I'm done, splayed on the too-firm bed with too-soft pillows, she tells me exactly what I don't want to hear.

"I hate to say it," she starts. "But I'm kind of on Finn's side here."

I choke out a laugh. "I'm . . . not sure how to react to that."

Her sigh crackles through the phone. "You haven't prioritized your writing in so long. Are you sure you even want it anymore?"

"Yes. Of course I do." *More than almost anything.* Not even to be published, but to have the satisfaction of completing my book, typing *THE END* and giving my characters the resolution they deserve. Anything that happened afterward would be icing.

It isn't that I disagree with her—not necessarily. I just hoped there was an easier solution here, one that didn't end with anyone heartbroken and my career left up to chance. I place a hand on my chest, rising and falling with the quickening of my breaths. The anxiety crawls up my throat, tightens my lungs.

I don't know how to explain that it's possible to want something without actively trying to get it. Although maybe she understands—after all, I did it with Wyatt for so many years. Even then, I convinced myself I was happy with what we were, because anything else would have required changing the status quo. It would have meant taking a risk, that thing I've avoided for so, so long.

"If you take this job," Noemie continues, "then nothing changes. You know how that story goes. And you can get a little codependent on your work."

"Pot, kettle."

A sigh. "I know, I know. But if you think about it, as stressful as your jobs have been sometimes, they've been comfortable. It's not one hundred percent what you want, but it's less scary than cutting ties and trying something new."

"What if that's it? What if—what if I'm just too fucking scared?" I say it too loudly, realizing that there are tears in my eyes. "What if I try and it doesn't work out?"

"Then you have a soft place to land." Her voice is gentle. "You have your family. You have me. And, well, I have a lot of time to talk during the next few weeks because . . ." A deep breath. "I got a new job. I start in January."

I sit up, crossing my legs and settling back against the headboard. "And you're only telling me now?"

"You were in panic mode. I was waiting for the right time," she says. "I'm going to be an in-house publicist at an organic snack-of-the-month subscription company. I didn't want to tell you until I had the offer because I didn't want to jinx it—and I just got it today."

And despite everything, I let out a laugh, because if that isn't the perfect job for her, nothing is. I can hear the excitement in her voice. "Nome. I am so, so happy for you. Truly."

"Thank you. And I hope you know . . . you have the room in my house as long as you need it," she says. "But Chandler? I hope you decide you don't need it. Not now—I'm not kicking you out or anything. But whenever you're ready."

We hang up with the promise of seeing each other soon. I should be used to hotel rooms by now, because in a way, they all kind of look the same. The same uncomfortable beds. Same soulless decor. All that's missing is my lesson plan and a familiar face across the hallway.

This whole trip, I've been fooling myself. I thought it would change me, that by the end of it, I'd know exactly what my next step would be.

If I take the job, I know what lies down that path. I've done it before.

But giving confidence to my writing, leaving my career up to chance . . .

My phone blinks with a new text.

Wherever you are, you get there okay?

I reply with a thumbs-up, which somehow seems a little too positive for the situation. **At a hotel. Just need some time to think,** I follow it up with.

If I go back to his place, then I'll give in. He'll be there with his lovely eyes and his arms that fit around me so perfectly, and it would be too easy to strap my career into the backseat.

For more than ten years, my life has been defined by deadlines, and I've taken pride in the fact that I've never missed a single one.

So I give myself a deadline. Once I finish the memoir, I'll make my decision about the job.

And about Finn.

Take as long as you need, he writes back.

It's better for both of us if I go back to Seattle now, put some space between us before the reunion taping next week.

I try to convince myself of that the entire flight home.

chapter

TWENTY-EIGHT

SEATTLE, WA

The *Seattle Times* is open on the kitchen table at my parents' house, slices of bread waiting in the toaster and a pan of scrambled eggs on the stove. This is the first place I went when my plane landed last night, dragging my suitcase up the stairs to my childhood bedroom, texting Noemie that I'd see her soon before I collapsed into bed.

I page through the newspaper, noting familiar bylines the way I've done since I decided to study journalism. There's no jealousy, though. No wistfulness. I don't wish I'd written that story about a recent music festival or the new light-rail station, the way I might have in college or in the years after, when I was still trying to find my footing.

My dad enters with his cane, plaid robe tied around his waist and gray-white stubble covering his face. "Morning! If you touched the crossword, there'll be hell to pay."

"Morning." I pass him the paper. "It's all yours."

He fills his plate as my mom comes downstairs, her long hair held back with a rainbow scrunchie. She hums an old Jefferson Airplane song as she waters a row of leafy plants at the kitchen window.

"You never pushed me to study journalism because it was more practical than writing novels," I say once we're all seated. "Did you?"

My mom pauses in the middle of buttering a slice of sourdough. "I can't imagine we would have," she says. "Maybe we were concerned about money, but I think *you* were the one who informed us journalism would make more sense."

I grimace. That does sound like me.

"I do miss those creepy mysteries you wrote, though." My dad takes a sip of coffee. "I have to admit, I liked them more than that water book." It takes me a moment to realize he means Maddy DeMarco's book. "Is there a reason you're asking?"

"Quarter-life crisis?" I suggest, and my dad cracks a smile.

"Nah, you're too young. By the time you're our age, the life expectancy will probably be one hundred and fifty, at least."

"You didn't like working on Finnegan's book?" my mom asks, brows creased with concern.

I liked it a little too much. I direct my gaze to my plate, hoping my face doesn't give me away. "No—it was good. Great. Almost done with it. Anyway," I say to my dad, desperate to change the subject, "you have a bone-density scan next week, right? I can take you. And maybe you can add me to your patient portal, just so I can check the results as soon as they come in?"

My dad coughs and my mom presses her lips together, staring pointedly at the ceiling. *Oh.* Maybe I've crossed some sort of boundary I wasn't aware of? They're pretty decent with technology, given their age, but surely it wouldn't hurt for me to get more involved. Especially now that I'm back.

"We've been meaning to talk to you about this," my dad says. "Your mom and I . . . well, we know we're no spring chickens."

My mom gives her hair a toss. "Speak for yourself," she says. "What we want to say is that we don't need you to bend over backward to help us. We got by just fine the past couple months when you were out of town."

I swallow hard. I wasn't prepared to hear that—that they hadn't needed me. "I was worried, though."

"We know you worry because you care," my dad says. "But it's just too much. We know you asked Noemie to check in on us a few times, and at a certain point, it felt a little like having a babysitter."

I wince. That wasn't what I'd wanted at all. "I'm so sorry. I guess I didn't exactly know what to do."

"I know there will come a time when we want your help," my dad says. "When we need it. It might be tomorrow, but it also might be years from now."

My mom pats my knee. "We're just not quite ready to let you parent us yet."

As we finish breakfast, something hits me with a striking clarity. I wonder if I haven't only been using ghostwriting as a crutch, like Finn said. How many jobs did I never apply for because they'd have meant leaving Seattle? How many opportunities did I miss out on because I was so intent on holding myself back? I've been so worried about people not needing me anymore that I tethered myself to them so tightly, I could hardly untie the knots.

I thought this place and these people were my whole world, and while I don't love them any less than I did before I took this assignment, the truth is that my world is larger than that. Again and again, I fell for new cities and new experiences—and most of all, the version of myself who could step outside her comfort zone.

Because the Chandler from back in September wouldn't be able to read a text from Wyatt, after weeks and weeks of silence, inviting me to a holiday party he's throwing later this month, and simply type, **Sorry, can't make it!** before deleting the entire thread.

I'M AVOIDING THE BOOK. IT'S DUE IN THREE DAYS, AND I'M AVOIDING IT.

I've finished watching *The Nocturnals* because that was easier than opening up the memoir, than confronting the end of this job and the start of something I haven't put a name to yet. I even went to a reverse running class with Noemie yesterday, hoping the backward jogging on treadmills would get the creativity flowing . . . and nothing.

But if I'm being realistic, it isn't the creativity. It's the fear. It's always, always the fear. Because even though we'll go through an editing process, finishing the book feels like the end of an era.

The truth is, the idea of writing another book based on a superficial connection is enough to make me want to sign up for the reverse running boot camp the instructor talked up earlier. As soon as I got off the phone with Stella, I knew I couldn't take that job. Maybe I've always known what I wanted, but I haven't been able to trust myself, and it's taken a while for my brain to catch up to my heart.

My new suitcase sits on the other side of my room, reminding me that this doesn't have to be an ending.

A deep breath, and I open Finn's book back up.

At first, I skim through everything I've written so far. And as I go, something strikes me—there's a strange current of emotion running throughout the book, from his acting to his Judaism to *Lord of the Rings*.

It's something like *love*.

I'm not sure how I missed it before when it's so tangled up in every chapter. His childhood in Reno and the dramatic readings he staged for his mom. His ill-fated portrayal of Cogsworth. How meticulously he researched Hux's science background for *The Nocturnals*, and his gradual understanding of his OCD and how to manage it.

Finnegan Walsh is earnest and *good* and worth every risk. And maybe we could have figured it out together, like he wanted to, but now I know I had to do it on my own first. I needed that space from him to truly see it.

I work for hours without pausing, without checking the clock or the word count. Maybe it's not a sun-drenched café in Silver Lake, but it's where I've written all my other books, and something about that brings me a comfort I've desperately needed since I touched down in Seattle.

I am a writer. I have always been a writer, but somewhere along the way, maybe to shield myself from the possibility of failure, I stopped writing for myself. I stopped writing for the pure love of it and let my voice disappear into someone else's.

Not anymore.

This book will have Finn's name on the cover—I've known that since the beginning.

And the next one, I'm determined, will have mine.

THE NOCTURNALS

Season 4, Episode 22: "Graduation, Part 2"

INT. OAKHURST QUAD—NIGHT

*CALEB RHODES, ALICE CHEN, OLIVER HUXLEY, MEG
LAWSON, SOFIA PEREZ, and WESLEY SINCLAIR stand in a
circle, watching the sky. The Raiders will show up
at any moment. Caleb and Alice are holding hands,
Hux and Meg are hugging, and Sofia is clutching the
Scarlet Talisman. Even Wesley looks serious for
what might be the first time in his life.*

> CALEB
> So . . . this is where it ends. Us
> against them. Funny, all I thought I'd
> be doing today was getting a piece of
> paper that said I managed to survive
> the past four years.

> WESLEY
> Don't tempt fate. You still might not.

> MEG
> I'm scared.

> HUX
> *He holds her closer and kisses the top of her head.*

> I know—I am, too. But I think it's less
> scary to be scared together, isn't it?

chapter
TWENTY-NINE

LOS ANGELES, CA

The studio is packed, swarms of fans dressed head to toe in fake fur, whiskers painted on their cheeks. They're brandishing homemade signs and grinning with plastic fangs and hugging each other tightly, squealing and shrieking and shedding a few tears because finally, *finally*, it's happening. Their favorite characters, back together for this one night.

Even after all the cons, it's still a sight to behold: all these people gathered here because of this thing they love so deeply.

I didn't exactly go all out, but at least my ship is obvious. I found an I'D MUCH RATHER BE UNUSUAL T-shirt on Etsy, which I've paired with Finn's dagger-patterned socks for a little extra strength. Though I can't count the number of planes I've been on since September, I white-knuckled the armrests the entire flight, with Noemie beside me offering whispered reassurances. That I haven't screwed things up. That Finn won't have changed his mind.

I understand if you can't make it, he texted last night. **But I really hope you will.**

I told him that of course I would be there. How could I miss it after everything we'd been through?

In her matching shirt, Noemie grips my wrist when we arrive at our reserved first-row seats. "Our names are on these," she says, stunned. "What is your life?"

Maybe at the end of the day, I'll have an answer for her.

The reunion opens with some footage from the show, a montage of its most memorable moments, punctuated by laughs and cheers from the audience. There's Caleb's first transformation, the scene he's forced to choose between Alice and Sofia, Hux and Meg's first kiss. A couple well-timed zingers from Wesley. There's the serum Hux develops at the end of the series that helps Meg control her werewolf side a bit more, enabling them to finally have a real relationship and for her to fearlessly pursue her passion for art history. Then the final shot of the show: all six characters standing in the rubble of what was once Oakhurst University on graduation day, after battling their villains one last time. They're bleeding and limping and covered with dirt, but they're victorious. And as they take a few moments to account for their injuries, making sure everyone's okay, the viewer knows it, too—that whatever's ahead for them, whatever the real and supernatural worlds throw their way, they're going to be able to handle it.

After the applause, the lights go up, revealing the six leads onstage. The audience rushes to their feet in a thunderous standing ovation, and by the time I sit down, my hands sting. Juliana and Cooper look a little bashful, Hallie and Bree grinning and waving, Ethan smirking.

And Finn.

He looks beautiful, of course, because he always does, dressed in a deep green button-up, gray tie, and a sweater vest that wardrobe debated for a solid half hour during rehearsals. He's the airbrushed version of himself, the one I got so used to seeing at cons and on my laptop screen—but there's something different about him. A weariness, maybe, that I haven't seen before, unless I'm imagining it just because of how much I've missed him.

Because if there was any doubt about it before I hopped on that flight, it doesn't exist now, my heart aching with the hope that he still wants me, even after I escaped back to Seattle.

The reunion is, in a word, delightful. The cast share their favorite moments, behind-the-scenes secrets, and answer questions, and the audience savors every minute of it.

Also delightful: the fact that Ethan makes an absolute idiot of himself onstage. The whole time, he seems distracted, rubbing at his elbow or reaching into his pocket, like he wants to check his phone but knows he can't.

"I would have been happy to keep both of them," he says with a sly smile when Zach Brayer, the series creator, asks him to settle a debate once and for all: Alice or Sofia. "But for some reason, Zach wasn't too keen on it."

Toward the end of the show, when it's time for audience questions, someone asks about rumors of a reboot or spin-off swirling around the internet. I've seen the rumors, too—they all seem to stem from the fact that Zach said last month that he'd love to write something else set in the *Nocturnals* universe, maybe even with some of the same characters.

"A reboot? I don't think so," Ethan says with a laugh. "No offense, but it would feel a little like going backward. I think I'm just at a different stage of my career right now."

A wave of gossipy murmurs moves through the audience.

"So he's just determined to be the worst, huh," Noemie mutters.

"I mean—" Ethan says, fumbling, clearly seeing the fans are souring on him, but Hallie's already talking over him.

"For those of us who aren't above the show that jump-started all of our careers, I would *love* to do a reboot. Or a spin-off," she says. "Meg at age thirty, trying to balance being a werewolf with her job as a museum curator? Here for it." This gets a few hoots and a round of applause.

But the best part is when Finn catches my eye, his gaze lingering on me for a long, lovely moment.

In that one glance, I can tell there's hope.

AFTERWARD, NOEMIE LEAVES TO GET DRINKS WITH SOME FANS SHE met years ago in a forum while I head backstage, searching for Finn's dressing room. The crew recognized me from rehearsals, waved me right back. The halls are narrow, my feet unsteady, and by the time I find the door with *Finn Walsh* scrawled on a moon-shaped placard, my heart is in my throat.

I smooth out a wrinkle in my shirt, adjust the heavy messenger bag I've been carrying, and knock.

"Just a minute," Finn calls. When he opens the door, jaw going slack, it's clear he wasn't expecting me. His face is a little pink, like he's just wiped off his makeup, and his fingers freeze in the middle of loosening his tie. I have to fight the urge to grab it myself and tug him closer, because suddenly that's all I want to do.

"You were amazing," I say instead.

"Thank you. Uh." He glances backward, rakes a hand through his hair. "Do you want to come in? It's not much, but . . ."

"Right, sure. Of course." This awkwardness between us is

new. He opens the door wider, revealing a vanity and costume rack, a half dozen flower arrangements crowding a tiny desk. The room is so small, I wonder if he can hear the racing of my pulse.

This is Finn, I remind myself. The man who has never given me a reason to feel anything but confident. *I can do this.*

He leans back against the vanity as I pull the spiral-bound manuscript from my bag. "I know no one uses hard copies anymore. But every time I imagined walking up to you like this, I was holding a massive stack of paper. For dramatic effect, and all that. Oh, and there might be a coffee stain on pages eighty-five and eighty-six—sorry about that." I pass it to him with trembling hands. "So . . . here it is. Your book."

A breath catches in his throat. He opens it up as though it's something delicate and not something I printed for forty dollars at Office Depot, his eyes lingering on some paragraphs longer than others. I hope he can see how much love for his work is in there. How much love for *him*, even when I tried to leave my own voice out of it. Because it's just like he said: I can't hide completely, and Finn is the last person I want to hide from.

When he speaks again, his voice is thick. Emotional. "No," he says, giving the plain white cover a pat. "*Our* book." For once, I don't fight him on it. "I love it. Some part of me feels like I don't deserve a book this good, but I'm not going to protest. I fucking love it, and you are fucking phenomenal."

"Thank you," I say, meaning it. "And you're welcome."

He places the book on the vanity, right next to a card that says HOWL NEVER FORGET YOU—XX BREE.

"I've been thinking a lot," he says, sliding his hands into his pockets, nudging my shoe with his. "And I know I might have sounded a little harsh that day at my house. I might have pushed you too much. Whatever you do, whether you're writing for your-

self or for other people, you're going to be incredible a
you've done for me, with this book . . . I'm not sure if 'th
will ever be enough. All of this has made me think I'm n
washed-up has-been. You helped me realize that."

"You've helped me, too." I pick at my nail polish. "I'm n
I've ever felt more confident in my writing than when you'
one reading it. And—I'm going to finish my book," I say,
determination in my voice. "After that, I'll see how it goes."

He nods. "I like the sound of that. And I like your shirt, too,
the way."

"Thanks, but . . . this isn't my ship."

"No?" A quirk of his mouth as he inches closer.

"I actually prefer Hux with someone else."

"Blasphemy."

I swallow hard. Because as much as I'd love to kiss him, there
are a few things I need to tell him first. Now or never, even if he
said I could take all the time I needed. I've known how I've felt for
weeks, maybe months, and it's time I say it. No flowery language,
no symbolism or hidden meaning. Just words—the right words.

"Over the past few months," I start, "we've really gotten to
know each other. Much better, in fact, than I know most people in
my life. I was supposed to be interviewing you, writing your life
story . . . but somehow we started interviewing each other. We
both opened up, shared things I'm not sure we've ever shared with
anyone else."

Even if we started off-balance, Finn has been all in on this
relationship for longer than I have. He's never wavered. And sure,
he's probably more famous than I'll ever be, even if he's not a
household name—but he's never made me feel like my career, as
nebulous as it is, doesn't matter.

"It was never just professional for me," I continue, "not even at

it. What
ank you'
ot just a

t sure
e the
ore

by

...ans I should have been fired. Maybe
...he job, but that would have meant that
...lose as we did. And—and I never would
...ake a step closer. "We never would have
...realized that while we can do great things
...nk we can also be pretty great together."

...s face could rip me apart and put me back to-
...yself not to glance away, to meet that gaze with
...ability. "I'm so deeply in love with you, and what-
...ooks like after this book—I want you in it."

...can take another breath, his arms are around me, heat
...ort and *relief.* "I love you so much, sweetheart," he says
...hair, his hand cradling the back of my neck. Thumb skim-
...up my ear. "I adore you. The amount of makeup they had to
...to hide my dark circles—I was so miserable after you left. I
...why you had to do it, but all I've been able to think about is
...nether you'd come back."

I bring a fingertip to the space beneath his eyes, brushing
along his skin. "You look pretty great to me."

When we kiss, it feels like the first deep breath I've taken all
week. Over and over, I tell him I love him, because suddenly I
can't stop saying it.

"So . . . long distance?" he asks. "Because I think we'd be really
fantastic at sexting."

I can't help laughing at that—he's probably right. "We'll figure
it out," I tell him, because the uncertainty doesn't scare me anymore. "But I'm not ready to live together just yet."

"Okay, but I will be over frequently. In your bed. And maybe
in the kitchen shirtless making pancakes and veggie bacon on
weekends."

"I am not opposed to any of that."

He holds me tighter, letting me burrow into his che. glad you took the risk," he whispers into my ear.

"That's the thing," I say to his heartbeat. Soft and stea true. "With you, it doesn't feel like one. It just feels like *hon*

t. "I'm so

dy and
e."

CREEN TO THE PAGE,
SH HAS RANGE

Walsh has a lot to smile about these days. The former *Noc-turnals* star's memoir debuted at number four on the *New York Times* bestseller list last month, with proceeds going to his new nonprofit Healthy Minds, which is designed to make therapy accessible to creatives with financial barriers. He's also been spotted across the country with his girlfriend of a year, writer Chandler Cohen, although the two are tight-lipped about how they met.

Fresh off a two-week-long book tour, Walsh is already diving back in to work. "I haven't been this busy in years," he said from his home in Los Angeles. "I feel so lucky to love what I'm doing."

Walsh's memoir, *Glasses Off*, chronicles his experience with OCD, his early days in Hollywood, and his life since *The Nocturnals* went off the air, all through a series of compelling vignettes. It's a must-read for fans of the teen paranormal drama but has significant broad appeal beyond that audience. Written in a gentle, irreverent manner, the book feels as though he's speaking directly to the reader as a close friend.

"The writing process was such a roller coaster," he said, unable to hide the joy in his voice. "And it was the most fun I've ever had."

EPILOGUE

SEATTLE, WA

Even from the other side of the bookstore, I can spot *Glasses Off*, and only partially because my favorite person is on the cover. Finn stands in a library, pinned against a deep-blue background, crushing a pair of broken spectacles and glancing at something off camera. The memoir anchors a display of the latest bestsellers, literary fiction and brightly colored cookbooks and celebrity tell-alls—written by other people, I'm sure.

I've been back to this store a few times since The Great Bookstore Theft that plunged my life into beautiful chaos, but tonight—tonight is different. Tonight, I'm forcing myself not to pick at my nails painted dark purple to match the cover, willing the nerves not to get the best of me. So I head toward the bar that holds the kind of memories I keep safely tucked next to my heart.

"Liquid courage?" someone asks from behind me.

I turn around, shaking my head. "No. Just contemplating the nature of fate, the intricacies of the universe, and how we got here."

"So nothing too profound then." Finn bumps my hip as he takes the stool next to me. There's more gray in his hair now, something I love to tease him about and that he doesn't mind at all.

"I wasn't expecting there to be so many people. Why are there so many people? Did they get the night wrong and think they're here to see Tana French instead? Is it too late to get her?"

Finn drapes an arm across my shoulder, pulls me close. "You can do this," he says, and because I half believe him, I give him a quick kiss. "You're going to be fantastic."

We head to the stage, our friends and family already waiting in the audience. Noemie and my parents and my aunts, Finn's mom and Krishanu and Derek. Then, with one final squeeze of my hand, Finn takes a seat in the front row while I make my way to the podium alone, drawing as much confidence as I can from my new black velvet blazer and fresh haircut.

"Thank you all so much for being here," I say after a bookseller introduces me. "It feels a little surreal, saying that, but I mean it: I had no idea if I'd ever get to this place, and I don't take any of it for granted." I hold up the book, a paperback with a smooth matte cover that I still can't believe has my name on it. "*The Poisoned Pen* isn't quite a cozy mystery, though I think it's plenty cozy—there's certainly enough romance in it to keep you warm. The ideal place to read it, as with any book, is by a fireplace with a mug of hot chocolate." At that, Finn's eyes spark with recognition.

"I started writing this book a long time ago," I continue, "but it didn't really coalesce for me until I was working on something completely different."

Only a handful of people here know what that something different was. A year after publication, two years since we started working on it, Finn's memoir is still featured prominently in the majority of bookstores. It went into a second printing before it was even released, and we've both already seen royalties from it. We talked about whether we wanted to go public with the fact that I'd written it, ultimately deciding to keep it a secret. Finn said it was entirely up to me, and I liked that it belonged to just us. A lovely, crucial piece of our history.

"I hope you enjoy it—or if you don't, please don't tell me." A few laughs. "But most of all, if you read it, I hope it lets you escape the real world for a while."

Afterward, there's cake and champagne and a signing line longer than I have any right for it to be. Sure, some people are probably here hoping to get a glimpse of Oliver Huxley, but for the most part, Finn and I have managed to live a quiet life. True to his word, he cut back on the con circuit and adopted a rescue dog named Bonnie who would always be happier to see me than him, which he'd defend by saying, "She sees me every day. Of course she *seems* more excited to see you when you're here." We split our time between Seattle and LA before we decided to rent out Finn's Los Feliz house and move in together this year, a quaint two-bedroom only a ten-minute drive from Noemie.

Stella sold *The Poisoned Pen* in a two-book deal shortly after I finished it, in large part thanks to the relationships I'd built through ghostwriting. The sequel is coming out next year, so I've been immersed in writing and working a part-time job at a bookstore near our apartment. Finn's wrapping production on a Hanukkah-themed romantic comedy, the first one for a network known mainly for Christmas movies. Plus, he's often traveling for stakeholder meetings for his nonprofit, Healthy Minds, which already has a dozen therapists on staff. Our lives are busier than they've ever been, and I can't imagine them any other way.

My parents are deeply amused by the whole thing, including

the fact that their daughter is in a relationship with someone they've watched on TV. My dad called him Hux for a full three months after I introduced him and still has the occasional slip.

"I still can't believe you haven't let us read it yet," my mom says after wrapping me in a hug. "We've read all the others!"

"Yes, but this one is different. Just to be safe, I think you should skip chapters three, eleven, fourteen, the last few pages of eighteen, and half of twenty." I consider this as I sign their copy. "And definitely twenty-two and twenty-four. Actually, maybe I should just hold on to this and redact some of those parts?"

"Those are all the good parts," Noemie stage-whispers, and I mime smacking her with the book.

Just when I think I've signed everything and all my friends and family have moved the party over to the bar, one last person approaches my table.

"Who should I make it out to?" I ask, the words still sounding strange but starting to feel more familiar.

"Your fiancé," Finn says as he slides the book forward.

Another word I haven't gotten used to, and I love the way it sounds in his voice. I glance down at the ring on my finger, warmth blooming in my chest. The engagement: a quiet, perfect moment between us a few months ago before we put his house up for rent. Glasses of wine, soft jazz playing from his sound system, Bonnie dozing in my lap. "Not being married to you feels like a complete waste of time," he said, toying with a strand of my hair. "I think we should fix that."

Now he watches me swipe my pen over the title page, nothing but the purest admiration in his eyes.

"My signature is a mess," I declare. The two C's aren't uniform, and it looks a little like I'm practicing cursive on one of those gridded worksheets for third graders. "After a while, I started thinking that it looked like I was signing 'Charlie Chaplin,' and then I got so overwhelmed that I might have actually signed a couple *as* Charlie Chaplin."

Finn looks down at it. "It looks pretty great to me," he says. "But if you want . . . I have a fair bit of experience with this sort of thing." His gaze slides back to mine, mouth quirking into my favorite kind of smile. "Maybe I could give you a few pointers?"

ACKNOWLEDGMENTS

To my editor, Kristine Swartz: Thank you for helping me find the heart of this book. As always, I'm deeply grateful for your insight, especially when it comes to topics both of us feel so strongly about. Working with you is an absolute dream.

At Berkley, tremendous thank-yous to Mary Baker, Jessica Plummer, Yazmine Hassan, Kristin Cipolla, Daniel Brount, and Megha Jain. Vi-An Nguyen, for another stunning cover. Across the pond, I'm so thrilled my books have found a UK home with Madeleine Woodfield and the Michael Joseph team! Thank you to Tawanna Sullivan for making it happen. Laura Bradford, for answering my neurotic emails and always knowing what I need to hear. And I owe so much gratitude to Taryn Fagerness for placing my books at publishers around the world. I can't adequately express how surreal it is to see them in stores. Thank you, too, to Hannah Vaughn and Alice Lawson at The Gersh Agency for being such fantastic champions of my books.

A good chunk of this book was written in the company of two people I admire very much: Vicki Campbell and Riv Begun; that week in Scotland was beyond perfect. Shout-out to Duncan for letting us back into the Airbnb when we locked ourselves out and for not being mad about it. Sarah Suk, Marisa Kanter, Carlyn Greenwald, and Kelsey Rodkey: I adore you. Thank you for the early reads, advice, and hand-holding. And thank you so much to Christina Lauren, Alicia Thompson, and Elissa Sussman for their time and kind words!

There are many excellent books that explore the topics Chandler is passionate about, and the two that helped me most during the writing process were *Come As You Are: The Surprising New Science that Will Transform Your Sex Life* by Emily Nagoski and *The Turnaway Study: Ten Years, a Thousand Women, and the Consequences of Having—or Being Denied—an Abortion* by Diana Greene Foster.

To Ivan, for everything, and for the theme songs. Even/especially the bad ones. Love you.

BUSINESS
— *or* —
PLEASURE

RACHEL LYNN SOLOMON

DISCUSSION QUESTIONS

1. Chandler begins the book in a state of despair about both her professional and personal life. How does this enable her to say yes to the job with Finn, in addition to going along with their scheme?

2. When Chandler suggests she give Finn some advice in the bedroom, she's certain she means it as a joke. Do you think she went into that scene hoping for a round two, or was it truly something that arose organically?

3. Sex is portrayed in vastly different ways across pop culture, from adult films to romance novels and everything in between. Chandler and Finn spend some time discussing how the media has shaped their own views on sex and intimacy. How has this kind of media impacted you, and how has that changed over the years?

4. OCD is another topic explored in the book that brings with it a host of misconceptions. Finn even remarks that he has "imposter syndrome" about his own mental illness. Where else have you seen OCD portrayed, and did it seem authentic? What distinguishes a positive portrayal of mental illness from one that might be harmful, and how would you classify this book's portrayal?

5. As a ghostwriter, Chandler is skilled in capturing her authors' voices. What are your feelings on ghostwritten books? If you know that a book is ghostwritten, how does it impact your enjoyment, if at all?

6. Despite not being a household name, Finn maintains throughout the book that he is content with his career and level of fame. What types of challenges does this create for his relationship with Chandler?

7. At what point do you think Finn starts falling for Chandler, and vice versa? Who do you think falls first?

8. Chandler and Finn's bedroom lessons are able to remain a secret for the entire book. What might have happened if this had been leaked to the press?

9. If you could read this book from Finn's point of view, what do you think his character arc would be? How would it differ from Chandler's?

10. What do you think the future holds for Chandler and Finn?

Photo by Sabreen Lakhani

RACHEL LYNN SOLOMON is the *New York Times* bestselling author of *The Ex Talk*, *Weather Girl*, and other romantic comedies for teens and adults. Originally from Seattle, she's currently navigating expat life in Amsterdam, where she can often be found exploring the city, collecting stationery, and working up the courage to knit her first sweater.

CONNECT ONLINE

RachelSolomonBooks.com

🐦 📷 RLynn_Solomon

Ready to find
your next great read?

Let us help.

Visit prh.com/nextread

Penguin
Random
House

The Mormon Papers

Are the Mormon Scriptures Reliable?

Harry L. Ropp

InterVarsity Press
Downers Grove
Illinois 60515

InterVarsity Press is the book publishing division
of Inter-Varsity Christian Fellowship,
a student movement active on campus at hundreds
of universities, colleges and schools of
nursing. For information about local and regional
activities, write IVCF, 233 Langdon St.,
Madison, WI 53703.

ISBN 0-87784-789-4
Library of Congress Catalog Card Number: 77-002681

Printed in the United States of America

Acknowledgements

I wish to express my gratitude to Lincoln Christian Seminary for permission to publish my M.A. thesis in this expanded form. I also wish to thank Dr. James D. Strauss and Mr. Donald C. Smith for their assistance in writing the thesis and this book. My wife, Karen, has also contributed greatly through her active support of the project.

58734

Introduction

The first fifty years of the nineteenth century gave birth to several new religious movements and witnessed widespread growth among the various Protestant denominations. In 1817, Jemima Wilkinson, who thought she was the Christ, founded a religious colony just twenty-five miles south of Palmyra, New York, in a community named Jerusalem. Jemima's group became known as the Public Universal Friends. The Baptists entered New York State and began to split into small sects. Between 1814 and 1830 the Reformed Baptists, Hard-shell Baptists, Free-will Baptists, Seventh-Day Baptists, Footwashers and other Baptist groups were formed.

In the late 1830s the Methodists became the largest denomination in America, growing from less than 15,000 in 1785 to nearly 900,000 by 1839. The Presbyterians at the beginning of the nineteenth century were located mainly on the East Coast with some churches in Kentucky and

Pennsylvania. By 1820 they had evangelized west of the Alleghenies enough to warrant the establishment of the Synod of Pittsburgh. As it began, this synod contained 216 congregations and 94 ministers.

In the midst of this religious ferment Joseph Smith grew to manhood. Young Joseph had moved with his family from Vermont to Palmyra, New York, in 1816. Between 1820 and 1830, Joseph laid the foundation for what has become one of the largest and fastest-growing religions in the world—the Church of Jesus Christ of Latter-day Saints, commonly called the Mormon Church. Beginning in 1830 with only six members, it has grown to an organization of 3,742,749. (Also according to Jerry Cahill [head of public communications department of the LDS Church] the total of 1976 converts was 133,959.) During the years 1966-1976, it increased by 1,130,000 members. This computes to 113,000 baptisms per year or over 300 per day during that span.

The Latter-day Saints Church is presently estimated to be the fifth largest religious body in the United States. The *1976 Yearbook of American and Canadian Churches* reported that "the six fastest-growing churches in the United States and their percentages of increase were: The Church of Jesus Christ of the Latter-day Saints, 21.5; Jehovah's Witnesses, 14.09; Assemblies of God, 5.27; Church of God (Cleveland), 4.97; Seventh-Day Adventists, 3.3; Church of the Nazarene, 3.04."

This expansion can be accounted for by the Mormon missionary system. In 1961 there were 10,300 full-time Mormon missionaries in the field; by 1969 there were 13,000. Presently the Mormons have over 26,000 full-time missionaries.

The Mormons have also experienced rapid growth in the British Isles and Europe. From 48,000 in 1960 they have increased to over 175,000 in 1976. Their missionary force is probably in excess of 4,000 in that area. Africa and the communist countries are the only portions of the world that have not seen a similar Mormon advance.

It is the Mormons' success in proselytizing that makes this book necessary. In 1831, Alexander Campbell wrote the first able review of the *Book of Mormon*. At the end of that review, Campbell apologized for even taking notice of the *Book of Mormon*: "Such is an analysis of the book of Mormon, the Bible of the Mormonites. For noticing of which I would have asked forgiveness from all my readers, had not several hundred persons of different denominations believed in it. On this account alone has it become necessary to notice it, and for the same reasons we must examine its pretentions to divine authority; for it purports to be a revelation from God."[1] Since Campbell made this statement, millions of people have made their way into Mormonism.

The purpose of this book is similar to Alexander Campbell's, namely, to examine the Mormon Church's claim to divine authority. Millions of people are in the Church of Jesus Christ of Latter-day Saints. If this Church is the only true church, as its missionaries assert, then these millions should be joined by millions more. But is the Mormon Church the only true church?

(We are talking throughout this book about the Church of Jesus Christ of Latter-day Saints, whose headquarters is in Salt Lake City, Utah. Several splinter groups have formed from the original company led by Joseph Smith. The only other offshoot of major consequence is the Reorganized Church of Jesus Christ of Latter-day Saints, whose headquarters is in Independence, Missouri. Although there are many similarities between these groups, there are also significant differences. One should be sure to learn about these variations before attempting to share the information in this book with members of the Reorganized Church.)

Many Christians today accept Mormons as brothers and sisters in the faith. This is an issue that must be dealt with immediately; so chapter one addresses the question, "Is Mormonism Christian?" Having seen that Mormons are not Christians, we must next ask, "Are the extrabiblical scriptures the Mormons hold sacred really the Word of God?" We will examine the *Book of Mormon*, the *Book of Commandments* and the *Doctrine and Covenants,* and the *Pearl of Great Price* in that order (chapters 2—5). In the final chapter we will consider how to witness to Mormons. This topic comes last because a Christian who wants to witness effectively to Mormons needs to have a solid background in the Mormon scriptures. That forty people are won into Mormonism for every one that is led out bears witness to the difficulty of the task.

My hope is that those who read this book will not only be strengthened to resist Mormon proselytizing but also be motivated and helped to turn Mormons to the truth.

Chapter **1.**

Is Mormonism Christian?

Over the past several years Mormonism has been trying to gain acceptance as a Christian denomination. Historically it has been denied that position. In recent days, by downplaying strong doctrinal teaching and inaugurating extensive television and radio campaigns, the Mormons have reached their goal in the minds of many. Since people in general are not sure what it means to be a Christian and since the Mormons talk about Christ, Mormons are easily assumed to be Christians. But are they?

To determine whether Mormonism is Christian, we will consider its teachings on three of the most important Christian doctrines—the doctrines of God, Christ and salvation, and the Bible.

God
Who does the Mormon Church say God is? The first lesson of the Mormon missionary handbook (*The Uniform System for*

Teaching Families) says, "God and Jesus Christ are separate and distinct persons, each has a glorified body of flesh and bone.... The father and his Son, Jesus Christ, are separate and distinct individuals and not just different manifestations of the same person.... Their bodies are much like ours, but are glorified and perfected."[1] Thus the Mormons declare that God and Jesus are two different gods. Joseph Smith also taught, "In the beginning, the head of the Gods called a council of the Gods; and they came together and concocted a plan to create the world and people it."[2]

Mormonism has an answer to the age-old question of where God came from. Joseph Smith said,

I am going to inquire after God; for I want you all to know him and to be familiar with him; ... I will go back before the beginning, before the world was, to show you what kind of being God is. God himself was once as we are now, and is an exalted Man and sits enthroned in yonder heavens.... I say, if you were to see him today, you would see him like a man in form—like yourselves, in all the person, image, and very form of man....

I am going to tell you how God came to be God. We have imagined and supposed that God was God from all eternity, I will refute that idea, and take away and do away the vail [sic], so that you may see.

Here, then, is eternal life—to know the only wise and true God; and you have got to learn how to be Gods yourselves, and to be kings and priests to God, the same as all Gods have done before you, namely, by going from one small degree to another, and from a small capacity to a great one, from grace to grace, from exaltation to exaltation, until you attain to the resurrection of the dead and are able to dwell in everlasting burnings and sit in glory, as do these who sit enthroned in everlasting power.[3]

Mormons believe that God used to be a man but was able to

learn how to be a god, and all Mormon men are planning on becoming gods just as they say our heavenly Father did. (The Mormons call this doctrine *eternal progression*.) Milton Hunter, a current Mormon writer, explains further, "Mormon prophets have continuously taught the sublime truth that God the Eternal Father was once a mortal man who passed through the school of earthlife similar to that through which we are now passing. He became God—an exalted being—through obedience to the same eternal Gospel truth that we are given opportunity today to obey."[4] Brigham Young, the second prophet, seer and revelator of the Mormon Church, said, "Gods exist and we had better strive to prepare to become one with them."[5] One of the most famous statements on this subject was made by Lorenzo Snow, former President and Prophet of the Mormon Church: "As man now is, God once was; as God now is, man may be."[6]

Mormons believe that God the Father has a wife with him in heaven. God is cohabiting with his wife and producing spirit-children who are then born into the bodies of earthly children. In other words, each of us is the result of two births, a spiritual birth in heaven and a physical birth on this earth. Both births are the result of sexual relations between each of our two sets of parents. In the second Mormon missionary lesson potential converts are taught, "Every person ever born on this earth lived in this premortal existence. We did not have physical bodies of flesh and bone as we now have. We lived as spirit-children of our Heavenly Father. . . . We testify to you that God is the father of our spirits, and that we lived with him before this life."[7]

Bruce McConkie, a prolific Mormon writer and apologist, states,

> Implicit in the Christian verity that all men are spirit children of an *Eternal Father* is the usually unspoken truth that they are also the offspring of an *Eternal Mother*. An exalted and glorified Man of Holiness (Moses 6:57)

could not be a Father unless a Woman of like glory, perfection, and holiness was associated with him as a Mother. The begetting of children makes a man a father and a woman a mother whether we are dealing in his mortal or immortal state.[8]

On April 9, 1852, Brigham Young introduced the Adam-God doctrine into Mormonism. From him we learn that God not only has a wife but is a polygamist, and that Adam and God are one and the same: "When our father Adam came into the garden of Eden, he came into it with a *celestial body*, and brought Eve, one of his wives, with him. . . . He *is our* Father and our God, and the only God with whom we have to do."[9]

To summarize: Jesus and God the Father are two distinct gods, both of them possessing glorified physical bodies. Besides these two perhaps hundreds or thousands of additional gods exist in the universe. God alone was not responsible for the creation of our world but was just the head of a council of gods who planned the earth. God is merely a man who went through an earthly life similar to ours and became exalted through a system like the one Mormons offer people today. In other words, man came from God, who was a man, who came from another god, and so forth. Mormons can offer no ultimate cause for existence but only an endless series of births. God is not alone in heaven but has many wives. He is continually having sex with his wives to produce spirit-children to be born into the bodies of earthly babies. This god came to earth as Adam and began the human race.

The Bible answers Mormon doctrine in terms that cannot be misunderstood. Deuteronomy 6:4 says, "Hear, O Israel! The Lord is our God, the Lord is one!" Again, in Isaiah 44:6, 8, "I am the first and I am the last, And there is no God besides Me. . . . Is there any God besides Me, Or is there any other Rock? I know of none."

The New Testament likewise confirms Christian monotheism. Paul teaches in 1 Timothy 2:5, "There is one God."

Occasionally Mormons will go to 1 Corinthians 8:5-6 to support their belief in many gods. But a close examination of these verses shows that Paul is actually asserting monotheism, not polytheism. Human beings may try to make gods out of many things, but that does not make these things truly gods.

Mormons declare that God has a physical body and that he is merely an exalted man. But Jesus says in John 4:24 that "God is spirit." Adding to this Jesus' teaching in Luke 24:39 that a spirit does not have flesh and bones shows us we must trust either Jesus or Joseph Smith. We cannot believe both.

Christ and Salvation

According to Mormon teaching, Jesus Christ's spirit, like ours, was pre-existent. Therefore, we are all literally brothers and sisters of Jesus and of each other. Jesus, though, is set apart since he was the first-born of the spirit-children of God. *Doctrine and Covenants* makes this clear in 93:21-23: "And now, verily I say unto you, I was in the beginning with the Father, and am the Firstborn; And all those who are begotten through me are partakers of the glory of the same, and are the church of the Firstborn. Ye were also in the beginning with the Father."

If all of us, including Jesus, were born spiritually in heaven before we were born physically, what sets Jesus apart from us besides his being the first-born spirit? Mormons teach it is the manner of Jesus' physical birth that makes him different.

Matthew 1:18-20 says that Mary was pregnant and that the Holy Spirit was the cause of that pregnancy. The remaining verses in the chapter explain that Mary was a virgin and remained a virgin until Jesus' birth. Although Mormons claim to believe this, they persistently deny that Mary conceived through the Holy Spirit. Brigham Young stated, "Now, remember from this time forth, and forever, that

Jesus Christ was not begotten by the Holy Ghost."[10]

Strangely enough, the *Book of Mormon* agrees with the Bible. In Alma 7:10 we read, "And behold, he shall be born of Mary, at Jerusalem which is the land of our forefathers, she being a virgin, a precious and chosen vessel, who shall be overshadowed and conceive by the power of the Holy Ghost, and bring forth a son, yea, even the Son of God." Yet despite the clear meaning of this verse, Joseph Fielding Smith, Tenth President of the Mormon Church, said, "They tell us the *Book of Mormon* states that Jesus was begotten of the Holy Ghost. I challenge that statement. The *Book of Mormon* teaches no such thing! Neither does the Bible."[11]

According to Mormon theology, God the Father, Jesus Christ, and the Holy Spirit are three separate and distinct individuals. So Jesus could not be the Son of God if the Holy Spirit was responsible for his conception. In order to make Jesus the Son of God, Mormons teach that God was responsible for the physical as well as the spiritual birth of Jesus. Brigham Young explained it this way: "The birth of the Savior was as natural as are the births of our children; it was the result of a natural action. He partook of flesh and blood— was begotten of his Father, as we were of our fathers."[12]

An early Mormon apostle, Orson Pratt, explained how God could have sexual relations with the wife of another man and not be considered sinful:

It was the personage of the Father who begat the body of Jesus; and for this reason Jesus is called "the Only Begotten of the Father;" . . . But God having created all men and women, had the most perfect right to do with His own creation, according to His holy will and pleasure: He had a lawful right to overshadow the Virgin Mary in the capacity of a husband, and beget a Son, although she was espoused to another; for the law which He gave to govern men and women was not intended to govern Himself, or to prescribe rules for his own conduct.[13]

From these statements it is difficult to understand how the Mormons can refer to Jesus as having been born of a virgin. And it is easy to see why this entire line of reasoning makes Christians shudder. This supposed Christian theology smacks of ancient pagan mythology and in no way accords with the God revealed in the Bible.

The Mormon view of Jesus' role in our salvation can be seen by referring to figure 1, "The Mormon Idea of Heaven." (This is a reproduction of a chart obtained at the Mormon Temple in Oakland, California.) The circle labeled "First Estate" represents the abode of God, the place in which we supposedly lived until we were born into an earthly body. At birth each of us entered the "Second Estate," or earth-life, which is a testing ground to determine where each of us will spend eternity. In other words, as the Mormon missionary handbook puts it, "Mortality is a probationary period during which we prepare to meet God again."[14]

From earth the way we go depends on us. The Mormons offer these options: The Telestial Kingdom, the Terrestrial Kingdom, and the Celestial Kingdom. Mormons teach that all people will go to one of them: "The gift of the resurrection will come to all men because of the death and resurrection of Christ. . . . Christ taught that we will go to different places after the resurrection, depending on how well we have kept his commandments."[15]

The "dishonest, liars, sorcerers, adulterers and whoremongers," and the like, will gain the Telestial Kingdom for eternity. People who are basically good, but being "blinded by the craftiness of men" do not become Mormons, are sent to the Terrestrial Kingdom. A person who wants to end up in the Celestial Kingdom must go through a rigid system of works. Placing one's faith in Christ as Savior, repentance, baptism and receiving the Holy Ghost—referred to by Mormons as the "first principles and ordinances of the Gospel" —are merely the entrance to the Straight and Narrow Way

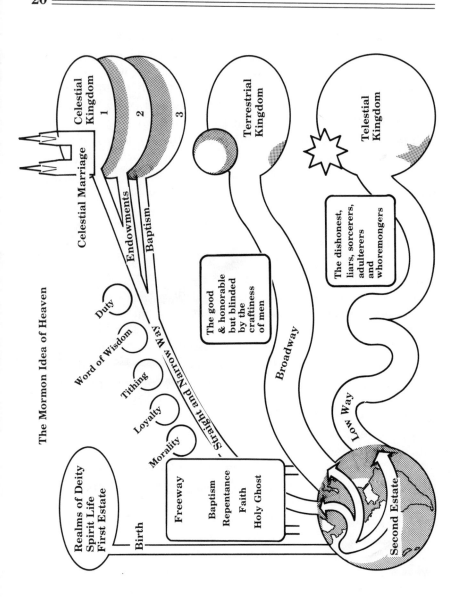

Figure 1. The Mormon Idea of Heaven

that leads to the Celestial Kingdom. To attain to the Celestial Kingdom, temple work (such as celestial marriage, baptism for the dead and endowments) must be performed. Not every Mormon is able to get into a temple to perform these rituals; only Mormons in good standing can gain entrance.

To be a Mormon in good standing one must lead a moral life, be loyal to the Church, give a minimum of ten per cent of one's gross income to the Church, keep the Word of Wisdom (abstaining from coffee, tea, alcohol and tobacco) and perform other duties at the request of the Church. If a Mormon does not keep these ordinances, his local bishop will not give him a recomment (pass) to enter a temple. Every Mormon is responsible to work out his own salvation beyond what Christ has done for him. This is made quite evident in the missionary lessons: "The Lord has made you responsible for preparing yourself to enter his kingdom. Mr. Brown, do you feel that each person should be responsible for his own salvation?"[16]

The Bible, however, does not place us in such a position. The Bible declares, "By the works of the Law no flesh will be justified in His sight" (Rom. 3:20). It is futile for us to strive to make ourselves right with God; we cannot do it. Paul taught the Christians at Ephesus: "By grace you have been saved through faith; and that not of yourselves, it is the gift of God; not as a result of works, that no one should boast" (Eph. 2:8-9). The use of the perfect participle—literally "having been saved"—indicates that salvation precedes good works. Verse 10 then states that good works are the result of a life that has been remade by Jesus Christ. Good works cannot earn merit for us but they are the outward manifestation of a life made new by Christ. Christians indeed are commanded to live a life befitting their relationship to a holy God. But justification is by God's grace through faith. As Christians we have assurance that the shed blood of Jesus "cleanses us from all sin."

Unfortunately, the blood of the Jesus in which the Mormons believe is not that powerful. Brigham Young maintained, "It is true that the blood of the Son of God was shed for sins through the fall and those committed by men, yet men can commit sins which it can never remit. There are sins that can be atoned for by an offering upon an altar, as in ancient days; and there are sins that the blood of a lamb, of a calf or of turtle doves, cannot remit, but they must be atoned for by the blood of man."[17] Mormons in the time of Brigham Young practiced "Blood Atonement" openly. Although Mormons do not do this today, they still believe there are some sins that are beyond the atoning work of Christ.

This atonement is codified in the Mormon practice of "Blood Atonement," in which a person's blood is shed for his own sin. Even in modern times, for example, a condemned criminal in Utah may choose hanging or the firing squad, thus giving a Mormon the option to have his own blood shed to accomplish atonement for sins not covered by the death of Christ. Brigham Young says, "There is not a man or woman, who violates the covenants made with their God, that will not be required to pay the debt. The blood of Christ will never wipe that out, your own blood must atone for it."

The Bible

When asked if they accept the Bible as the Word of God, most Mormons respond by quoting article eight in their Articles of Faith: "We believe the Bible to be the word of God as far as it is translated correctly." At first glance that sounds orthodox, but it does not accurately represent the Mormon attitude toward the Bible. Mormons quote much from the Bible. The King James is their favorite version and is, in fact, their only officially accepted translation. Despite their extensive use of the Bible, however, they do not really trust it.

Joseph Smith himself had reservations about the Bible. He once stated, "I believe the Bible as it read when it came from the pen of the original writers. Ignorant translators, careless transcribers, or designing and corrupt priests have committed many errors."[18]

The *Book of Mormon* reflects this same attitude:

And after they go forth by the hand of the twelve apostles of the Lamb, from the Jews unto the Gentiles, thou seest the foundation of a great and abominable church, which is most abominable above all other churches; for behold, they have taken away from the gospel of the Lamb many parts which are plain and most precious; and also many covenants of the Lord have they taken away. (1 Nephi 13:26)

James E. Talmage, in his book *The Articles of Faith*, says,

There will be, there can be no absolutely reliable translation of these or other scriptures unless it is effected through the gift of translation, as one of the endowments of the Holy Ghost. . . . Let the Bible then be read reverently and with prayerful care, the reader ever seeking the light of the Spirit that he may discern between the truth and the errors of men.[19]

Talmage says "there can be no absolutely reliable translation." The reason we cannot have a reliable translation is not that we do not have adequate scholarship but that the materials from which we must translate have been corrupted. Orson Pratt wrote, "Who knows that even one verse of the whole Bible has escaped pollution, so as to convey the same sense now that it did in the original?"[20]

The question then arises as to who made these changes. In 1 Nephi 13:26, the responsibility for them is placed on the "great and abominable church." In the *Missionary Pal*, Mormon Keith Marston suggests that the Roman Catholic Church is that "great and abominable church."[21] Being more direct in the *Divine Authenticity of the Book of Mormon*, Orson Pratt states quite plainly that the "Romanists" are responsible for the corruptions in the Bible manuscripts.[22]

Mormon missionaries, as well as many other Mormons, quote the Bible freely, which is rather strange in light of their insistence that it is basically untrustworthy. In their proselytizing activities they imply that they wholeheartedly accept the Bible; but when presented with a contradiction between the Bible and Mormon doctrine, they refer to article eight in the Articles of Faith and say that the only reason there appears to be a contradiction is that the Bible is translated incorrectly at that point.

While the issue of the accuracy of the Bible text as we have it today may not be as crucial as the doctrines of God and Christ, it is nonetheless important because it bears on one's view of the final authority in religious debate. Christians have historically affirmed that each of the Bible's books "is inspired by God and profitable for teaching, for reproof, for correction, for training in righteousness" (2 Tim. 3:16), and few, if any, believe today that the Bible text has been so corrupted that it is an unreliable source of doctrine. The reasons we can have confidence in the accurate transmission of the original texts will be outlined in chapter six.

Thus, their views of God, of Christ and his role in securing our salvation, and of the Bible set Mormons apart from orthodox Christians. In fact, Mormons desperately need to know the way of salvation. But before we can share it with them effectively we must understand the problems with the Mormon system of belief. Who was this Joseph Smith, and why can we be sure the documents he produced were not divinely inspired? We will begin by discussing the origin of the *Book of Mormon* and the difficulties that stand in the way of affirming it as a revelation from God.

Chapter 2.

The Book of Mormon

There are several theories about the origin of the *Book of Mormon*. According to the official version, the year of 1820 was one of extensive religious activity in the Palmyra, New York area, with the Methodists and Presbyterians holding revivals all over western New York. In this climate, young Joseph Smith found himself uncertain about which church was doctrinally correct. Early one spring morning in 1820 he decided to claim the promise for wisdom in James 1:5. He went into the woods to seek guidance about which church to join.

While he was praying, a pillar of light began to shine around him and he saw two people in the pillar. One spoke to him and said, "This is My Beloved Son. Hear Him!" When Joseph asked which of the sects was right, he was instructed to join none of them, because "they draw near to me with their lips, but their hearts are far from me; they teach for doctrines the commandments of men, having a form of godliness, but they deny the power thereof " (Writings of Joseph Smith 2:19).

This was just the first of several visions Joseph was to have. The next was on September 21, 1823. This time an angel appeared to Joseph and told him about some gold plates he was to translate. These plates, the angel said, contained the "fullness of the gospel" as revealed to the former inhabitants of this continent by Jesus Christ himself. The angel also told Joseph that the Urim and Thummim, two seer stones, were with the plates and were to be used to translate them from Reformed Egyptian to English.

On September 22, 1823, Joseph Smith had another vision in which the angel Moroni told him where to find the golden plates containing a record of the former inhabitants of this continent. A man named Mormon was largely responsible for the content and preservation of these plates; thus, when they were translated by Joseph Smith the book took on his name.

When Joseph arrived at the place, the hill Cumorah, he moved a large stone and thus uncovered a stone box holding the golden plates, a breastplate and the two stones set in silver bows (that is, like spectacles). He was prevented from taking the plates from the box and was told he must undergo four years probation before he would be allowed to remove them. The plates were finally delivered to him on September 22, 1827, with this charge (in Joseph Smith's own words): "That I should be responsible for them; that if I should let them go carelessly, or through any neglect of mine, I should be cut off; but that if I would use all my endeavors to preserve them until he, the messenger, should call for them, they should be protected" (Writings of Joseph Smith 2:59).

Not long after he received the plates Joseph and his wife Emma moved to her father's home in Harmony, Pennsylvania, hoping to find a peaceful place to work on translating the plates. While in Pennsylvania, Joseph was called on by

Martin Harris, a wealthy farmer from near Joseph's home in New York. Harris was so impressed with the work that he proceeded to assist Joseph in the translating. By June 14, 1828, Harris had written 116 pages of manuscript, as dictated by Joseph.

To convince his wife of the genuineness of the venture, he persuaded Joseph to allow him to take the manuscript home for her examination. While the manuscript was with Harris, it was stolen and never recovered. Because the manuscript had been lost, God, so Smith claimed, would not allow that part of the plates to be retranslated. Though Harris was never again allowed to help in the process of translation, he played an important part in the movement Joseph soon began.

Oliver Cowdery was the next scribe Joseph Smith used when he resumed the translation work in April of 1829. When the two men learned that the *Book of Mormon* taught baptism for the remission of sins, they went to the woods to pray about this revelation because Smith had never been baptized. On May 15, 1829, while they were praying, a heavenly messenger appeared to them and identified himself as John the Baptist. He stated, as he laid his hands on them, that he was ordaining them into the Aaronic priesthood, and that afterwards they should baptize each other. They were given the keys to the ministerings of angels and the authority to baptize for the remission of sins, but not the authority to confer the Holy Spirit by the laying on of hands—a gift they would receive at some time in the future. The messenger said he was acting in the name of the Messiah and under the direction of Peter, James and John, who held the keys to the priesthood of Melchizedek which would also be given to them later (Writings of Joseph Smith 2:72).

In June of 1829 the work of translating was completed. Up to this time, because the process of translation went on with Joseph and the plates behind a curtain and the scribe on the other side taking dictation, no one but Joseph had actually seen the plates. In the course of the translating, the record itself revealed that the plates were to be shown to others: "Three witnesses shall behold it by the power of God, besides him to whom the book shall be delivered; and they shall testify to the truth of the book and the things therein. And there is none other which shall view it, save it be a few according to the will of God, to bear testimony of his word unto the children of men; for the Lord God hath said that the words of the faithful should speak as if it were from the dead" (2 Nephi 27:12-13).

This gave rise to "The Testimony of Three Witnesses" and later "The Testimony of Eight Witnesses." The three witnesses were Oliver Cowdery, David Whitmer and Martin Harris. The eight witnesses were Christian, Jacob, Peter and John Whitmer, Hyrum Page, Joseph Smith's father and Joseph's brothers Hyrum and Samuel. (These two testimonies are still found in every copy of the *Book of Mormon*.)

Soon E. B. Grandin of Palmyra was hired to print five thousand copies of the book. The completed volume contained nearly six hundred pages and came off the press in the spring of 1830. Thus, according to the Mormon Church, the *Book of Mormon* came into being.

To summarize briefly, the basic story of the *Book of Mormon* involves the migration of two groups of people from the Near East to the North American continent. The first migration was supposed to have occurred just before the confusion of the languages at the Tower of Babel. The second departure was from Jerusalem immediately prior to its destruction (in approximately 600 B. C.). A third migration was small and unimportant.

The story of the second migration and the resultant civilization comprise the bulk of the book. After arriving in North America, these people divided into two tribes, one following Nephi and the other his brother Laman. Eventually the

Lamanites turned against God and warred with the Nephites. God cursed the Lamanites with a dark skin. The dark-skinned Lamanites eventually killed all the fair-skinned Nephites and were discovered by Columbus and called Indians. The last remaining Nephite prophet, Moroni, hid the golden plates on which the Nephites' records were kept so Joseph Smith could find them and bring them to light.

The First Vision

Since Joseph's first vision supposedly initiated his divine calling, it deserves at least a brief consideration before we take an extensive look at the revelation which came less than a decade after it.

In recent years much information has come to light about the official Latter-day Saints version of Joseph Smith's first vision. Jerald and Sandra Tanner are responsible for bringing much of the information available on Mormonism to light. They are ex-Mormons who live in Salt Lake City just thirteen blocks from the Salt Lake Temple. Because of their previous connections with the Mormon Church, they have had access to many rare documents and information to which others would have been denied access. They have written in excess of twenty-five books and pamphlets on Mormonism and printed them in their garage. In a recent book, *The First Vision Examined*, the Tanners inform us that there are many conflicting statements regarding this first vision. According to Joseph Smith, he was born on December 23, 1805 (Writings of Joseph Smith 2:3). This would have made him fourteen years old when he received his first vision, according to the official account. The Tanners have reproduced a photocopy of a record of the first vision, dictated by Joseph Smith, in which he states he was "in the 16th year of my age." In this version, Joseph only relates seeing one person ("I saw the Lord") while in the official account he says, "I saw two personages." A photocopy of this differing narrative was published in the Spring, 1969, edition of *Brigham Young University Studies.*

The Tanners also have reproduced another description of the first vision as it was told and recorded in 1835. In this second unofficial narrative, Joseph Smith gives his age as "about 14 years old," which is in harmony with the official account. But he nowhere mentions seeing the Father or the Son. Rather, he relates that he saw many angels, one of whom forgave his sins and testified that Jesus is the Son of God. In neither of the other two versions are angels mentioned. A photocopy of this version also appeared in the Spring, 1969, edition of *Brigham Young University Studies.*

Another important part of the official account of the first vision is the date on which it took place. Joseph Smith indicated that a general religious revival in the Palmyra, New York area in 1820 led to his first vision. Wesley P. Walters, in 1967, published evidence that there was no revival in the Palmyra vicinity between 1819 and 1824. Not until fall, 1824, did a revival occur.[1]

These disparities make us wonder if Joseph Smith really had a first vision or if he later elaborated on some "half-remembered dream" or created a sheer invention to enhance his reputation with the faithful.[2]

The Origin of the Book of Mormon

Not only is the first vision in doubt, but the source of the *Book of Mormon* is not as certain as the Mormon Church would have us believe. Several alternative explanations are live options. We shall examine the theories set forth by Fawn Brodie, George Arbaugh and Hal Hougey. Each of these three theories respond to Mormon claims and expose problems in the *Book of Mormon* text.

Fawn Brodie's Theory. In 1943, Fawn Brodie received an Alfred A. Knopf Fellowship in Biography. The result of this fellowship was *No Man Knows My History,* the finest and most comprehensive biography of Joseph Smith written to date.

Fawn Brodie was born and raised a Mormon. She cannot remember the first time she heard of Joseph Smith and his visions and his golden plates. "I seem always to have known him," she has said. The amount of research that went into her biography is staggering. The result of her efforts is the most authoritative work on the life of Joseph Smith available, one essential to any student of Mormonism.

Brodie's basic conclusion is that Joseph Smith himself was the author of the *Book of Mormon*. She considers Joseph to have been a genius and a born leader. Here is an example of her attitude after extensive research: "Scholars of American literary history have remained persistently uninterested in the *Book of Mormon*. Their indifference is most surprising since the book is one of the earliest examples of frontier fiction, the first long Yankee narrative that owes nothing to English literary fashions. Except for the borrowings from the King James Bible, its sources are absolutely American."[3]

Brodie explains the content of the *Book of Mormon* from the historical setting of the author, seeing it as an "obscure compound of folklore, moral platitude, mysticism, and millennialism." The book was an attempt to answer those questions most in the minds of Joseph's contemporaries, especially about the origin of the American Indian, the secrets of the Masonic Lodge and Calvinism versus Arminianism.

Brodie suggests Joseph wrote the Nephite and Lamanite history first, but as discussion about the Indians' origin continued, the time span this history covered (namely, 600 B.C. to A.D. 400) seemed to him inadequate. Speculation that the Indians had migrated to this continent as early as the time of Noah was set forth in 1820 by Caleb Atwater. In 1823, Ethan Smith published *View of the Hebrews,* in which he quoted several Indian legends that were similar to the

Old Testament flood account. Even the title of Ethan Smith's book suggests that Joseph was not the only one who had theorized that the Indians might have descended from the Hebrews.

To fill in the void, Joseph wrote the history of Jared and his descendants. They built boats described similarly to Noah's ark and filled them with animals, food and seed. Brodie points out that Joseph was careless in his choice of domestic animals, for he had them bring horses, swine, sheep, cattle and asses. It was widely known even in Joseph's day that Columbus had not found any of these animals when he landed in the Americas.[4] Joseph also, by the way, made the mistake of having the Nephites produce wheat and barley instead of the indigenous maize and potatoes.[5]

Realizing there were imperfections in his work, Joseph sought to cover them with explanations within the book itself. Brodie cites three places in which this seems to be the motive behind particular verses. In one place, Mormon apologizes for having to use Reformed Egyptian because he had no room to write in Hebrew. This, he says, is the reason for the imperfections. In two other places, the *Book of Mormon* asserts that if it has any imperfections they are the mistakes of men.[6]

It is through Joseph's magnetic personality and his intuitive understanding of his followers that Brodie accounts for the visions Joseph's followers had. She labels this "the talent for making men see visions." Among these visions she includes Cowdery's seeing of John the Baptist and the viewing of the golden plates by the three witnesses and the eight witnesses.

One of the best examples of this talent is an account of the eight witnesses and their testimony to the existence of the plates:

The witnesses were "set to continual prayer, and other spiritual exercises." Then at last "he [Joseph] assembled them in a room, and produced a box, which he said contained the precious treasure. The lid was opened; the witnesses peeped into it, but making no discovery, for the box was empty, they said, 'Brother Joseph, we do not see the plates.' The prophet answered them, 'O ye of little faith! how long will God bear with this wicked and perverse generation? Down on your knees . . . pray . . . for a holy and living faith.' " After over two hours of prayer, looking again into the box they were persuaded that they saw the plates.[7]

Fawn Brodie sees the *Book of Mormon* as the product of one man, Joseph Smith. His genius alone accounts for its existence. All of those involved in the forming of the Mormon Church were victims of Joseph's powerful and persuasive personality.

George Arbaugh's Theory. George Arbaugh is so certain of the so-called Spaulding-Rigdon theory that in the opening pages of his work on Mormon revelation he declares that Sidney Rigdon was the founder of Mormonism and that Rigdon chose Joseph Smith to be its prophet.[8] The bulk of the information available on this theory has been collected by Charles Shook in his *True Origin of the Book of Mormon.* It contains affidavits and letters written between 1833 and 1900 which Shook organized and published in 1914. Arbaugh's section on the origin of the *Book of Mormon* uses Shook's book for most of its information.

The theory presents the Reverend Solomon Spaulding as the writer of a romance explaining the origin of the American Indians. He began to write this novel when he lived in Conneaut, Ohio, in 1809. In 1812, Spaulding and his family moved to Pittsburgh, and there he turned his manuscript over to Robert Patterson, a local printer, to be published. Patterson had an employee, J. H. Harrison, who was a friend of Sidney Rigdon. Rigdon frequently lounged around the printing office, and when the manuscript came up missing,

Rigdon was suspected of the theft. Rigdon reworked the manuscript with the aid of Smith and Cowdery, and thus we have what is known as the *Book of Mormon*.[9]

The affidavits and letters Shook gathered contain an abundance of material to support this theory. This evidence comes from Solomon Spaulding's immediate family, from other relatives, close and distant, and from other people who came into contact with his writings. Shook's collection also includes information that pertains to Sidney Rigdon and his whereabouts at crucial points in the story. Further, it has material that tries to establish contact between Sidney Rigdon and Joseph Smith before Rigdon's conversion to Mormonism in the early 1830s.

Fawn Brodie deals with the Spaulding-Rigdon theory in Appendix B of her biography. She denies the conclusiveness of the evidence Shook presents. She contends that Joseph Smith was himself capable of writing the book and that Rigdon could not have had any contact with Smith before 1830.

In Appendix B, Brodie gives a list of the activities of Rigdon from November 2, 1826, to November 14, 1830. In examining this list, we see several gaps of unaccounted-for time—gaps which coincide with several important events in the life of Smith and his activities in translating the *Book of Mormon*. The first gap is from August 23 to October 9, 1827. This includes the date of September 22, 1827, when Smith claimed he received the plates.

Another gap occurs in Rigdon's activities between May and July, 1829. It was on May 15 that John the Baptist supposedly visited Smith and Cowdery. Some months later, Cowdery, on meeting Sidney Rigdon, was amazed at the similarity between Rigdon's voice and the voice of John the Baptist. In addition, during the first week of June, the translation was completed. While Brodie does not think this theory is correct, her own evidence heavily supports it.

Hal Hougey's Theory. While Hal Hougey was not the first to set forth the similarity between the *Book of Mormon* and Ethan Smith's *View of the Hebrews,* he has, in his booklet *"A Parallel"–The Basis of the Book of Mormon*, enlarged the amount of information available.

Hougey shows that prior to Joseph Smith's publication of the *Book of Mormon* several books had advanced the theory that the American Indians were of Hebrew descent. Hougey also reports frequent newspaper articles on the subject to which Joseph Smith had access. It seems to have been a common topic of conversation. Joseph's interest in the matter is borne out by his mother: "During our evening conversations, Joseph would occasionally give us some of the most amusing recitals that could be imagined. He would describe the ancient inhabitants of this continent, their dress, mode of traveling, and the animals upon which they rode; their cities, their buildings, with every particular; their mode of warfare; and also their religious worship. This he would do with as much ease, seemingly, as if he had spent his whole life with them."[10] Such statements, according to Joseph's mother, were made by Joseph in 1824, several years before he translated the *Book of Mormon.*

Much of the information Hougey uses was compiled by B. H. Roberts, a Mormon apostle and historian. After Roberts's death, his son made public mimeographed copies of his father's list of parallels between the *Book of Mormon* and Ethan Smith's *View of the Hebrews.* The list offers a large number of important items. These are a few of them:

1. Both set forth the Hebrew origin of the American Indian.

2. Both talk of an ancient book hidden—buried in the ground.

3. Both speak of prophets and seers.

4. Both mention the Urim and Thummin and a breastplate.

5. Both speak of ancient Egyptian inscriptions.

6. Both talk of a civilized and a barbaric element in the population.

7. Both have references to the destruction of Jerusalem.

8. Both talk of the gathering of Israel "in the last days."

9. Both quote extensively from Isaiah.

10. Both speak of a great gentile nation rising up in America in the last days to save Israel.

11. Both speak of the practice of polygamy among the early people.

12. Both speak of widespread ancient civilization on the American continent.

13. Both speak of an appearance of a white God on the American continent.[11]

Hougey says that *View of the Hebrews* was published seven years prior to the *Book of Mormon*; the first edition was printed in 1823 and the second in 1825. The book was published in Poultney, Vermont, where Oliver Cowdery lived before he moved to New York in 1825 and came into contact with the Smith family. It is therefore possible for Cowdery to have carried a copy of the second edition of *View of the Hebrews* with him to New York.

It is possible that all three of the theories we have just described are correct. Hougey rightly states, "The possibility of Joseph's having used *View of the Hebrews* in no way precludes his using other possible sources in writing the *Book of Mormon*. He may very well have used a number of sources."[12] In other words, Joseph Smith could have used his own natural genius and both the Spaulding manuscript and *View of the Hebrews*, as well as other materials, to produce the *Book of Mormon*.

Changes in the Book of Mormon

The most important claim made for the *Book of Mormon* is that it is the Word of God. If it can stand as the Word of God, then we would do well to study and accept it as such. Inherent in this claim is the claim to perfection Joseph Smith made for it when he stated, "I told the brethren that the Book of Mormon was the most correct of any book on earth."[13]

Joseph Fielding Smith, Tenth President of the Mormon Church, likewise maintained,

> Inspiration is discovered in the fact that each part, as it was revealed, dovetailed perfectly with what had come before. There was no need for eliminating, changing, or adjusting any part to make it fit; but each new revelation on doctrine and priesthood fitted into its place perfectly to complete the whole structure, as it has been prepared by the Master Builder.[14]

In 1881 Oliver Huntington recorded that another Joseph Fielding Smith, the Sixth President of the Mormon Church, stated in a sermon:

> Joseph did not render the writing on the gold plates into the English language in his own style of language as many people believe, but every word and letter was given to him by the gift and power of God. . . . The Lord caused each word spelled as it is in the book to appear on the stones in short sentences or words, and when Joseph had uttered the sentence or word before him and the scribe had written it properly, that sentence would disappear and another would appear. And if there was a word wrongly written or even a letter incorrect, the writing on the stones would remain there. Then Joseph would require the scribe to spell the reading of the last spoken and thus find the mistake and when corrected the sentence would disappear as usual.[15]

David Whitmer, one of the three witnesses to the *Book of Mormon*, gave a basically identical account of the translation in his *Address to All Believers in Christ*:

> I will now give you a description of the manner in which the Book of Mormon was translated. Joseph Smith would

put the seer stone into a hat, and put his face in the hat, drawing it closely around his face to exclude the light; and in the darkness the spiritual light would shine. A piece of something resembling parchment would appear, and on that appeared the writing. One character at a time would appear, and under it was the interpretation in English. Brother Joseph would read off the English to Oliver Cowdery, who was his principal scribe, and when it was written down and repeated to Brother Joseph to see if it was correct, then it would disappear, and another character with the interpretation would appear. Thus the Book of Mormon was translated by the gift and power of God, and not by any power of man.[16]

Most Mormons still believe that Joseph Smith was an unlearned man and that God did the translating through the stones.

Since God made the translation, we would expect the 1830 edition of the *Book of Mormon* to be exactly as God wanted it to be. It should therefore be the same in the current edition. But, in fact, there have been hundreds of changes. As early as 1898, Lamoni Call had counted two thousand alterations in what Joseph Smith called the "most correct of any book on earth." A more recent study by the Tanners has shown that at least 3,913 changes have been made in the *Book of Mormon* since it was first published.[17]

The bulk of the changes are corrections of grammar or spelling, but some alter the meaning of the text. We shall look first at a few grammatical and spelling errors, then at some more substantive matters.

Like many who are not well-versed in grammar, Joseph Smith had trouble with the verb *to be*. Here are six errors from the first edition of the *Book of Mormon* which have been corrected in later editions. Since the first edition of the *Book of Mormon* was not divided into chapters and verses, the page on which each example is found follows the example.

1. "Adam and Eve, which was our first parents" (p. 15).
2. "and loosed the bands which was upon my wrists" (p. 49).
3. "but it all were in vain" (p. 142).
4. "it were easy to guard them" (p. 375).
5. "the words which is expedient" (p. 67).
6. "here is our weapons of war" (p. 346).

Another common mistake which later editions have repaired is the addition of unnecessary words. The following are five examples in which the word *a* has since been deleted from the original text.

1. "As I was a journeying" (p. 249).
2. "And as I was a going thither" (p. 249).
3. "Moroni was a coming against them" (p. 403).
4. "he found Muloki a preaching" (p. 284).
5. "the Lamanites a marching" (p. 529).

The first edition of the *Book of Mormon* uses many words incorrectly. It would be impractical to include them all here. To illustrate the variety of the errors, a list of eight of the most common ones is presented below. In each example the word used incorrectly is italicized and followed by the correct word in brackets. In each case the word has been corrected in later editions of the *Book of Mormon*.

1. "lest he should not look for that he *had not ought* [ought not] and he should perish" (p. 173).
2. "having no *respects* [respect] to persons" (p. 224).
3. "I have *wrote* [written] unto you somewhat" (p. 377).
4. "they were *exceeding fraid* [exceedingly afraid]" (p. 354).
5. "they had *began* [begun] to possess the land of Amulon, and had *began* [begun] to till the ground" (p. 204).
6. "this he *done* [did] that he might overthrow" (p. 140).
7. "we have *took* [taken] of their wine" (p. 379).
8. "they did not fight against God *no* [any] more" (p. 290).

If we accept the mechanical view of revelation described

above, we must conclude that God either wanted all the errors (or at least colloquial forms of English) found in the first edition of the *Book of Mormon* to be there or that God is not well-versed in the English language. Evidently the Mormons do not accept the first solution because they have proceeded to correct the errors. The latter solution is absurd.

While it is true that Joseph Smith made many of the corrections in the *Book of Mormon* himself, it is possible to show by comparing various editions of the *Book of Mormon* that many changes were made after his death. Dr. Sidney B. Sperry, a prominent Mormon apologist, admits that many of the changes were made by Dr. James Talmadge, a Mormon Apostle, and were first incorporated into the 1920 edition of the *Book of Mormon*.[18]

Mormons often rationalize that Joseph Smith had the right to revise his grammar and other mistakes in the *Book of Mormon*. If Joseph Smith were the author or even translator (by his own linguistic ability), then he would have had such a right. The original claim was that Joseph was only a tool used by God and God himself was actually the translator. Therefore, neither Joseph Smith nor anyone else, for that matter, had the right to change God's translation.

It is one thing to correct God's grammar, but it takes a bold person indeed to alter the meaning of what he believes is God's Word. Yet this is what has happened in the following five cases. The Mormon Church made the first four changes to support a doctrine it developed at a later date, and it made the fifth to avoid an internal contradiction. Because the first four deal with the same subject, we shall consider them together and then look at the fifth.

The current Mormon doctrine of God is one of a plurality of gods. To understand this doctrine, we must remember that the Mormons make a distinction between Jesus and the Father, claiming that they are two different gods. Jesus, they say, is Jehovah (the divine name, Yahweh) while his

Father is Elohim (simply the Hebrew word for God). In brief, Jesus Jehovah is the son of the heavenly Father, Elohim.[19]

But the founders of the movement apparently had no such doctrine in mind. The concluding statement in the "Testimony of Three Witnesses," found even in the current edition of the *Book of Mormon* reads, "And the honor be to the Father, and to the Son, and to the Holy Ghost, which is one God." Likewise, 2 Nephi 31:21 says, "And now, behold, this is the doctrine of Christ, and the only and true doctrine of the Father, and of the Son, and of the Holy Ghost, which is one God, without end. Amen." At the bottom of the page on which this verse is found in the 1961 edition is a list of six similar verses.

In the 1830 edition, in 1 Nephi we read, "And the angel spake unto me, saying: These last records . . . shall make known to all kindreds, tongues, and people, that the Lamb of God is the Eternal Father and the Saviour of the world; and that all men must come unto Him, or they cannot be saved" (p. 32). In the 1961 edition of the *Book of Mormon* the same passage says, "And the angel spake unto me, saying: These last records . . . shall make known to all kindreds, tongues, and people, that the Lamb of God is *the Son of* the Eternal Father, and the Saviour of the world; and that all men must come unto him, or they cannot be saved" (1 Nephi 13:40). Who added the words *the Son of* to the later edition, or when they added them, we do not know; but the result is clear: a contradiction with the doctrine of the plurality of the gods is avoided.

The next two changes in the 1830 edition are made within the same conversation. "And he said unto me, Behold, the virgin which thou seest, is the mother of God, after the manner of the flesh. . . . And I looked and beheld the virgin again, bearing a child in her arms. And the angel said unto me, behold the Lamb of God, yea, even the Eternal Father!" (p. 25). This verse equates the baby Jesus with the Eternal

Father. Since it does not square with Mormon doctrine, later editions of the *Book of Mormon* have changed the equation: "And he said unto me: Behold, the virgin whom thou seest is the mother of *the Son of* God, after the manner of flesh. . . . And I looked and beheld the virgin again, bearing a child in her arms. And the angel said unto me: Behold the Lamb of God, yea, even *the Son of* the Eternal Father!" (1 Nephi 11: 18-21). By the addition of the words *the Son of* the meaning of the verse has been changed.

Later the same chapter of 1 Nephi says, "And I looked and beheld the Lamb of God, that he was taken by the people; yea, the Everlasting God was judged of the world" (p. 26). When this verse was printed in later editions of the *Book of Mormon*, it also contained the words *the Son of*: "And I looked and beheld the Lamb of God, that he was taken by the people; yea, *the Son of* the Everlasting God was judged of the world" (1 Nephi 11:32).

Some Mormon apologists assert that the phrases in question were in the original handwritten copies of the *Book of Mormon* (Joseph had his scribes produce two copies so that, in case of theft, one would be preserved) and were omitted by the printer.[20] The Reorganized Church of Jesus Christ of Latter-day Saints is now in possession of one of the originals in the handwriting of Oliver Cowdery. In this manuscript two of the verses in question have the words *the Son of* added between the lines. In the other two verses nothing has been added, and they read exactly as in the first edition of the *Book of Mormon*.[21]

The Church Historian's Library (an official arm of the Church of Jesus Christ of Latter-day Saints) has a portion of the second manuscript. It contains three of the four verses in question, and these three are in exact agreement with the first edition.[22] This rules out the possibility of a printing error.

Often Mormons who are not aware of the existence of the

handwritten copies of the *Book of Mormon* explain changes in the *Book of Mormon* by saying the printer who produced the first edition made typographical errors we should allow to be corrected. Comparing the original handwritten copies with the 1830 edition of the *Book of Mormon*, however, we see that the typographical errors were remarkably few for the country press that did the typesetting and proofreading. The late Mormon historian B. H. Roberts admitted this was the case. When speaking of the vast majority of the changes in the *Book of Mormon* text, he said,

> Such is the nature of the errors in question, and so interwoven are they throughout the diction of the book, that they may not be disposed of by saying they result from inefficient proof-reading or referring them to the mischievous disposition of the "typos," or the unfriendliness of the publishing house. The errors are constitutional in their character; they are of the web and woof of the style and not such errors as may be classed as typographical. Indeed, the first edition of the Book of Mormon is singularly free from typographical errors.[23]

The fifth example of a substantive change deals with a different subject. On page 200 of the 1830 edition of the *Book of Mormon*, the name of the king under discussion is Benjamin. In the 1961 edition, the same section names the king as Mosiah (Mosiah 21:28). It would appear from the chronology in Mosiah 6 and 7 that King Benjamin had been dead for some time. Evidently, some Church leaders at some time felt it was better to erase the error by changing Benjamin to Mosiah.[24]

Sidney B. Sperry, professor emeritus at Brigham Young University, has responded to the attacks on the *Book of Mormon* resulting from this change. Sperry says this was an inadvertent slip of the tongue on Joseph's part as he was dictating to Cowdery, or perhaps it was a mistake made by Mormon when he abridged the gold plates. Despite this,

Sperry admits, "the reading king Benjamin is an out and out error, because the king had been dead for some time."[25]

Neither of the two possibilities Sperry proposes go well for the Mormon view of revelation. If we accept the first solution, we find that the *Book of Mormon* was not translated mechanically by the gift and power of God and may therefore contain countless errors. If we lay the blame on Mormon, we are in a similar dilemma because Mormon may have made other mistakes we have no way of detecting. Either horn of this dilemma is less than adequate to sustain the Mormon view of revelation.

To escape from the embarrassments that necessitated these various changes, modern, more liberal, Mormon apologists are beginning to reject the mechanical theory of translation. B. H. Roberts was one of the first to suggest abandoning it. Roberts said Joseph Smith had to ponder over each part of the translation and then pray to ascertain its correctness, as Oliver Cowdery had been instructed to do. (*Doctrine and Covenants* 9 and *Book of Commandments* 8 tell how Cowdery was supposed to play his part in the translation process.) Therefore, Roberts concludes, "It is undoubtedly the manner in which Joseph Smith did translate the Book of Mormon through the medium of the Urim and Thummim." Roberts further argues that since Joseph was used to thinking in poor grammar, he expressed himself in poor grammar. Then as Smith became more correct in grammar later in his life, he was able to fix his grammatical mistakes in subsequent editions of the *Book of Mormon*.[26] There have been several more recent attempts to explain the changes in the *Book of Mormon*, but nearly all of them have followed Roberts's line of reasoning.

There are problems with Roberts's theory, however. It is built on two assumptions: that Joseph used the same method of translation that Oliver Cowdery was told to use and that the Urim and Thummim were part of this method. Both of these assumptions the *Doctrine and Covenants* and the *Book of Commandments* disallow. First of all, the portions of the *Doctrine and Covenants* that come from this period nowhere indicate that these gifts were the same for Oliver and Joseph. The text is also silent about Oliver's use of the Urim and Thummim. The verse Roberts quotes to show how Oliver used the Urim and Thummim (*Doctrine and Covenants* 8:2) does not mention them or even imply they were part of the process. On the contrary, it strongly suggests direct revelation: "Yea, behold, I will tell you in your mind and in your heart, by the Holy Ghost, which shall come upon you and which shall dwell in your heart."

Joseph Smith, on the other hand, states that the Urim and Thummim were very much a part of his translation work. In the Writings of Joseph Smith, during his recital of the events leading up to his receiving and translating the golden plates, Joseph says this about the Urim and Thummim: "There were two stones in silver bows—and these stones, fastened to a breastplate, constituted what is called the Urim and Thummim—deposited with the plates; and the possession and use of these stones were what constituted 'seers' in ancient or former times; and that God had prepared them for the purpose of translating the book" (Writings of Joseph Smith 2:35). Several verses later he says, "I commenced copying the characters off the plates. I copied a considerable number of them, and by means of the Urim and Thummim I translated some of them" (Writings of Joseph Smith 2:62).

The translation process made use of the Urim and Thummim in a seemingly indispensable way. If we accept Roberts's theory that God through the Holy Ghost told Joseph the meaning in his mind and heart, then the stones become an unnecessary step in the process. Roberts's theory just does not fit all the facts.

Roberts's theory is an argument from silence. There is nowhere an account of the translation process that resembles the one he sets forth, yet there are several that describe the mechanical view of translation. We have already seen statements by David Whitmer (one of the "three witnesses" to the *Book of Mormon*) and Joseph Fielding Smith (the "living prophet" of his time) that attest to it.

With regard to Whitmer's statement, it should be noted that Peter Whitmer, David's father, allowed Joseph Smith to live in the Whitmer home during part of the time Joseph worked on the translation. In *Address to All Believers in Christ*, Whitmer implies that one of the reasons he accepts the *Book of Mormon* as the Word of God is that it was translated in such a miraculous way.

Mormons try to discount these records by saying they are not official accounts. Whether or not they are official has nothing to do with their truthfulness. Whitmer's statement was printed in 1887, and Joseph Fielding Smith's was dated 1881. If these statements were incorrect, and were actually in opposition to the truth, why did no one respond to them before Roberts in the late 1940s?

Current Mormon apologists have no basis for dismissing the mechanical method of the translation process. This leaves the Mormons with their dilemma: Either Joseph Smith copied mistakes that were on the plates, which are not now available for examination, or the *Book of Mormon* was not translated by the gift and power of God and may, therefore, contain countless errors. Either way, this should cause even the most devout Mormon to question the integrity of the *Book of Mormon* in its present form and in its original construction.

Chapter **3.**

The Book of Mormon & New World Archaeology

Since the Mormons—in several tracts and in the current missionary edition of the *Book of Mormon*—use archaeology to win many into the Mormon Church, we must take a close look at the archaeological evidence they claim supports the *Book of Mormon*. According to Joseph Smith, when he first learned about the existence of the golden plates, the angel Moroni told him they contained "an account of the former inhabitants of this continent" (Writings of Joseph Smith 2:34). This tells us the geographical area within which we should look for data. Let us see how the *Book of Mormon* describes these ancient people so we will know what kind of evidence to look for.

According to the *Book of Mormon*, each of the two waves of Jewish migrants built a large and prosperous civilization. The earlier one, which became extinct after a number of generations, had many farming utensils: tools with which to plow, sow, reap, hoe and thrash, and "all manner of tools with which they did work their beasts" (Ether 10:25-26). In addition, these Jaredites had "all manner of fruit, and of grain, and of silks and of fine linen, and of gold, and of silver, and of precious things; and also all manner of cattle, of oxen, and cows, and of sheep, and of swine, and of goats, and also many other kinds of animals which were useful for the food of man. And they also had horses, and asses, and there were elephants and cureloms and cumoms" (Ether 9:17-19).

The later civilization, which endured from about 600 B.C. to A.D. 400, "multiplied exceedingly, and spread upon the face of the land, and became exceedingly rich" (Jarom 1:8). It "began to cover the face of the whole earth, from the sea south to the sea north, from the sea west to the sea east" Helaman 3:8). The text of the *Book of Mormon* names at least thirty-seven cities and recounts that in the final battle between the Lamanites and the Nephites, over two-hundred-thirty thousand Nephites were killed on or near the hill Cumorah (Mormon 6:10-15).

Not only was there a population explosion, but "the whole face of the land had become covered with buildings" (Mormon 1:7). Not only did the people build buildings, but they also made ships, temples, synagogues, sanctuaries (Helaman 3:14), coins of gold and silver (Alma 11:4), and weapons of war (according to Alma 43:18-20, swords, cimeters [scimitars], breast-plates, arm-shields, head-shields, bows, arrows, stones and slings). Nephi describes one of the temples this way: "And I Nephi, did build a temple; and I did construct it after the manner of the temple of Solomon save it were not built of so many precious things; for they were not to be found upon the land, wherefore, it could not be built like unto Solomon's temple. But the manner of the construction was like unto the temple of Solomon; and the workmanship thereof was exceeding fine" (2 Nephi 5:16).

Is There Any Evidence?

If these accounts are true, then we should find ample archaeological evidence to support them. Ross T. Christensen, a
Mormon anthropologist, admits that the *Book of Mormon*
stands or falls on the historicity of its statements:

The Book of Mormon is of such a nature that its validity
can be submitted to a thorough and objective scientific
test. . . .

If the Book's history is fallacious, its doctrine cannot
be genuine. On the other hand, if the historical content
proves to be correct, by inference, it is impossible that the
doctrine could be incorrect.

. . . I am fully confident that the nature of the Book is
such that a definitive archaeological test can be applied
to it.[1]

We must now apply the test to which Christensen refers.

Mormon missionaries have often claimed that the Smithsonian Institution uses the *Book of Mormon* as a guide to its
archaeological research. This claim is untrue. Appendix A
contains a letter and statement the Smithsonian Institution
has produced as a response to hundreds of inquiries made in
recent years. To summarize, the Smithsonian Institution
states that it has never used the *Book of Mormon* as a
scientific guide and that Smithsonian Institution scientists
see "no connection between the archaeology of the New
World and the subject matter of the Book."

Joseph Smith claimed that the golden plates from which
the *Book of Mormon* was translated were written in "Reformed Egyptian." If this were true, we would expect to find
other examples of Egyptian writing in the Americas. The
Smithsonian letter attests to the lack of any such evidence.
In a recent article which appeared in *Dialogue: A Journal on
Mormon Thought*, Michael Coe, who describes himself as "a
sympathetic and interested outsider," discusses the Kinderhook Plates, supposedly records in Egyptian discovered by

Robert Wiley in 1843. Wiley reported he dug up the plates while excavating an Indian mound near Kinderhook, Illinois. When they were shown to him, Joseph Smith pronounced the hieroglyphs on the six bell-shaped brass plates to be the records of the descendants of Ham. About this pronouncement Michael Coe says, "Let me now state uncategorically that as far as I know there is not one professionally trained archaeologist, who is not a Mormon, who sees any scientific justification for believing the foregoing to be true, and I would like to state that there are quite a few Mormon archaeologists who join this group."[2]

W. P. Harris, one of the men involved in the supposed find, wrote in 1855 that Wiley had etched the hieroglyphs on the plates with beeswax and nitric acid. One of the plates was recently rediscovered, and a member of the University Archaeology Society at Brigham Young University had the metal tested at Princeton University. The tests showed that it was a low-zinc brass or a bronze, that "the dimensions, tolerances, composition and workmanship are consistent with the facilities of an 1843 blacksmith shop and with the fraud stories of the original participants,"[3] and that the inscriptions were most certainly produced by the beeswax-acid etching technique. So with this find discredited, there still have been no discoveries of Reformed Egyptian or Hebrew writing on this continent.

Near the end of his article, Coe draws the following conclusion: "The bare facts of the matter are that nothing, absolutely nothing, has ever shown up in any New World excavation which would suggest to a dispassionate observer that the Book of Mormon, as claimed by Joseph Smith, is a historical document relating to the history of early migrants to our hemisphere."[4]

Amateur Mormon Archaeologists
Despite the absence of archaeological support for the *Book of*

Mormon, Mormons continue to produce a spate of archaeological works. Most are nonsense written by amateurs.

Not until 1938 did the first Mormon earn a doctorate in archaeology, and today only a few hold this degree. Many are honest scientists who study the facts and try to set forth the truth as they see it, even when it means raising a storm of protest from Mormon leaders. In reacting to the work of widely read but amateur Mormon archaeologists, John L. Sorenson, a Mormon elder who was assistant professor of anthropology and sociology at Brigham Young University, says, "Few of the writings they have produced are of genuine consequence in archaeological terms. Some are clearly on the odd-ball fringe; others have credible qualifications. Two of the most prolific are Professor Hugh Nibley and Milton R. Hunter; however, they are not qualified to handle the archaeological materials their works often involve."[5]

Dee Green, formerly assistant professor of anthropology at Weber State College, holds an M.A. degree from Brigham Young University in archaeology. He was a general officer of the University Archaeological Society and editor of the *U.A.S. Newsletter.* Agreeing with Sorenson, he states,

Those volumes which most flagrantly ignore time and space and most radically distort, misinterpret, or ignore portions of the archaeological evidence are the popular Farnsworth volumes. Also inadequate, from a professional archaeologist's point of view, are the well intentioned volumes by Milton R. Hunter and a number of smaller pamphlets and works by various authors. . . .

New World-Old World comparisons have been less popular but equally fraught with problems. The best known examples are the two volumes by [Hugh] Nibley which suffer from an overdose of "Old Worlditis." . . . He does not know New World culture history well, and his writing ignores the considerable indigenous elements in favor of exclusive Old World patterns.[6]

Keep in mind that these are Mormon scientists, not critical non-Mormon polemicists, making these statements.

The Mormon apologists being criticized attempt to show from available archaeological material that many of the anachronisms in the *Book of Mormon* are not anachronisms at all. Milton R. Hunter, for example, has attempted to demonstrate that the ancient Americans had horses prior to the coming of the Spaniards.[7] Although the Mormon Church takes no official position in such matters, many Mormons accept such "proof" without question.

Other popular Mormon apologists claim that the locations mentioned in the *Book of Mormon* can be shown on a map. In response to such claims, Dee Green comments,

There have been no spectacular finds (from the Book of Mormon point of view), no Zarahemlas discovered, no gold plates brought to light, no horses uncovered, and King Benjamin's tomb remains unexcavated. . . .

The first myth that we need to eliminate is that Book of Mormon archaeology exists. Titles on books full of archaeological half-truths, dilettanti on the peripheries of American archaeology calling themselves Book of Mormon archaeologists regardless of their education, and a Department of Archaeology at BYU devoted to the production of Book of Mormon archaeologists do not insure that Book of Mormon archaeology really exists. If one is to study Book of Mormon archaeology, then one must have a corpus of data with which to deal. We do not. The *Book of Mormon* is really there so one *can* have Book of Mormon studies, and archaeology is really there so one can study archaeology, but the two are not wed. *At least they are not wed in reality since no Book of Mormon location is known with reference to modern topography.* Biblical archaeology can be studied because we do know where Jerusalem and Jericho were and are, but we do not know where Zarahemla and Bountiful (nor any other location for that matter) were or are. It would seem then that a concentration on geography should be the first order of business, but we have already seen that twenty years of such an approach has left us empty-handed.[8]

As the position of Mormon archaeologists becomes clear, it is easy to see how John L. Sorenson could say,

> In situations where sources of religious and secular authority conflict with each other, a Latter-day Saint sometimes finds himself in a quandary. He has been assured by a folklore transmitted in lessons, talks and church literature that archaeologists (usually Gentile) are steadily proving the Book of Mormon authentic, while through his formal education and secular literature he has become aware that in actuality "the experts" seem to contradict the scripture.[9]

The Mormons have made several attempts to show that some artifacts have been discovered that support the *Book of Mormon*. One of the most popular is the "Lehi Tree of Life Stone." In 1941 an expedition from the National Geographic Society and the Smithsonian Institution uncovered a stone monument in Izapa, Chiapas, Mexico, and designated it Stela 5, Izapa. Mormons first began showing interest in the stone in 1953 and have since maintained that the carving on the stela depicts the dream of Lehi, one of the Jewish immigrants to this continent. M. Wells Jakeman has been one of the chief proponents of the theory.

Dee Green warns against accepting Jakeman's theory as proof too quickly, submitting that the only way we could know if the artist or artists had Lehi's dream in mind would be to ask them. At this point popular Mormon apologist Hugh Nibley agrees with Green:

> Science does not arrive at its conclusions by syllogism, and no people on earth deplore proof demonstration by syllogism more loudly than real archaeologists do. Yet Mr. Jakeman's study is nothing but an elaborate syllo-

gistic stew. The only clear and positive thing about the whole study is the objective the author is determined to reach. With naive exuberance, he repeatedly announces that he has found exactly what we would expect to find. Inevitably there emerges from this dim and jumbled relief exactly what Mr. Jakeman is looking for.[10] Green adds that Jakeman's hand-drawn version, the one to which Mormons most frequently refer, was drawn from a photograph and not from the stone. Green examined the photograph, compared it to Jakeman's drawing, and concluded that the drawing is not accurate. Green further states that one should "not compare photo 109 in Ferguson's *One Fold and One Shepherd* nor the plaster reproduction of Stela 5 in the BYU Archaeology Museum since Ferguson's photograph is of the cast and the cast itself has been altered by Jakeman after his interpretation."[11]

In this quote, Green refers to Thomas Stewart Ferguson. Ferguson founded the New World Archaeological Foundation, an organization through which Brigham Young University has conducted several archaeological expeditions, and he wrote three books trying to prove the *Book of Mormon* true on the basis of archaeology. But after publishing them, Ferguson decided he had not really found conclusive evidence and left the Latter-day Saints in the early 1970s.

We conclude with Ferguson that archaeology has not verified the *Book of Mormon*. Dee Green sums it up well when he says, "I strongly suspect that the Lord, at least for some time to come, will still require faith, not 'proof,'—and Moroni 10:4 ('he will manifest the truth of it unto you, by the power of the Holy Ghost'), not archaeology, will continue to be the key for those who really care to understand the contents of the *Book of Mormon* and desire to know its truth."[12] In other words, there is no objective, external verification for the *Book of Mormon*. One must believe it by unsubstantiated faith. Chapter six evaluates this subjectivism in more detail.

Chapter **4.**

The Book of Commandments & The Doctrine & Covenants

If the *Book of Mormon* were the only extrabiblical revelation claimed by the Mormon Church, Mormon theology would have few major differences from orthodox Christianity. But the Mormon Church takes very few of its doctrines from the *Book of Mormon*. Some of the teachings most vital and most peculiar to Mormonism not found in the *Book of Mormon* are (1) the organizational structure of the church, (2) the Melchizedekian priesthood, (3) the Aaronic priesthood, (4) the plurality of gods, (5) God as an exalted man, (6) a human being's ability to become a god, (7) the three degrees of heaven, (8) the plurality of wives, (9) the Word of Wisdom, (10) the pre-existence of the human spirit, (11) eternal progression, (12) baptism for the dead and (13) celestial marriage.[1]

The source of these doctrines is either the *Book of Commandments* or the *Doctrine and Covenants*. (The *Book of Commandments* deals with some of these doctrines; the *Doc-*

trine and Covenants mentions all of them.) The *Book of Commandments*, the first published collection of the revelations Joseph Smith received during and after the translation of the *Book of Mormon*, was printed in 1833 and then enlarged and reprinted in 1835 under the title *Doctrine and Covenants*. While the *Book of Commandments* contains only the sixty-five revelations that came between July, 1828, and September, 1831, the *Doctrine and Covenants* contains an additional seventy-one sections. A comparison of the two documents reveals that drastic changes have been made from the one to the other. Some verses are rewritten; some are omitted; others are added. Yet both books claim to be the Word of God:

> Search these commandments, for they are true and faithful, and the prophecies and promises which are in them shall all be fulfilled. What I the Lord have spoken, I have spoken, and I excuse not myself; and though the heavens and the earth pass away, my word shall not pass away, but shall all be fulfilled, whether by my own voice or by the voice of my servants, it is the same. For behold, and lo, the Lord is God, and the Spirit beareth record, and the record is true, and the truth abideth forever and ever. Amen. (*Book of Commandments* 1:7; *Doctrine and Covenants* 1:37-39)

Changes in the Revelations

Why the differences between the two books? Some of the revelations were added to support doctrines Joseph Smith had begun teaching. Other revelations were expanded to make new doctrines seem to have an earlier origin than they in fact had. Some of the initial revelations contained statements that contradicted later doctrines, and so parts of them were omitted. Several specific cases will illustrate the nature of the changes:

1. At least fifty changes have been made in the first four

verses of the fourth chapter of *Book of Commandments*. One in particular, 4:2, will concern us: "He [Joseph Smith] has no power over them [the gold plates] except I grant it unto him; and he has a gift to translate the book, and I have command-ed him that he shall pretend to no other gift, for I will grant him no other gift." Here Joseph was claiming, first, that his gift to translate the plates was from God, and second, that this was the only gift he was to receive.

Had Joseph heeded this revelation, he would have stopped writing scripture when he finished the *Book of Mormon*. Later, however, when he began to compile the revelations, those familiar with them argued that God never meant them to be printed.[2] Joseph continued to force the issue until he won out, and the reason for his insistence soon became clear: he, Rigdon and a few others were to receive the profits from the book's sale, as a reward for their hard work (*Doctrine and Covenants* 70:5-8, 15-18).

After the printing of the *Book of Commandments*, Joseph apparently realized that the very existence of the book was a contradiction of *Book of Commandments* 4:2. If this verse was left in its original form, then it would be obvious that those who opposed the printing had been right and Joseph had been wrong. The verse as it now stands in *Doctrine and Covenants* 5:4 reads this way (the italicized words are the words that have either been added or changed in some way since the original printing): "And *you have* a gift to translate the *plates*; and *this is the first gift that I bestowed upon you*; and I have commanded that *you* shall pretend to no other gift *until my purpose is fulfilled in this*; for I will grant *unto you* no other gift until *it is finished*." These changes reverse the meaning of the original version. By making them, Joseph opened the door for further additions to be made to the scrip-ture of his church.

2. *Book of Commandments* 6, when published in 1833, contained 143 words. When reprinted (*Doctrine and Cove-*

nants 33:1-3), it had 252 words. The preface to this chapter in the *Book of Commandments* indicates it is a translation through the Urim and Thummim of a "parchment, written and hid up" by the apostle John. It is this claim that creates the most difficult problem. How could a translation expand by 109 words? The Tanners suggest there are only three possible explanations: (1) The Lord may have revealed to Joseph that the first translation was incorrect and that many words had been left out. This would cast doubt on Joseph's ability as a translator and hence on his other translations. (2) Before reprinting this translation, Joseph Smith decided to attribute words to John which John did not write. This would make Joseph a deceiver. (3) Joseph contrived the entire revelation but suppressed part of it in the first printing only to add it two years later. This, too, would make Joseph a deceiver.[3]

3. In June, 1829, Joseph Smith received instructions about the new church he was to establish. The structure of this new church was to be found in the "fullness of the gospel" as it had been revealed in the *Book of Mormon*: "You rely upon the things which are written; for in them are all things written, concerning my church, my gospel, and my rock. Wherefore if you shall build up my church, and my gospel, and my rock, the gates of hell shall not prevail against you" (*Book of Commandments* 15:3-4).

This verse does not mention the *Book of Mormon* by name but refers instead to "the things which are written." The introduction to this revelation says it was given to Oliver Cowdery while he was acting as scribe for Joseph Smith. In verses 2 and 3 of this revelation God tells Oliver that the things he has written—that is, the *Book of Mormon*—are true; therefore, he should rely on them.

Many Mormons claim that the "things written" include all revelation from God. This cannot be supported from the context. Sidney B. Sperry, in his *Doctrine and Covenants*

Compendium, says that the "things written" are "doubtless in the *Book of Mormon*."[4] We would expect, therefore, to find all the doctrines, offices and structures of the Mormon Church in the *Book of Mormon*.

But, as noted at the beginning of this chapter, such is not the case. The *Book of Mormon* does not reveal many of the Church's doctrines, nor does it contain most of the Church's offices or structures. If Joseph's early revelation about the new church he was to establish were true, and the *Book of Mormon* contained all that is necessary for the Latter-day Saints Church, then the Church would have to deny all of the thirteen doctrines we listed.

Recognizing this problem, Joseph Smith solved it by re-writing the revelation to allow for future revelation. When reprinted in *Doctrine and Covenants*, the passage quoted above from the *Book of Commandments* read, "You rely upon the things which are written; for in them are all things written concerning *the foundation of* my church, my gospel, and my rock. Wherefore, if you shall build up my church, *upon the foundation* of my gospel and my rock, the gates of hell shall not prevail against you" (*Doctrine and Covenants* 18:3-5). The word *foundation* has been inserted twice, which changes the meaning of the revelation. The *Book of Mormon* no longer contains "all things" about the Church, but now only the "foundation" of the Church. Thus, Joseph Smith made it possible for additional doctrines to be revealed.[5]

4. In August of 1830, Sidney Rigdon broke off relations with Alexander Campbell over the issue of re-establishing a communal society in the Disciples of Christ churches. On his own, Rigdon began a communal society at Kirtland, Ohio, near Cleveland. Not long after the split, Mormon missionaries arrived in Kirtland, and in less than three weeks Rigdon and his whole community had become Mormons.[6]

In February of the following year, 1831, a revelation was received that gave the Lord's endorsement to the communal effort. The passage about communal life is found in the middle of a rather lengthy revelation on the "law for the governing of the church." *Book of Commandments* 44:26-29 describes how "all" the properties of the church members are to be consecrated to the Church and given to each "as he stands in need."

By the time the *Doctrine and Covenants* was printed, the Mormon communal society had failed. It was necessary to alter only a few words of the revelation to shift its meaning. The word *all* was changed to *of*, so the phrase in which it was included now reads in *Doctrine and Covenants* 42:30, "And behold, thou wilt *remember the poor*, and consecrate *of* thy properties *for their support*." The words *remember the poor* and *for their support* were added to make the poor, and not every member of the Church, the recipients of the consecrated goods. The passage has shifted from being the ground rules of a communal society to being those of a church welfare program, clearly an attempt to hide the communal ideals present in the Kirtland Church.

5. Several changes have been made in the revelations concerning the priesthood. David Whitmer, one of the three witnesses to the *Book of Mormon*, rebelled against these changes and made the following statement about instituting the high priesthood: "The office of high priests was never spoken of, and never thought of being established in the church until Rigdon came in. Remember that we had been preaching from August, 1829, until June, 1831— almost two years—and had baptized about 2,000 members into the Church of Christ, and had not one high priest."[7]

Whitmer further related that "Brother Joseph" had often referred to "elder" as being the highest office in the Mormon Church. As implied in the quote, Whitmer credited Rigdon with having introduced the high, or Melchizedekian, priesthood into the Latter-day Saints Church, claiming that Rigdon would expound to Joseph the Old Testament Scriptures about the high priest and the priesthood and would persuade Joseph to inquire of the Lord about them. Promptly, Joseph would receive a revelation sustaining the view Rigdon had set forth. In this way the high priesthood entered the Latter-day Saints Church.

Book of Commandments 28, a revelation given on September 4, 1830, contains seven short verses with a total of twenty-three lines. Its general theme is the "sacrament" (the Mormon term for the Lord's Supper), and nowhere does it mention the priesthood. The parallel passage in *Doctrine and Covenants* 27:1-18 has eighteen verses and more than twice the number of words than the original version. It prescribes two ordinations: (1) the ordination into the Aaronic priesthood and (2) the ordination to apostleship by Peter, James and John. Mormon apologists today claim this second ordination was to confer the Melchizedekian priesthood.[8]

With regard to the priesthood, the following changes were also made in later editions of *Doctrine and Covenants:* (1) *Book of Commandments* 24:44-45 makes no mention of these offices: presiding elders, traveling bishops, high counselors, high priests and presidents of the high priesthood. *Doctrine and Covenants* 20:49-68 adds all of them. (2) *Book of Commandments* 44:26-29 makes no mention of high priests, high councils, or counselors, but *Doctrine and Covenants* 42:31-34 includes them. (3) *Book of Commandments* 44:54-55 makes no mention of high priests, counselors or bishops, but *Doctrine and Covenants* 42:62-73 has all three, equating the elders with high priests.

We have not examined all of the changes that have been made in the *Book of Commandments*, but we have seen enough to know that these supposed revelations from God do not measure up to the standard they set for themselves. They do not fulfill the claim that "though the heavens and the earth pass away, my word shall not pass away" and that "the record is true, and the truth abideth forever and ever. Amen."

To admit that the changes were made by Joseph Smith would be to admit that God is not their author. To claim that God authorized the changes presents other problems. For God to change his mind and reverse his position on matters of doctrine is hard to conceive. Joseph Smith would have us believe, for instance, that (1) at one time God said the *Book of Mormon* was all that was necessary for the restoration of the Church but later decided it was not enough; (2) once God said Joseph's only gift was the ability to translate the gold plates, but then chose to make that only the first endowment; and (3) God first commanded the Mormons to establish a communal society, but changed his design to a welfare program when the communal effort failed. Apparently, it is not just that God has given new revelation for a new age but that he or his prophets have "rewritten" the old revelation so that it squares with the new. It is easier to attribute this doctoring of the records to man rather than God. We must conclude that the revelations on which the essential Mormon doctrines are based originated not with God, but with Joseph Smith.

False Prophecies
While many of the revelations recorded in the *Doctrine and Covenants* were commands, some of them were predictions about the future. We shall look at two of the several prophecies Joseph Smith made that did not come to pass. The first one concerns the building of a temple and the gathering of Israel. The second is about the Civil War.

In *Doctrine and Covenants* 84:2-5 and 31 prophecy projects the building of a city called New Jerusalem and a temple. This new city and temple were to be built "in the western boundaries of the State of Missouri, and dedicated by the hand of Joseph Smith." The sons of Moses and Aaron, it was foretold, would "offer an acceptable offering and sacrifice in the house of the Lord, which house shall be built unto the Lord in this generation."

This prophecy was given on September 22 and 23, 1832. At that time the Mormons were anticipating a move to western Missouri, though they did not begin to move to Missouri in large numbers until 1836. In 1838, Joseph Smith and his chief lieutenants moved to Missouri when they were forced out of Kirtland. After severe persecution, the Mormons were driven from Missouri in early 1839. They fled to Quincy, Illinois, and never had a chance to build in Missouri the temple they had anticipated erecting.[9]

The prophecy contained things that were not and cannot now be fulfilled. Not only was a temple never built in the western part of Missouri, but the only generation that could have built it is now dead. Furthermore, the temple was not dedicated by Joseph Smith and the city of New Jerusalem was not established.

One reason it is not possible for Mormon apologists to pull this prophecy out of its time limitations is that Joseph Smith did prepare to build the temple in question—the four cornerstones were laid—but he never completed it. Mormon apologists have tried to extend the length of a generation to 125 years so that the prophecy could be fulfilled.[10] But this effort was abandoned when Joseph Fielding Smith admitted that no one who was in the Church when this revelation was given remained alive.[11]

Another false prophecy, found in *Doctrine and Covenants* 87, concerns the Civil War. The details of the revelation are (1) the rebellion would begin in South Carolina; (2) it would shortly come to pass; (3) "war will be poured out upon all nations, beginning at this place"; (4) slaves would rebel against their masters; (5) famine, plague and earthquake would come from God; and (6) all nations would come to an end. This prophecy was given on December 25, 1832.

The Tanners have shown that Joseph Smith, prior to receiving this revelation, could have known that President Andrew Jackson had alerted the nation's troops in response to South Carolina's declaring a tariff act null and void.[12] The nation was fully expecting a civil war to begin promptly in South Carolina. This fact is borne out by a story in the February, 1833, edition of the Mormon monthly, the *Evening and Morning Star*, in an article titled "Rebellion in South Carolina." This article stated, "In addition to the above tribulations, South Carolina has rebelled against the laws of the United States; held a state convention, and passed ordinances, the same as declaring herself an independent nation." The article further reported that Jackson had ordered several companies of artillery to Charleston to prepare for the war that seemed imminent. Since the *Evening and Morning Star* was a monthly publication, the news could have been available to Joseph as much as a month before the printing of this story. The idea of a civil war was not original to him.

The revelation stated that these events were to come to pass shortly, yet not until 1861 did South Carolina actually secede from the union and the war begin. It foretold, too, that war would be "poured out upon all nations," yet the Civil War did not evolve into a worldwide conflict. Also, the Civil War did not result in the "end of all nations."

Was Joseph Smith a prophet of God? In the *Inspired Version of the Holy Scriptures*, the version on which Joseph Smith himself put his seal of approval, Deuteronomy 18:20-22 reads (just as it does in the King James):

But the prophet, which shall presume to speak a word in my name, which I have not commanded him to speak, or that shall speak in the name of other gods, even that prophet shall die. And if thou say in thine heart, How shall we know the word which the Lord hath not spoken? When a prophet speaketh in the name of the Lord, if the thing follow not, nor come to pass, that is the thing which the Lord hath not spoken, but the prophet hath spoken it presumptuously: thou shalt not be afraid of him.

On the basis of Scripture, Joseph Smith cannot stand as a true prophet, for when a true prophet gives God's word, it cannot fail to come to pass.

Contradictions between the Doctrine and Covenants and the Book of Mormon

Several of the revelations in the *Doctrine and Covenants* contradict the teachings in the *Book of Mormon*. One example concerns the purpose of baptism and its relation to forgiveness of sins and the gift of the Holy Spirit; the other, plural marriage.

1. *Doctrine and Covenants* 20:37 indicates that those who repent of their sins and show by works that they have received the Holy Spirit "shall be received by baptism into his church."[13] It is the order of events that is important here. This verse commands that a person have his sins remitted and receive the Holy Spirit before he is baptized.

The *Book of Mormon* teaches exactly the opposite: "For the gate by which ye should enter is repentance and baptism by water; and then cometh a remission of your sins by fire and by the Holy Ghost" (2 Nephi 31:17). In Mosiah 18:14, Alma is baptized and then receives the Spirit. In 3 Nephi 12:2, remission of sins follows baptism.[14] The materials currently used by Mormon missionaries also follow this view: "When we are baptised [*sic*] . . . the Lord promises that all our sins will be forgiven, and that he will send his spirit to guide and counsel us."[15]

If the *Doctrine and Covenants* ordering of events is authoritative, then those who are baptized by Mormon missionaries and taught that they must be baptized in order to have the Holy Spirit and forgiveness of sins are being taught false doctrine. If they have been baptized under this misconception, then their baptism is not valid because they have not met the prerequisites for baptism. This serious contradiction is damaging to the Mormon claim that both of these books are divinely inspired.

2. Although the Mormon Church today officially opposes plural marriage, the contradiction on the subject between the *Doctrine and Covenants* and the *Book of Mormon* still remains. *Doctrine and Covenants* 132:4 declares plural marriage to be "a new and an everlasting covenant," which even brings damnation on those who do not accept it. This revelation also explains how Abraham, Isaac, Jacob, Moses and David were justified in having many wives and concubines (*Doctrine and Covenants* 132:29-39). Verses 61-62 of the same chapter describe how this doctrine is to be implemented: A man may take as many wives as he wishes as long as each one is a virgin and is not espoused to another man.

Several passages in the *Book of Mormon* conflict with this revelation. Ether 10:5 says, "And it came to pass that Riplakish did not do that which was right in the sight of the Lord, for he did have many wives and concubines." And Jacob 2:23-24 reads, "They seek to excuse themselves in committing whoredoms, because of the things which were written concerning David, and Solomon his son. Behold, David and Solomon truly had many wives and concubines, which thing was abominable before me, saith the Lord." Another verse (Jacob 3:5) commands that a man have only one wife and no concubines. If both the *Doctrine and Covenants* and the *Book of Mormon* are divinely inspired, then the Mormon god, it seems, has a hard time deciding whether polygamy is good or evil, whether he should command or condemn it.

These are only two of several contradictions between the *Doctrine and Covenants* and the *Book of Mormon*, but they should cause even the most devoted Mormon to doubt that the scriptures he believes have been revealed by God.

The Lectures of Faith

The Lectures of Faith were a series of theological lectures Joseph Smith gave to the elders of the Church in the Kirtland Temple, Kirtland, Ohio. They were first printed in the 1835 edition of the *Doctrine and Covenants* and appeared in all subsequent editions prior to 1921. They have not appeared in the *Doctrine and Covenants* since 1921. The title page of the 1835 edition makes no distinction between the rest of the revelations and these lectures. The preface implies that both the revelations and the lectures should be accepted as scripture. The last paragraph of the preface says, "We do not present this little volume with any other expectation than that we are to be called to answer to every principle advanced." The preface was signed by Joseph Smith, Oliver Cowdery, Sidney Rigdon and F. G. Williams.

Although the modern Mormon leaders admit that the lectures have been removed, they offer no adequate explanation for their removal; but when the doctrines taught in the lectures are compared to current Mormon doctrine, the reason is evident. The Lectures of Faith propounded things contrary to present Mormon teaching.

Very early in the lectures, Joseph set forth the doctrine of God. In the Lecture Second, verse 2, we read, "We here observe that God is the only supreme governor, and independent being, in whom all fullness and perfection dwells; who is omnipotent, omnipresent, and omnicient; without beginning of days or end of life." In Lecture Third, verse 15, we discover, "thirdly, that he changes not, neither is there variableness with him; but he is the same from everlasting to everlasting, being the same yesterday today and forever; and that his course is one eternal round, without variation." The current Mormon doctrine of God's being born of a man in another world and progressing to godhood (see p. 14) is not consistent with the God the Lectures Second and Third describe, who has no beginning or end and is changeless.

Lecture Third goes on to state that it is only because God is unchangeable that people can have faith in him. "For without the idea of unchangibleness [sic] in the character of Deity, doubt would take the place of faith." Modern Mormons teach that God is continually progressing. Mormon men are planning to become "like God" but never equal to God, for he has a head start and they can never catch him. Can God be eternally unchanging and at the same time constantly changing?

In Lecture Fifth, Joseph considered the attributes of God further. In describing the Father and the Son he said, "The Father being a personage of spirit, glory and power; possessing all perfection and fullness; The son, who was in the bosom of the Father, *a personage of tabernacle*, made, or fashioned like unto man, or being in the form and likeness of man . . . and is called the Son *because of the flesh*" (emphasis added). According to present-day Mormon teaching, God the Father has a tangible body of flesh and bone while the lecture just quoted says the body of the Son is what makes him different from the Father. God the Father cannot both have flesh and not have flesh at the same time.

Clearly, current Mormon doctrine does not coincide perfectly with the Lectures of Faith, which for nearly one hundred years Mormons accepted as authoritative. Mormon apostle Mark E. Petersen stated in his book, *As Translated Correctly*, "It seems unthinkable to the honest and devout mind that any man or set of men would deliberately change any of the text of the word of God to further their own peculiar purposes."[16] Yet Mormon leaders decided to delete the Lectures of Faith from their sacred books because portions of it contradicted doctrines they wanted to promulgate from the *Doctrine and Covenants*. This action highlights the confusion in the revelations the Mormons claim were given Joseph Smith by God, and points to their human origin.

Chapter **5.**

The Pearl of Great Price

The *Pearl of Great Price* is the shortest of the four standard works of Mormonism. Actually it is a compilation of three different works: (1) the Book of Moses, (2) the Book of Abraham, and (3) the Writings of Joseph Smith. The Book of Moses was originally in two parts: (a) Visions of Moses and (b) Writings of Moses. Joseph received the former revelation in June, 1830; the latter, in December, 1830. Mormons hold the Book of Abraham to be "a Translation of some Ancient Records, that have fallen into our hands from the Catacombs of Egypt, the Writings of Abraham while he was in Egypt, called the Book of Abraham, written by his own hand, upon Papyrus. Translated from the Papyrus by Joseph Smith."[1] The Writings of Joseph Smith contain Joseph's translation of the twenty-fourth chapter of Matthew and portions of Joseph's personal history.

The Mormons consider the *Pearl of Great Price* to be as divinely inspired as the Bible. We would expect it, then, to be free from error. But the evidence against the Book of Abraham is by itself so damaging that we can be certain the book is not flawless.

Revelation in the Book of Abraham

The Book of Abraham is unique among the extrabiblical scriptures of the Mormons. It alone purports to be a translation of ancient records that are extant. That means it is the only work which came from Joseph Smith that we can study in light of the original papyrus.

How did Joseph Smith acquire the papyrus which he translated and named the Book of Abraham? On July 3, 1885, Michael H. Chandler opened an exhibit in Kirtland, Ohio, which contained four mummies and several papyri covered with hieroglyphics. Joseph, with the help of some of his followers, purchased the mummies and the manuscripts. When Joseph examined the papyri, he declared that one contained the writings of Abraham while he was in Egypt and that another was the work of Joseph, son of Jacob. During the first few months after the purchase, Joseph translated the Book of Abraham—a translation which now appears in the *Pearl of Great Price*.[2]

After Joseph's death, his family sold the papyri, which finally ended up in a Chicago museum.[3] It was thought that the manuscripts were lost in the Chicago fire of 1871 until the following article appeared in the *Deseret News* on November 27, 1967:

New York—A collection of pa[p]yrus manuscripts, long believed to have been destroyed in the Chicago fire of 1871, was presented to the Church of Jesus Christ of Latter-day Saints here Monday by the Metropolitan Museum of Art.

Included in the papyri is a manuscript identified as the original document from which Joseph Smith had copied the drawing which he called "Facsimile No. 1" and published with the Book of Abraham.[4]

Since these manuscripts have come to light, extensive work has been done on them by Dee Jay Nelson, a philologist by vocation and an internationally known Egyptologist. Mormon leaders such as Hugh Nibley and N. Eldon Tanner (one of the three most powerful men in the Mormon Church) recommended that he receive copies of the papyri to translate.[5] When Joseph Smith first wrote down his translation of the Book of Abraham, he placed Egyptian characters at intervals in the left margin. By comparing the Egyptian letters with those on the papyri rediscovered in 1967, Nelson determined that the fragment labeled "XI. Small 'Sensen' text" was the papyrus Joseph used as the basis for the Book of Abraham.[6]

A large portion of Joseph's translation has survived in his original hand (see figure 2A). Immediately noticeable is the large number of words Joseph Smith used to render each Egyptian character. In the surviving portion, 1,125 words correspond to 46 Egyptian characters. This is a ratio of 25:1.

Figures 2A and 2B show the rediscovered papyrus along with the portion of the original handwritten translation by Joseph Smith.[7] Arrow 1 points to the same Egyptian character as it appears in both. It is ㄱ. Nelson says it is correctly written 〰〰〰. According to him, this character is only one part of a word which means "lake" or "pool." To translate this character, Joseph Smith used 76 words and 334 letters. The translation reads:

> It was made after the form of a bedstead, such as was had among the Chaldeans, and it stood before the gods of Elkenah, Libnah, Mahmackrah, Korash, and also a god like unto that of Pharoah, king of Egypt. That you may have an understanding of these gods, I have given you the fashion of them in the figures at the beginning, which manner of the figures is called by the Chaldeans Rahleenos, which signifies hieroglyphics. (Abraham 1:13-14)

Figure 2A. A Portion of Joseph Smith's Translation of the Book of
Abraham in Joseph Smith's Handwriting.

To translate the remainder of this Egyptian word, Joseph used an additional 59 words, making a total of 136 English words from the one Egyptian word.

Another Egyptian character on the first line of the Sensen papyrus is ⵕ. Nelson identifies it as the demonstrative pronoun *this* or *the*. From this pronoun Joseph Smith translated most of Abraham 1:11: "Now, this priest had offered upon this altar three virgins at one time, who were the daughters of Onitah, one of the royal descent directly from the loins of Ham. These virgins were offered up because of their virtue; they would not bow down to worship gods of wood or of stone, therefore, they were killed upon this altar." Thus, 59 words come from the Egyptian equivalent of the English word *this*.

Figure 2B. A portion of the "XI. Small 'Sensen' text."

The phrase ⌐𝔸 in the second line of the Sensen text is best translated into English by "born to" or "born of." If the sex of the offspring is known, then it is possible to render it "daughter of " or "son of." In Joseph Smith's translation, three verses (Abraham 1:29-31, with the exception of the last 24 words of verse 31), or 131 words, translate these three Egyptian characters.

Three Egyptologists translate the next word in the Sensen text as a proper name. Nelson translates it Tai-Khebit, while Klaus Baer renders it Tikhebyt, and Richard Parker, Taykhebyt. The differences in the spelling can be accounted for by the lack of vocalizations in the Egyptian hieroglyphics. When Joseph Smith came to this name, he divided it into three parts. The first part, 𝔸 , became, "and I shall endeavor to write some of these things upon this record, for the benefit of my posterity that shall come after me" (Abraham 1:31). The second part, 𝔸 , became, "Now the Lord God caused the famine to wax sore in the land of Ur, insomuch that Haran, my brother, died; but Terah, my father, yet lived in the land of Ur, of the Chaldees. And it came to pass that I, Abraham, took Sarai to wife, and Nehor, my brother, took Milcah to wife" (Abraham 2:1-2a). (This is a total of 55 words from the center portion of one Egyptian name.) And the third part, 𝔸 , became "who were the daughters of Haran" (Abraham 2:2b).

The third line of the Sensen text has the word 𝔸 . Joseph translated Abraham 2:12-13 from three of the four letters of this Egyptian term. Dee Jay Nelson says this word may be translated either "his heart" or "his breast." Nelson adds that this spelling was never used prior to 400 B.C., contradicting the claim that it was written by Abraham, who lived approximately 2000 B.C.

We could continue to make comparisons of the Book of Abraham with the Egyptian text, but we have already seen enough to know that Joseph's translation in no way corresponds to the writing on the papyrus. From the 46 characters in the manuscript, Smith produced 1,125 English words, including over 65 proper names. In English, this represents approximately 296 vocables, and this count does not include those of a connecting type that are least audible.

One further point: in language translation proper names are most often transliterated rather than translated. In Joseph Smith's version, the name Mahmackrah appears three times with seven vocables each time. Shagreel, a proper name with six vocables, occurs once. Elkenah has five vocables and appears five separate times. That makes a total of 52 vocables for those three names alone. Therefore, the 46 characters that Joseph translated cannot even account for the nine occurrences of these three words, much less the remaining 1,073 words.

If the Sensen text Joseph used to produce the Book of Abraham does not really contain the words of Abraham, then what would an accurate translation of the Sensen text be? Dee Jay Nelson translates it this way:

... the pool of The Traveler, Khensu ... [Osiris Hor, who is true of word], born of Tai-Khebit, who is true of word likewise. After ... seized, the two arms with his heart are wrapped up with the Book of Breathings made by [Isis] and which is with writing on the inside and outside of royal linen. It is placed near and wrapped up on the left side in alignment with his heart. This having been done at his final wrapping for burial. If this book is made for him then he (will) breathe like the soul[s of the gods] for ever and ever.[8]

The title of the scroll of which this fragment is a part is found in the text of the fragment. It was called the *Book of Breathings*. We know from a similar papyrus in the Louvre which includes the preamble to the *Book of Breathings* that the purpose of the papyrus was to aid the deceased on their journey through the afterlife.

Book of Abraham Facsimiles

When Joseph Smith received the mummies and papyri, several of the papyri had only pictures on them. In preparing the Book of Abraham for publication, he had three of these Egyptian papyri transferred to woodcuts and printed in the text as illustrations of the narration in the Book of Abraham. He called them *Facsimiles 1, 2, and 3*.

We must keep in mind that the Small Sensen text, which we have just examined, was found with the mummies. From Nelson's translation of it, we know that the entire *Book of Breathings* was to be placed with a corpse for protection and guidance in the afterlife. Klaus Baer, of the University of Chicago, concluded after careful study that the fragments— the Small Sensen text, the Larger Sensen text and the fragment Joseph Smith identified as the original of Facsimile 1 —were all part of the same scroll.[9] This is significant for our study, because if these pieces were all part of the same scroll, Facsimile 1 must also belong to the *Book of Breathings*. When compared to the copy of the *Book of Breathings* in the British Museum, it seems quite probable that the picture Joseph called Facsimile 3 was also attached to the same scroll by a piece of the papyrus that is now missing.[10]

Scholars have long considered Facsimile 2 in the Book of Abraham to be a hypocephalus, a disk that was placed under the head of a mummy.[11] Since the hypocephalus is not considered a part of the *Book of Breathings* scroll, we shall consider it separately, and then return to Facsimiles 1 and 3.

Facsimile 2, as it appears in the Book of Abraham, has been found by prominent Egyptologists to contain many inaccuracies and adulterations. For example, a line of hieroglyphics that runs along the rim of this disk-shaped pictograph is interrupted by hieratic writing. This in itself is unusual, to say the least, and even more surprising is that the hieratic writing has been inserted upside down.[12]

For some time it was not known where the hieratic letters

Figure 3. Facsimile 2, Hypocephalus

came from. After the papyri became available in 1967, the Tanners compared the hieratic letters with the writing on the Small Sensen text and found that in several places groups of letters matched perfectly.[13] They could see no reason, though, for these insertions until they were able to obtain copies of *Joseph Smith's Egyptian Alphabet Grammar.* In it Joseph Smith had copied the original hypocephalus (see figure 4). The original, it turns out, was incomplete, indicating that the papyrus had been damaged before Joseph Smith purchased it. Comparing it with the woodcut of the same hypocephalus in the Book of Abraham, the Tanners found that the letters and pictures the Egyptologists had considered adulterations were missing.[14]

When Joseph Smith placed Facsimile 2 in the Book of Abraham, he labeled various parts of it and included a translation of several of these parts. Some of the parts he labeled (1) "Ought not to be revealed at this present time"; (2) "If the world can find out these numbers, so let it be"; and (3) "will be given in the own due time of the Lord." It is obvious that Joseph Smith had no idea what these parts of the hypocephalus meant.[15] Dee Jay Nelson has wryly commented, "The time seems to have arrived as I have succeeded after many years of work; . . . in translating 94 percent of the text on this circular drawing."[16]

In Joseph Smith's explanation of this hypocephalus, he used proper names like Abraham, Adam, Seth, Noah, Melchizedek and Kolob. Nelson's translation has no names that remotely resemble them.[17] It is hard to reach any other conclusion than that Joseph Smith's explanations were products of his creative imagination.

Facsimiles 1 and 3, as previously mentioned, are probably part of the same scroll. Number 1, according to Joseph Smith, is a drawing of the priest of Elkenah attempting to offer Abraham as a sacrifice to the gods Elkenah, Libnah, Mahmackrah, Korash and Pharaoh.[18] When Dee

Jay Nelson examined Facsimile 1, he made these observations:

> This scene is intimately familiar to me. . . . In one temple
> alone . . . are twenty-nine wall bas-reliefs . . . which ex-
> actly resemble the one on this papyrus fragment. . . . One
> of them has the following similarities. I should say, pre-
> cise equivalents: 1. The bier has a lion's head and an up-
> turned tail. 2. A person is lying on the bier, face up. 3.
> The hands of the reclining person are held above his face,
> palms downward (the sign of grief). 4. The reclining fig-
> ure stands near the foot of the bier facing the head of the
> couch. 6. A hawk-headed (ba) hovers over the reclining
> figure.[19]

Nelson has also observed that the four jars under the bier
with humanoid and animalistic heads were jars that were
used to contain the soft body parts of the embalmed person.
Nelson's observations are completely at variance with the
interpretation the Book of Abraham gives.

The papyrus fragment of this scene has several items that
are not shown on the copy in the Book of Abraham. It has
several rows of Egyptian characters on the sides and a small
portion of what appears to have been a row of characters
across the top. In these characters are several names. Two
of them are Anubis and Osiris. These same names are found
on other copies of the *Book of Breathings.* Another name
that appears on this facsimile is the name for the falcon-god
Horus, which most Egyptologists render Hor. This name
appears on both of the Sensen fragments and Facsimile 3.[20]
Although Hor appears on three of the four fragments, it is
not found anywhere in Joseph Smith's work, nor are the
other two names, Anubis or Osiris.

Facsimile 3 is a drawing with six figures, five standing
and one seated. In his explanation of this drawing, Joseph
Smith names and numbers each of these figures. Figure 1 is
Abraham, 2 is Pharaoh, 3 signifies Abraham in Egypt, 4 is

Figure 4. Facsimile 1.

the Prince of Pharaoh, 5 is Shulem and 6 is Olimlah the slave.[21] After Dee Jay Nelson had examined Facsimile 3, he suggested a totally different set of names. Figure 1 is the god Osiris, 2 is the goddess Isis, 3 is a small altar, 4 is the goddess Maat, 5 is Hor and 6 is the god Anubis.[22]

Nelson is not alone in his identification of these figures. Klaus Baer gives us this interpretation:

"Facsimile No. 3" shows a man (5), his hand raised in adoration, and a cone of perfume grease and a lotus flower on his head (ancient Egyptian festival attire), being introduced by Maat (4), the goddess of justice, and Anubis (6),

Figure 5. Facsimile 3.

the guide of the dead, into the presence of Osiris (1), enthroned as king of the Netherworld. Behind Osiris stands Isis (2), and in front of him is an offering-stand (3) with a jug [?] and some flowers on it. Over the whole scene is a canope with stars painted on it to represent the sky.

The scene comes from a mortuary papyrus. . . . It is a summary in one illustration of what the *Breathing Permit* promised: The deceased, after successfully undergoing the judgment, is welcomed into the presence of Osiris.[23]

Joseph Smith's explanation is far from accurate. All three of the facsimiles have a significance that in no way relates to the meaning he poured into them.

Speaking of Dee Jay Nelson's work on the papyri, Hugh Nibley said, "Latter-day Saints owe a debt of gratitude to Mr. Dee Jay Nelson. . . . This is a conscientious and courageous piece of work . . . supplying students with a usable and reliable translation."[24] Nelson, at the time of his work, was an elder in the Latter-day Saints Church, but he has refused to compromise on his findings. After several years of contemplation, he and his family wrote to the First Presidency of the Mormon Church the letter of resignation found in Appendix B. Nelson reached a conclusion with which we must concur: The Book of Abraham is a false translation of the papyrus Joseph Smith had in his possession and not the Word of God.

Chapter **6.**

Witnessing to Mormons

Mormonism is not Christian. And the documents out of which its unorthodox doctrines come are not divinely inspired. Being sure of this ourselves, how can we persuade those who are not convinced? How can we use the information we have to lead Mormons to a true knowledge of Christ?

This is not an easy subject to approach. Since each Mormon is an individual with unique needs and at a unique stage of doubting or accepting Mormonism, we cannot develop a step-by-step approach that will work with all Mormons at all times. If we are witnessing to a Mormon bishop, our approach will necessarily be different from the way we deal with a recent Mormon convert. We can, however, lay down some general principles to adapt to specific situations.

The New Testament gives us the essential principles in 2 Timothy 2:24-26. In this passage the apostle Paul is telling Timothy how to interact with those who oppose him:

And the Lord's bond-servant must not be quarrelsome,

but be kind to all, able to teach, patient when wronged, with gentleness correcting those who are in opposition, if perhaps God may grant them repentance leading to the knowledge of the truth, and they may come to their senses and escape from the snare of the devil, having been held captive by him to do his will.

Paul addresses these instructions to the Lord's *bond-servant.* The Greek word is the common term for a slave. When applied to a relation between God and a human being, it refers to a person whom God owns body and soul. Paul uses it here and in other passages to mean any follower of Christ. All Christians, then, should heed these principles in their witnessing.

The Lord's bond-servant must not be quarrelsome. To be *quarrelsome* means "to do verbal battle." We are not to engage in verbal warfare with those to whom we witness. Enemies, not friends, are made when an encounter turns into an argument. To maintain the long-term friendship with a Mormon that is necessary for a fruitful witness, we cannot sacrifice friendship to make a point.

Friendship is of the utmost importance in witnessing to most Mormons. For one thing, as we get to know a person more intimately, we are better able to discern which information, of all the information we could give him, he most needs to hear. I recently met a man who had been a Christian minister for nearly twenty-five years before becoming a Mormon. He revealed that there were several Christian doctrines he would never be able to give up and that the Mormon Church accepted these doctrines. One of them was the virgin birth. He had not learned that the Mormons believe God the Father had physical relations with Mary. This was, therefore, a good place to start in trying to win him back to Christianity. Planting one doubt about Mormon doctrine or the Mormon scriptures may raise a harvest of further questioning.

Being *kind*, rather than argumentative, does not rule out being a bold witness for the Lord; instead, it implies being tactful, saying the right thing in the right way at the right time. We cannot compromise the truth, but it does no good to pistol-whip a Mormon with the Bible. John L. Smith, a student of Mormonism for more than twenty-five years, makes a relevant comment about the many occurrences of the word *boldness* in Acts:

The words translated "boldly and boldness" here came from words that mean "outspoken, frankness, bluntness, and by implication, assurance. To be frank in utterance or confident in spirit and demeanor."

A witness to Mormons must be bold. The Mormon is bold—often almost to the point of arrogance—and any successful witness to him must be courageous and forward. Any hesitation on the part of the witness is interpreted by the Mormon as weakness and error. He is used to seeing non-Mormons who are timid and unsure of themselves. He sees the Mormon self-assuredness as an indication of his being "right." Therefore, the fearful, timid, flinching, fainthearted witness has already almost defeated his effort by his lack of "boldness."[1]

Smith adds that he is not advocating either harshness or arrogance as New Testament *boldness*.

The Lord's bond-servant must also be *able to teach*. A witness who does not know his material will not easily succeed. In talking with a Mormon, we must know more than just the Bible. The Bible is essential and should take the foremost position, but we must know the Mormon outlook as well.

Paul showed by his approach in Acts 17:16-34 that he understood Stoic and Epicurean philosophy. He did not learn these Greek world views in his Bible. Yet it was because he understood how the pagan mind worked that he was able to see results from his bold encounter with the Court of the

Areopagus. Paul had to pave the way for their reception of God's truth by showing these philosophers that their ideas were inadequate. As a result of Paul's witness "some men joined him and believed, among whom also was Dionysius the Areopagite and a woman named Damaris and others with them" (Acts 17:34).

If we are gentle yet bold, and able to teach, God may perhaps use our words to convince people of the truth.

Where Should You Start?

If you are new at witnessing to Mormons, you should not try to witness to Mormon missionaries. There are several reasons for this. One is that Mormon missionaries usually work in pairs, which gives them an advantage in dealing with a single Christian. Another is that Mormon missionaries are told they should not spend time with anyone they do not think they can convert. If you resist their doctrine, they probably will not return for a second conversation. If you succeed in raising a question that causes them to check with their superiors, they will in all likelihood be transferred to a new area.

A person with enough experience can accomplish with Mormon missionaries what Charles Crane, a man who has witnessed to Mormons for twenty-five years, calls "knocking the polish off their testimony." By this, Crane means getting a Mormon to doubt Mormonism enough that he will have a hard time telling potential converts he "knows" the *Book of Mormon* and the Mormon Church are true. This will greatly decrease his effectiveness in leading people into Mormonism.

The best place for you to start is probably with a Mormon friend or relative with whom you are comfortable and whom you know well. This enables you to know how to approach the person and how far you can go without starting an argument and losing a friend.

The plan that seems most effective in talking with Mormons involves these three steps: (1) showing that the Bible is trustworthy, (2) showing that the *Book of Mormon*, the *Doctrine and Covenants* and the *Pearl of Great Price* are not God's Word, and (3) getting a Mormon to realize that his faith in the *Book of Mormon* and Mormonism is purely subjective. Let us examine each of these three steps more closely.

As we discussed in chapter one, Mormons believe the Bible is unreliable because the Bible manuscripts have been almost hopelessly corrupted in transmission. You must, therefore, support the Bible's integrity before you use any verses from it. If you fail to do this, any verse you quote that contradicts Mormon doctrine will simply be written off as one of those places at which the Bible cannot be trusted.

Many Mormons have discovered the errors of Mormonism without the aid of a Christian. This was the case with archaeologist Thomas Stewart Ferguson who left Mormonism because of the evidence against it. But Ferguson also abandoned the Bible! Mormons already distrust the Bible. If you do not build up their confidence in it, you may turn them against Christianity as well as Mormonism.

Evidence for the trustworthiness of the Bible is plentiful. In the following several paragraphs we will survey the kind of information you can share with a Mormon.

Most of the important evidence for the accurate transmission of the Old Testament comes from the Dead Sea Scrolls. The first pieces were discovered in 1946 when a shepherd boy threw a rock into a cave near the Dead Sea and heard a jar break. This led to a series of excavations that uncovered one of the richest biblical manuscript finds ever.

The Dead Sea Scrolls contain portions of every Old Testament book except Esther. Until the discovery of these manuscripts, the oldest Old Testament manuscript in existence dated from around A.D. 900. The Dead Sea Scrolls were produced between 200 B.C. and A.D. 68. That means the Dead Sea Scrolls are from 900 to 1,100 years older than the oldest previously existing manuscript. The Mormons' claim that the Bible (in this case the Old Testament) was changed and corrupted by the Catholic Church, can now be tested.

To illustrate the *accuracy* of the transmission of the Hebrew Old Testament, consider how the Masoretic text of Isaiah 53 (produced in A.D. 916 and used in making most English translations) compares with Isaiah 53 in a portion of the Dead Sea Scrolls (dated 125 B.C.):

Of the 166 words in Isaiah 53, there are only seventeen letters in question. Ten of these letters are simply a matter of spelling, which does not affect the sense. Four more letters are minor stylistic changes, such as conjunctions. The remaining three letters comprise the word "light," which is added in verse 11, and does not affect the meaning greatly. . . . Thus, in one chapter of 166 words, there is only one word (three letters) in question after a thousand years of transmission and this word does not significantly change the meaning of the passage.[2]

Gleason Archer states that the Isaiah scroll is word-for-word identical with our standard Hebrew Old Testament in over ninety-five per cent of the text. He attributes the five per cent variation to obvious slips of the pen and variations in spelling.[3]

The accuracy of the transmission of the Old Testament text can be accounted for by the strict regulations under which Jewish scribes worked. Samuel Davidson describes how the Talmudist went about making a copy of the Old Testament text. The minute regulations were as follows:

(1) A synagogue roll must be written on the skins of clean animals, (2) prepared for particular use of the synagogue by a Jew. (3) These must be fastened together with strings taken from clean animals. (4) Every skin must contain a certain number of columns, equal throughout the entire

codex. (5) The length of each column must not extend over less than 48 or more than 60 lines; and the breadth must consist of thirty letters. (6) The whole copy must be first-lined; and if three words be written without a line, it is worthless. (7) The ink should be black, neither red, green, nor any other colour, and be prepared according to a definite recipe. (8) An authentic copy must be the examplar, from which the transcriber ought not in the least deviate. (9) No word or letter, not even a yod, must be written from memory, the scribe not having looked at the codex before him. . . . (10) Between every consonant the space of a hair or thread must intervene. (11) Between every new parashah, or section, the breadth of nine consonants; (12) between every book, three lines. (13) The fifth book of Moses must terminate exactly with a line; but the rest need not do so. (14) Besides this, the copyist must sit in full Jewish dress, (15) wash his whole body, (16) not begin to write the name of God with a pen newly dipped in ink, (17) and should a king address him while writing that name he must take no notice of him.[4]

Rolls that did not measure up to the standards were destroyed.

The Old Testament we have today is for all practical purposes identical to the texts used before Jesus' time. This is fatal to the Mormon claim that the Catholic Church has made it impossible for us to have a correct Bible. Even if we had found significant doctrinal differences between the Dead Sea Scrolls and our Old Testament, we would now have the older manuscripts with which to correct our current text.

There is an even greater abundance of manuscript evidence for the accuracy of the transmission of the New Testament. According to Bruce Metzger, we now have nearly five thousand manuscripts that contain all or part of the New Testament. They date from approximately A.D. 130 to A.D.

1200. Considering that these manuscripts were written in a span of over a thousand years by thousands of different scribes all over the world, we would expect a large number of variations in the readings. There are, in fact, in excess of 150,000 textual variants. Yet, as Geisler and Nix point out, "There is an ambiguity in saying there are some 200,000 variants in the existing manuscripts of the New Testament, since they represent only 10,000 places in the New Testament. If one single word is misspelled in 3,000 different manuscripts, this is counted as 3,000 variants or readings."[5]

F. F. Bruce, with keen insight into the discipline of textual criticism, concludes, "When we have documents like our New Testament writings copied and recopied thousands of times, the scope for copyists' errors is so enormously increased it is surprising there are no more than there actually are. Fortunately, if the great number of manuscripts increases the number of scribal errors, it increases proportionately the means of correcting such errors, so that the margin of doubt left in the process of recovering the exact original wording is not so large as might be feared; it is in truth remarkably small."[6]

Based on the observations of F. J. A. Hort, who spent his life studying the manuscripts, Geisler and Nix conclude that about one-eighth of the variants are of any material substance, or about one-sixtieth of the entire text. "Mathematically this would compute to a text that is 98.33 percent pure."[7]

Several of the best and most complete manuscripts have a rather early date; two of them—the Codex Vaticanus and the Codex Sinaiticus—are as early as A.D. 350. Also important is the Chester Beatty Papyri, consisting of parts of eleven codices, three of which contain most of the New Testament writings. These codices have been assigned dates ranging from A.D. 250 to 350. The John Rylands papyrus is probably the oldest New Testament manuscript yet found. It contains portions of John 18:31-33, 37-38. It is dated about A.D. 130. Also supporting our present Gospel of John is the Bodmer II Papyrus. It has the first fourteen chapters of John and much of the remaining seven chapters and is dated about A.D. 200, little more than one hundred years after the original composition.[8]

With these thousands of manuscripts with hundreds of thousands of variations, it is striking that no important doctrinal issues are at stake in any of the disputed readings. Philip Schaff maintains that not one of the variations alters "an article of faith or a precept of duty which is not abundantly sustained by other and undoubted passages, or by the whole tenor of Scripture teaching."[9]

We must agree therefore with the late Sir Frederic Kenyon:

> The interval between the dates of the original composition and the earliest extant evidence becomes so small as to be in fact negligible, and the last foundation for any doubt that the Scriptures have come down to us substantially as they were written has now been removed. Both the authenticity and the general integrity of the books of the New Testament may be regarded as finally established.[10]

Joseph Smith and other early Mormon leaders did not have sufficient evidence to make the claims they made about the Bible. Modern scholarship has established the reliability of the Old and New Testament manuscript traditions beyond question.

Creating Doubt

You must use evidence like this to remove a Mormon's doubt about the trustworthiness of the Bible and then replace that doubt with doubt in the extrabiblical documents the Mormons regard as sacred. Creating doubt plays a large part in an effective witness to a Mormon. You must be in continual prayer that God's Spirit will lead you to raise the right questions. Once a Mormon has begun to doubt, evidence that never carried any weight before suddenly begins to make sense. You can then share additional facts as fast as the person can receive them without becoming overwhelmed or angry with you.

One way to raise doubt about whether the *Book of Mormon* is the Word of God is to point out serious differences between its teachings and Mormon doctrine. As we have learned, the *Book of Mormon* does not contain basic Mormon doctrine. As a matter of fact, the *Book of Mormon* often contradicts it and teaches orthodox Christian positions.

An important example of this is the doctrine of God. Mormons believe in a God that has a body of flesh and bone, who lives in heaven (the First Estate) with his wives, who is procreating spirit-children, who is completely separate and distinct from Jesus, who is perhaps just one of thousands of gods that exist in the universe, who is literally the father of Jesus both in spirit and the flesh, and who has progressed from being a man to being a God and will continue to progress through eternity. These teachings are totally absent from the *Book of Mormon*. (Most Mormons are not aware of this.) On the contrary, the *Book of Mormon* teaches the Christian doctrine of God, as these verses show:

(1) Only one God: Alma 11:21-22, 28-31; 3 Nephi 11:27, 36; 2 Nephi 11:7; 2 Nephi 31:21; Mosiah 15:1-5; Mosiah 16:15; (2) God the Father and Son have been God eternally: Alma 11:38-39, 44; 2 Nephi 26:12; (3) God is unchanging: Mormon 9:9-11; Moroni 7:22; Moroni 8:18; (4) God is a Spirit: Alma 18:24-28; Alma 22:9-11.

If you are serious about witnessing to Mormons, you should study each of these verses in its context. With the aid of a concordance to the *Book of Mormon*, you can add to this list or produce a similar list on other doctrines. Most copies of the *Book of Mormon* contain a concordance and cross-reference system.

A good way to present these verses is to ask a Mormon what he believes about God. Get him to say it out loud. Many times a Mormon will be reluctant to do this because he knows his beliefs about God will be repulsive to a Christian. But prod him if necessary, because it is important that he state his beliefs.

If he does not object, jot down his doctrine of God as he gives it. When his ideas are out in the open, ask him to show you some verses in the *Book of Mormon* that support them. He will hunt in vain—for there are none. (As far as I know, he could appeal to only one chapter in the *Book of Mormon*, Ether 3. Several times this section mentions the finger of God. But this anthropomorphism does not prove that God has a physical body any more than Psalm 91:4 (KJV), "He shall cover thee with his feathers and under his wings shalt thou trust," proves that God is a cosmic chicken.)

Then use the verses listed above to show that the *Book of Mormon* actually teaches the Christian doctrine of God. You might say something like this, "I know that you accept the *Book of Mormon* as the Word of God, but I do not. I do believe, though, that it contains some true statements about God. If I can show you that the *Book of Mormon* teaches my doctrine of God, and not yours, will you accept that doctrine?" While doing this, make use of what you wrote down as the Mormon was explaining his concept of God, refuting these ideas point by point.

The first verses in the list are powerful when taken in context. In Alma 11:21-29 is a conversation between Amulek, a prophet of God, and Zeezrom, a "man who was expert in the devices of the devil, that he might destroy that which was good." Zeezrom, hoping to trick Amulek into betraying God, begins to question him: "Will ye answer the questions which I shall put unto you?" And Amulek said unto him:

"Yea, if it be according to the Spirit of the Lord, which is in me; for I shall say nothing which is contrary to the Spirit of the Lord." Zeezrom asks Amulek point-blank, "Is there more than one God?" And Amulek answers, "No."

Point out to your friend that he has just told you there are many gods in the universe and that Jesus and the Father are separate and distinct gods. How can he square that belief with this statement by a prophet of God? Some Mormons will answer, "What the prophet meant was that there is only one God with whom we have anything to do. To which you can respond, "If that is what he meant, why isn't that what he said?" Also, Mormons do not really believe this answer, for they think that Jesus and the Father are two completely separate gods and that we have something to do with both of them. Press the issue gently, "Which do you accept, the *Book of Mormon* or Mormon doctrine? You cannot believe both."

Another key verse is 2 Nephi 31:21: "And now, behold, this is the doctrine of Christ, and the only and true doctrine of the Father, and of the Son, and of the Holy Ghost, which is one God, without end." You need to emphasize two things in this verse. First, it purports to teach "the only true doctrine" about the person of God. Second, it teaches the essential oneness of the three persons of the Godhead.

The standard Mormon objection is that this verse is pointing to the fact that they are one in purpose. Again, if this is what the author meant, why isn't it what the author said? In fact, not one verse in the *Book of Mormon* says they are only one in purpose.

Eternal progression, the concept that God is a man who has progressed to godhood and that any man today can also achieve godhood, is an important Mormon idea about God that is absent from and even opposed by the *Book of Mormon*.[11] Consider Mormon 9:9-10, for example: "For do we not read that God is the same yesterday, today, and forever, and in him there is no variableness neither shadow of changing? And now if ye have imagined up unto yourselves a god who doth vary, and in whom there is shadow of changing, then have ye imagined up unto yourselves a god who is not a God of miracles." In the same context, Mormon 9:19 asserts, "And behold, I say unto you he changeth not; if so he would cease to be God." Moroni 8:18 further widens the gap between Mormon doctrine and the *Book of Mormon*: "For I know that God is not a partial God, neither a changeable being; but is unchangeable from all eternity to all eternity."

You cannot stress this contradiction enough. Mormon doctrine teaches that God has changed and will continue to change forever according to the law of eternal progression, while the *Book of Mormon* teaches that God has been the same for all eternity past and will be the same for all eternity to come. Mormons must give up either Mormon doctrine, or the *Book of Mormon*, or both.

Most Mormons will want to use the *Doctrine and Covenants* when they can find no ready help in the *Book of Mormon*. In such a case, you should refer the Mormon to *Doctrine and Covenants* 18:1-5, which claims that the *Book of Mormon* contains "all things written concerning the foundation of my church, my gospel, and my rock." The doctrine of God would seem to be a foundation doctrine and crucial to understanding the gospel; therefore, it should be found in the *Book of Mormon*.

Once your Mormon friend has begun to see the contradictions between Mormon doctrine and the *Book of Mormon*, you can share more of the material we have already discussed in this book. The changes in the *Book of Commandments* are a good topic to turn to next. Realizing a few things about the changes will help you in presenting them.

One of the most important verses to use is *Book of Commandments* 1:7 and the duplicate statement in *Doctrine and Covenants* 1:37-39. You must emphasize that these verses assert that *Book of Commandments* and *Doctrine and Covenants* are God's Word and will stand forever. Whenever you point out a change in one of the revelations, you should remind your hearer about these verses to show that these books do not measure up to their own claims.

The three most important changes to share are those between *Book of Commandments* 4:2 and *Doctrine and Covenants* 5:4; *Book of Commandments* 6 and *Doctrine and Covenants* 7; and *Book of Commandments* 15:1-4 and *Doctrine and Covenants* 18:1-5.

The first change undercuts the inspiration of all books written by Joseph Smith except the *Book of Mormon*. Actually, two of the three extrabiblical scriptures the Mormons claim are God's Word stand or fall with this change. The second change concerns the reliability of the *Book of Commandments*, the *Doctrine and Covenants* and the *Book of Mormon*. If Joseph could not even translate a three-verse passage correctly with the Urim and Thummim, how can we trust the nearly six hundred pages of the *Book of Mormon* that were translated in the same way? The third change is important because it deals with the content of the *Book of Mormon*. Does the *Book of Mormon* contain all things or not? When using this change be sure to use the entire context or the Mormon will say the "things written" are all the extrabiblical Mormon scriptures.

Ask your Mormon friend, "If these revelations are God's Word as you claim, why haven't they remained unchanged as *Book of Commandments* 1:7 and *Doctrine and Covenants* 1:37-39 claimed they would?" Press home the importance of these three changes; all of Mormonism stands or falls on them. (To help the serious student study changes not discussed in this book and to facilitate comparing verses in the *Book of Commandments* and the *Doctrine and Covenants*, a chart showing the parallel chapters in each is included in Appendix C.)

The third important element of a witness to a Mormon is showing him that his faith in the *Book of Mormon* and Mormonism is subjective. In the front of most of the missionary editions of the *Book of Mormon* is printed Moroni 10:4-5, which reads, "And when ye receive these things, I would exhort you that ye would ask God, the Eternal Father, in the name of Christ, if these things are not true; and if ye shall ask with a sincere heart, with real intent, having faith in Christ, he will manifest the truth of it unto you, by the power of the Holy Ghost. And by the power of the Holy Ghost ye may know the truth of all things." Most Mormons use these verses as a basis for their faith.

Most Mormons claim to have received a testimony as a result of following these instructions. They often refer to it as a "burning feeling" that told them the *Book of Mormon* is true. In the Mormon missionary lessons the potential convert is asked to read the *Book of Mormon* and then pray according to Moroni 10:4-5. The missionaries claim, "I know you will feel the truth of our message if you will make the effort to ponder these things and will seek the Lord in sincere prayer."[12]

The missionaries use the right word when they say *feel*. This plea is found in the first lesson of the materials and the rest of the process of conversion into Mormonism depends on this feeling. There are Christians who have prayed sincerely and have received a feeling that the *Book of Mormon* is false. Who is to say which feeling, if either, came from God? We must encourage Mormons to abandon this subjective basis for their faith and examine the *Book of Mormon* and Mormonism with their minds.

If you do not overcome this subjectivism, your efforts may be in vain. Many Mormons have been presented with mountains of evidence against the *Book of Mormon* and Mormonism only to respond, "But God has told me that it is true. There must be an answer to your claims." Sometimes it may take months or even years for a Mormon to abandon this subjectivism. Sandra Tanner was no exception. A few years after she left the Mormon Church she said, "It was a long time before I could admit I didn't believe the *Book of Mormon*.... It was weeks after that before I could say it out loud."[13]

What Should You Do Next?

If you have been successful up to this point—if you have created confidence in the Bible while creating doubts about the Mormon documents and emphasizing the subjective basis for Mormon faith—what should you do next? If God has used you to open the person's eyes, to create a desire to know the truth, then share Bible passages that teach sound Christian doctrine. Center your message on the person and work of Jesus Christ, making clear that he can provide forgiveness for all sins.

If possible, get your Mormon friend into a Bible study on basic Christian doctrine. Assume he has no correct understanding of any biblical concept unless he demonstrates he has. This is necessary to prevent his combining Mormon and Christian ideas. He needs to study subjects like the nature of God, the nature of sin, the person and work of Christ, salvation and conversion. In most cases it will take a long while for a Mormon to accept these teachings. Take your time, get into the Bible yourself and allow the Holy Spirit to work through you.

You can get help with Bible study from many sources. Margaret Erb's *Basic Christianity* contains Bible studies on most of the essential topics. Also useful is John Stott's book with the same title. Stott discusses the person and work of Christ, the nature of sin, and the necessary response. Paul Little's *How to Give Away Your Faith* makes general suggestions on how to witness, most of which you can readily adapt to witnessing to Mormons.[14]

Do not be discouraged if you are unable to involve your

friend in a study of the Scriptures right away. Several months or years may pass before your witness bears fruit. Even though your witness seems to be having no effect, keep the communication lines open and keep sharing. Many times it will take a crisis in the life of a Mormon to make him realize that Mormonism is false.

I have a friend who spent nearly two years witnessing to a young Mormon businessman. Slowly he shared the problems with the Mormon scriptures, but his Mormon friend seemed unaffected. Evidently, though, the Mormon was beginning to have some doubts he did not share with anyone. As he began to doubt, his giving to the Church began to decrease. The more he doubted, the less he gave. Finally, his bishop called on him to see why he had not been giving his full tithe. That was the last straw. He asked the bishop to leave, called my friend and within two weeks gave his life to Christ.

Remember, the Mormons base their faith on a feeling. Often the facts a Christian presents seem to be ignored. But when a crisis comes, the subjectivism may not be enough to sustain the Mormon and he will call on a Christian friend for help and guidance.

In addition to information from the Bible, your personal testimony can have an effect. Mormons need to know that Christians have an experience with God. We must be careful, of course, to define our terms so our listener does not give them Mormon meanings.

I have also found it helpful not to refer to anything that a Mormon would consider anti-Mormon literature. A refutation of Mormon doctrine like the Tanners' *Mormonism: Shadow or Reality?* you should digest before the encounter. Your arguments will be more effective if you use Mormon books to refute Mormon doctrine.

Extremely useful are the reprints of the 1830 edition of the *Book of Mormon*, the 1833 edition of the *Book of Commandments* and the 1835 edition of the *Doctrine and Cove-*

nants. These are published in two volumes by the Deseret News Press, the official Latter-day Saints Church press, under the title *Joseph Smith Begins His Work* by W. C. Wood and are thoroughly documented photoreproductions of the originals. They are distributed by Bookcraft Publishers Inc., Salt Lake City, Utah, on a wholesale basis. They are available in some Latter-day Saints bookstores and from the author of this book on a retail basis. (For order information, write P.O. Box 322, Roy, Utah 84067.) You can look up in these reprints the sections discussed in chapters two and four and compare them with current editions, available from Mormon missionaries or Latter-day Saints bookstores.

A final hint would be that it is not usually worthwhile to argue with a Mormon over controversial issues that have often been at the center of discussion in the past. Some of these are baptism for the dead, the stick of Joseph and the stick of Judah, the lifestyle and character of Joseph Smith, and polygamy. (Since we have not discussed many of these items in the body of this book, a brief description of them has been relegated to the glossary.) Such matters are not the primary problems. The main question is: are three books— the *Book of Mormon*, the *Doctrine and Covenants*, and the *Pearl of Great Price*—really God's Word? Our conclusions on the rest of the disputed matters depend on our view of these books.

Witnessing to Mormons is not easy. Yet, because of the threat they pose to the body of Christ and because of our love for them, we must accept the responsibility of trying to help them see the truth.

Appendixes

Appendix A
Letter and Statement from the Smithsonian Institution, Department of Anthropology

Your recent inquiry concerning the Book of Mormon has been received in the Smithsonian Department of Anthropology.

The Book of Mormon is a religious document and not a scientific guide. The Smithsonian Institution does not use it in any way in archaeological research. Because the Smithsonian Institution receives many inquiries in this regard and in connection with Mormon statements about the origin and relationships of the American Indian, we have prepared a "Statement Regarding the Book of Mormon," a copy of which is enclosed for your information.

Statement Regarding the Book of Mormon

The Smithsonian Institution has received hundreds of inquiries in recent years regarding the use of the Book of Mormon as a guide to archaeological researches. Answers to questions most commonly asked are as follows:

1. The Smithsonian Institution has never used the Book of Mormon in any way as a scientific guide. Smithsonian archeologists see no connection between the archaeology of the New World and the subject matter of the Book.

2. The physical type of the American Indian is basically Mongoloid, being most closely related to that of the peoples of eastern, central, and northeastern Asia. Archaeological evidence indicates that the ancestors of the present Indians came into the New World—probably over a land bridge known to have existed in the Bering Strait region during the last Ice Age—in a continuing series of small migrations beginning about 30,000 years ago.

3. Present evidence indicates that the first people to reach this continent from the East were the Norsemen who arrived in the northeastern part of North America around A.D. 1000. There is nothing to show that they reached Mexico or Central America.

4. There is a possibility that the spread of cultural traits across the Pacific to MesoAmerica and the northwestern coast of South America began several thousand years before the Christian era. However, these appear to be the result of accidental voyages originating in eastern and southern Asia and show no relationship to ancient Egyptian or Hebrew cultures.

5. We know of no authentic cases of ancient Egyptian or Hebrew writ-

ing having been found in the New World. Reports of findings of Egyptian influence in the Mexican and Central American areas have been published in newspapers and magazines from time to time, but thus far no reputable Egyptologist has been able to discover any relationship between Mexican remains and those in Egypt.

6. There are two copies of the Book of Mormon (and part of a third copy) in the National Museum of Natural History, and another copy was sent by the Smithsonian Library to the Library of Congress for deposit. Two of these were gift copies, and one was received by transfer from another government agency. One or two members of the staff have personal copies that were presented to them by Mormons.

Suggested Reading

Coe, Michael D.
1962. *Mexico.* 245 pp., 75 pls., 32 figs., 8 maps, 1 table. Frederick A. Praeger, New York (Ancient Peoples and Places Series, vol. 29). (A well-written and authoritative summary of Mexican archaeology.)

Ferguson, Thomas S.
1958. *One Fold and One Shepherd.* 405 pp., illus. Books of California, San Francisco. (A book presenting the Mormon point of view.)

Hunter, Milton R., and Ferguson, Thomas S.
1950. *Ancient America and the Book of Mormon.* 450 pp., 53 figs., Kolob Book Co., Oakland, California. (Another book presenting the Mormon point of view.)

Jennings, Jesse D., and Norbeck, Edward
1963. *Prehistoric Man in the New World.* 633 pp., illus. University of Chicago Press, Chicago. (The most recent and thorough survey of New World archaeology, written by leading American archaeologists.)

MacGowan, Kenneth, and Hester, Joseph A., Jr.
1962. *Early Man in the New World.* Rev. ed. 333 pp., illus. Anchor Books, Doubleday & Co., Garden City, New Jersey (The Natural History Library). (Good general reading; also provides some Old World background.)

Morley, Sylvanus G.
1956. *The Ancient Maya.* 494 pp., 102 pls., 57 figs. (3rd ed., rev. by George W. Brainerd.) Stanford University Press, Stanford, California. (Maya history: origin of their civilization, its rise, first florescence, first decline, renaissance and final decline, Spanish conquest.)

Thompson, J. Eric
1954. *The Rise and Fall of Maya Civilization.* 287 pp., 24 pl., 20 figs., map. University of Oklahoma Press, Norman. (An important account of Maya civilization based on archaeological discoveries.)

Appendix B
Dee Jay Nelson's Letter of Resignation

PROF. DEE JAY NELSON
Lecturer
Egyptologist
719 HIGHLAND PARK DRIVE
BILLINGS, MONTANA 59102

FIELD ADDRESS:
NILE HILTON
CAIRO, EGYPT, U.A.R.

Attention: First Presidency
Church of Jesus Christ of Latter Day Saints
Church Office Building
Salt Lake City, Utah

This letter is to inform you that it is our considered desire that my
own name and those of my wife and daughter be removed from the member-
ship rolls of the Latter Day Saint Church.

We:
     Dee Jay Nelson
     Katherine G. Nelson (Mrs. Dee Jay Nelson)
     Kim Cherie Nelson
          do freely, and with full understanding of the implications
of the step, require that our names be removed from all member records
of the L.D.S. Church.

I, Dee Jay Nelson, do herby renounce and relinquish the priesthood
which I now hold.

Following my translation (the first to be published) of the bulk of
the hieratic and hieroglyphic Egyptian texts upon the Metropolitan-
Joseph Smith Papyri Fragments three of the most eminent Egyptologists
now living published corroborating translations. These amply prove
the fraudulent nature of the Book of Abraham, in which lies the un-
just assertion that negros are unworthy of participation in the highest
privileges of the L.D.S. Church.

We do not wish to be associated with a religious organization which
teaches lies and adheres to policies so blatantly opposed to the
civil and religious rights of some citizens of the United States.

By affixing our signatures to this document we exercise our constitut-
ional rights of religious freedom and separate ourselves from the
Church of Jesus Christ of Latter Day Saints.

Dee Jay Nelson

Katherine G. Nelson

Kim Cherie Nelson

Date: Dec. 8, 1975

Appendix C
Cross-reference between Book of Commandments
and Doctrine and Covenants.

The following is a chart comparing the revelations in the Book of Commandments *with their counterparts in the* Doctrine and Covenants. *This chart is helpful because the order of the revelations have been changed several times. Fortunately there is an introductory paragraph with each revelation that makes it possible to compare them in each edition.*

BC = *Book of Commandments*
DC = *Doctrine and Covenants*

1. BC 1, DC 1
2. DC 2, not in BC
3. BC 2, DC 3
4. BC 3, DC 4
5. BC 4, DC 5
6. BC 5, DC 6
7. BC 6, DC 7
8. BC 7, DC 8
9. BC 8, DC 9
10. BC 9, DC 10
11. BC 10, DC 11
12. BC 11, DC 12
13. DC 13, not in BC
14. BC 12, DC 14
15. BC 13, DC 15
16. BC 14, DC 16
17. DC 17, not in BC
18. BC 15, DC 18
19. BC 16, DC 19
20. BC 17—21, DC 23
21. BC 22, DC 21
22. BC 23, DC 22
23. BC 24, DC 20
24. BC 25, DC 24
25. BC 26, DC 25
26. BC 27, DC 26
27. BC 28, DC 27
28. BC 29, DC 29
29. BC 30, DC 28
30. BC 31—33, DC 30
31. BC 34, DC 31
32. DC 32, not in BC
33. BC 35, DC 33
34. BC 36, DC 34
35. BC 37, DC 35
36. BC 38, DC 36
37. BC 39, DC 37
38. BC 40, DC 38
39. BC 41, DC 39
40. BC 42, DC 40
41. BC 43, DC 41
42. BC 44, DC 42:1-73
43. BC 45, DC 43
44. BC 46, DC 44
45. BC 47, DC 42:74-93
46. BC 48, DC 45
47. BC 49, DC 46
48. BC 50, DC 47
49. BC 51, DC 48
50. BC 52, DC 49
51. BC 53, DC 50
52. DC 51, not in BC
53. BC 54, DC 52
54. BC 55, DC 53
55. BC 56, DC 54
56. BC 57, DC 55
57. BC 58, DC 56
58. DC 57, not in BC
59. BC 59, DC 58
60. BC 60, DC 59
61. BC 61, DC 60
62. BC 62, DC 61
63. BC 63, DC 62
64. BC 64, DC 63
65. BC 65, DC 64

Appendix D
New Developments in the Spaulding-Rigdon Theory

As this book was going to press, the news media (see *Time*, July 11, 1977; *Christianity Today*, July 8, 1977) reported new evidence regarding the Spaulding-Rigdon Theory of the origin of the *Book of Mormon* (see pp. 33-34). Based on recent handwriting analysis, Howard A. Davis, Donald R. Scales and Wayne L. Cowdrey contend that twelve pages of the original handwritten manuscript of the *Book of Mormon* are actually in the handwriting of Solomon Spaulding. These researchers have what has been termed "a firm case" supporting the Spaulding origin of at least a portion of the *Book of Mormon* manuscript. This conclusion was reached after three expert handwriting analysts had compared twelve pages of the *Book of Mormon* manuscript with a known Spaulding manuscript.

I have examined firsthand the pages of the manuscripts in question in the office of Donald Schmidt of the Historical Department of the LDS Church in Salt Lake City. In addition to the *Book of Mormon* manuscript and a Spaulding manuscript, we requested to see and were allowed to examine a third manuscript. Schmidt allowed us to compare a photocopy of a manuscript represented as the original manuscript of *Doctrine and Covenants* 56 which was dated 1831. The Mormons claim that this manuscript was written by the same unknown scribe who penned the twelve disputed pages in the *Book of Mormon*.

It is significant to note that this third manuscript has not yet been studied by the handwriting analysts who have come out in support of the new theory. The LDS Church has not yet released copies of this 1831 manuscript, but they will allow it to be examined by competent analysts in the LDS office. Though I am not a specialist in handwriting analysis, even to the untrained eye the *Book of Mormon* manuscript and the 1831 *Doctrine and Covenants* manuscript are remarkably similar. If the manuscript of *Doctrine and Covenants* 56 was in fact written in 1831 (*after* Spaulding's death) and if it and the *Book of Mormon* manuscript are found to be in the same handwriting, then the new theory of Davis, Cowdrey and Scales could not be supported.

Because this 1831 document has not yet been examined by the experts, we urge Christians to suspend judgment until all the evidence is in. Making claims that could later be proven false by the LDS Church could be very detrimental to Christian witnessing. On the other hand, if the 1831 document is not genuine or is shown to be in another hand, this new evidence would be a very powerful argument against the credibility of the *Book of Mormon* and Joseph Smith's claim to be a prophet of God.

Notes

Introduction

[1]*Alexander Campbell*, "Delusions," Millennial Harbinger, *II, February 1831.*

Chapter 1

[1]Uniform System for Teaching Families *(Salt Lake City: Corp. of Pres. of Church of Jesus Christ of Latter-day Saints, 1973), p. C-31.*

[2]*Joseph Smith*, Journal of Discourses *(Liverpool: F. D. Richards, 1855), VI, 5.*

[3]*Ibid., pp. 3-4.*

[4]*Milton R. Hunter*, The Gospel through the Ages *(Salt Lake City: Deseret Book Co., 1969), pp. 104-05.*

[5]*Brigham Young*, Discourses of Brigham Young *(Salt Lake City: Deseret News Press, 1825), p. 351.*

[6]*Brigham Young, ed.*, Millennial Star, *54 (Liverpool: Brigham Young, 1892), p. 404.*

[7]Uniform System for Teaching Families, *pp. D-3, 5.*

[8]*Bruce McConkie*, Mormon Doctrine *(Salt Lake City: Bookcraft, 1958), p. 467.*

[9]*Brigham Young*, Journal of Discourses *(Liverpool: F.D. Richards, 1855), I, 50-51.*

[10]*Ibid.*

[11]*Joseph Fielding Smith*, Doctrines of Salvation, *(Salt Lake City: Bookcraft, 1969), I, 19.*

[12]*Brigham Young*, Journal of Discourses *(Liverpool: F.D. Richards, 1855),VIII, 115.*

[13]*Orson Pratt*, The Seer *(Washington, DC: Orson Pratt, Oct. 1853), p. 158.*

[14]Uniform System for Teaching Families, *p. D-7.*

[15]*Ibid., pp. D-13, 17.*

[16]*Ibid., p. E-23.*

[17]*Brigham Young*, Journal of Discourses, *IV, 54.*

[18]*Joseph Fielding Smith*, Teachings of the Prophet Joseph Smith *(Salt Lake City: Deseret News Press, 1958), p. 327.*

[19]*James E. Talmage*, The Articles of Faith *(Salt Lake City: Deseret News Press, 1968), p. 237.*

[20]*Orson Pratt*, Orson Pratt's Works *(Salt Lake City: Deseret News Press, 1945), p. 196.*

[21]*Keith Marston*, Missionary Pal *(Salt Lake City: Publishers Press, 1959), pp. 73-75.*

[22]*Pratt*, Works, *pp. 175-196.*

Chapter 2

[1]*Wesley P. Walters*, New Light on Mormon Origins *(Salt Lake City: Modern Microfilm Co., 1967), p. 3.*

[2]*The phrase is Fawn Brodie's.*

[3]*Fawn Brodie*, No Man Knows My History *(New York: Alfred A. Knopf, 1967), p. 67.*

[4]*Ibid., pp. 70-72.*

[5]*Ibid. Also, see Gordon Fraser*, What Does the Book of Mormon Teach? *(Chicago: Moody Press, 1864), pp. 86-91.*

[6]*Mormon 8:17; 9:32ff.; Ether 12:22-28.*

[7]*Brodie, pp. 79-80.*

[8]*George Arbaugh,* Revelation in Mormonism *(Chicago: University of Chicago Press, 1932), p. 9.*

[9]*Ibid.*

[10]*Lucy Mack Smith,* Biographical Sketches of Joseph Smith the Prophet and His Progenitors for Many Generations *(Liverpool: S. W. Richards, 1853), p. 85, as quoted in Hal Hougey,* "A Parallel"—The Basis of the Book of Mormon *(Concord, CA: Pacific Publishing Co., 1963), p. 5.*

[11]*B. H. Roberts, as reproduced in Hougey,* "A Parallel," *pp. 7-20.*

[12]*Hougey,* "A Parallel," *p. 21.*

[13]*Joseph Smith,* The History of the Church of Jesus Christ of Latter-day Saints *(Salt Lake City: Deseret News Press, 1902), IV, 461.*

[14]*Joseph Fielding Smith,* Doctrines of Salvation *(Salt Lake City: Bookcraft, 1954), I, 170.*

[15]*This quote is found in the journal of Oliver Huntington, p. 168. He attended the meeting at which the statement by Joseph Fielding Smith was made. A typed copy of his journal is on deposit with the Utah State Historical Society. Photocopies are available.*

[16]*David Whitmer,* An Address to All Believers in Christ *(Concord, CA: Pacific Publishing Co., 1976), p. 12.*

[17]*Jerald and Sandra Tanner,* Mormonism: Shadow or Reality? *(Salt Lake City: Modern Microfilm Co., 1972), p. 89. For a complete list of the changes in the* Book of Mormon *since the first edition, see Jerald and Sandra Tanner,* 3,913 Changes in the Book of Mormon *(Salt Lake City: Modern Microfilm Co., 1965). This is a photoreproduction of the first edition of the* Book of Mormon *with the changes marked in the text. Also see William Brodie Crouch,* The Myth of Mormon Inspiration *(Shreveport, LA: Lamberts Book House, 1968), pp. 248-68.*

[18]*Tanner,* Mormonism, *p. 90.*

[19]*James E. Talmage,* Articles of Faith *(Salt Lake City: The Church of Jesus Christ of Latter-day Saints, 1968), pp. 466-67.*

[20]*Tanner,* Mormonism, *pp. 165-66.*

[21]*Ibid.*

[22]*Ibid.*

[23]*Francis W. Kirkham,* A New Witness for Christ in America, The Book of Mormon *(Independence, MO: Zion's Printing and Pub. Co., 1942), pp. 200-01).*

[24]*Tanner,* Mormonism, *p. 90.*

[25]*Ibid. Sidney B. Sperry's article can be found in the* Brigham Young University Bulletin: Graduate School Issue, *1972-73, p. 176.*

[26]*Kirkham, pp. 199-201. See also B. H. Roberts,* Defense of the Faith *(Salt Lake City: Deseret News Press, 1907), p. 278-79.*

Chapter 3

[1]*Ross T. Christensen,* University Archaeological Society Newsletter, *30 Jan. 1960, pp. 3-6.*

[2]*Michael Coe,* "Mormons and Archaeology: An Outside View," *in* Dialogue: A Journal on Mormon Thought, *7, No. 2 (Los Angeles: Dialogue Foundation), 42.*

[3]*Ibid., p. 42.*

⁴*Ibid., p. 46.*

⁵*Quoted in Hal Hougey*, Archaeology and the Book of Mormon *(Concord, CA: Pacific Publishing Co., 1976), pp. 6-7. Original article in* Dialogue: A Journal on Mormon Thought, *Spring 1966, pp. 145-246.*

⁶*Dee Green, "Book of Mormon Archaeology: The Myths and the Alternatives," in* Dialogue: A Journal on Mormon Thought, *4, No. 2 (Los Angeles: Dialogue Foundation), 74.*

⁷*Milton R. Hunter,* Archaeology and the Book of Mormon *(Salt Lake City: Deseret Book Co., 1972), pp. 1-10.*

⁸*Dee Green, "Book of Mormon Archaeology," pp. 77-78.*

⁹*John L. Sorenson, "Ancient American and the Book of Mormon Revisited," in* Dialogue: A Journal on Mormon Thought, *4, No. 2 (Los Angeles: Dialogue Foundation), 81.*

¹⁰*Dee Green, "Book of Mormon Archaeology," p. 75.*

¹¹*Ibid., p. 75.*

¹²*Ibid., p. 80.*

¹³*Hal Hougey has done an excellent survey of all the pertinent information relating to the Lehi Tree of Life Stone in* The Truth about the Lehi Tree-of-Life Stone *(Concord, CA: Pacific Publishing Co., n.d.).*

Chapter 4

¹*Arthur Budvarson,* Changes in Mormonism *(La Mesa, CA: Utah Christian Tract Society, n.d.), pp. 6-7.*

²*David Whitmer,* An Address to All Believers in Christ *(Richmond, MO: David Whitmer, 1887), pp. 54-55.*

³*Tanner,* Mormonism, *pp. 27-28.*

⁴*Sidney B. Sperry,* Doctrine and Covenants Compendium *(Salt Lake City: Book-craft, 1960), p. 85.*

⁵*David Whitmer, in his* Address, *pp. 58-59, attributes these new doctrines and changes to the influence of Sidney Rigdon. See also F. M. McKernan,* Sidney Rigdon 1792-1876 *(Lawrence, KS: Coronado Press, 1972).*

⁶*Brodie,* No Man Knows My History, *pp. 94-113. This section deals with the new society the Mormons built, the communal element, and Rigdon's influence. See also Arbaugh,* Revelation in Mormonism, *pp. 10ff.*

⁷*Whitmer,* Address, *p. 35.*

⁸*Tanner,* Mormonism, *p. 180.*

⁹*Joseph Fielding Smith,* Essentials in Church History *(Salt Lake City: Deseret Book Co., 1972). See chapters 22-26 for the history of this period. This is an official Mormon view of Mormon history and is one of the books that the First Presidency of the Church places in libraries all over the world free of cost.*

¹⁰*Hyrum M. Smith,* Doctrine and Covenants Commentary *(Salt Lake City: Deseret Book Co., 1968), p. 497.*

¹¹*Joseph Fielding Smith,* Answers to Gospel Questions *(Salt Lake City: Deseret Book Co., 1963), IV, 112.*

¹²*Tanner,* Mormonism, *p. 190.*

¹³*For an authoritative discussion on this verse from the Mormon view, see Smith,* Doctrine and Covenants Commentary, *p. 105.*

[14]*For more verses that support this view, see page 68, footnote u, in the 1961 edition of the* Book of Mormon.

[15]Uniform System for Families, *pp. 25, 27, 31. On page 31 the first paragraph under "Concept 11" confirms the order taught by Mormon missionaries.*

[16]*Tanner,* Mormonism, *p. 30.*

Chapter 5

[1]Pearl of Great Price, *1891 edition, p. iv.*

[2]*Joseph Fielding Smith,* Essentials in Church History, *p. 154.*

[3]*LeGrand Richards,* A Marvelous Work and a Wonder *(Salt Lake City: Deseret Book Co., 1971), p. 427. Richards gives a good but brief account of the history of the mummies and the papyri and of how they fell into the hands of Joseph Smith.*

[4]*Jerald and Sandra Tanner,* The Case Against Mormonism *(Salt Lake City: Modern Microfilm Co., 1968), II, 113.*

[5]*Tanner,* Mormonism, *p. 310. See also Dee Jay Nelson,* The Joseph Smith Papyri, *Part 2 (Salt Lake City: Modern Microfilm Co., 1968).*

[6]*Tanner,* Mormonism, *p. 311. The Tanners have also been able to obtain photocopies of the original manuscript of the translation by Joseph Smith. These photocopies cover Abraham 1:1–2:18. (Tanner,* The Case Against Mormonism, *pp. 2:146-151. Follow the translation through the fourth line of the "Small Sensen text.")*

[7]*Photocopies of several of the pages of the original handwritten manuscripts are available from the Tanners on request. The discussion that follows relies primarily on Tanner,* The Case Against Mormonism, *II, and Nelson,* The Joseph Smith Papyri, *Part 2.*

[8]*Nelson,* The Joseph Smith Papyri, *Part 2, p. 21.*

[9]*Tanner,* Mormonism, *pp. 333-34.*

[10]*Ibid.*

[11]*Dee Jay Nelson,* Joseph Smith's "Eye of Ra" *(Salt Lake City: Modern Microfilm Co., 1968), p. 1. This is an invaluable study devoted entirely to the translation of Facsimile No. 2. It is fully illustrated and understandable to the general reader. It may be purchased from the Tanners.*

[12]*Tanner,* Mormonism, *pp. 335-39.*

[13]*Ibid.*

[14]*Ibid.*

[15]Pearl of Great Price, *p. 34.*

[16]*Nelson,* Joseph Smith's "Eye of Ra," *p. 1.*

[17]*Ibid., p. 28.*

[18]Pearl of Great Price, *p. 28.*

[19]*Quoted in Tanner,* The Case Against Mormonism, *III, 35.*

[20]*Ibid., p. 34.*

[21]Pearl of Great Price, *p. 42.*

[22]*Dee Jay Nelson,* A Translation and Study of Facsimile No. 3 in the Book of Abraham *(Salt Lake City: Modern Microfilm Co., 1969), p. 13.*

[23]*Tanner,* The Case Against Mormonism, *III, 49.*

[24]*Tanner,* Mormonism, *p. 310.*

Chapter 6

¹*John L. Smith,* Witnessing Effectively to Mormons *(Marlow, OK: Utah Missions Inc., 1975), pp. 29-30.*

²*Geisler and Nix,* A General Introduction to the Bible *(Chicago: Moody Press, 1968), p. 263.*

³*Gleason Archer,* A Survey of the Old Testament *(Chicago: Moody Press, 1964), p. 19.*

⁴*Quoted in Josh McDowell,* Evidence That Demands a Verdict *(Campus Crusade For Christ International, 1972), pp. 56-67.*

⁵*Geisler and Nix,* A General Introduction to the Bible, *p. 361.*

⁶*F. F. Bruce,* The New Testament Documents: Are They Reliable? *(Downers Grove, IL: InterVarsity Press, 1960), p. 19.*

⁷*Geisler and Nix,* A General Introduction to the Bible, *p. 365.*

⁸*Bruce, pp. 16-18; J. A. Thompson,* The Bible and Archaeology *(Grand Rapids: Eerdmans, 1962), p. 437.*

⁹*Quoted in McDowell,* Evidence, *pp. 44.*

¹⁰*Quoted in Bruce, p. 20.*

¹¹*Milton Hunter, in his book* The Gospel through the Ages, *explains this doctrine fully:*

> *In the first stage, man was an eternally existent being termed an intelligence. The next realm where man dwelt was the spirit world. According to Mormon concept eternally-existing intelligences were clothed with spirit bodies in the mansion of their Eternal Father.... [They are] born to heavenly parents into that eternal family in the spirit world. There in the spirit world they were reared to maturity, becoming grown spirit men and women prior to coming upon this earth.... Here he receives a physical body and undergoes the experiences of mortality.... Eventually, however, mortal death comes upon all. This eternal spirit goes to the spirit world to await resurrection and judgment. ... There some of them will become Angels, and others priests and Kings, or in other words Gods. (Hunter,* Gospel, *p. 126-29.)*

> *Hunter further states that progression applies to God: "Our Eternal Father has attained His position of exaltation and Godhood by obedience to the great law of progression." (Hunter,* Gospel, *p. 12.)*

¹²Uniform System for Teaching Families, *pp. C-27-29.*

¹³*Tanner,* Mormonism, *pp. v-vi.*

¹⁴*All of the titles mentioned in this paragraph are available from InterVarsity Press.*

Glossary of Mormon Terms

Many Mormon terms have not been mentioned or discussed at length in this book because they are not essential for an effective witness to Mormons. We define several of them here in case you come upon them in your conversation or reading and need to know their meaning. The meaning given is the Mormon, not the Christian one.

Apostle: one of the twelve men who serve under the First Presidency. They have various responsibilities within the Mormon Church, such as missions, visitor centers, finances.

Apostate: one who has left the Mormon Church.

Baptism for the Dead: immersion in water on behalf of a deceased person, who can accept or reject its benefit. The Mormons have nearly five billion names on microfilm in their genealogical records so that church members can search out their ancestors and be baptized for them. This doctrine is · based on an incorrect understanding of 1 Corinthians 15:29.

Bishop: the nonpaid leader of a Mormon ward, the closest parallel to a Christian minister.

Branch: a Mormon congregation not large enough to be called a ward; a mission congregation.

Chapel: a ward meetinghouse.

Church: Mormonism; the Mormon headquarters in Salt Lake City.

Deacon: an office given to Mormon boys at age 12.

Elder: a relatively minor office in the Mormon Church held by Mormon missionaries and other men. More influential officers who are not bishops, even apostles, may be referred to as elders.

Endowments: a secret ceremony revealing information and powers to priesthood holders. It takes place in a temple prior to eternal marriage or the sending out of a missionary to a foreign field.

First Presidency: the Mormon Prophet, or President, and his two counselors.

General Authorities: the First Presidency and apostles.

Gentile: any non-Mormon.

Institute of Religion: the Mormon college and university ministry; a free educational program used by Mormons to attract converts on the campuses. These programs are becoming widespread throughout the United States.

M. I. A.: Mutual Improvement Association, the Mormon youth organization.

Negro Doctrine: the Mormon teaching that blacks cannot hold the priesthood because they were sinful in their pre-existent state; therefore, God has cursed them with a black skin. Since they are denied the priesthood, they cannot be saved to the highest degree of the Mormon Heaven. This doctrine comes from the Book of Abraham and was supposed to have been recorded on a portion of the papyrus that is missing.

Patriarchal Blessing: a prophecy concerning the future of a young, faithful Mormon given by one of the older men in each congregation called a Ward Patriarch.

Polygamy: the practice of having more than one wife, either in this life or in the life to come. See *Doctrine and Covenants*, section 132.

Priesthood: the authority to act for God. Nearly every male Mormon from 12 years old on up is said to hold the priesthood.

Primary: the Mormon organization for grade-school children.

Relief Society: the Mormon women's organization.

Sacrament: communion or the Lord's Supper. Mormons use water and light bread as the elements.

Saints: Mormons.

Seminary: an educational program on the high-school level. Often adjacent to the public schools in the west, the teachers usually have a current state certificate and are paid according to public school pay scales.

Stake: a geographic area with several wards.

The "Stick of Joseph" and the "Stick of Judah": the *Book of Mormon* and the Bible respectively. Labels based on a false interpretation of Ezekiel 37:18-23.

Temple: a building in which Mormons perform secret ceremonies, eternal marriages and baptisms for the dead. The Mormons have sixteen temples throughout the world with two new ones under construction in Tokyo and São Paulo. Only Mormons in good standing may enter a temple.

Ward: a local Mormon congregation.

Word of Wisdom: section 89 in the *Doctrine and Covenants*, which forbids the use of "hot drinks" (coffee and tea), tobacco and alcohol as beverages.

Selected and Annotated Bibliography

This bibliography includes the most important items for further study from both Mormon and non-Mormon sources. Some of these books are available in Christian bookstores. Others are difficult to find and may be ordered from Mission to Mormons, *the ministry of the author. For current prices and an order form, write to Harry L. Ropp, P. O. Box 322, Roy, UT 84067.*

Non-Mormon Publications

Brodie, Fawn M. *No Man Knows My History*. New York: Alfred A. Knopf, 1967. The best biography of Joseph Smith. Brodie was excommunicated from the Mormon Church for writing it.

Bruce, F. F. *The New Testament Documents: Are They Reliable?* Downers Grove, IL: InterVarsity Press, 1973. An extremely helpful book for supporting the accuracy of the New Testament.

Hoekema, Anthony A. *The Four Major Cults*. Grand Rapids: Eerdmans, 1970. A work whose section on Mormonism is very valuable. Also contains extensive bibliography both pro and con.

Hougey, Hal. *Archaeology and the Book of Mormon*. Concord, CA: Pacific Publishing Co., 1975. An inexpensive booklet that covers the topic well.

McDowell, Josh. *Evidence That Demands a Verdict*. Campus Crusade for Christ, 1972. An apologetic containing much material about the reasons for our confidence in both the New and Old Testaments.

Martin, Walter R. *The Kingdom of the Cults*. Minneapolis: Bethany Fellowship, 1970. A good study of Mormon doctrine with extensive bibliography.

Tanner, Jerald and Sandra. *Mormonism: Shadow or Reality?* Salt Lake City: Modern Microfilm Co., 1972. The most extensive reference work available on Mormonism (nearly six hundred pages). The Tanners, former Mormons, have written over thirty books and pamphlets that are available directly from them at Box 1884, Salt Lake City, UT 84110.

Mormon Publications

Book of Mormon. Salt Lake City: Church of Jesus Christ of Latter-day Saints, 1961.

Doctrine and Covenants/Pearl of Great Price. Salt Lake City: Church of Jesus Christ of Latter-day Saints, 1968.

Hinkley, Gordon B. *Truth Restored*. Salt Lake City: Church of Jesus Christ of Latter-day Saints, 1969. A short history of the Mormon Church as told by a Latter-day Saints apostle.

Richards, LeGrand. *A Marvelous Work and a Wonder*. Salt Lake City: Deseret News Press, 1971. A work designed to help a Mormon missionary with his apologetics.

Talmage, James E. *Study of the Articles of Faith*. Salt Lake City: Church of Jesus Christ of Latter-day Saints, 1968. A discussion of the primary Mormon doctrines.

Wood, Wilford C. *Joseph Smith Begins His Work.* 2 vols. Salt Lake City: Deseret News Press, 1963. Valuable photoreprints of the 1830 edition of the *Book of Mormon*, the 1833 edition of the *Book of Commandments* and the 1835 edition of the *Doctrine and Covenants*.

Where Does It Say That? Scottsdale, AZ: Christian Communications Incorporated, 1977. Nearly two hundred pages of photo-reproductions of early Mormon literature showing doctrines which have been modified or abandoned. This material is otherwise extremely difficult or expensive to obtain. Write Christian Communications Incorporated, P. O. Box 80, Scottsdale, AZ 85252.

About the Author

Harry L. Ropp (A.B. Taylor University, 1969; M.A. and M.Div. in doctrine and philosophy Lincoln Christian Seminary in Lincoln, Illinois, 1974) is director of Mission to Mormons. The bulk of his M.A. work dealt with the Mormon doctrine of revelation. This book is an expansion of his masters thesis. Ropp has ministered to churches in Indiana and Illinois and is presently serving in Roy, Utah. He travels extensively, holding workshops and seminars for churches and college groups across the country. Through these workshops he seeks to stem the flow of converts from Christian churches to Mormonism and help Christians witness effectively to Mormons. Questions about these workshops and any correspondence concerning Mormonism may be addressed to: Harry L. Ropp, Box 322, Roy, Utah 84067.